P9-DNL-902

BY TESS GERRITSEN

Rizzoli & Isles Novels

The Surgeon

The Apprentice

The Sinner

Body Double

Vanish

The Mephisto Club

The Keepsake

Ice Cold

The Silent Girl

Rizzoli & Isles: Last to Die

Rizzoli & Isles: Die Again

Other Novels

Girl Missing

Harvest

Life Support

Bloodstream

Gravity

The Bone Garden

RIZZOLI & ISLES:

DIE AGAIN

RIZZOLI & ISLES:

DIE AGAIN

A NOVEL

TESS GERRITSEN

BALLANTINE BOOKS NEW YORK

Rizzoli & Isles: Die Again is a work of fiction. Names, characters, places, and incidents are the products of the author's imagination or are used fictitiously. Any resemblance to actual events, locales, or persons, living or dead, is entirely coincidental.

Published in the United States by Ballantine Books, an imprint of Random House, a division of Random House LLC, a Penguin Random House Company, New York.

BALLANTINE and the HOUSE colophon are registered trademarks of Random House LLC.

LIBRARY OF CONGRESS CATALOGING-IN-PUBLICATION DATA
Gerritsen, Tess.
Rizzoli & Isles : die again : a novel / Tess Gerritsen.
pages; cm.—(Rizzoli & Isles)
ISBN 978-0-345-54385-1
eBook ISBN 978-0-345-54386-8
1. Rizzoli, Jane, Detective (Fictitious character)—Fiction. 2. Isles, Maura (Fictitious character)—Fiction. 3. Policewomen—Fiction. 4. Women forensic scientists—Fiction.
I. Title. II. Title: Die again.
PS3557.E687R585 2014 813'.54—dc23 2014032292

Printed in the United States of America on acid-free paper

www.ballantinebooks.com

2 4 6 8 9 7 5 3 1

First Edition

To Levina

RIZZOLI & ISLES:
DIE AGAIN

ONE

OKAVANGO DELTA, BOTSWANA

IN THE SLANTING LIGHT OF DAWN I SPOT IT, SUBTLE AS A WATERMARK, pressed into the bare patch of dirt. Were it midday, when the African sun glares down hot and bright, I might have missed it entirely, but in early morning, even the faintest dips and depressions cast shadows, and as I emerge from our tent that lone footprint catches my eye. I crouch down beside it and feel a sudden chill when I realize that only a thin layer of canvas shielded us while we slept.

Richard emerges through the tent flap and gives a happy grunt as he stands and stretches, inhaling the scents of dew-laden grass and wood smoke and breakfast cooking on the campfire. The smells of Africa. This adventure is Richard's dream; it has always been Richard's, not mine. I'm the good-sport girlfriend whose default mode is *Of course I'll do it, darling.* Even when it means twenty-eight hours and three different planes, from London to Johannesburg to Maun and then into the bush, the last plane a rickety crate flown by a hungover pilot. Even when it means two weeks in a tent, swatting mosquitoes and peeing behind bushes.

Even if it means I could die, which is what I'm thinking as I stare down at that footprint, pressed into the dirt barely three feet from where Richard and I were sleeping last night.

"Smell the air, Millie!" Richard crows. "Nowhere else does it smell like this!"

"There was a lion here," I say.

"I wish I could bottle it and bring it home. What a souvenir that would be. The smell of the bush!"

He isn't listening to me. He's too high on Africa, too wrapped up in his great-white-adventurer fantasy where everything is *brilliant* and *fantastic,* even last night's meal of tinned pork and beans, which he declared the "splendid-est supper ever!"

I repeat, louder: "There was a lion here, Richard. It was right next to our tent. It could have clawed its way in." I want to alarm him, want him to say, *Oh my God, Millie, this is serious.*

Instead he blithely calls out to the nearest members of our group: "Hey, come take a look! We had a lion here last night!"

First to join us are the two girls from Cape Town, whose tent is pitched beside ours. Sylvia and Vivian have Dutch last names that I can neither spell nor pronounce. They're both in their twenties, tan and long-legged and blond, and at first I had trouble telling them apart, until Sylvia finally snapped at me in exasperation: "It's not like we're twins, Millie! Can't you see that Vivian has blue eyes and I have green?" As the girls kneel on either side of me to examine the paw print, I notice that they smell different, too. Vivian-with-the-blue-eyes smells like sweet grass, the fresh, unsoured scent of youth. Sylvia smells like the citronella lotion she's always slathering on to repel the mosquitoes, because *DEET is a poison. You do know that, don't you?* They flank me like blond-goddess bookends, and I can't help but see that Richard is once again eyeing Sylvia's cleavage, which is so blatantly displayed in her low-cut tank top. For a girl so conscientious about coating herself in mosquito repellent, she exposes an alarming amount of bitable skin.

Naturally Elliot is quick to join us, too. He's never far from the blondes, whom he met only a few weeks ago in Cape Town. He's since attached himself to them like a loyal puppy, hoping for a scrap of attention.

"Is that a fresh print?" Elliot asks, sounding worried. At least someone else shares my sense of alarm.

"I didn't see it here yesterday," says Richard. "The lion must have come through last night. Imagine stepping out to answer the call of nature and running into *that.*" He yowls and swipes a clawed hand at Elliot, who flinches away. This makes Richard and the blondes laugh, because Elliot is everyone's comic relief, the anxious American whose pockets bulge with tissues and bug spray, sunscreen and sanitizer, allergy pills, iodine tablets, and every other possible necessity for staying alive.

I don't join in their laughter. "Someone could have been killed out here," I point out.

"But this is what happens on a real safari, hey?" says Sylvia brightly. "You're out in the bush with lions."

"Doesn't look like a very big lion," says Vivian, leaning in to study the print. "Maybe a female, do you think?"

"Male or female, they can both kill you," says Elliot.

Sylvia gives him a playful slap. "Ooh. Are you scared?"

"No. No, I just assumed that Johnny was exaggerating when he gave us that talk the first day. *Stay in the jeep. Stay in the tent. Or you die.*"

"If you want to play it perfectly safe, Elliot, maybe you should have gone to the zoo instead," Richard says, and the blondes laugh at his cutting remark. All hail Richard, the alpha male. Just like the heroes he writes about in his novels, he's the man who takes charge and saves the day. Or thinks he is. Out here in the wild, he's really just another clueless Londoner, yet he manages to sound like an expert at staying alive. It's yet another thing that irritates me this morning, on top of the fact I'm hungry, I didn't sleep well, and now the mosquitoes have found me. Mosquitoes always find me. Whenever I step outside, it's as if they can hear their dinner bell ring, and already I'm slapping at my neck and face.

Richard calls out to the African tracker, "Clarence, come here! Look what came through camp last night."

Clarence has been sipping coffee by the campfire with Mr. and Mrs. Matsunaga. Now he ambles toward us, carrying his tin coffee cup, and crouches down to look at the footprint.

"It's fresh," says Richard, the new bush expert. "The lion must have come through just last night."

"Not a lion," says Clarence. He squints up at us, his ebony face agleam in the morning sun. "Leopard."

"How can you be so sure? It's just one paw print."

Clarence sketches the air above the print. "You see, this is the front paw. The shape is round, like a leopard's." He rises and scans the area. "And it is only one animal, so this one hunts alone. Yes, this is a leopard."

Mr. Matsunaga snaps photos of the print with his giant Nikon, which has a telephoto lens that looks like something you'd launch into space. He and his wife wear identical safari jackets and khaki pants and cotton scarves with wide-brimmed hats. Down to the last detail, they are sartorially matched. In holiday spots around the world you find couples just like them, dressed in the same outlandish prints. It makes you wonder: Do they wake up one morning and think, *Let's give the world a laugh today*?

As the sun lifts higher, washing out the shadows that so clearly defined the paw print, the others snap photos, racing against the brightening glare. Even Elliot pulls out his pocket camera, but I think it's simply because everyone else is doing it, and he doesn't like to be the odd man out.

I'm the only one who doesn't bother to fetch my camera. Richard is taking enough photos for both of us, and he's using his Canon, *the same camera* National Geographic *photographers use!* I move into the shade, but even here, out of the sun, I feel sweat trickle from my armpits. Already the heat is building. Every day in the bush is hot.

"Now you see why I tell you to stay in your tents at night," Johnny Posthumus says.

Our bush guide has approached so quietly that I didn't realize he'd returned from the river. I turn to see Johnny standing right behind me. Such a grim-sounding name, Posthumus, but he told us it's a common enough surname among Afrikaans settlers, from which he's descended. In his features I see the bloodline of his sturdy Dutch ancestors. He has sun-streaked blond hair, blue eyes, and tree-trunk legs that are deeply tanned in khaki shorts. Mosquitoes don't seem to bother him, nor does the heat, and he wears no hat, slathers on no repellent. Growing up in Africa has toughened his hide, immunized him against its discomforts.

"She came through here just before dawn," Johnny says, and points to a thicket on the periphery of our camp. "Stepped out of those bushes, strolled toward the fire, and looked me over. Gorgeous girl, big and healthy."

I'm astonished by how calm he is. "You actually saw her?"

"I was out here building the fire for breakfast when she showed up."

"What did you do?"

"I did what I've told all of you to do in that situation. I stood tall. Gave her a good view of my face. Prey animals such as zebras and antelope have eyes at the sides of their heads, but a predator's eyes face forward. Always show the cat your face. Let her see where your eyes are, and she'll know you're a predator, too. She'll think twice before attacking." Johnny looks around at the seven clients who are paying him to keep them alive in this remote place. "Remember that, hey? We'll see more big cats as we go deeper into the bush. If you encounter one, stand tall and make yourself look as large as you can. Face them straight-on. And whatever you do, don't run. You'll have a better chance of surviving."

"You were out here, face-to-face with a leopard," says Elliot. "Why didn't you use *that*?" He points to the rifle that's always slung over Johnny's shoulder.

Johnny shakes his head. "I won't shoot a leopard. I won't kill any big cat."

"But isn't that what the gun's for? To protect yourself?"

"There aren't enough of them left in the world. They own this land, and we're the intruders here. If a leopard charged me, I don't think I could kill it. Not even to save my own life."

"But that doesn't apply to us, right?" Elliot gives a nervous laugh and looks around at our traveling party. "You'd shoot a leopard to protect *us,* wouldn't you?"

Johnny answers with an ironic smile. "We'll see."

BY NOON WE'RE PACKED up and ready to push deeper into the wild. Johnny drives the truck while Clarence rides in the tracker's seat, which juts out in front of the bumper. It seems a precarious perch to me, out there with his legs swinging in the open, easy meat for any lion who can snag him. But Johnny assures us that as long as we stay attached to the vehicle, we're safe, because predators think we're all part of one huge animal. *But step out of the truck and you're dinner. Got that, everyone?*

Yes sir. Message received.

There are no roads at all out here, only a faint flattening of the grass where the passage of earlier tires has compacted the poor soil. The damage caused by a single truck can scar the landscape for months, Johnny says, but I cannot imagine many of them make it this far into the Delta. We're three days' drive from the bush landing strip where we were dropped off, and we've spotted no other vehicles in this wilderness.

Wilderness was not something I actually believed in four months ago, sitting in our London flat, the rain spitting against the windows. When Richard called me over to his computer and showed me the Botswana safari he wanted to book for our holiday, I saw photos of lions and hippos, rhinos and leopards, the same familiar animals you can find in zoos and game parks. That's what I imagined, a giant game park with comfortable lodges and roads. At a minimum, roads. According to the website, there'd be "bush camping" involved, but I pictured lovely big tents with showers and flush toilets. I didn't think I'd be paying for the privilege of squatting in the bushes.

Richard doesn't mind roughing it in the least. He's high on Africa, higher than Mount Kilimanjaro, his camera constantly clicking away as we drive. In the seat behind us, Mr. Matsunaga's camera matches Richard's, click for click, but with a longer lens. Richard won't admit it, but he has lens envy, and when we get back to London he'll probably go straight online to price Mr. Matsunaga's gear. This is the way modern men do battle, not with spear and sword, but with credit cards. My platinum beats your gold. Poor Elliot with his unisex Minolta is left in the dust, but I don't think he minds, because once again he's snuggled in the last row with Vivian and Sylvia. I glance back at the three of them and catch a glimpse of Mrs. Matsunaga's resolute face. She's another good sport. I'm sure that shitting in the bushes wasn't her idea of a great holiday, either.

"Lions! Lions!" shouts Richard. "Over there!"

Cameras click faster as we pull so close I can see black flies clinging to the flank of the male lion. Nearby are three females, lolling in the shade of a leadwood tree. Suddenly there's an outburst of Japanese behind me, and I turn to see that Mr. Matsunaga has leaped to his feet. His wife hangs on to the back of his safari jacket, desperate to stop him from leaping out of the truck for a better photo.

"Sit. Down!" Johnny booms out in a voice that no one, man or beast, could possibly ignore. *"Now!"*

Instantly Mr. Matsunaga drops back into his seat. Even the lions seem startled, and they all stare at the mechanical monster with eighteen pairs of arms.

"Remember what I told you, Isao?" scolds Johnny. "If you step out of this truck, you're *dead.*"

"I get excited. I forget," murmurs Mr. Matsunaga, apologetically bowing his head.

"Look, I'm only trying to keep you safe." Johnny releases a deep breath and says quietly: "I'm sorry for shouting. But last year, a colleague was on a game drive with two clients. Before he could stop them, they both jumped out of the truck to take photos. The lions had them in a flash."

"You mean—they were killed?" says Elliot.

"That's what lions are programmed to do, Elliot. So please, enjoy the view, but from inside the truck, hey?" Johnny gives a laugh to defuse the tension, but we're all still cowed, a group of misbehaving children who've just been disciplined. The camera clicks are half-hearted now, photos taken to cover our discomfort. We're all shocked by how hard Johnny came down on Mr. Matsunaga. I stare at Johnny's back, which looms right in front of me, and the muscles of his neck stick out like thick vines. He starts the engine again. We leave the lions and drive on, to our next campsite.

AT SUNSET, THE LIQUOR comes out. After the five tents are pitched and the campfire is lit, Clarence the tracker opens the aluminum cocktail case that has bounced in the back of the truck all day, and sets out the bottles of gin and whiskey, vodka and Amarula. The last I've grown particularly fond of, a sweet cream liqueur made from the African marula tree. It tastes like a thousand boozy calories of coffee and chocolate, like something a child would sneak a sip of when his mother's back is turned. Clarence winks at me as he hands me my glass, as if I'm the naughty child of the bunch because everyone else sips grown-up drinks like warm gin and tonic or whiskey, neat. This is the part of the day when I think, Yes, it's good to be in Africa. When the day's discomforts and the bugs and the tension between me and Richard all dissolve in a pleasant, tipsy haze and I can settle into a camp chair and watch the sun go down. As Clarence prepares a simple evening meal of meat stew and bread and fruit, Johnny strings up the perimeter wire, hung with little bells to alert us should anything wander into camp. I notice Johnny's silhouette suddenly go still against the sunset's glow, and he raises his head as if he's sniffing the air, taking in a thousand scents that I'm not even aware of. He's like another bush creature, so at home in this wild place that I almost expect him to open his mouth and roar like a lion.

I turn to Clarence, who's stirring the pot of bubbling stew. "How long have you worked with Johnny?" I ask.

"With Johnny? First time."

"You've never been his tracker before?"

Clarence briskly shakes pepper into the stew. "My cousin is Johnny's tracker. But this week Abraham is in his village for a funeral. He asked me to take his place."

"And what did Abraham say about Johnny?"

Clarence grins, his white teeth gleaming in the twilight. "Oh, my cousin tells many stories about him. Many stories. He thinks Johnny should have been born Shangaan, because he's just like us. But with a white face."

"Shangaan? Is that your tribe?"

He nods. "We come from Limpopo Province. In South Africa."

"Is that the language I hear you two speaking sometimes?"

He gives a guilty laugh. "When we don't want you to know what we say."

I imagine that none of it is flattering. I look at the others seated around the campfire. Mr. and Mrs. Matsunaga are diligently reviewing the day's photos on his camera. Vivian and Sylvia lounge in their low-cut tank tops, oozing pheromones that make poor, awkward Elliot grovel for attention as usual. *Are you gals chilly? Can I get your sweaters? How about another gin and tonic?*

Richard emerges from our tent with a fresh shirt. There's an empty chair waiting for him beside me, but he walks right past it. He sits down next to Vivian instead, and proceeds to dial up the charm. *How are you enjoying our safari? Do you ever make it to London? I'd be happy to send you and Sylvia autographed copies of* Blackjack *when it's published.*

Of course they all now know who he is. Within the first hour of meeting everyone, Richard subtly slipped in the fact that he is thriller writer Richard Renwick, creator of MI5 hero Jackman Tripp. Unfortunately none of them had ever heard of Richard or his hero, which led to a prickly first day on safari. But now he's back in form, doing what he does best: charming his audience. Laying it on too thick, I think. Far too thick. But if I complain about it later, I know exactly what he'll say. *It's what writers have to do, Millie. We have to be sociable and bring in new readers.* Funny how Richard never wastes his time being sociable with grandmotherly types, only with young, preferably pretty girls. I remember how he'd turned that same charm on me four years ago, when he'd signed copies of *Kill Option* at the bookshop where I work. When Richard's on his game, he's impossible to resist, and now I see him looking at Vivian in a way he hasn't looked at me in years. He slips a Gauloise between his lips and tilts forward to cup the flame from his sterling-silver lighter, the way his hero Jackman Tripp would, with masculine panache.

The empty chair next to me feels like a black hole, sucking all the joy out of my mood. I'm ready to get up and go back to my tent when suddenly Johnny settles into that chair beside me. He doesn't say anything, just scans the group as if taking our measure. I think he is always taking our measure, and I wonder what he sees when he looks at me. Am I like all the other resigned wives and girlfriends who've been dragged into the bush to humor the safari fantasies of their men?

His gaze rattles me, and I'm compelled to fill the silence. "Do those bells on the perimeter wire actually work?" I ask. "Or are they just there to make us feel safer?"

"They serve as a first alert."

"I didn't hear them last night, when the leopard came into camp."

"I did." He leans forward, tosses more wood on the fire. "We'll probably hear those bells again tonight."

"You think there are more leopards lurking about?"

"Hyenas this time." He points at the darkness looming beyond our firelit circle. "There's about half a dozen of them watching us right now."

"What?" I peer into the night. Only then do I spot the reflected gleam of eyes staring back.

"They're patient. Waiting to see if there's a meal to be scavenged. Walk out there alone, and they'll make *you* their meal." He shrugs. "Which is why you hired me."

"To keep us from ending up as dinner."

"I wouldn't get paid if I lost too many clients."

"How many is too many?"

"You'd only be the third."

"That's a joke, right?"

He smiles. Though he's about the same age as Richard, a lifetime in the African sun has etched lines around Johnny's eyes. He lays a reassuring hand on my arm, which startles me because he's not a man who offers unnecessary touches. "Yes, it's a joke. I've never lost a client."

"I find it hard to tell when you're serious."

"When I'm serious, you'll know it." He turns to Clarence, who's just said something to him in Shangaan. "Supper's ready."

I glance at Richard, to see if he's noticed Johnny talking to me, Johnny's hand on my arm. But Richard's so focused on Vivian that I might as well be invisible.

"IT'S WHAT WRITERS HAVE to do," Richard predictably says as we lie in our tents that night. "I'm only bringing in new readers." We speak in whispers, because the canvas is thin, the tents close together. "Besides, I feel a little protective. They're on their own, just two girls out in the bush. Rather adventurous when they're only twenty-something, don't you think? You have to admire them for that."

"Elliot obviously admires them," I observe.

"Elliot would admire anything with two X chromosomes."

"So they're not exactly on their own. He signed on to the trip to keep them company."

"And God, that must get tiresome for them. Having him hanging around all the time, making cow eyes."

"The girls invited him. That's what Elliot says."

"Invited him out of pity. He chats them up in some nightclub, hears they're going on safari. They probably said, *Hey, you should think about coming into the bush, too!* I'm sure they never imagined he'd actually sign on."

"Why do you always put him down? He seems like a very nice man. And he knows an awful lot about birds."

Richard snorts. “That’s always *so* attractive in a man.”

“What is the matter with you? Why are you so cranky?”

“I could say the same about you. All I do is chat up a young woman and you can’t deal with it. At least *those* girls know how to have a good time. They’re in the spirit of things.”

“I’m trying to enjoy myself, I really am. But I didn’t think it would be so rough out here. I expected—”

“Fluffy towels and chocolates on the pillow.”

“Give me some credit. I’m here, aren’t I?”

“Complaining all the way. This safari was my dream, Millie. Don’t ruin it for me.”

We’re no longer whispering and I’m sure the others can hear us, if they’re still awake. I know that Johnny is, because he’s on first watch. I imagine him sitting by the campfire, listening to our voices, hearing the rising tension. Surely he’s already aware of it. Johnny Posthumus is the kind of man who misses nothing, which is how he survives in this place, where hearing the tinkle of a bell on a wire means the difference between life and death. What useless, shallow people we must seem to him. How many marriages has he watched fall apart, how many self-important men has he seen humbled by Africa? The bush is not merely a holiday destination; it’s where you learn how insignificant you truly are.

“I’m sorry,” I whisper, and reach out for Richard’s hand. “I don’t mean to spoil this for you.”

Though my fingers close around his, he doesn’t return the gesture. His hand feels like a dead thing in my grasp.

“You’ve put a damper on everything. Look, I know this trip wasn’t your idea of a holiday, but for God’s sake, enough of the glum face. Look how Sylvia and Vivian are enjoying themselves! Even Mrs. Matsunaga manages to be a good sport.”

“Maybe it’s all because of these malaria pills I’m taking,” I offer weakly. “The doctor said they can make you depressed. He said some people even go insane on them.”

"Well, the mefloquine isn't bothering *me.* The girls are taking it, too, and they're jolly enough."

The girls again. Always comparing me with the girls, who are nine years younger than I am, nine years slimmer and fresher. After four years of sharing the same flat, the same loo, how could any woman still seem fresh?

"I should stop taking the pills," I tell him.

"What, and get malaria? Oh right, that makes sense."

"What do you want me to do? Richard, tell me what you want me to do."

"I don't *know.*" He sighs and turns away from me. His back is like cold concrete, a wall that encases his heart, locking it beyond my reach. After a moment, he says softly: "I don't know where we're going, Millie."

But I know where Richard is going. Away from me. He's been pulling away from me for months, so subtly, so gradually that until now, I refused to see it. I could chalk it up to: *Oh, we're both so busy lately.* He's been scrambling to finish the revisions on *Blackjack.* I've been struggling through our annual inventory at the bookshop. All will be better between us when our lives slow down. That's what I kept telling myself.

Outside our tent, the night is alive with sounds of the Delta. We are camped not far from a river, where earlier we saw hippos. I think I can hear them now, along with the croaks and cries and grunts of countless other creatures.

But inside our tent, there is only silence.

So this is where love comes to die. In a tent, in the bush, in Africa. If we were back in London, I'd be out of bed, dressed and off to my girlfriend's flat for brandy and sympathy. But here I'm trapped inside canvas, surrounded by things that want to eat me. Sheer claustrophobia makes me desperate to claw my way out of the tent, to run screaming into the night. It must be these malaria pills, wreaking havoc with my brain. I want it to be the pills, because that means it's not my fault I'm feeling hopeless. I really must stop taking them.

Richard has fallen deeply asleep. How can he do that, just drop off so peacefully when I feel I'm about to shatter? I listen to him breathe in and out, so relaxed, so steady. The sound of him not caring.

He is still deeply asleep when I awake the next morning. As the pale light of dawn seeps through the seams of our tent, I think with dread of the day ahead. Another uneasy drive as we sit side by side, trying to be civil with each other. Another day of slapping mosquitoes and peeing in the bushes. Another evening of watching Richard flirt and feeling another piece of my heart crumble away. This holiday cannot possibly get worse, I think.

And then I hear the sound of a woman shrieking.

TWO

BOSTON

IT WAS THE MAILMAN WHO CALLED IT IN. ELEVEN FIFTEEN A.M., SHAKY voice on a cell phone: *I'm on Sanborn Avenue, West Roxbury, oh-two-one-three-two. The dog—I saw the dog in the window . . .* And that's how it came to the attention of Boston PD. A cascade of events that started with an alert mail carrier, one in an army of foot soldiers deployed six days a week in neighborhoods across America. They are the eyes of the nation, sometimes the only eyes that notice which elderly widow has not collected her mail, which old bachelor doesn't answer his doorbell, and which porch has a yellowing pile of newspapers.

The first clue that something was amiss inside the large house on Sanborn Avenue, zip code 02132, was the overstuffed mailbox, something that US postal carrier Luis Muniz first noticed on day number two. Two days' worth of uncollected mail wasn't necessarily a cause for alarm. People go away for the weekend. People forget to request a hold on home delivery.

But on day number three, Muniz started to worry.

On day number four, when Muniz opened the mailbox and found

it still jam-packed with catalogs and magazines and bills, he knew he had to take action.

"So he knocks on the front door," said Patrolman Gary Root. "Nobody answers. He figures he'll check with the next-door neighbor, see if she knows what's going on. Then he looks in the window and spots the dog."

"That dog over there?" asked Detective Jane Rizzoli, pointing to a friendly-looking golden retriever who was now tied to the mailbox.

"Yeah, that's him. The tag on his collar says his name's Bruno. I took him outta the house, before he could do any more . . ." Patrolman Root swallowed. "Damage."

"And the mail carrier? Where's he?"

"Took the rest of the day off. Probably getting a stiff drink somewhere. I got his contact info, but he probably can't tell you much more than what I just told you. He never went inside the house, just called nine one one. I was first on the scene, found the front door unlocked. Walked in and . . ." He shook his head. "Wish I hadn't."

"You talk to anyone else?"

"The nice lady next door. She came out when she saw the cruisers parked out here, wanted to know what was going on. All I told her was that her neighbor was dead."

Jane turned and faced the house where Bruno the friendly retriever had been trapped. It was an older two-story, single-family home with a porch, a two-car garage, and mature trees in front. The garage door was closed, and a black Ford Explorer, registered to the homeowner, was parked in the driveway. This morning, there would have been nothing to distinguish the residence from the other well-kept houses on Sanborn Avenue, nothing that would catch a cop's eye and make him think: Wait a minute, there's something wrong here. But now there were two patrol cars parked at the curb, rack lights flashing, which made it obvious to anyone passing by that yes, something was very wrong here. Something that Jane and her partner, Barry Frost, were about to confront. Across the street, a gathering crowd of neighbors stood gaping at the house. Had any of them noticed the occupant hadn't been seen in a few days, hadn't walked his dog or picked up his mail? Now they were probably telling one another: *Yeah, I knew something wasn't right.* Everyone's brilliant in retrospect.

"You want to walk us through the house?" Frost asked Patrolman Root.

"You know what?" said Root. "I'd rather not. I finally got the smell outta my nose, and I don't care for another whiff of it."

Frost swallowed. "Uh . . . that bad?"

"I was in there maybe thirty seconds, tops. My partner didn't last even that long. It's not like there's anything in there I need to point out to you. You can't miss it." He looked at the golden retriever, who responded with a playful bark. "Poor pup, trapped in there with nothing to eat. I know he had no choice, but still . . ."

Jane glanced at Frost, who was staring at the house like a condemned prisoner facing the gallows. "What'd you have for lunch?" she asked him.

"Turkey sandwich. Potato chips."

"Hope you enjoyed it."

"This isn't helping, Rizzoli."

They climbed the porch steps and paused to pull on gloves and shoe covers. "You know," she said, "there's this pill called Compazine."

"Yeah?"

"Works pretty good for morning sickness."

"Great. When I get knocked up, I'll give it a try."

They looked at each other and she saw him take a deep breath, just as she was doing. One last gulp of clean air. With a gloved hand she opened the door, and they stepped inside. Frost lifted his arm to cover his nose, blocking the smell that they were far too familiar with. Whether you called it *cadaverine,* or *putrescine,* or any other chemical name, it all came down to the stench of death. But it was not the smell that made Jane and Frost pause just inside the door; it was what they saw hanging on the walls.

Everywhere they looked, eyes stared back at them. A whole gallery of the dead, confronting these new intruders.

"Jesus," murmured Frost. "Was he some kind of big-game hunter?"

"Well, that is definitely big game," said Jane, staring up at the mounted head of a rhino and wondering what kind of bullet it took to kill such a creature. Or the Cape buffalo beside it. She moved slowly past the row of trophies, her shoe covers swishing across the wood floor, gaping at animal heads so life-like she almost expected the lion to roar. "Are these even legal? Who the hell shoots a leopard these days?"

"Look. The dog wasn't the only pet running around in here."

A variety of reddish-brown paw prints tracked across the wood floor. The larger set would match Bruno, the golden retriever, but there were smaller prints as well, dotted throughout the room. Brown smears on the windowsill marked where Bruno had propped up his front paws to look out at the mail carrier. But it wasn't merely the sight of a dog that caused Luis Muniz to dial 911; it was what protruded from that dog's mouth.

A human finger.

She and Frost followed the trail of paw prints, passing beneath the glassy eyes of a zebra and a lion, a hyena and a warthog. This collector did not discriminate by size; even the smallest creatures had their ignominious place on these walls, including four mice posed with tiny china cups, seated around a miniature table. A Mad Hatter's grotesque tea party.

As they moved through the living room and into a hallway, the stench of putrefaction grew stronger. Though she could not yet see its source, Jane could hear the ominous buzz of its supplicants. A fat fly buzzed a few lazy circles around her head and drifted away through a doorway.

Always follow the flies. They know where dinner is served.

The door hung ajar. Just as Jane pushed it wider, something white streaked out and shot past her feet.

"Holy crap!" yelled Frost.

Heart banging, Jane glanced back at the pair of eyes peering out from under the living room sofa. "It's just a cat." She gave a relieved laugh. "That explains the smaller paw prints."

"Wait, you hear that?" said Frost. "I think there's another cat in there."

Jane took a breath and stepped through the doorway, into the garage. A gray tabby trotted over to greet her and silkily threaded back and forth between her legs, but Jane ignored it. Her gaze was fixed on what hung from the ceiling hoist. The flies were so thick she could feel their hum in her bones as they swarmed around the ripe feast that had been flayed open for their convenience, exposing meat that now squirmed with maggots.

Frost lurched away, gagging.

The nude man hung upside down, his ankles bound with orange nylon cord. Like a pig carcass hanging in a slaughterhouse, his abdomen had been sliced open, the cavity stripped of all organs. Both arms dangled free, and the hands would have almost touched the floor—if the hands had still been attached. If hunger had not forced Bruno the dog, and maybe the two cats as well, to start gnawing off the flesh of their owner.

"So now we know where that finger came from," Frost said, his voice muffled behind his sleeve. "Jesus, it's everyone's worst nightmare. Getting eaten by your own cat . . ."

For three starving house pets, what now hung from the hoist would certainly look like a feast. The animals had already disarticulated the hands and stripped away so much skin and muscle and cartilage from the face that the white bone of one orbit was exposed, a pearly ridge peeking through shredded flesh. The facial features were gnawed beyond recognition, but the grotesquely swollen genitals left no doubt this was a man—an older one, judging by the silvery pubic hair.

"Hung and dressed like game," said a voice behind her.

Startled, Jane turned to see Dr. Maura Isles standing in the doorway. Even at a death scene as grotesque as this one, Maura managed to look elegant, her black hair as sleek as a gleaming helmet, her gray jacket and pants perfectly tailored to her slim waist and hips. She made Jane feel like the sloppy cousin with flyaway hair and scuffed shoes. Maura did not quail from the smell but moved straight to the carcass, heedless of the flies that were dive-bombing her head. "This is disturbing," she said.

"Disturbing?" Jane snorted. "I was thinking more along the lines of *totally fucked up.*"

The gray tabby abandoned Jane and went to Maura, where it rubbed back and forth against her leg, purring loudly. So much for feline loyalty.

Maura nudged the cat away with her foot, but her attention stayed focused on the body. "Abdominal and thoracic organs missing. The incision looks very decisive, from pubis down to xiphoid. It's what a hunter would do to a deer or a boar. Hang it, gut it, leave it to age." She glanced up at the ceiling hoist. "And that looks like something you'd use to hang game. Clearly this house belongs to a hunter."

"Those look like what a hunter would use, too," said Frost. He pointed to the garage workbench, where a magnetized rack held a dozen lethal-looking knives. All of them appeared clean, the blades bright and gleaming. Jane stared at the boning knife. Imagined that razor edge slicing through flesh as yielding as butter.

"Odd," said Maura, focusing on the torso. "These wounds here don't look like they're from a knife." She pointed to three incisions that sliced down the rib cage. "They're perfectly parallel, like blades mounted together."

"Looks like a claw mark," said Frost. "Could the animals have done that?"

"They're too deep for a cat or dog. These appear to be postmortem, with minimal oozing . . ." She straightened, focusing on the floor. "If he was butchered right here, the blood must have been hosed away. See that drain in the concrete? It's something a hunter would install if he used this space to hang and age meat."

"What's the thing about aging? I never understood the point of hanging meat," said Frost.

"Postmortem enzymes act as a natural tenderizer, but it's usually done at temperatures just above freezing. In here it feels like, what, about fifty degrees? Warm enough to get decomp. And maggots. I'm just glad it's November. It would smell a lot worse in August." With a pair of tweezers, Maura picked off one of the maggots and studied it as it squirmed in her gloved palm. "These look like third instar stage. Consistent with a time of death about four days ago."

"All those mounted heads in the living room," said Jane. "And he ends up hanging, like some dead animal. I'd say we've got a theme going here."

"Is this victim the homeowner? Have you confirmed his identity?"

"Kind of hard to make a visual ID with his hands and face gone. But I'd say the age matches. The homeowner of record is Leon Gott, age sixty-four. Divorced, lived alone."

"He certainly didn't die alone," said Maura, staring into the gaping incision at what was now little more than an empty shell. "Where are they?" she said, and suddenly turned to face Jane. "The killer hung the body here. What did he do with the organs?"

For a moment, the only sound in the garage was the humming of flies as Jane considered every urban legend she'd ever heard about stolen organs. Then she focused on the covered garbage can in the far corner. As she approached it, the stench of putrefaction grew even stronger, and flies swarmed in a hungry cloud. Grimacing, she lifted the edge of the lid. One quick glance was all she could stomach before the smell made her back away, gagging.

"I take it you found them," said Maura.

"Yeah," muttered Jane. "At least, the intestines. I'll leave the full inventory of guts to you."

"Neat."

"Oh yeah, it'll be lots of fun."

"No, what I mean is, the perp was neat. The incision. The removal of the viscera." Paper shoe covers crackled as Maura crossed to the trash can. Both Jane and Frost backed away when Maura pried open the lid, but even from the opposite side of the garage they caught the stomach-turning whiff of rotting organs. The odor seemed to excite the gray tabby, who was rubbing against Maura with even more fervor, mewing for attention.

"Got yourself a new friend," said Jane.

"Normal feline marking behavior. He's claiming me as his territory," said Maura as she plunged a gloved hand into the garbage can.

"I know you like to be thorough, Maura," said Jane. "But how about picking through those in the morgue? Like, in a biohazard room or something?"

"I need to be certain . . ."

"Of what? You can *smell* they're in there." To Jane's disgust, Maura bent over the garbage can and reached even deeper into the pile of entrails. In the morgue, she'd watched Maura slice open torsos and peel off scalps, de-flesh bones and buzz-saw through skulls, performing all these tasks with laser-guided concentration. That same icy focus was on Maura's face as she dug through the congealed mass in the trash can, heedless of the flies now crawling in her fashionably clipped dark hair. Was there anyone else who could look so elegant while doing something so disgusting?

"Come on, it's not like you haven't seen guts before," said Jane.

Maura didn't answer as she plunged her hands deeper.

"Okay." Jane sighed. "You don't need us for this. Frost and I will check out the rest of the—"

"There's too much," Maura muttered.

"Too much what?"

"This isn't a normal volume of viscera."

"You're the one who's always talking about bacterial gases. Bloating."

"Bloating doesn't explain *this.*" Maura straightened, and what she held in her gloved hand made Jane cringe.

"A heart?"

"This is not a normal heart, Jane," said Maura. "Yes, it has four chambers, but this aortic arch isn't right. And the great vessels don't look right, either."

"Leon Gott was sixty-four," said Frost. "Maybe he had a bad ticker."

"That's the problem. This doesn't look like a sixty-four-year-old man's heart." Maura reached into the garbage pail again. "But *this* one does," she said, and held out her other hand.

Jane looked back and forth between the two specimens. "Wait. There are *two* hearts in there?"

"And two complete sets of lungs."

Jane and Frost stared at each other. "Oh shit," he said.

THREE

FROST SEARCHED THE DOWNSTAIRS AND SHE TOOK THE UPSTAIRS. WENT room by room, opening closets and drawers, peering under beds. No gutted bodies anywhere, nor any signs of a struggle, but plenty of dust bunnies and cat hair. Mr. Gott—if indeed he was the man hanging in the garage—had been an indifferent housekeeper, and scattered across his dresser were old hardware store receipts, hearing aid batteries, a wallet with three credit cards and forty-eight dollars in cash, and a few stray bullets. Which told her that Mr. Gott was more than a little casual about firearms. She wasn't surprised to open his nightstand drawer and find a fully loaded Glock inside, with a round in the chamber, ready to fire. Just the tool for the paranoid homeowner.

Too bad the gun was upstairs while the homeowner was downstairs, getting his guts ripped out.

In the bathroom cabinet she found the expected array of pills for a man of sixty-four. Aspirin and Advil, Lipitor and Lopressor. And on the countertop was a pair of hearing aids—high-end ones. He hadn't been wearing them, which meant he might not have heard an intruder.

As she started downstairs, the telephone rang in the living room. By the time she reached it, the answering machine had already kicked in and she heard a man's voice leave a message.

Hey, Leon, you never got back to me about the trip to Colorado. Let me know if you want to join us. Should be a good time.

Jane was about to play the message again, to see the caller's phone number, when she noticed that the PLAY button was smeared with what looked like blood. According to the blinking display, there were two recorded messages, and she'd just heard the second one.

With a gloved finger she pressed PLAY.

November three, nine fifteen A.M.*: . . . and if you call immediately, we can lower your credit card rates. Don't miss this opportunity to take advantage of this special offer.*

November six, two P.M.*: Hey, Leon, you never got back to me about the trip to Colorado. Let me know if you want to join us. Should be a good time.*

November 3 was a Monday, today was a Thursday. That first message was still on the machine, unplayed, because at nine on Monday morning, Leon Gott was probably dead.

"Jane?" said Maura. The gray tabby had followed her into the hallway and was weaving figure of eights between her legs.

"There's blood on this answering machine," said Jane, turning to look at her. "Why would the perp touch it? Why would he check the victim's messages?"

"Come see what Frost found in the backyard."

Jane followed her into the kitchen and out the back door. In a fenced yard landscaped only with patchy grass stood an outbuilding with metal siding. Too big to be just a storage shed, the windowless structure looked large enough to hide any number of horrors. As Jane stepped inside, she smelled a chemical odor, alcohol-sharp. Fluorescent bulbs cast the interior in a cold, clinical glare.

Frost stood beside a large worktable, studying a fearsome-looking tool bolted to it. "I thought at first this was a table saw," he said. "But this blade doesn't look like any saw I've ever come across. And those cabinets over there?" He pointed across the workshop. "Take a look at what's inside them."

Through the glass cabinet doors, Jane saw boxes of latex gloves and an array of frightening-looking instruments laid out on the shelves. Scalpels and knives, probes and pliers and forceps. *Surgeon's tools.* Hanging from wall hooks were rubber aprons, splattered with what looked like bloodstains. With a shudder, she turned and stared at the plywood worktable, its surface scarred with nicks and gouges, and saw a clump of congealed, raw meat.

"Okay," Jane murmured. "Now I'm freaking out."

"This is like a serial killer's workshop," said Frost. "And this table is where he sliced and diced the bodies."

In the corner was a fifty-gallon white barrel mounted to an electrical motor. "What the hell is that thing for?"

Frost shook his head. "It looks big enough to hold . . ."

She crossed to the barrel. Paused as she spotted red droplets on the floor. A smear of it streaked the hatch door. "There's blood all around here."

"What's inside the barrel?" said Maura.

Jane gave the fastening bolt a hard pull. "And behind door number two is . . ." She peered into the open hatch. "Sawdust."

"That's all?"

Jane reached into the barrel and sifted through the flakes, stirring up a cloud of wood dust. "Just sawdust."

"So we're still missing the second victim," said Frost.

Maura went to the nightmarish tool that Frost had earlier thought was a table saw. As she examined the blade, the cat was at her heels again, rubbing against her pant legs, refusing to leave her alone. "Did you get a good look at this thing, Detective Frost?"

"I got as close as I wanted to get."

"Notice how this circular blade has a cutting edge that's bent sideways? Obviously this isn't meant for slicing."

Jane joined her at the table and gingerly touched the blade edge. "This thing looks like it'd rip you to shreds."

"And that's probably what it's for. I think it's called a flesher. It's used not to cut but to grind away flesh."

"They *make* a machine like that?"

Maura crossed to a closet and opened the door. Inside was a row of what looked like paint cans. Maura reached for one large container and turned it around to read the contents. "Bondo."

"An automotive product?" said Jane, glimpsing the image of a car on the label.

"The label says it's filler, for car body work. To repair dings and scratches." Maura set the can of Bondo back on the shelf. She couldn't shake the gray cat, who followed her as she went to the cabinet and peered through glass doors at the knives and probes, laid out like a surgeon's tool kit. "I think I know what this room was used for." She turned to Jane. "You know that second set of viscera in the trash can? I don't believe they're human."

"LEON GOTT WAS NOT a nice man. And I'm trying to be charitable," said Nora Bazarian as she wiped a mustache of creamed carrots from her one-year-old son's mouth. In her faded jeans and clinging T-shirt, with her blond hair pulled back in a girlish ponytail, she looked more like a teenager than a thirty-three-year-old mother of two. She had a mother's skill at multitasking, efficiently feeding spoonfuls of carrots into her son's open mouth between loading the dishwasher, checking on a cake in the oven, and answering Jane's questions. No wonder the woman had a teenager's waistline; she didn't sit still for five seconds.

"You know what he yelled at my six-year-old?" said Nora. "*Get off my lawn.* I used to think that was just a caricature of cranky old men, but Leon actually said that to my son. All because Timmy wandered next door to pet his dog." Nora closed the dishwasher with a bang. "Bruno has better manners than his owner did."

"How long did you know Mr. Gott?" asked Jane.

"We moved into this house six years ago, just after Timmy was born. We thought this was the perfect neighborhood for kids. You can see how well kept the yards are, for the most part, and there are other young families on this street, with kids Timmy's age." With balletic grace she pivoted to the coffeepot and refilled Jane's cup. "A few days after we moved in, I brought Leon a plate of brownies, just to say hello. He didn't even say thanks, just told me he didn't eat sweets, and handed them right back. Then he complained that my new baby was crying too much, and why couldn't I keep him quiet at night? Can you believe that?" She sat down and spooned more carrots into her son's mouth. "To top it off, there were all those dead animals hanging on his wall."

"So you've been inside his house."

"Only once. He sounded so proud when he told me he'd shot most of them himself. What kind of a person kills animals just to decorate his walls?" She wiped a carroty dribble from the baby's chin. "That's when I decided we'd just stay away from him. Right, Sam?" she cooed. "Just stay away from that mean man."

"When did you last see Mr. Gott?"

"I talked to Officer Root about all this. I last saw Leon over the weekend."

"Which day?"

"Sunday morning. I saw him in his driveway. He was carrying groceries into his house."

"Did you see anyone visit him that day?"

"I was gone for most of Sunday. My husband's in California this week, so I took the kids down to my mom's house in Falmouth. We didn't get home till late that night."

"What time?"

"Around nine thirty, ten."

"And that night, did you hear anything unusual next door? Shouts, loud voices?"

Nora set down the spoon and frowned at her. The baby gave a

hungry squawk, but Nora ignored him; her attention was entirely focused on Jane. "I thought—when Officer Root told me they found Leon hanging in his garage—I assumed it was a suicide."

"I'm afraid it's a homicide."

"You're certain? Absolutely?"

Oh yes. Absolutely. "Mrs. Bazarian, if you could think back to Sunday night—"

"My husband isn't coming home until Monday, and I'm alone here with the kids. Are we safe?"

"Tell me about Sunday night."

"Are my children *safe*?"

It was the first question any mother would ask. Jane thought about her own three-year-old daughter, Regina. Thought about how she would feel in Nora Bazarian's position, with two young children, living so close to a place of violence. Would she prefer reassurance, or the truth, which was that Jane didn't know the answer. She couldn't promise that anyone was ever safe.

"Until we know more," said Jane, "it would be a good idea to take precautions."

"What *do* you know?"

"We believe it happened sometime Sunday night."

"He's been dead all this time," Nora murmured. "Right next door, and I had no idea."

"You didn't see or hear anything unusual Sunday night?"

"You can see for yourself, he has a tall fence all around his yard, so we never knew what was going on there. Except when he was making that god-awful racket in his backyard workshop."

"What kind of noise?"

"This horrible whine, like a power saw. To think he had the nerve to complain about a crying baby!"

Jane remembered seeing Gott's hearing aids on the bathroom counter. If he'd been working with noisy machinery Sunday night, he'd certainly leave out those hearing aids. It was yet one more reason he would not have heard an intruder.

"You said you got home late Sunday night. Were Mr. Gott's lights on?"

Nora didn't even need to think about it. "Yes, they were," she said. "I remember being annoyed because the light on his backyard shed shines directly into my bedroom. But when I went to bed, around ten thirty, the light was finally off."

"What about the dog? Was he barking?"

"Oh, Bruno. He's *always* barking, that's the problem. He probably barks at houseflies."

Of which there were now plenty, thought Jane. Bruno was barking at that moment, in fact. Not in alarm, but with doggy excitement about the many strangers in his front yard.

Nora turned toward the sound. "What's going to happen to him?"

"I don't know. I guess we'll have to find someone to take him. And the cats as well."

"I'm not crazy about cats, but I wouldn't mind keeping the dog here. Bruno knows us, and he's always been friendly with my boys. I'd feel safer, having a dog here."

She might not feel the same way if she knew Bruno was even now digesting morsels of his dead owner's flesh.

"Do you know if Mr. Gott had any next of kin?" asked Jane.

"He had a son, but he died some years ago, on a foreign trip. His ex-wife's dead, too, and I've never seen any woman there." Nora shook her head. "It's an awful thing to think about. Dead for four days and no one even notices. That's how unconnected he seemed to be."

Through the kitchen window, Jane caught a glimpse of Maura, who'd just emerged from Gott's house and now stood on the sidewalk, checking messages on her cell phone. Like Gott, Maura lived alone, and even now she seemed an isolated figure, standing off by herself. Left to her solitary nature, might Maura one day evolve into another Leon Gott?

The morgue van had arrived, and the first TV crews were scrambling into position outside the police tape. But tonight, after all these cops and criminalists and reporters departed, the crime scene tape would remain, marking the home where a killer had visited. And here, right next door, was a mother alone with her two children.

"It wasn't just random, was it?" said Nora. "Was it someone he knew? What do you think you're dealing with?"

A monster was what Jane thought as she slipped her pen and notebook into her purse and stood up. "I notice you have a security system, ma'am," she said. "Use it."

FOUR

MAURA CARRIED THE CARDBOARD BOX FROM HER CAR INTO THE house and set it down on the kitchen floor. The gray tabby was mewing pitifully, begging to be released, but Maura kept him contained in the box as she hunted in her pantry for a cat-appropriate meal. She'd had no chance to stop at the grocery store for cat food, had impulsively taken on the tabby because no one else would, and the only alternative was the animal shelter.

And because the cat, by practically grafting himself to her leg, had clearly adopted *her*.

In the pantry Maura found a bag of dry dog food, left over from Julian's last visit with his dog, Bear. Would a cat eat dog food? She wasn't sure. She reached for a can of sardines instead.

The tabby's cries turned frantic as Maura opened the can, releasing its fishy fragrance. She emptied the sardines into a bowl and opened the cardboard box. The cat shot out and attacked the fish so ravenously that the bowl skittered across the kitchen tiles.

"Guess sardines taste better than human, huh?" She stroked the tabby's back, and his tail arched up in pleasure. She had never owned a cat. She'd never had the time or the inclination to adopt any pet, unless she counted the brief and ultimately tragic experience with the Siamese fighting fish. She wasn't certain she wanted this pet, either, but here he was, purring like an outboard motor as his tongue licked the china bowl—the same bowl she used for her breakfast cereal. That was a disturbing thing to consider. Man-eating cat. Cross-contamination. She thought of all the diseases that felines were known to harbor: Cat scratch fever. *Toxoplasma gondii.* Feline leukemia. Rabies and roundworms and salmonella. Cats were veritable cesspools of infection, and one was now eating out of her cereal bowl.

The tabby lapped up the last fragment of sardine and looked up at Maura with crystal-green eyes, his gaze so intent that he seemed to be reading her mind, recognizing a kindred spirit. This is how crazy cat ladies are created, she thought. They look into an animal's eyes and think they see a soul looking back. And what did this cat see when he looked at Maura? The human with the can opener.

"If only you could talk," she said. "If only you could tell us what you saw."

But this tabby was keeping his secrets. He allowed her to give him a few more strokes, then he sauntered away into a corner, where he proceeded to wash himself. So much for feline affection. It was *Feed me, now leave me alone.* Maybe he truly was the perfect pet for her, both of them loners, unsuited for long-term companionship.

Since he was ignoring her, she ignored him and attended to her own dinner. She slid a leftover casserole of eggplant Parmesan into the oven, poured a glass of Pinot Noir, and sat down at her laptop to upload the photos from the Gott crime scene. On screen she saw once again the gutted body, the face stripped to bone, the blowfly larvae gorged on flesh, and she remembered all too vividly the smells of that house, the hum of the flies. It would not be a pleasant autopsy tomorrow. Slowly she clicked through the images, searching for details that she might have overlooked while at the scene, where the presence of cops and criminalists was a noisy distraction. She saw nothing that was inconsistent with her postmortem interval estimate of four to five days. The extensive injuries to the face, neck, and upper limbs could be attributed to scavenger damage. And that means *you,* she thought, glancing at the tabby, who was serenely licking his paws. What was his name? She had no idea, but she couldn't just keep calling him Cat.

The next photo was of the mound of viscera inside the trash can, a congealed mass that she would need to soak and peel apart before she could adequately examine the individual organs. It would be the most repellent part of the autopsy, because it was in the viscera where putrefaction started, where bacteria thrived and multiplied. She clicked through the next few images, then stopped, focusing on yet another view of the viscera in the trash can. The lighting was different in this image because the flash had not gone off, and in the slanting light, new curves and fissures were revealed on the surface.

The doorbell rang.

She wasn't expecting visitors. Certainly she didn't expect to find Jane Rizzoli standing on her front porch.

"Thought you might need this," said Jane, holding out a shopping bag.

"Need what?"

"Kitty litter, and a box of Friskies. Frost feels guilty that you're the one who got stuck with the cat, so I told him I'd drop this off. Has he torn up your furniture yet?"

"Demolished a can of sardines, that's about it. Come in, you can see for yourself how he's doing."

"Probably a lot better than the other one."

"Gott's white cat? What did you do with it?"

"No one can catch it. It's still hiding somewhere in that house."

"I hope you gave it some fresh food and water."

"Frost has taken charge, of course. Claims he can't stand cats, but you should've seen him down on his hands and knees, begging kitty, *pretty please!* to come out from under the bed. He'll go back tomorrow and change the litter box."

"I think he could really use a pet. He's got to be pretty lonely these days."

"Is that why *you* took one home?"

"Of course not. I took him home because . . ." Maura sighed. "I have no idea why. Because he wouldn't leave me alone."

"Yeah, he knows a patsy when he sees one," Jane said with a laugh as she followed Maura to the kitchen. "There's the lady who'll feed me cream and pâté."

In the kitchen Maura stared in dismay at the tabby, who was on top of the kitchen table, his front paws planted on her laptop keyboard. "Shoo," she snapped. "Get off!"

The cat yawned and rolled onto his side.

Maura scooped him up and dropped him onto the floor. "And *stay* off."

"You know, he can't really hurt your computer," said Jane.

"It's not the computer, it's the table. I eat at that table." Maura grabbed a sponge, squirted it with spray cleaner, and began wiping the tabletop.

"I think you might have missed a microbe there."

"Not funny. Think of where that cat's been. What his feet have been walking through in the past four days. Would you want to eat at that table?"

"He's probably cleaner than my three-year-old."

"No disagreement there. Children are like fomites."

"What?"

"Spreading infections everywhere they go." Maura gave the table one last vigorous swipe and threw the sponge in the trash can.

"I'll remember that when I get home. *Come to Mommy, my sweet little fomite.*" Jane opened the bag of kitty litter and poured it into the plastic litter box she'd also brought. "Where do you want to put this?"

"I was hoping I could just let him out and he'd do his business in the yard."

"Let him out and he might not come back." Jane clapped litter dust from her hands and straightened. "Or maybe that's a good thing?"

"I don't know what I was thinking, bringing him home. Just because he attached himself to me. It's not as if I wanted a cat."

"You just said Frost needed a pet. Why not you?"

"Frost just got divorced. He's not used to being alone."

"And you are."

"I have been for years, and I don't think that's going to change anytime soon." Maura looked around at the spotless countertops, the scrubbed sink. "Unless some miracle man suddenly appears."

"Hey, that's what you should call him," said Jane, pointing to the cat. "Miracle Man."

"That is *not* going to be his name." The kitchen timer beeped, and Maura opened the oven to check on the casserole.

"Smells good."

"It's eggplant Parmesan. I couldn't stomach the thought of eating meat tonight. Are you hungry? There's enough here for two of us."

"I'm going to my mom's for dinner. Gabriel's still in DC, and Mom can't stand the thought of me and Regina by ourselves." Jane paused. "Maybe you want to join us, just for the company?"

"It's nice of you to ask, but my dinner's already heated up."

"Not necessarily tonight, but in general. Anytime you need a family to hang out with."

Maura gave her a long look. "Are you adopting me?"

Jane pulled out a chair and sat down at the kitchen table. "Look, I feel we still need to clear the air between us. We haven't talked much since the Teddy Clock case, and I know the last few months have been tough on you. I should have asked you to dinner a long time ago."

"I should have invited you, too. We've both been busy, that's all."

"You know, it really worried me, Maura, when you said you were thinking about leaving Boston."

"Why would it worry you?"

"After all we've been through together, how can you just walk away? We've lived through things no one else could possibly understand. Like *that.*" Jane pointed to Maura's computer, where the photo of entrails was still on screen. "Tell me, who else am I gonna talk to about guts in a trash can? It's not something that normal people would do."

"Meaning, I'm not normal."

"You don't honestly think that I am, do you?" Jane laughed. "We're both sick and twisted. That's the only explanation for why we're in this business. And why we make such a good team."

It was something Maura could not have predicted when she'd first met Jane.

She'd earlier heard of Jane's reputation, muttered by the male cops: *Bitch. Ballbuster. Always on the rag.* The woman who strode onto the crime scene that day had certainly been blunt, focused, and relentless. She was also one of the best detectives Maura had ever encountered.

"You once told me you didn't have anything keeping you here in Boston," said Jane. "I'm just reminding you it's not true. You and I, we've got a history together."

"Right." Maura snorted. "Of getting into trouble."

"And getting ourselves out of it, together. What's waiting for you in San Francisco?"

"I did get an offer from an old colleague there. A teaching position at UC."

"What about Julian? You're the closest thing to a mother that boy has. You go off to California, he'll feel like you're abandoning him here."

"I hardly get a chance to see him as it is. Julian's seventeen, and he'll be applying for college. Who knows where he'll end up, and there are some fine schools in California. I can't hitch my life to a boy who's just starting his own."

"This job offer in San Francisco. Does it pay better? Is that it?"

"That's not why I'd take it."

"It's about running away, isn't it? Getting the hell out of Dodge." Jane paused. "Does *he* know you might leave Boston?"

He. Abruptly Maura turned away and refilled her wineglass. Driven to drink, just by the mention of Daniel Brophy. "I haven't spoken to Daniel in months."

"But you see him."

"Of course. When I walk onto a crime scene, I never know if he'll be there. Comforting the family, praying for the victim. We move in the same circles, Jane. The circle of the dead." She took a deep sip of wine. "It would be a relief to escape it."

"So going to California is all about avoiding him."

"And temptation," Maura said softly.

"To go back to him?" Jane shook her head. "You made your decision. Stick with it and move on. That's what I would do."

And that's what made them so different from each other. Jane was quick to act, and always certain about what needed to be done. She wasted no sleep second-guessing herself. But uncertainty was what kept Maura awake at night, mulling over choices, considering their consequences. If only life were like a mathematical formula, with just one answer.

Jane stood up. "Think about what I said, okay? It'd be way too much work for me to break in another ME. So I'm counting on you to stay." She touched Maura's arm and added quietly: "I'm asking you to stay." Then, in typical Jane Rizzoli fashion, she brusquely turned to leave. "See you tomorrow."

"Autopsy's in the morning," said Maura as they walked to the front door.

"I'd rather skip it. I've seen more than enough maggots, thank you."

"Surprises might turn up. You wouldn't want to miss it."

"The only surprise," Jane said as she stepped outside, "will be if Frost shows up."

Maura locked the door and returned to the kitchen, where the eggplant casserole had cooled. She slid it back into the oven to reheat. The cat had once again jumped onto the table and draped himself over the laptop keyboard, as if to say: *No more work tonight.* Maura snatched him up and dropped him to the floor. Someone had to exert authority in this house, and it most certainly was not going to be a cat. He'd reawakened the screen, which was now lit with the last image she'd been studying. It was the photo of the viscera, the undulated surface emphasized by shadows cast in the slanting light. She was about to close the laptop when she focused on the liver. Frowning, she zoomed in and stared at the surface curves and fissures. It was not just a trick of the light. Nor was it distortion caused by bacterial swelling.

This liver has six lobes.

She reached for the phone.

FIVE

BOTSWANA

"WHERE IS HE?" SYLVIA IS SCREAMING. *"WHERE'S THE REST OF HIM?"*

She and Vivian stand a few dozen yards away, under the trees. They are staring down at the ground, at something hidden from my view by knee-high grass. I step over the camp's perimeter wire, where the bells still hang, bells that gave no warning clang in the night. Instead it is Sylvia who has given the alarm, her shrieks pulling us out of our tents in various states of undress. Mr. Matsunaga is still zipping up his trousers as he lurches out through his tent flap. Elliot doesn't even bother to pull on pants, but stumbles out into the cold dawn wearing only boxer shorts and sandals. I've managed to snatch up one of Richard's shirts and I pull it over my nightdress as I wade into the grass, my boots still untied, a trapped pebble biting into my bare sole. I spot a bloody shred of khaki, tangled like a snake around the branch of a bush. Another few steps closer, and I see more ripped cloth, and a clump of what looks like black wool. I take another few steps, and I see what the girls are staring at. Now I know why Sylvia is screaming.

Vivian turns and throws up into the bushes.

I am too numb to move. Even as Sylvia whimpers and hyperventilates beside me, I am studying the various bones scattered in that flattened area of grass, feeling strangely remote, as if I am inhabiting someone else's body. A scientist's, perhaps. An anatomist, who looks at bones and feels compelled to fit them together, to announce: *This is the right fibula and that is the ulna and that is from the fifth right toe. Yes, definitely the right toe.* Although in truth I can identify almost nothing of what I'm looking at, because there is so little left, and it is all in pieces. All I can be sure of is that there is a rib, because it looks like ribs that I have eaten, slathered in sauce. But this is not a pork rib, oh no, this gnawed and splintered bone is human, and it belonged to someone I knew, someone I spoke to not nine hours ago.

"Oh Jesus," groans Elliot. "What happened? What the fuck happened?"

Johnny's voice booms out: "Get back. Everyone *get back.*"

I turn to see Johnny pushing into our circle. We are all here now—Vivian and Sylvia, Elliot and Richard, the Matsunagas. Only one person is missing, but not really, because here is his rib and a clump of Clarence's hair. The smell of death is in the air, the smell of fear and fresh meat and Africa.

Johnny crouches down over the bones and for a moment does not speak. No one does. Even the birds are quiet, rattled by this human disturbance, and all I hear is the grass rustling in the wind and the faint rush of the river.

"Did any of you see anything last night? Hear anything?" Johnny asks. He looks up, and I notice that his shirt is unbuttoned, his face unshaven. His eyes lock on mine. All I can do is shake my head.

"Anyone?" Johnny scans our faces.

"I slept like a rock," says Elliot. "I didn't hear—"

"We didn't, either," says Richard. Answering, in his usual annoying way, for both of us.

"Who found him?"

Vivian's answer comes out barely a whisper. "We did. Sylvia and I. We both had to use the toilet. It was already getting light, and we thought it would be safe to come out. Clarence usually has the fire started by now, and . . ." She stops, looking sick that she has said his name. *Clarence.*

Johnny rises to his feet. I am standing closest to him, and I take in every detail, from his sleep-fluffed hair to the thickly knotted scar on his abdomen, a scar I'm seeing for the first time. He has no interest in us now, because we can't tell him anything. Instead his attention is focused on the ground, on the scattered remnants of the kill. He glances first toward the camp perimeter, where the wire is strung. "The bells didn't ring," he says. "I would have heard it. Clarence would have heard it."

"So it—whatever it was—didn't come into camp?" Richard says.

Johnny ignores him. He begins to pace an ever-expanding circle, impatiently pushing aside anyone who stands in his path. There is no bare earth, only grass, and no footprints or animal tracks to offer any clues. "He took over watch at two A.M., and I went straight to sleep. The fire's almost dead, so no wood's been added for hours. Why would he leave it? Why would he step out of the perimeter?" He glances around. "And where's the rifle?"

"The rifle is there," says Mr. Matsunaga, and he points toward the ring of stones where the campfire has now gone out. "I saw it, lying on the ground."

"He just *left* it there?" says Richard. "He walks away from the fire and wanders into the dark without his gun? Why would Clarence do that?"

"He wouldn't" is Johnny's quietly chilling answer. He is circling again, scanning the grass. Finding scraps of cloth, a shoe, but little else. He moves farther away, toward the river. Suddenly he drops to his knees, and over the grass I can just see the top of his blond head. His stillness makes us all uneasy. No one is eager to find out what he's now staring at; we have already seen more than enough. But his silence calls to me with a gravitational force that pulls me toward him.

He looks up at me. "Hyenas."

"How do you know they did it?"

He points to grayish clumps on the ground. "That's spotted hyena scat. You see the animal hair, the bits of bone mixed in?"

"Oh God. It's not his, is it?"

"No, this scat is a few days old. But we know hyenas are here." He points to a tattered piece of bloody fabric. "And they found him."

"But I thought hyenas were only scavengers."

"I can't prove they took him down. But I think it's clear they fed on him."

"There's so little of him left," I murmur, looking at the fragments of cloth. "It's as if he just . . . disappeared."

"Scavengers waste nothing, leave nothing behind. They probably dragged the rest of him to their den. I don't understand why Clarence died without making a sound. Why I didn't hear the kill." Johnny stays crouched over those gray lumps of scat, but his eyes are scanning the area, seeing things that I'm not even aware of. His stillness unnerves me; he is like no other man I've met, so in tune with his environment that he seems a part of it, as rooted to this land as the trees and the gently waving grasses. He is not at all like Richard, whose eternal dissatisfaction with life keeps him searching the Internet for a better flat, a better holiday spot, maybe even a better girlfriend. Richard doesn't know what he wants or where he belongs, the way Johnny does. Johnny, whose prolonged silence makes me want to rush into the gap with some inane comment, as if it is my duty to keep up the conversation. But the discomfort is solely my own, not Johnny's.

He says, quietly: "We need to gather up everything we can find."

"You mean . . . Clarence?"

"For his family. They'll want it for the funeral. Something tangible, something for them to mourn over."

I look down in horror at the bloody scrap of clothing. I don't want to touch it; I certainly don't want to pick up those scattered bits of bone and hair. But I nod and say, "I'll help you. We can use one of the burlap sacks in the truck."

He rises and looks at me. "You're not like the others."

"What do you mean?"

"You don't even want to be here, do you? In the bush."

I hug myself. "No. This was Richard's idea of a holiday."

"And your idea of a holiday?"

"Hot showers. Flush toilets, maybe a massage. But here I am, always the good sport."

"You are a good sport, Millie. You know that, don't you?" He looks into the distance and says, so softly that I almost miss it: "Better than he deserves."

I wonder if he intended for me to hear that. Or maybe he's been in the bush so long that he regularly talks aloud to himself out here, because no one is usually around to hear him.

I try to read his face, but he bends down to pick up something. When he rises again, he has it in his hand.

A bone.

"YOU ALL UNDERSTAND, THIS expedition is at an end," says Johnny. "I need everyone to pitch in so we can break camp by noon and be on our way."

"On our way where?" says Richard. "The plane isn't due back at the airstrip for another week."

Johnny has gathered us around the cold campfire, to tell us what happens next. I look at the other members of our safari, tourists who signed up for a wildlife adventure and got more than they bargained for. A real kill, a dead man. Not exactly the jolly thrills you see on television nature programs. Instead there is a sad burlap sack containing pitifully few bones and shreds of clothing and torn pieces of scalp, all the mortal remains we could find of our tracker Clarence. The rest of him, Johnny says, is lost forever. This is how it is in the bush, where every creature that's born will ultimately be eaten, digested, and recycled into scat, into soil, into grass. Grazed upon and reborn as yet another animal. It seems beautiful in principle, but when you come face-to-face with the hard reality, that bag of Clarence's bones, you understand that the circle of life is also a circle of death. We are here to eat and be eaten, and we are nothing but meat. Eight of us left now, meat on the bone, surrounded by carnivores.

"If we drive back to the landing strip now," says Richard, "we'll just have to sit there and wait days for the plane. How is that better than continuing the trip as planned?"

"I'm not taking you any deeper into the bush," says Johnny.

"What about using the radio?" Vivian asks. "You could call the pilot to pick us up early."

Johnny shakes his head. "We're beyond radio range here. There's no way to contact him until we get back to the airstrip, and that's a three-day drive to the west. Which is why we'll head east instead. Two days' hard drive, no stops for sightseeing, and we'll reach one of the game lodges. They have a telephone, and there's a road out. I'll arrange to have you driven back to Maun."

"Why?" asks Richard. "I hate to sound callous, but there's not a thing we can do for Clarence now. I don't see the point of rushing back."

"You'll get a refund, Mr. Renwick."

"It's not the money. It's just that Millie and I came all this way from London. Elliot had to come from Boston. Not to mention how far the Matsunagas had to fly."

"Jesus, Richard," Elliot cuts in. "The man's *dead.*"

"I know, but we're already here. We might as well carry on."

"I can't do that," says Johnny.

"Why not?"

"I can't guarantee your safety, much less your comfort. I can't stay alert twenty-four hours a day. It takes two of us to stand watch overnight and to keep the fire burning. To break camp and set it up again. Clarence didn't just cook your meals; he was another set of eyes and ears. I need a second man when I'm hauling around people who don't know a rifle from a walking stick."

"So teach *me.* I'll help you stand watch." Richard looks around at the rest of us, as if to confirm that he's the only one who's man enough for the task.

Mr. Matsunaga says, "I know how to shoot. I can take watch, too."

We all look at the Japanese banker, whose only shooting skills we've witnessed so far have been with his mile-long telephoto lens.

Richard can't suppress a disbelieving laugh. "You do mean *real* guns, Isao?"

"I belong to the Tokyo shooting club," says Mr. Matsunaga, unruffled by Richard's snide tone. He points to his wife and adds, to our astonishment, "Keiko, she belongs, too."

"I'm glad that lets me off the hook," says Elliot. "'Cause I don't even want to touch the damn thing."

"So you see, we have enough hands on deck," Richard says to Johnny. "We can take turns on watch and keep the fire going all night. This is what a real safari's all about, isn't it? Rising to the occasion. Proving our mettle."

Oh yes, Richard the expert, who spends his year sitting so heroically at his computer, spinning testosterone-fueled fantasies. Now those fantasies have come true, and he can play the hero of his own thriller. Best of all, he has an audience that includes two gorgeous blondes, who are the ones he's really playing to, because I'm past the point of being impressed by him, and he knows it.

"A pretty speech, but it changes nothing. Pack up your things, we're headed east." Johnny walks away to take down his tent.

"Thank God he's ending this," says Elliot.

"He has to." Richard snorts. "Now that he's bloody well botched it."

"You can't blame him for what happened to Clarence."

"Who's ultimately responsible? He hired a tracker he's never worked with before." Richard turns to me. "That's what Clarence told you. Said he'd never worked with Johnny until this trip."

"But they had connections," I point out. "And Clarence worked as a tracker before. Johnny wouldn't have hired him if he wasn't experienced."

"That's what you'd *think,* but look what happened. Our so-called experienced tracker puts down his rifle and walks into a pack of hyenas. Does that sound like someone who knew what he was doing?"

"What's the point of all this, Richard?" Elliot asks wearily.

"The point is, we can't trust his judgment. That's all I'm saying."

"Well, I think Johnny's right. We can't just *carry on,* as you put it. A dead man kind of ruins the mood, you know?" Elliot turns toward his tent. "It's time to get out of here and go home."

Home. As I stuff clothes and toiletries into my duffel bag, I think about London and gray skies and cappuccino. In ten days, Africa will seem like a golden-hued dream, a place of heat and glaring sunlight, life and death in all its vivid colors. Yesterday I wanted nothing more than to be back home in our flat, in the land of hot showers. But now that we're leaving the bush, I feel it holding on to me, its tendrils winding around my ankles, threatening to root me to this soil. I zip up my knapsack, which contains the "essentials," all the things I thought I absolutely needed to survive in the wild: PowerBars and toilet paper, pre-moistened hand wipes and sunscreen, tampons and my mobile. How different the word *essential* seems when you're beyond the reach of any phone tower.

By the time Richard and I have packed up our tent, Johnny has already loaded up the truck with his own gear as well as the cooking equipment and camp chairs. We've all been amazingly quick, even Elliot, who struggled to dismantle his tent and needed Vivian and Sylvia to help him fold it. Clarence's death hangs over us, stifling idle chatter, making us focus on our tasks. When I load our tent into the back of the truck, I notice the burlap bag with Clarence's remains tucked beside Johnny's backpack. It unnerves me to see it stowed there, with the rest of our gear. *Tents, check. Stove, check. Dead man, check.*

I climb into the truck and sit down beside Richard. Clarence's empty seat is in view, a stark reminder that he's gone, his bones scattered, flesh digested. Johnny is the last one to climb into the truck, and as his door slams shut I look around at our now cleared campsite, thinking: Soon there'll be no trace that we were ever here. We'll have moved on, but Clarence never will.

Suddenly Johnny swears and climbs out of the driver's seat. Something is wrong.

He stalks to the front and lifts the truck bonnet to inspect the engine. Moments tick by. His head is hidden by the raised bonnet, so we can't see his face, but his silence alarms me. He offers no reassuring *It's just a loose wire* or *Yes, I see the problem.*

"Now what?" mutters Richard. He, too, climbs out of the truck, although I don't know what advice he can possibly offer. Beyond reading the petrol gauge, he knows nothing about cars. I hear him offering suggestions. Battery? Spark plugs? Loose connection? Johnny answers in barely audible monosyllables, which only alarms me more, because I've learned that the more dire the situation, the quieter Johnny becomes.

It is hot in the open truck, almost noon, with the sun beating down. The rest of us climb out and move into the shade of the trees. I see Johnny's head pop up as he orders: "Don't wander too far!" Not that anyone intends to; we've seen what can happen when you do. Mr. Matsunaga and Elliot join Richard at the truck, to offer their advice, because of course all men, even men who never get their hands greasy, understand machinery. Or think they do.

We women wait in the shade, swatting away bugs, continually searching for any telltale trembling in the grass, which could be our only warning that a predator approaches. Even in the shade, it is hot, and I settle onto the ground. Through the branches above I see vultures circling, watching us. They are strangely beautiful, black wings sketching lazy loops in the sky as they wait to feast. *On what?*

Richard stalks toward us, muttering: "Well, *this* is a brilliant development. Bloody thing won't start. Won't even turn over."

I sit up straight. "It was fine yesterday."

"Everything was fine yesterday." Richard huffs out a breath. "We're stranded."

The blondes give simultaneous gasps of alarm. "We *can't* be stranded," blurts Sylvia. "I'm due back at work next Thursday!"

"Me, too!" says Vivian.

Mrs. Matsunaga shakes her head in disbelief. "How can this be? It is not possible!"

As their voices blend into a chorus of rising agitation, I can't help noticing that the vultures overhead are tracing tighter and tighter circles, as if homing in on our distress.

"Listen. All of you, *listen,*" Johnny commands.

We turn to look at him.

"This is not the time to panic," he says. "There's absolutely no reason to. We're next to the river, so we have plenty of water. We have shelter. We have ammunition and a ready supply of game for food."

Elliot gives a laugh that's thin with fear. "So . . . what? We hang around out here and go all Stone Age?"

"The plane is scheduled to meet you at the landing strip in a week. When we don't show up as expected, there'll be a search. They'll find us soon enough. It's what you all signed up for, isn't it? An authentic experience in the bush?" He regards us one by one, taking our measure, deciding if we're up to the challenge. Searching for which one of us will crumble, which one he can count on. "I'll keep working on the truck. Maybe I can fix it, maybe I can't."

"Do you even know what's wrong with it?" Elliot asks.

Johnny pins him with a hard glare. "It's never broken down before. I can't explain it." He scans our circle, as if searching for the answer in our faces. "In the meantime, we need to pitch camp again. Get out the tents. This is where we stay."

SIX

BOSTON

PSYCHOLOGISTS CALL IT RESISTANCE WHEN A PATIENT FAILS TO TURN UP on time because he doesn't really want to address his problems. It also explained why Jane was late walking out her front door that morning; she *really* didn't want to view Leon Gott's autopsy. She took her time dressing her daughter in the same Red Sox T-shirt and grass-stained overalls that Regina had insisted on wearing for the past five days. They lingered too long over their breakfast of Lucky Charms and toast, which made them twenty minutes late walking out the apartment door. Add a traffic-choked drive to Revere, where Jane's mother lived, and by the time she pulled up outside Angela's house, Jane was a full half hour behind schedule.

Her mother's house seemed smaller every year, as though it were shrinking with age. Walking up to the front door with Regina in tow, Jane saw that the porch needed fresh paint, the gutters were clogged with autumn leaves, and the perennials in front still needed to be clipped back for the winter. She'd have to get on the phone with her brothers and see if they could all pitch in for a weekend, because Angela obviously needed the help.

She could also use a good night's sleep, thought Jane when Angela opened the front door. Jane was startled by how tired her mother looked. Everything about her seemed worn down, from her faded blouse to her baggy jeans. When Angela bent down to pick up Regina, Jane spotted gray roots on her mother's scalp, a startling sight because Angela was meticulous about her hairdresser appointments. Was this the same woman who'd shown up at a restaurant just last summer wearing red lipstick and spike heels?

"Here's my little pumpkin," Angela cooed as she carried Regina into the house. "Nonna's so glad to see you. Let's go shopping today, why don't we? Aren't you tired of these dirty overalls? We'll buy you something new and pretty."

"Don't *like* pretty!"

"A dress, what do you think? A fancy princess dress."

"Don't *like* princess."

"But every girl wants to be a princess!"

"I think she'd rather be the frog," said Jane.

"Oh for heaven's sake, she's just like you." Angela sighed in frustration. "You wouldn't let me put you in a dress, either."

"Not everyone's a princess, Ma."

"Or ends up with Prince Charming," muttered Angela as she walked away carrying her granddaughter.

Jane followed her into the kitchen. "What's going on?"

"I'm going to make some more coffee. You want some?"

"Ma, I can see that something's going on."

"You've gotta go to work." Angela set Regina in her high chair. "Go, catch some bad guys."

"Is it too much work for you, babysitting? You know you don't have to do it. She's old enough for day care now."

"My granddaughter in day care? Not gonna happen."

"Gabriel and I have been talking about it. You've already done so much for us, and we think you deserve a break. Enjoy your life."

"*She* is the one thing I look forward to every day," said Angela, pointing to her granddaughter. "The one thing that keeps my mind off . . ."

"Dad?"

Angela turned away and began filling the coffee reservoir with water.

"Ever since he came back," said Jane, "I haven't seen you look happy. Not one single day."

"It's gotten so complicated, having to make a choice. I'm getting pulled back and forth, stretched like taffy. I wish someone would just tell me what to do, so I wouldn't have to choose between them."

"You're the one who has to make the choice. Dad or Korsak. I think you should choose the man who makes you happy."

Angela turned a tormented face to hers. "How can I be happy if I spend the rest of my life feeling guilty? Having your brothers tell me that I *chose* to break up the family?"

"You didn't choose to walk out. Dad did."

"And now he's back and he wants us all to be together again."

"You have a right to move on."

"When both my sons are insisting I give your father another chance? Father Donnelly says it's what a good wife *should* do."

Oh great, thought Jane. Catholic guilt was the most powerful guilt of all.

Jane's cell phone rang. She glanced down and saw it was Maura calling; she let it go to voice mail.

"And poor Vince," said Angela. "I feel guilty about him, too. All the wedding plans we made."

"It could still happen."

"I don't see how, not now." Angela sagged back against the kitchen counter as the coffeemaker gurgled and hissed behind her. "Last night I finally told him. Janie, it was the hardest thing I've ever done in my whole life." And it showed on her face. The puffy eyes, the drooping mouth—was this the new and future Angela Rizzoli, sainted wife and mother?

There are already too many martyrs in the world, thought Jane. The idea that her mother would willingly join those legions made her angry.

"Ma, if this decision makes you miserable, you need to remember that it's *your* decision. You're choosing *not* to be happy. No one can make you do that."

"How can you say that?"

"Because it's true. You're the one in control, and you have to take the wheel." Her phone pinged with a text message, and she saw it was Maura again. STARTING AUTOPSY. RU COMING?

"Go on, go to work." Angela waved her away. "You don't need to bother yourself with this."

"I want you to be happy, Ma." Jane turned to leave, then looked back at Angela. "But you have to want it, too."

It was a relief for Jane to step outside, take a breath of fresh cold air, and purge the gloom of the house from her lungs. But she couldn't shake off her annoyance at her dad, at her brothers, at Father Donnelly, at every man who presumed to tell a woman what her duty was.

When her phone rang again, she answered with an irritated: "Rizzoli!"

"Uh, it's me," said Frost.

"Yeah, I'm on my way to the morgue. I'll be there in twenty minutes."

"You're not there already?"

"I got held up at my mom's. Why aren't *you* there?"

"I thought it might be more efficient if I, uh, followed up on a few other things."

"Instead of barfing into a sink all morning. Good choice."

"I'm still waiting for the phone carrier to release Gott's call log. Meantime, here's something interesting I pulled off Google. Back in May, Gott was featured in *Hub Magazine.* Title of the article was: 'The Trophy Master: An Interview with Boston's Master Taxidermist.'"

"Yeah, I saw a framed copy of that interview hanging in his house.

It's all about his hunting adventures. Shooting elephants in Africa, elk in Montana."

"Well, you should read the online comments about that article. They're posted on the magazine's website. Apparently, he got the lettuce eaters—that's what Gott called the anti-hunting crowd—all pissed off. Here's one comment, posted by Anonymous: 'Leon Gott should be hung and gutted, like the fucking animal he is.' "

"Hung and gutted? That sounds like a threat," she said.

"Yeah. And maybe someone delivered."

WHEN JANE SAW WHAT was displayed on the morgue table, she almost turned and walked right back out again. Even the sharp odor of formalin could not mask the stench of the viscera splayed across the steel table. Maura wore no respiratory hood, only her usual mask and plastic face guard. She was so focused on the intellectual puzzle posed by the entrails that she seemed immune to the smell. Standing beside her was a tall man with silvery eyebrows whom Jane did not recognize, and like Maura he was eagerly probing the array of viscera.

"Let's start with the large bowel here," he said, gloved hands sliding across the intestine. "We have cecum, ascending colon, transverse, descending colon . . ."

"But there's no sigmoid colon," said Maura.

"Right. The rectum is here, but there's no sigmoid. That's our first clue."

"And it's unlike the other specimen, which does have a sigmoid colon."

The man gave a delighted chuckle. "I'm certainly glad you called me to see this. It's not often I come across something this fascinating. I could dine out for months on this story."

"Wouldn't wanna be part of *that* dinner conversation," said Jane. "I guess this is what they mean by *reading the entrails.*"

Maura turned. "Jane, we're just comparing the two sets of viscera. This is Professor Guy Gibbeson. And this is Detective Rizzoli, homicide."

Professor Gibbeson gave Jane a disinterested nod and dropped his gaze back to the intestines, which he obviously found far more fascinating.

"Professor of what subject?" asked Jane, still standing back from the table. From the smell.

"Comparative anatomy. Harvard," he said without looking at her, his attention fixed on the bowel. "This second set of intestines, the one with the sigmoid colon, belongs to the victim, I presume?" he asked Maura.

"It appears so. The incised edges match up, but we'd need DNA to confirm it."

"Now, turning our attention to the lungs, I can point out some pretty definitive clues."

"Clues to what?" said Jane.

"To who owned this first set of lungs." He picked up one pair of lungs, held them for a moment. Set them down and lifted the second set. "Similar sizes, so I'm guessing similar body masses."

"According to the victim's driver's license, he was five foot eight and a hundred forty pounds."

"Well, these would be his," Gibbeson said, looking at the lungs he was holding. He put them down, picked up the other pair. "These are the lungs that really interest me."

"What's so interesting about them?" said Jane.

"Take a look, Detective. Oh, you'll have to come much closer to see it."

Suppressing a gag, Jane approached the butcher's array of offal laid across the table. Detached from their owners, all sets of viscera looked alike to Jane, consisting of the same interchangeable parts that she, too, possessed. She remembered a poster of "The Visible Woman" hanging in her high school health class, revealing the organs in their anatomical positions. Ugly or beautiful, every woman is merely a package of organs encased in a shell of flesh and bone.

"Can you see the difference?" asked Gibbeson. He pointed to the first set of lungs. "That left lung has an upper lobe and a lower lobe.

The right lung has both upper and lower lobes, plus a middle lobe. Which makes how many lobes in all?"

"Five," said Jane.

"That's normal human anatomy. Two lungs, five lobes. Now look at this second pair found in the same garbage pail. They're of similar size and weight, but with an essential difference. You see it?"

Jane frowned. "It has more lobes."

"Two extra lobes, to be exact. The right lung has four, the left has three. This is not an anatomical anomaly." He paused. "Which means it's not human."

"That's why I called Professor Gibbeson," said Maura. "To help me identify which species we're dealing with."

"A large one," said Gibbeson. "Human-sized, I'd say, judging by the heart and lungs. Now let's see if we can find any answers in the liver." He moved to the far end of the table, where the two livers were displayed side by side. "Specimen one has left and right lobes. Quadrate and caudate lobes . . ."

"That one's human," said Maura.

"But this other specimen . . ." Gibbeson picked up the second liver and flipped it over to examine the reverse side. "It has six lobes."

Maura looked at Jane. "Again, not human."

"So we've got two sets of guts," said Jane. "One belonging to the victim, we assume. The other belonging to . . . what? A deer? A pig?"

"Neither," said Gibbeson. "Based on the lack of sigmoid colon, the seven-lobed lungs, the six-lobed liver, I believe this viscera comes from a member of the family Felidae."

"Which is?"

"The cat family."

Jane looked at the liver. "That'd be one damn big kitty."

"It's an extensive family, Detective. It includes lions, tigers, cougars, leopards, and cheetahs."

"But we didn't find any carcass like that at the scene."

"Did you check the freezer?" asked Gibbeson. "Find any meat you can't identify?"

Jane gave an appalled laugh. "We didn't find any tiger steaks. Who'd want to eat one, anyway?"

"There's definitely a market for exotic meats. The more unusual the better. People pay for the experience of dining on just about anything, from rattlesnake to bear. The question is, where did this animal come from? Was it hunted illegally? And how on earth did it end up gutted in a house in Boston?"

"He was a taxidermist," said Jane, turning to look at Leon Gott's body, which lay on an adjacent table. Maura had already wielded her scalpel and bone saw, and in the bucket nearby Gott's brain was steeping in a bath of preservative. "He's probably gutted hundreds, maybe thousands of animals. Probably never imagined he'd end up just like them."

"Actually, taxidermists process the body in a completely different way," said Maura. "I did some research on the subject last night and learned that large-animal taxidermists prefer not to gut the animal before skinning, because body fluids can spoil the pelt. They make their first incision along the spine, and peel the skin away from the carcass in one piece. So evisceration would have occurred after the pelt was removed."

"Fascinating," said Gibbeson. "I didn't know that."

"That's Dr. Isles for you. Full of all sorts of fun facts," said Jane. She nodded to Gott's corpse. "Speaking of facts, do you have a cause of death?"

"I believe I do," said Maura, stripping off blood-smeared gloves. "The extensive scavenger damage to his face and neck obscured the antemortem injuries. But his X rays gave us some answers." She went to the computer screen and clicked through a series of X-ray images. "I saw no foreign objects, nothing to indicate the use of a firearm. But I did find this." She pointed to the skull radiograph. "It's very subtle, which is why I didn't detect it on palpation. It's a linear fracture of the right parietal bone. His scalp and hair may have cushioned the blow enough so that we don't see any concave deformation, but just the presence of a fracture tells us there was significant force involved."

"So it's not from falling."

"The side of the head is an odd location for a fracture caused by a fall. Your shoulder would cushion you as you hit the ground, or you'd reach out to catch yourself. No, I'm inclined to think this was from a blow to the head. It was hard enough to stun him and take him down."

"Hard enough to kill him?"

"No. While there is a small amount of subdural blood inside the cranium, it wouldn't have been fatal. It also tells us that after the blow, his heart was still beating. For a few minutes, at least, he was alive."

Jane looked at the body, now merely an empty vessel robbed of its internal machinery. "Jesus. Don't tell me he was alive when the killer started gutting him."

"I don't believe evisceration was the cause of death, either." Maura clicked past the skull films, and two new images appeared on the monitor. "This was."

The bones of Gott's neck glowed on the screen, views of his vertebrae both head-on and from the side.

"There are fractures and displacement of the superior horns of the thyroid cartilage as well as the hyoid bone. There's massive disruption of the larynx." Maura paused. "His throat was crushed, most likely while he was lying supine. A hard blow, maybe from the weight of a shoe, straight to the thyroid cartilage. It ruptured his larynx and epiglottis, lacerated major vessels. It all became clear when I did the neck dissection. Mr. Gott died of aspiration, choking on his own blood. The lack of arterial splatter on the walls indicates the evisceration was done postmortem."

Jane was silent, her gaze fixed on the screen. How much easier it was to focus on a coldly clinical X ray than to confront what was lying on the table. X rays conveniently stripped away skin and flesh, leaving only bloodless architecture, the posts and beams of a human body. She thought of what it took to slam your heel down on a man's neck. And what did the killer feel when that throat cracked under his shoe, and he watched consciousness fade from Gott's eyes? Rage? Power? Satisfaction?

"One more thing," said Maura, clicking to a new X-ray image, this one of the chest. With all the other damage done to the body, it was startling how normal the bony structures appeared, ribs and sternum exactly where they should be. But the cavity was weirdly empty, missing its usual foggy shadows of hearts and lungs. "This," said Maura.

Jane moved closer. "Those faint scratches on the ribs?"

"Yes. I pointed it out on the body yesterday. Three parallel lacerations. They go so deep, they actually penetrated to bone. Now look at this." Maura clicked to another X ray, and the facial bones appeared, sunken orbits and shadowy sinuses.

Jane frowned. "Those three scratches again."

"Both sides of the face, penetrating to bone. Three parallel nicks. Because of the soft-tissue damage by the owner's pets, I couldn't see them. Until I looked at these X rays."

"What kind of tool would do that?"

"I don't know. I didn't see anything in his workshop that would make these marks."

"You said yesterday it looked like it was done postmortem."

"Yes."

"So what's the point of these lacerations if it's not to kill or to inflict pain?"

Maura thought about it. "Ritual," she said.

For a moment there was only silence in the room. Jane thought of other crime scenes, other rituals. She thought of the scars she would always carry on her hands, souvenirs of a killer who'd had rituals of his own, and she felt those scars ache again.

The buzz of the intercom almost made her jump.

"Dr. Isles?" said Maura's secretary. "Phone call for you from a Dr. Mikovitz. He says you left a message this morning with one of his colleagues."

"Oh, of course." Maura picked up the phone. "This is Dr. Isles."

Jane turned her gaze back to the X ray, to those three parallel nicks on the cheekbones. She tried to imagine what could have left such a mark. It was a tool that neither she nor Maura had encountered before.

Maura hung up and turned to Dr. Gibbeson. "You were absolutely right," she said. "That was the Suffolk Zoo. Kovo's carcass was delivered to Leon Gott on Sunday."

"Hold on," said Jane. "What the hell is Kovo?"

Maura pointed to the unidentified set of entrails on the morgue table. "That's Kovo. A snow leopard."

SEVEN

"KOVO WAS ONE OF OUR MOST POPULAR EXHIBITS. HE WAS WITH US nearly eighteen years, so we were all heartbroken when he had to be euthanized." Dr. Mikovitz spoke in the hushed voice of a grieving family member, and judging by the many photos displayed on the walls of his office, the animals in the Suffolk Zoo were indeed like family to him. With his wiry red hair and wisp of a goatee, Dr. Mikovitz looked like a zoo denizen himself, perhaps some exotic species of monkey with wise dark eyes that now regarded Jane and Frost across his desk. "We haven't yet issued any press release about it, so I was startled when Dr. Isles inquired whether we'd had any recent losses in our large-cat collection. How on earth did she know?"

"Dr. Isles is good at sniffing out all sorts of obscure information," said Jane.

"Yes, well, she certainly caught us by surprise. It's something of a, well, sensitive matter."

"The death of a zoo animal? Why?"

"Because he had to be euthanized. That always gets negative reactions. And Kovo was a very rare animal."

"What day was this done?"

"It was Sunday morning. Our veterinarian Dr. Oberlin came in to administer the lethal injection. Kovo's kidneys had been failing for some time and he'd lost a great deal of weight. Dr. Rhodes pulled him off exhibit a month ago, to spare him the stress of being in public. We hoped we could pull him through this illness, but Dr. Oberlin and Dr. Rhodes finally agreed that it was time to do it. Much as it grieved them both."

"Dr. Rhodes is another veterinarian?"

"No, Alan is an expert on large-cat behavior. He knew Kovo better than anyone else did. He's the one who delivered Kovo to the taxidermist." Dr. Mikovitz glanced up at a knock on his door. "Ah, here's Alan now."

The title *Large-Cat Expert* conjured up images of a rugged outdoorsman in safari clothes. The man who walked into the office was indeed wearing a khaki uniform with dusty trousers and stray burrs clinging to his fleece jacket, as if he'd just come off a hiking trail, but there was nothing particularly rugged about Rhodes's pleasantly open face. In his late thirties, with springy dark hair, he had the block-shaped head of Frankenstein's monster, but a friendly version.

"Sorry I'm late," said Rhodes, clapping dust from his pant legs. "We had an incident at the lion enclosure."

"Nothing serious, I hope?" said Dr. Mikovitz.

"No fault of the cats. It's the damn kids. Some teenager thought he'd prove his manhood, so he climbed the outer fence and fell into the moat. I had to go in and drag him out."

"Oh my God. Are we going to have any liability issues?"

"I doubt it. He was never in any real danger, and I think he found it so humiliating he'll never tell a soul." Rhodes gave a pained smile to Jane and Frost. "Just another fun day with idiot humans. My lions, at least, have more than an ounce of common sense."

"This is Detective Rizzoli, Detective Frost," said Mikovitz.

Rhodes extended a callused hand to them. "I'm Dr. Alan Rhodes.

I'm a wildlife biologist specializing in felid behavior. All cats, large and small." He glanced at Mikovitz. "So have they found Kovo?"

"I don't know, Alan. They just arrived, and we haven't gotten to that subject yet."

"Well, we need to know." Rhodes turned back to Jane and Frost. "Animal pelts deteriorate quite rapidly after death. If it isn't immediately harvested and processed, it loses its value."

"How valuable is a snow leopard pelt?" asked Frost.

"Considering how few of the animals there are in the world?" Rhodes shook his head. "I'd say priceless."

"And that's why you wanted the animal stuffed."

"*Stuffed* is rather an inelegant term," said Mikovitz. "We wanted Kovo preserved in all his beauty."

"And that's why you brought him to Leon Gott."

"For skinning and mounting. Mr. Gott is—was—one of the best taxidermists in the country."

"Did you know him personally?" asked Jane.

"Only by reputation."

Jane looked at the large-cat expert. "And you, Dr. Rhodes?"

"I met him for the first time when Debra and I delivered Kovo to his house," said Rhodes. "I was shocked this morning when I heard about his murder. I mean, we'd just seen him alive on Sunday."

"Tell me about that day. What you saw, what you heard at his house."

Rhodes glanced at Mikovitz, as if to confirm he should answer their questions.

"Go ahead, Alan," said Mikovitz. "It's a murder investigation, after all."

"Okay." Rhodes took a breath. "On Sunday morning, Greg—Dr. Oberlin, our veterinarian—euthanized Kovo. According to the agreement, we had to deliver the carcass immediately to the taxidermist. Kovo weighed over a hundred pounds, so one of our zookeepers, Debra Lopez, assisted me. It was a pretty sad drive. I worked with that cat for twelve years, and we had a bond, the two of us. Which sounds insane, because you can't really trust a leopard. Even a supposedly tame one can kill you, and Kovo was certainly large enough to bring down a man. But I never felt threatened by him. I never sensed any aggression in him at all. It's almost as if he understood I was his friend."

"What time did you arrive at Mr. Gott's house on Sunday?"

"Around ten A.M., I guess. Debra and I brought him straight there, because the carcass needs to be skinned as soon as possible."

"Did you talk much with Mr. Gott?"

"We stayed awhile. He was really excited about working on a snow leopard. It's such a rare animal, he'd never handled one before."

"Did he seem at all worried about anything?"

"No. Just euphoric about the opportunity. We carried Kovo into his garage, then he brought us into the house to show us the animals he's mounted over the years." Rhodes shook his head. "I know he was proud of his work, but I found it sad. All those beautiful creatures killed just to be trophies. But then, I'm a biologist."

"I'm not a biologist," said Frost. "But I found it pretty sad, too."

"That's their culture. Most taxidermists are also hunters, and they don't understand why anyone would object to it. Debra and I tried to be polite about it. We left his house around eleven, and that was it. I don't know what else I can tell you." He looked back and forth at Jane and Frost. "So what about the pelt? I'm anxious to know whether you found it, because it's worth a hell of a lot to—"

"Alan," said Mikovitz.

The two men glanced at each other, and both fell silent. For a few seconds, no one said anything, a pause so significant that it might as well have come with a blinking alert: *Something is wrong. There's something they're trying to hide.*

"This pelt is worth a hell of a lot to whom?" said Jane.

Mikovitz answered, too glibly: "Everyone. These animals are extremely rare."

"How rare, exactly?"

"Kovo was a snow leopard," said Rhodes. "*Panthera uncia,* from the mountainous regions of Central Asia. Their fur is thicker and paler than an African leopard's, and there are fewer than five thousand left in the world. They're like phantoms, solitary and hard to spot, and they're getting more and more rare by the day. It's illegal to import their skins. It's even illegal to sell a pelt, new or old, across state lines. You can't buy or sell them on the open market. That's why we're anxious to know. Did you find Kovo's?"

Instead of answering his question, Jane asked another. "You mentioned something earlier, Dr. Rhodes. About an agreement."

"What?"

"You said you delivered Kovo to the taxidermist as part of *the agreement.* What agreement are you talking about?"

Rhodes and Mikovitz both avoided her eyes.

"Gentlemen, this is a homicide case," Jane said. "We're going to find this out anyway, and you *really* don't want to get on my bad side."

"Tell them," said Rhodes. "They need to know."

"If this gets out, Alan, the publicity will kill us."

"Tell them."

"All right, all right." Mikovitz gave Jane an unhappy look. "Last month, we got an offer we couldn't refuse, from a prospective donor. He knew that Kovo was ill, and would most likely be euthanized. In exchange for the animal's fresh, intact carcass, he would make a substantial donation to the Suffolk Zoo."

"How substantial a donation?"

"Five million dollars."

Jane stared at him. "Is a snow leopard really worth that much?"

"To this particular donor, it is. It's a win–win proposition. Kovo was doomed anyway. We get a big influx of cash to stay afloat, and the donor gets a rare prize for his trophy room. His only stipulation was that it be kept quiet. And he specified Leon Gott as his taxidermist, because Gott is one of the best. And I believe they're already acquainted." Mikovitz sighed. "Anyway, that's why I was reluctant to mention it. The arrangement is sensitive. It could put our institution in a bad light."

"Because you're selling rare animals to the highest bidder?"

"I was against this deal from the start," Rhodes said to Mikovitz. "I told you it would come back to bite us in the ass. Now we're going to get a shitload of publicity."

"Look, if we can keep it quiet, we can salvage this. I just need to know that the pelt is safe. That it's properly handled and cared for."

"I'm sorry to tell you this, Dr. Mikovitz," said Frost, "but we found no pelt."

"What?"

"There was no leopard pelt in Gott's residence."

"You mean—it was *stolen*?"

"We don't know. It's just not there."

Mikovitz slumped back in his chair, stunned. "Oh God. It's all fallen apart. Now we'll have to return his money."

"Who is your donor?" asked Jane.

"This information can't get out. The public can't know about it."

"Who is he?"

It was Rhodes who answered, with undisguised scorn in his voice. "Jerry O'Brien."

Jane and Frost glanced at each other in surprise. "You mean *the* Jerry O'Brien? The guy on the radio?" asked Frost.

"Boston's own Big Mouth O'Brien. How do you think our animal-loving patrons are going to feel when they hear we cut a deal with the shock jock? The guy who brags about his hunting trips to Africa? About the fun he has blasting elephants to smithereens? His whole persona is about glorifying blood sport." Rhodes gave a snort of disgust. "If only those poor animals could shoot back."

"Sometimes, Alan, we have to make a deal with the devil," said Mikovitz.

"Well, the deal's off now, since we have nothing to offer him."

Mikovitz groaned. "This is a disaster."

"Didn't I predict that?"

"Easy for you to stay above it all! You have only your damn cats to worry about. I'm charged with the survival of this institution."

"Yeah, that's the advantage of working with cats. I *know* I can't trust them. And they don't try to convince me otherwise." Rhodes glanced down at his ringing cell phone. Almost simultaneously the office door flew open and the secretary burst into the room.

"Dr. Rhodes! They need you there *now.*"

"What is it?"

"There's been an accident at the leopard enclosure. One of the keepers—they need the rifle!"

"No. *No.*" Rhodes sprang from his chair and pushed past her, out of the office.

It took only an instant for Jane to decide. She jumped up and followed him. By the time she made it down the stairs and out of the building, Rhodes was already far ahead of her, racing past startled zoo visitors. Jane had to sprint to keep up. As she rounded a curve in the path, she came up against a dense wall of people standing outside the leopard enclosure.

"Oh my God," someone gasped. "Is she *dead*?"

Jane shoved her way through the crowd until she reached the railing. At first all she saw through the cage bars was the camouflaging habitat of greenery and fake boulders. Then, almost hidden among the branches, something moved. It was a tail, twitching atop a rocky ledge.

Jane moved sideways, trying to get a better view of the animal. Only as she reached the very edge of the enclosure did she see the blood: a ribbon of it, bright and glistening, streaming down the boulder. Dangling from the rocky shelf above was a human arm. A woman's arm. Crouched over its kill, the leopard stared straight at Jane, as if daring her to steal its prize.

Jane raised her weapon and paused, her finger on the trigger. Was the victim in her line of fire? She could not see past the lip of the ledge, could not tell if the woman was even alive.

"Don't shoot!" she heard Dr. Rhodes yell from the rear of the cage. "I'm going to lure him into the night room!"

"There's no time, Rhodes. We need to get her out of there!"

"I don't want him killed."

"What about *her*?"

Rhodes banged on the bars. "Rafiki, meat! Come on, come into the night cage!"

Fuck this, thought Jane, and once again she raised her weapon. The animal was in plain view, a straight shot to the head. There was a chance the bullet might hit the woman as well, but if they didn't get her out of there soon, she was dead anyway. With both hands steady on the grip, Jane slowly squeezed the trigger. Before she could fire, the crack of a rifle startled her.

The leopard dropped and tumbled off the ledge, into the bushes.

Seconds later a blond man dressed in a zoo uniform darted across the cage, toward the boulders. "Debbie?" he called out. *"Debbie!"*

Jane glanced around for a way into the cage and spotted a side path labeled STAFF ONLY. She followed it around to the rear of the enclosure, where the door into the cage hung ajar.

She stepped inside and saw a congealed pool of red beside a bucket and fallen rake. Blood smeared the concrete pathway in an ominous trail of drag marks, punctuated by paw prints. The trail led toward the artificial boulders at the rear of the cage.

At the base of those boulders, Rhodes and the blond man crouched over the woman's body, which they'd pulled down from the rock ledge.

"Breathe, Debbie," the blond man pleaded. "Please, *breathe.*"

"I'm not getting a pulse," said Rhodes.

"Where's the ambulance?" The blond man looked around in panic. "We need an ambulance!"

"It's coming. But Greg, I don't think there's anything . . ."

The blond man planted both palms on the woman's chest and began pumping in quick, desperate bursts to restart the heart. "Help me, Alan. Do mouth-to-mouth. We need to do this together!"

"I think we're too late," said Rhodes. He placed a hand on the blond man's shoulder. "Greg."

"Fuck off, Alan! I'll do this myself!" He placed his mouth against the woman's, forced air past pale lips, and began pumping again. Already, the woman's eyes were clouding over.

Rhodes looked up at Jane and shook his head.

EIGHT

MAURA'S LAST VISIT TO THE SUFFOLK ZOO HAD BEEN ON A WARM summer weekend, when the walkways were crowded with children dripping ice cream and young parents pushing baby strollers. But on this chilly November day, Maura found the zoo eerily deserted. In the flamingo enclosure, the birds preened in peace. Peacocks strutted on the path, unmolested by pursuing cameras and toddlers. How nice it would be to stroll here alone and linger at each exhibit, but Death had called her here today, and she had no time to enjoy the visit. The zoo employee led her at a brisk pace past primate cages and toward the wild dog enclosures. Carnivore territory. Her escort was a young woman named Jen, uniformed in khaki, with a blond ponytail and a healthy tan. She would have looked right at home on a Nat Geo wildlife documentary.

"We shut down the zoo right after the incident," said Jen. "It took us about an hour to get all the visitors out. I still can't believe this happened. We've never had to deal with anything like it before."

"How long have you worked here?" asked Maura.

"Almost four years. When I was a kid, I dreamed about working in a zoo. I tried getting into vet school, but I just didn't have the grades. Still, I get to do what I love. You have to love this job, 'cause you sure don't do it for the pay."

"Did you know the victim?"

"Yeah, we're a pretty tight group." She shook her head. "I just can't figure out how Debbie could have made this mistake. Dr. Rhodes always warned us about Rafiki. *Never turn your back on him. Never trust a leopard,* he told us. And here I thought he was exaggerating."

"Doesn't it worry you? Working so closely with large predators?"

"It didn't worry me before. But this changes everything." They rounded a curve, and Jen said: "That's the enclosure where it happened."

There was no need for her to point it out; the grim faces of those who stood gathered outside the cage told Maura she had arrived at her destination. Among the group was Jane, who broke away to greet Maura.

"This is one case you're not likely to see again," said Jane.

"Are you investigating this death?"

"No, I was just about to leave. From what I've gathered, it's an accident."

"What happened, exactly?"

"It looks like the victim was cleaning the exhibit area when the cat attacked. She must have forgotten to secure the night cage, and the animal got into the main enclosure. By the time I got here, it was long over." Jane shook her head. "Reminds you exactly where we stand in the food chain."

"What kind of cat did it?"

"An African leopard. There was one large male in the cage."

"Has he been secured?"

"He's dead. Dr. Oberlin—he's that blond guy standing over there—he tried to hit him with the dart gun, but he missed both times. He had to shoot him."

"So it's safe to go in now."

"Yeah, but it's a frigging mess. There's buckets of blood in there."

Jane looked down at her stained footwear and shook her head. "I liked these shoes. Oh well. I'll call you later."

"Who's going to walk me through the scene?"

"Alan Rhodes can do it."

"Who?"

"He's their large-cat expert." Jane called out to the group of men gathered near the exhibit: "Dr. Rhodes? Dr. Isles is here, from the ME's office. She needs to see the body."

The dark-haired man who came toward them still looked shell-shocked by the tragedy. The trousers of his zoo uniform were bloodstained, and his attempt at a smile couldn't disguise the strain in his face. Automatically he reached out to greet her, then realized there was dried blood on his hand, and he dropped his arm back to his side. "I'm sorry you have to see this," he said. "I know you've probably encountered some terrible things, but this is awful."

"I've never dealt with a large-cat attack before," said Maura.

"This is my first time as well. I never want to see another one." He pulled out a key ring. "I'll take you around back, to the staff area. That's where the gate is."

Maura waved goodbye to Jane and followed Rhodes down the shrubbery-lined pathway marked STAFF ONLY. The walkway cut between neighboring exhibits and led to the rear of the enclosure, which was hidden from public view.

Rhodes unlocked the gate. "This will take us through the squeeze cage. There are two inner gates on either end of this cage. One leads to the public exhibit area. The other gate leads to the night room."

"Why is it called a squeeze cage?"

"It's a collapsible section we can use to control the cat for veterinary purposes. When he walks through this section, we push on the cage wall and it traps him against the bars. Makes it easy to vaccinate him or inject other meds in his shoulder. Minimum stress for the animal and maximum safety for the staff."

"Is this where the victim would have entered?"

"Her name was Debra Lopez."

"I'm sorry. Is this how Ms. Lopez entered?"

"It's one of the access points. There's also a separate entrance for the night room, where the animal stays during off-exhibit hours." They walked into the cage and Rhodes shut the door behind them, trapping them in the claustrophobically narrow passage. "As you can see, there are gates at both ends. Before you enter any cage, you confirm the animal is secured in the opposite section. That's Zoo Safety One Oh One: Always know where the cat is. Especially Rafiki."

"Was he particularly dangerous?"

"Every leopard is potentially dangerous, especially *Panthera pardus.* The African leopard. They're smaller than lions or tigers, but they're silent and unpredictable and powerful. A leopard can drag a carcass much heavier than he is straight up a tree. Rafiki was in his prime, and extremely aggressive. He was kept in solitary because he attacked the female leopard we tried to place with him in this exhibit. Debbie knew how dangerous he was. We all did."

"So how could she make this kind of mistake? Was she new to the job?"

"Debbie worked here at least seven years, so it certainly wasn't lack of experience. But even veteran zookeepers sometimes get careless. They fail to confirm the animal's whereabouts, or they forget to latch a gate. Greg told me that when he got here, he found the gate to the night cage wide open."

"Greg?"

"Dr. Greg Oberlin, our veterinarian."

Maura focused on the night cage gate. "This latch didn't malfunction?"

"I tested it. So did Detective Rizzoli. It's in working order."

"Dr. Rhodes, I'm having a lot of trouble understanding how an experienced zookeeper leaves a leopard's cage door wide open."

"It's hard to believe, I know. But I can show you a spreadsheet of similar accidents involving big cats. It's happened in zoos around the world. Since 1990, there've been more than seven hundred incidents in the US alone, with twenty-two people killed. Just last year, in Germany and the UK, experienced zookeepers were killed by tigers. In both cases, they simply forgot to lock the gates. People get distracted or careless. Or they start to believe the cats are friends who'd never hurt them. I keep telling our staff, *never* trust a big cat. Never turn your back. These are not pet kitties."

Maura thought about the gray tabby she'd just adopted, the cat whose affections she was now trying to win with expensive sardines and bowls of half-and-half. He was just another wily predator who had claimed Maura as his personal servant. If he were a hundred pounds heavier, she had little doubt he'd see her not as a friend, but as a tasty source of meat. Could anyone truly trust a cat?

Rhodes unlocked the inner gate, which led to the public exhibit. "This is the way Debbie would have entered," he said. "We found a lot of blood next to the bucket and broom, so she was probably attacked while doing morning cleanup."

"What time would this have been?"

"Around eight or nine o'clock. The zoo opens at nine for visitors. Rafiki's fed in the night room before he's let into the exhibit."

"Are there any security cameras back here?"

"Unfortunately not, so we have no footage of the incident, or what preceded it."

"What about the victim's—Debbie's—state of mind? Was she depressed? Troubled about anything?"

"Detective Rizzoli asked that same question. *Was this a suicide by cat?*" Rhodes shook his head. "She was such a positive, optimistic woman. I can't imagine her committing suicide, despite what was going on in her life."

"*Was* something going on?"

He paused, his hand still on the gate. "Isn't there *always* something going on in people's lives? I know she'd just broken up with Greg."

"That's Dr. Oberlin, the veterinarian?"

He nodded. "Debbie and I talked about it on Sunday, when we brought Kovo's body to the taxidermist. She didn't seem too upset about it. More . . . relieved. I think Greg took it a lot harder. It didn't make things easy for him, since they both work here and they see each other at least once a week."

"Yet they got along?"

"As far as I could tell. Detective Rizzoli spoke to Greg, and he's pretty devastated about this. And before you ask the obvious question, Greg said he was nowhere near this cage when it happened. He said he came running when he heard the screams."

"Debbie's?"

Rhodes looked pained. "I doubt she lived long enough to make a sound. No, it was some visitor screaming. She saw blood and started yelling for help." He swung open the exhibit gate. "She's lying in the back, near the boulders."

Only three paces into the enclosure, Maura halted, disturbed by the evidence of carnage. This was what Jane had described as "buckets of blood," and it was splashed across foliage, congealed in pools on the concrete pathway. Arterial splatters arced in multiple directions, sprayed out by the victim's last, desperate heartbeats.

Rhodes looked down at the toppled bucket and rake. "She probably never saw him coming."

The human body contains five liters of blood, and this was where Debbie Lopez had spilled most of hers. It had still been wet when others walked through it; Maura saw multiple footprints and smears across the concrete. "If he attacked her here," she said, "why did he drag her to the back of the cage? Why not consume her where she fell?"

"Because a leopard's instinct is to guard his kill. In the wild, there'd be scavengers who'd fight him for it. Lions and hyenas. So leopards move their kill out of reach."

Blood smears marked the leopard's progress as he had dragged his prize of human flesh along the concrete path. In that trail of streaks and swipes, one clear paw print stood out, startling evidence of the size and power of this killer. The trail led to the rear of the enclosure. At the base of a massive artificial boulder lay the body, covered with an olive-green blanket. The dead leopard sprawled nearby, jaws gaping open.

"He dragged the body up onto the ledge," said Rhodes. "We pulled her down to do CPR."

Maura looked up at the boulder and saw the dried stream of blood that had trickled from the ledge. "He got her all the way up there?"

Rhodes nodded. "That's how powerful they are. They can haul a heavy kudu into a tree. Their instinct is to go high and leave the carcass hanging over a branch, where they can gorge undisturbed. That's what he was about to do when Greg shot him. By then, Debbie was already gone."

Maura donned gloves and crouched down to pull aside the blanket. One glance at what was left of the victim's throat told her that the attack was not survivable. In appalled silence she stared at the crushed larynx and exposed trachea, at a neck ripped open so deeply that the head lolled back, nearly decapitated.

"That's how they do it," said Rhodes, his gaze averted, his voice unsteady. "Cats are designed by nature to be perfect killing machines, and they go straight for the throat. They crush the spine, tear open the jugular and carotids. At least they make sure their prey's dead before they start feeding. I'm told it's a quick death. Exsanguination."

Not quick enough. Maura pictured Debbie Lopez's agonal seconds, the blood pulsing like a water cannon from her severed carotids. It would also flood into her torn trachea, drowning her lungs. A rapid death, yes, but for this victim, those final seconds of terror and suffocation must have seemed an eternity.

She pulled the blanket back over the dead woman's face and turned her attention to the leopard. It was a magnificent animal, with a massive chest and a lustrous pelt that gleamed in the dappled sunlight. She stared at razor-sharp teeth and imagined how easily they would crush and tear a woman's throat. With a shudder she rose to her feet and saw, through the exhibit bars, that the morgue retrieval team had arrived.

"She loved this cat," said Rhodes, gazing down at Rafiki. "After he was born, she bottle-fed him like a baby. I don't think she ever imagined he'd do this to her. And that's what really killed her. She forgot he was the predator, and we're his prey."

Maura peeled off her gloves. "Has the family been notified?"

"She has a mother in St. Louis. Our director, Dr. Mikovitz, has already called her."

"My office will need her contact information. For the funeral arrangements after the autopsy."

"Is an autopsy really necessary?"

"The cause of death seems obvious, but there are always questions that need to be answered. Why did she make this fatal mistake? Was she impaired by drugs or alcohol or some medical condition?"

He nodded. "Of course. I didn't even think of that. But I'd be shocked if you found any drugs in her system. That just wouldn't be the woman I knew."

The woman you believed you knew, thought Maura as she walked out of the cage. Every human on this earth had secrets. She thought of her own, so closely guarded, and how startled her colleagues would be to learn of them. Even Jane, who knew her best of all.

As the morgue retrieval team wheeled the stretcher into the enclosure, Maura stood on the public pathway, gazing over the railing at what the visitors would have seen. The spot where the leopard first attacked was out of view, hidden by a wall, and shrubbery would have obscured the dragging of the body. But the rock ledge where he'd guarded his kill was clearly visible, and it was now marked by the gruesome trail of blood that had dripped down the boulder.

No wonder people had been shrieking.

A shiver rippled across Maura's skin, like the chill breath of a predator. Turning, she glanced around. Saw Dr. Rhodes huddled in conversation with worried zoo officials. Saw a pair of zookeepers comforting each other. No one was looking at Maura; no one even seemed to notice she was there. But she could not shake the sensation of being watched.

Then she spotted him, through the bars of a nearby enclosure. His tawny coat was almost invisible against the sand-colored boulder where he crouched. His powerful muscles were poised to spring. Silently tracking his prey, his eyes were fixed on her. Only on her.

She looked at the placard mounted on the railing. *PUMA CONCOLOR*. A cougar.

And she thought: I never would have seen him coming, either.

NINE

"JERRY O'BRIEN'S A BOMB THROWER. OR HE PLAYS ONE ON THE RADIO, anyway," said Frost as they drove northwest into Middlesex County, Jane at the wheel. "On his show last week, he was ranting about the animal rights crowd. Compared them to grass-eating rodents, and wondered how dumb bunnies got to be so vicious." Frost laughed as he pulled up the audio file on his laptop. "Here's the part you've got to hear, about hunting."

"You think he really believes the shit he says?" she asked.

"Who knows? It gets him an audience, anyway, 'cause he's syndicated all the way to the moon." Frost tapped on his keyboard. "Okay, this is last week's show. Listen to this."

> Maybe you eat chicken or enjoy a steak once in a while. You pick it up at the grocery store, wrapped up nicely in plastic. What makes you think you're morally superior to the hunter who hauls himself out of bed at four A.M., who endures the cold and exhaustion to hike through the woods with a heavy gun? Who waits patiently in the brush, maybe for hours?

Who spends a lifetime honing his skill with a firearm—and trust me, people, it is a skill to be able to hit a target. Who on God's green earth has the right to begrudge the hunter his right to engage in an ancient, honored occupation that has fed families since the beginning of human history? These metrosexual snobs who have no problem eating their steak frites in a fancy French restaurant have the audacity to tell us red-blooded hunters we're cruel for killing a deer. Where do they think meat comes from?

And don't get me started on wild-eyed vegetarians. Hey, animal lovers! You got a cat or a dog, right? What do you feed your beloved pooch or puss? Meat. M. E. A. T. You might as well take your anger out on Fluffy!

Frost paused the recording. "Which reminds me, I dropped by Gott's house this morning. Didn't see the white cat, but all the food I left last night was gone. I refilled the bowl and changed the litter box."

"And Detective Frost gets the merit badge for pet care."

"What're we gonna do about him? You think Dr. Isles wants another cat?"

"I think she already regrets the one she has. Why don't you adopt it?"

"I'm a guy."

"So?"

"So it'd feel weird, having a cat."

"What, do they steal your manhood?"

"It's all about image, you know? If I bring home a girl, what's she gonna think when she sees I have a fluffy white cat?"

"Oh yeah, like your goldfish gives a *much* better impression." She nodded at his laptop. "So what else does O'Brien have to say?"

"Listen to this part," said Frost, and clicked PLAY.

. . . but no, these grass-eating rodents, vicious bunnies who dine every day on lettuce, they're more bloodthirsty than any

> carnivore. And believe me, friends, I hear from them. They threaten to string me up and gut me like a deer. Threaten to burn me, cut me, strangle me, crush me. Would you believe this comes from the lips of *vegetarians*? Friends, beware the lettuce eaters. There's no one on earth more dangerous than your so-called *animal lovers.*

Jane looked at Frost. "Maybe they're even more dangerous than he realizes," she said.

WITH A WEEKLY SHOW syndicated to six hundred radio stations, reaching an audience of over twenty million listeners, Jerry "Big Mouth" O'Brien could afford the best, a fact made abundantly clear from the moment Jane and Frost drove past the guarded gatehouse onto O'Brien's estate. The rolling pastures and grazing horses could be on a farm somewhere in Virginia or Kentucky; it was an unexpectedly bucolic setting only an hour outside Boston. They drove past a farm pond and up a grassy slope dotted with white sheep, to the massive log-built residence at the top of the hill. With its wide porches and massive timber posts, it looked more like a hunting lodge than a private home.

They had just pulled up to the building when they heard the first gunshots.

"What the hell?" said Frost as they both unsnapped their holsters.

More gunshots rang out in rapid succession, then silence. Too long a silence.

Jane and Frost lurched out of the car and were already bounding up the porch steps, guns drawn, when the front door suddenly swung open.

A chubby-cheeked man greeted them with a pasted-on smile so big it had to be fake. He saw the two Glocks pointed at his chest and said, with a laugh: "Whoa now, there's no need for *that.* You must be Detectives Rizzoli and Frost."

Jane kept her weapon level. "We heard gunshots."

"It's only target practice. Jerry's got a nice shooting range downstairs. I'm his personal assistant, Rick Dolan. Come on in."

Another burst of gunfire rang out. Jane and Frost glanced at each other, then simultaneously reholstered their weapons.

"Sounds like some major firepower," said Jane.

"You're welcome to check it out. Jerry loves to show off his arsenal."

They stepped into a soaring entrance hall where the natural pine walls were hung with Native American rugs. Dolan reached into a hall cabinet and tossed ear protectors to his guests.

"Jerry's rules," he said, slipping a pair of protectors over his own head. "He went to a few too many rock concerts as a kid, and as he likes to say, *Deafness is forever.*"

Dolan swung open a door that was thickly padded with soundproofing. Jane and Frost hesitated as gunfire thundered up from the basement.

"Oh, it's perfectly safe down there," he said. "Jerry spared no expense when he designed it. Basement walls are sand-filled blocks, ceiling's pre-stressed concrete, topped with four inches of steel. He's got fully enclosed bullet traps, and the underground exhaust system vents all the smoke and residue to the outside. I'm telling you, it's the best of the best. You gotta take a look."

Jane and Frost put on the ear protectors and followed him down the stairs.

Under the harsh glare of fluorescent lights, Jerry O'Brien stood with his back turned to them. He was dressed incongruously in blue jeans and a garish aloha shirt, which generously draped his barrel-shaped torso in flowered fabric. He did not immediately acknowledge his visitors, but kept his focus on the target of a human silhouette as he fired repeatedly. Only when he'd emptied his magazine did he turn to face Jane and Frost.

"Ah, Boston PD's here." O'Brien pulled off his ear protectors. "Welcome to my little corner of Paradise."

Frost surveyed the array of handguns and rifles displayed on the table. "Wow. Quite a collection you have here."

"Trust me, they're all legal. No magazine with more than ten rounds. I keep them all in a fully secured storage locker, and I have a Class A CCW permit. You can check with my local police chief." He picked up another handgun and held it out to Frost. "This one's my favorite. Care to try it out, Detective?"

"Uh, no thanks."

"Not even tempted? Probably won't get another chance to fire one of these babies anytime soon."

"We're here to ask you about Leon Gott," said Jane.

O'Brien turned his attention to her. "Detective Rizzoli, right? So are you into guns?"

"When I need them."

"You hunt?"

"No sir."

"Ever hunted?"

"Only people. It's more exciting 'cause they shoot back."

O'Brien laughed. "My kinda gal. Not like any of my frigging exwives." He removed the magazine, checked the chamber for any remaining bullets. "So let me tell you about Leon. He wouldn't have gone down without a fight. Given half a chance, I know he would've blown the fucker's brains out." He looked at Jane. "So did he get half a chance?"

"How deaf was he?"

"What's that got to do with it?"

"He wasn't wearing his hearing aids."

"Oh. Well, that changes the picture. Without his hearing aids, he wouldn't have heard a moose clomping up the stairs."

"Sounds like you knew him pretty well."

"Well enough to trust him as a hunter. I brought him out to Kenya twice. Last year he took down one hell of a nice buffalo, one shot. Didn't hesitate, didn't blink. You get to know a lot about a person when you go hunting with him. You find out if they're just talk and no action. If you can trust 'em enough to turn your back. If they've got the spine to face down a charging elephant. Leon proved himself, and I respected him. I don't say that about many people." O'Brien set the gun on the table and looked at Jane. "Why don't we talk about this upstairs? I keep coffee brewing twenty-four seven, if you want any." He tossed a key to his personal assistant. "Rick, you wanna lock up these guns for me? We'll be in the den."

O'Brien led the way, moving slowly and ponderously up the stairs in his garish tent of a shirt. By the time they reached the hallway, he was wheezing. *The den* was where he'd said they were headed, but the room he led them to was no mere man cave; instead it was a two-story cavern with massive oak beams and a fieldstone fireplace. Everywhere Jane looked she saw mounted game animals, the taxidermied evidence of O'Brien's skill as a marksman. Jane had been startled by Leon Gott's collection, but this room made her jaw drop.

"You shot all of these yourself?" asked Frost.

"Almost all," said O'Brien. "A few of these animals are endangered and impossible to hunt, so I had to get 'em the old-fashioned way. By opening my wallet. That Amur leopard, for instance." He pointed to a mounted head with one badly tattered ear. "It's probably forty years old, and you won't find them anymore. I paid good money to a collector for that sorry specimen."

"And the point would be?" asked Jane.

"What, you never had stuffed animals as a kid, Detective? Not even a teddy bear?"

"I didn't have to shoot my teddy bear."

"Well, this Amur leopard is *my* stuffed animal. I wanted it because it's a spectacular predator. Beautiful. Lethal. Designed by nature as a killing machine." He pointed to the wall of trophies facing them, a gallery of heads bristling with fangs and tusks. "I still take down the occasional deer, 'cause there's no better eating than deer tenderloin. But I really prize the animals that scare me. I'd love to get my hands on a Bengal tiger. And that snow leopard was another one

I really wanted. Frigging shame the skin's gone missing. It was worth a lot to me, and obviously worth it to the asshole who killed Leon."

"You think that's the motive?" asked Frost.

"Sure. You police need to watch the black market, and if a pelt comes up for sale, you'll have your perp. I'd be glad to assist you. It's my civic duty, and I owe it to Leon."

"Who knew he was working on a snow leopard?"

"Lots of people. Very few taxidermists get to handle such a rare animal, and he was crowing about it on Internet hunting forums. We're all fascinated by big cats. By animals who can kill us. I know I am." He looked up at his trophies. "This is how I honor them."

"By hanging their heads on your wall?"

"No worse than what they'd do to me if they got the chance. That's life in the jungle, Detective. Dog eat dog, survival of the fittest." He looked around his trophy room, a king surveying his conquered subjects. "It's in our nature to kill. People don't acknowledge that. If I so much as take a slingshot to a squirrel here, you can bet that my loony granola neighbors will squawk. Crazy lady next door yelled at me to pack up and move the hell to Wyoming."

"You could," observed Frost.

O'Brien laughed. "Naw, I'd rather stay and be a thorn in their side. Anyway, why should I? I grew up in Lowell, right up the road. Crappy neighborhood next to the mill. I stay here because it reminds me how far I've come." He crossed to a liquor cabinet and uncorked a bottle of whiskey. "Can I offer you some?"

"No sir," said Frost.

"Yeah, I know. On duty and all that." He poured a few fingers' worth into a glass. "I own my business, so I get to make the rules. And I say cocktail hour starts at three."

Frost moved closer to the display of predators and studied the full-body mount of a leopard. It was poised on a tree branch, its body coiled as if ready to pounce. "Is this an African leopard?"

O'Brien turned, glass in hand. "Yeah. Shot that a few years ago, in

Zimbabwe. Leopards are tricky. Secretive and solitary. When they're up in the branches, they can take you by surprise. As cats go, they're not all that big, but they're strong enough to drag you up a tree." He took a sip of whiskey as he admired the animal. "Leon mounted that one for me. You can see the quality of his work. He also did that lion, and that grizzly over there. He was good, but he didn't come cheap." O'Brien crossed to a full-body mount of a cougar. "This was the first one he did for me, about fifteen years ago. Looks so real, it still gives me a start when I see it in the dark."

"So Leon was your hunting buddy and your taxidermist," said Jane.

"Not just *any* taxidermist. His work is legendary."

"We saw an article about him in *Hub Magazine.* 'The Trophy Master.' "

O'Brien laughed. "He liked that piece. Had it framed and hanging on his wall."

"That article got a lot of comments. Including a few pretty nasty ones, about hunting."

O'Brien shrugged. "Comes with the territory. I get threats, too. People calling in to the show, wanting to stick me like a pig."

"Yeah, I've heard some of those calls," said Frost.

O'Brien's head perked up, like a bulldog hearing a supersonic whistle. "You listen to me, huh?"

What he wanted Frost to say was, *Of course I do! I love your show and I'm your biggest fan!* A man who lived this large and flamboyantly, a man who seemed to delight in extending his middle finger to all who despised him, was also a man starved for validation.

"Tell us about these people who've threatened you," said Jane.

O'Brien laughed. "My show reaches a lot of people, and some of 'em don't like what I have to say."

"Any of those threats worry you? Say, from the anti-hunting crowd?"

"You saw my arsenal. Let 'em try and take me down."

"Leon Gott had an arsenal, too."

He paused, whiskey glass at his lips. He lowered it and frowned at her. "You think it was some wacko animal lover?"

"We're looking at all angles. That's why we want to hear about any threats you're getting."

"Which ones? Every time I open my mouth, I piss off certain listeners."

"Any of them say they want to see you hung and gutted?"

"Oh yeah, that's so original. Like she'd ever come up with anything new."

"She?"

"One of my regular dipshits. Suzy something, calls all the time. *Animals have souls! Humans are the real savages!* Blah, blah, blah."

"Anyone else make that particular threat? About hanging and gutting?"

"Yeah, and it's almost always gals. They go into great bloodthirsty detail, like only women can." He paused, suddenly struck by the significance of Jane's question. "You're not saying that's what happened to Leon? Did someone gut him?"

"How about keeping track of those callers for us? Next time you get a threat like that, give us a log of the phone numbers."

O'Brien looked at his personal assistant, who'd just walked into the room. "Rick, can you take care of that? Get 'em names and numbers?"

"Sure thing, Jerry."

"But I can't see any of those weirdos following through on their threats," O'Brien said. "They're just a bunch of hot air."

"I'd take any threat seriously," said Jane.

"Oh, I'll take it dead seriously." He tugged up the edge of his billowing aloha shirt to reveal a Glock in his under-the-waistband holster. "No point having a CCW if I don't keep one on me, right?"

"Did Leon say he was getting any threats?" asked Frost.

"Nothing that worried him."

"Any enemies? Any colleagues or family members who might profit from his death?"

O'Brien paused, lips pursed like a bullfrog. He'd picked up his whiskey glass again and sat staring at it for a moment. "Only family member he ever talked about was his son."

"The one who passed away."

"Yeah. Talked about him a lot on our last trip to Kenya. You sit around a campfire with a bottle of whiskey, you get to talking about a lot of things. Bag your game, dine on bush meat, talk under the stars. For men, that's what it's all about." He glanced at his personal assistant. "Right, Rick?"

"You said it, Jerry," Dolan answered, smoothly refilling his boss's whiskey.

"No women go on these trips?" Jane asked.

O'Brien gave her a look usually reserved for the insane. "Why would I want to ruin a perfectly good time? Women only screw things up." He nodded. "Present company excepted. I've had four wives, and they're still bleeding me dry. Leon had his own lousy marriage. Wife left with their only son, turned the boy against him. Broke Leon's heart. Even after the bitch died, that son went out of his way to piss off Leon. Makes me glad I never had kids." He sipped his whiskey and shook his head. "Damn, I'm gonna miss him. How can I help you catch the bastard who did it?"

"Just keep answering our questions."

"I'm not, like, a suspect am I?"

"Should you be?"

"No games, okay? Just ask your questions."

"The Suffolk Zoo says you agreed to donate five million dollars in exchange for the snow leopard."

"Absolutely true. I told 'em I'd allow only one taxidermist to do the mounting, and that was Leon."

"And the last time you spoke to Mr. Gott?"

"We heard from him on Sunday, when he called to tell us he'd skinned and gutted the animal, and did we want the carcass?"

"What time was this call?"

"Around noon or so." O'Brien paused. "Come on, you guys must already have the phone records. You know about that call."

Jane and Frost exchanged irritated looks. Despite a subpoena for Gott's phone records, the carrier hadn't delivered. With nearly a thousand daily requests from police departments across the country, it might take days, even weeks, for a phone company to comply.

"So he called you about the carcass," said Frost. "What happened then?"

"I drove over and picked it up," said O'Brien's assistant. "Got to Leon's place about two P.M., loaded the animal into my truck. Brought it straight back here."

"Why? I mean, you wouldn't want to *eat* leopard meat, would you?"

O'Brien said, "I'll try any meat at least once. Hell, I'd chomp down on a juicy human butt roast if it's offered to me. But no, I wouldn't eat an animal that's been euthanized with drugs. I wanted it for the skeleton. After Rick brought it back, we dug a hole and buried it. Give it a few months, let Mother Nature and the worms do their work, and I'll have bones to mount."

And that's why they'd found only the leopard's internal organs, thought Jane. Because the carcass was already here on O'Brien's property, decomposing in a grave.

"Did you and Mr. Gott talk when you were there on Sunday?" Jane asked Dolan.

"Hardly. He was on the phone with someone. I waited around for a few minutes, but he just waved me away. So I took the carcass and left."

"Who was he talking to?"

"I don't know. He said something about wanting more photos of Elliot in Africa. 'Everything you've got,' he said."

"Elliot?" Jane looked at O'Brien.

"That was his dead son," said O'Brien. "Like I said, he'd been talking about Elliot a lot lately. It happened six years ago, but I think the guilt was finally getting to him."

"Why would Leon feel guilty?"

"Because he had almost nothing to do with him after the divorce. His ex-wife raised the boy, turned him into a *girlie-man,* according to Leon. The kid hooked up with some wacko PETA girlfriend, probably just to piss off his old man. Leon tried to make contact, but his son wasn't too keen on staying in touch. So when Elliot died, it really hit Leon hard. All he had left of his son was a photo. Had it hanging in his house, one of the last pictures ever taken of Elliot."

"How did Elliot die? You said it happened six years ago."

"Yeah, the kid got it in his fool head to go to Africa. He wanted to see the animals before they got wiped out by hunters like me. Interpol says he met a couple of girls in Cape Town, and the three of them flew off to Botswana for a safari."

"And what happened?"

O'Brien drained his whiskey glass and looked at her. "They were never seen again."

TEN

BOTSWANA

JOHNNY PRESSES THE TIP OF HIS KNIFE AGAINST THE IMPALA'S ABDOMEN and slices through hide and fat, to the greasy caul that drapes the organs beneath. Only moments ago he brought down the beast with a single gunshot, and as he guts it I watch the impala's eye cloud over, as if Death has breathed a cold mist across it, glazing it with frost. Johnny works with the swift efficiency of a hunter who's done this many times before. With one hand he slits open the belly; with his other he pushes the entrails away from the blade to avoid puncturing organs and contaminating the meat. The work is gruesome yet delicate. Mrs. Matsunaga turns away in disgust, but the rest of us cannot stop watching. This is what we have come to Africa to witness: life and death in the bush. Tonight we'll feast on impala roasted over the fire, and the price of our meal is the death of this animal, now being gutted and butchered. The smell of blood rises from the warm carcass, a scent so powerful that all around us, scavengers are stirring. I think I can hear them now, rustling closer in the grass.

Above us, the ever-present vultures are circling.

"The gut's full of bacteria, so I remove this to keep the meat from spoiling," Johnny explains as he slices. "It also lightens the load, makes it easier to carry. Nothing will go to waste, nothing goes uneaten. Scavengers will clean up whatever we leave behind. Better to do it out here, so we don't attract them back to camp." He reaches into the thorax to tug on the heart and lungs. With a few strokes of the knife, he severs the windpipe and great vessels and the chest organs slide out like a newborn, slimy with blood.

"Oh God," groans Vivian.

Johnny looks up. "You eat meat, don't you?"

"After watching this? I don't know if I can."

"I think we all *need* to watch this," says Richard. "We need to know where our meal comes from."

Johnny nods. "Exactly right. It's our duty, as carnivores, to know what's involved in getting that steak to your plate. The stalking, the killing. The gutting and butchering. Humans are hunters, and this is what we've done since the beginning." He reaches into the pelvis to strip out the bladder and uterus, then grasps handfuls of intestines and tosses them onto the grass. "Modern men have lost touch with what it means to survive. They go into the supermarket and open their wallet to pay for a steak. That's not the meaning of meat." He stands up, bare arms streaked with blood, and looks down at the gutted impala. "*This* is."

We stand in a circle around the kill as the last blood drains from the open cavity. Already the discarded organs are drying out in the sun and the vultures grow thicker overhead, anxious to rip into this ripening mound of carrion.

"The meaning of meat," Elliot says. "I never thought of it that way."

"The bush makes you see your real place in the world," says Johnny. "Here, you're reminded of what you really are."

"Animals," Elliot murmurs.

Johnny nods. "Animals."

AND THAT'S WHAT I see when I look around the campfire that night. A circle of feeding animals, teeth ripping into chunks of roasted impala meat. Just one day after being stranded in the wild, we have devolved into savage versions of ourselves, eating with our bare hands as juices drip down our chins, our faces streaked with black from charred fat. At least we do not worry about starving out here in the bush, which teems with meat on the hoof and on the wing. With his rifle and skinning knife, Johnny will keep us well fed.

He sits in the shadows just outside our circle, watching us gorge. I wish I could read his face, but it's closed to me tonight. Does he look at us with contempt, these clueless clients, helpless as baby birds, who need him to put food in our mouths? Does he blame us somehow for Clarence's death? He picks up the empty bottle of whiskey that Sylvia has just tossed aside and deposits it in the burlap sack where we store our rubbish, which he insists we must haul out. *Leave no trace,* he says; *that is how we respect the land.* Already the rubbish bag clinks with glass empties, but there is no danger we'll run out of booze anytime soon. Mrs. Matsunaga is allergic to alcohol, Elliot drinks only sparingly, and Johnny seems determined to stay stone-cold sober until we are rescued.

He returns to the fire and, to my surprise, he sits down beside me.

I look at him, but his eyes stay on the flames as he says quietly: "You're handling the situation well."

"Am I? I didn't think so. Not particularly."

"I appreciated your help today. Skinning the impala, breaking down the carcass. You're a natural in the bush."

That makes me laugh. "I'm the one who didn't want to be here. The one who insists on hot showers and proper toilets. This trip was about me being a good sport."

"To please Richard."

"Who else?"

"I hope he's impressed."

I glance sideways at Richard, who is not looking at me. He's too busy chatting up Vivian, whose formfitting T-shirt leaves no doubt that she's braless. I focus, once again, on the fire. "Being a good sport only gets you so far in life."

"I hear from Richard that you're a bookseller."

"Yes, I manage a bookshop in London. In the real world."

"This isn't the real world?"

I glance around at the shadows surrounding our campfire. "This is a fantasy, Johnny. Something out of a Hemingway novel. I guarantee, it's going to show up in one of Richard's thrillers someday." I laugh. "Don't be surprised if he makes you the villain."

"What part do you play in his novels?"

I study the fire. And say, wistfully: "I used to be the love interest."

"No longer?"

"Nothing stays the same, does it?" No, now I'm the millstone. The inconvenient girlfriend who'll have to be dispatched by the villain, so the hero can pursue some new romantic interest. Oh, I know all about how things work in men's thrillers because I sell those novels to countless pale, flabby men who are all, in their minds, James Bond.

Richard knows just how to tap into their fantasies because he shares them. Even now, as he reaches over with his silver lighter to light Mr. Matsunaga's cigarette, he is playing the suave hero. James Bond would never fuss with a mere match.

Johnny picks up a stick and prods the fire, pushing a log deeper into the flames. "For Richard, this may be only a fantasy. But this one has real teeth."

"Yes, of course you're right. It's not a fantasy. It's a bloody nightmare."

"Then you understand the situation," he murmurs.

"I understand that everything's changed. It's not a holiday any longer." I add, softly: "And I'm frightened."

"You don't have to be, Millie. Watchful, yes, but not frightened. Now, a city like Johannesburg, *that's* a scary place. But here?" He shakes his head and smiles. "Here, everything's just trying to survive. Understand that, and you will, too."

"Easy for you to say. You grew up in this world."

He nods. "My parents had a farm in Limpopo Province. Every

day, when I walked out into the fields, I'd pass leopards perched in trees, watching me. I got to know them all, and they knew me."

"They never attacked?"

"I like to think we had an agreement, those leopards and I. It was respect between predators. But it didn't mean we ever trusted each other."

"I'd be afraid to step out of my house. There are so many ways to die here. Lions. Leopards. Snakes."

"I have a healthy respect for them all, because I know what they're capable of." He grins at the fire. "When I was fourteen, I was bitten by a pit viper."

I stare at him. "And you're smiling about it?"

"It was entirely my fault. I collected snakes as a kid. Caught them myself, and kept them in various containers in my bedroom. But one day I got cocky and my viper bit me."

"Good God. What happened then?"

"Luckily it was a dry bite, with no venom. But that taught me there's a penalty for carelessness." He gives a regretful shake of the head. "The worst part was, my mother made me give up my snakes."

"I can't believe she let you collect them in the first place. Or that she ever let you step foot outside with leopards around."

"But that's what our ancestors did, Millie. This is where we all come from. Some part of you, some ancient memory deep in your brain, recognizes this continent as home. Most people have lost touch with it, but the instincts are still there." Gently he reaches out and touches my forehead. "That's how you stay alive here, by reaching deep for those ancient memories. I'll help you find them."

Suddenly I feel Richard's eyes on us. Johnny feels it, too, and instantly conjures up a big smile, as if a switch has been flipped. "Wild game roasting on the fire. Nothing to beat it, eh, everybody?" he calls out.

"Way more tender than I ever expected," Elliot says, licking juices from his fingers. "I feel like I'm getting in touch with my inner caveman!"

"How about you and Richard do the butchering when I bring down the next one?"

Elliot looks startled. "Uh . . . me?"

"You've seen how it's done." Johnny looks at Richard. "Think you can do it?"

"Of course we can," says Richard, staring straight back at Johnny. I'm sitting between the two of them, and although Richard has ignored me for most of the meal, he now slings an arm around my shoulder, as if to declare ownership. As if he considers Johnny a romantic rival who would steal me away.

The thought makes my face flush hot.

"In fact," says Richard, "all of us are ready to pitch in. We can start tonight, by keeping watch." He holds out his hands for the rifle, which is always at Johnny's side. "You can't go all night without sleeping."

"But you've never shot a rifle like that," I point out.

"I'll learn."

"Don't you think that's up to Johnny to decide?"

"No, Millie. I do *not* think he should be the only one in control of the gun."

"What are you doing, Richard?" I whisper.

"I could ask the same of you." The look he gives me is radioactive. Everyone around the campfire goes quiet, and in the silence we hear the distant whoops of hyenas, feasting on the gift of entrails we left behind.

Johnny says, calmly: "I've already asked Isao to take the second watch tonight."

Richard looks in surprise at Mr. Matsunaga. "Why *him*?"

"He knows his way around a rifle. I checked him out earlier."

"I am the number one marksman in the Tokyo shooting club," says Mr. Matsunaga, smiling proudly. "What time do you wish me to stand watch?"

"I'll wake you up at two, Isao," says Johnny. "You'd best get to bed early."

. . .

THE RAGE IN OUR tent is like a living thing, a monster with glowing eyes that waits to attack. I am the one in its sight, the victim in whom its claws will sink, and I keep my voice low and calm, hoping the claws will pass me by, that those eyes will burn themselves out. But Richard won't let it die.

"What's he been saying to you? What were you two talking about so lovingly?" he demands.

"What do you *think* we were talking about? How we can make it through this week alive."

"So it was all about survival, was it?"

"Yes."

"And Johnny's so bloody good at it, we're now stranded."

"You blame *him* for this?"

"He's proved to us he can't be trusted. But of course you can't see that." He laughs. "There's a term for it, you know. They call it khaki fever."

"What?"

"It's when women fall into lust for their bush guides. All it takes is the sight of a man wearing khaki, and they'll spread their legs for him."

It's the crudest insult he could fling at me, yet I manage to remain calm because nothing he says can hurt me now. I simply don't care. Instead I laugh. "You know, I've just realized something about you. You really *are* a bastard."

"At least I'm not the one who wants to fuck the bush guide."

"How do you know I haven't already?"

He flings himself onto his side, turning his back to me. I know he wants to storm out of this tent as much as I do, but it's not safe to even step outside. Anyway, we have nowhere else to go. All I can do is move as far away from him as I can and stay silent. I no longer know who this man is. Something has changed inside him, some transformation that happened while I wasn't watching. The bush has done this. Africa has done this. Richard is now a stranger, or perhaps he was always a stranger. Can you ever really know a person? I once read about a wife who was married for a decade before she discovered her husband was a serial killer. How could she not know it? I thought when I read that article.

But now I do understand how it can happen. I'm lying in a tent with a man I've known for four years, a man I thought I loved, and I feel like the serial killer's wife, the truth about her husband finally laid bare.

Outside our tent, there's a thump, a crackle, and the fire flares brighter. Johnny has just added wood to the flames to keep the animals at bay. Did he hear us talking? Does he know this argument is about him? Perhaps he's seen this happen countless times before on other safaris. Couples dissolving, accusations flying. *Khaki fever.* A phenomenon so common it's earned a name of its own.

I close my eyes and an image appears in my mind. Johnny standing in the tall grass at dawn, his shoulders silhouetted by sunrise. Am I infected, just a little, by the fever? He is the one who protects us, who keeps us alive. At the moment he sighted the impala, I was standing right beside him, so close that I saw the muscles snap taut on his arm as he raised the rifle. Once again I feel the thrill of the explosion, as if I myself had pulled the trigger, I had brought down the impala. A shared kill, binding us with blood.

Oh yes, Africa has changed me, too.

I hold my breath as Johnny's silhouette pauses outside our tent. Then he moves past and his shadow glides away. When I fall asleep, it's not Richard I dream about, but Johnny, standing tall and straight in the grass. Johnny, who makes me feel safe.

Until the next morning, when I wake up to the news that Isao Matsunaga has vanished.

ELEVEN

KEIKO KNEELS IN THE GRASS, SOBBING SOFTLY AS SHE ROCKS BACK and forth like a metronome ticking off a rhythm of despair. We've found the rifle, lying just beyond the bell-strung perimeter, but we have not yet found her husband. She knows what that means. We all know.

I stand over Keiko, uselessly stroking her shoulder because I don't know what else to do. I've never been good at comforting people. After my father died, and my mother sat weeping in his hospital room, all I could do was rub her arm, rub, rub, rub, until she finally cried out: "Stop it, Millie! That's so annoying!" I think Keiko is too distraught to even notice that I'm touching her. Looking down at her bowed head, I see white roots peeking through her black hair. With her pale, smooth skin, she seemed so much younger than her husband, but now I realize she's not young at all. That a few months out here will reveal her true age as her black hair turns to silver, as her skin darkens and wrinkles in the sun. Already she seems to be shriveling before my eyes.

"I'm going to search by the river," says Johnny, and he picks up the rifle. "All of you, stay here. Better yet, wait in the truck."

"The *truck*?" Richard says. "You mean that piece of junk you can't even start?"

"If you stay in the truck, nothing will hurt you. I can't search for Isao and protect you at the same time."

"Wait. Johnny," I speak up. "Should you be out there by yourself?"

"He's got the fucking gun, Millie," Richard says. "We've got nothing."

"While he's hunting for tracks, someone needs to watch his back," I point out.

Johnny gives a curt nod. "Okay, you're my spotter, Millie. Stay close."

As I step over the perimeter wire, my boot bumps the strand and the bells tinkle. Such a sweet ringing, like a wind chime on the breeze, but out here it means the enemy has invaded and my heart gives a reflexive kick of alarm at the sound. I take a deep breath and follow Johnny into the grass.

I was right to come with him. His attention is fixed on the ground as he searches for clues, and he could very well miss seeing the flick of a lion's tail off in the underbrush. As we move forward I am constantly scanning behind us, all around us. The grass is tall, up to my hips, and I think of puff adders and how you might step on one and not know it until fangs sink into your leg.

"Here," Johnny says quietly.

I look where the grass has been flattened and see a bare patch of soil and a scrape mark left by something being dragged across it. Johnny's already moving again, following the trail of flattened grass.

"Did the hyenas take him?"

"Not hyenas. Not this time."

"How do you know?"

He doesn't answer, but keeps moving toward a grove of trees, which I'm now able to recognize as sycamore figs and jackal berries. Though

I cannot see the river, I hear it rushing somewhere close by, and I think of crocodiles. Everywhere you look in this place, in the trees, in the river, in the grass, teeth are waiting to bite, and Johnny relies on me to spot them. Fear sharpens my senses and I'm aware of details I've never noticed before. The kiss of river-chilled wind against my cheek. The way freshly trampled grass smells like onions. I am looking, listening, smelling. We are a team, Johnny and I, and I won't fail him.

Suddenly I sense the change in him. His soft intake of breath, his abrupt stillness. He is no longer focused on the ground, but has straightened to his full height, shoulders squared.

At first I do not see her. Then I follow the direction of his gaze, to the tree that looms before us. It is a towering sycamore fig, a majestic specimen with wide-spreading branches and dense foliage, the kind of tree where you'd build a Swiss Family Robinson house.

"There you are," whispers Johnny. "Such a pretty girl."

Only then do I spot her, draped over a high branch. The leopard is almost invisible, so well does she blend into the leaf-dappled shade. All along she's been observing us, waiting patiently as we drew near, and now she watches with keen intelligence, weighing her next move, just as Johnny weighs his. Lazily she flicks her tail, but Johnny stays perfectly motionless. He is doing exactly what he advised us to do. *Let the cat see your face. Show it that your eyes are forward-facing, that you, too, are a predator.*

A moment passes, a moment when I have never felt so afraid or so alive. A moment when each heartbeat sends a sharp thrust of blood up my neck, whistling through my ears like wind. The leopard's gaze stays on Johnny. He is still gripping the rifle in front of him. Why doesn't he lift it to his shoulder? Why doesn't he fire?

"Back away," he whispers. "There's nothing we can do for Isao."

"You think the leopard killed him?"

"I know she did." He lifts his head, a subtle gesture that I almost miss. "Upper branch. To the left."

It has been hanging there the whole time, but I didn't notice it.

Just as I didn't at first notice the leopard. The arm dangles free like the strange fruit of a sausage tree, the hand gnawed down to a fingerless knob. Foliage masks the rest of Isao's body, but through the leaves I make out the shape of his torso, wedged in the crook of a branch, as if he'd dropped from the sky and landed like a broken doll in that tree.

"Oh my God," I whisper. "How are we going to get him—"

"Don't. Move."

The leopard has risen to a crouch, haunches tensed to spring. It's *me* she's staring at, her eyes fixed on mine. In an instant Johnny's rifle is up and ready to fire, but he doesn't pull the trigger.

"What are you waiting for?" I whisper.

"Back away. Together."

We take a step back. Another. The leopard settles back onto her branch, tail flicking.

"She's only protecting her kill," he says. "That's what leopards do, store their prey in a tree, where other scavengers can't get it. Look at the muscles in her shoulders. In her neck. That's real power for you. The power to drag a dead animal that outweighs her, all the way up to that high branch."

"For God's sake, Johnny. We need to get him down."

"He's already dead."

"We can't leave him up there."

"We get any closer, she'll spring on us. And I won't kill a leopard just to retrieve a corpse."

I remember what he once told us: that he would never kill a big cat. That he considered them sacred animals, too rare to sacrifice for any reason, not even to save his own life. Now he stands behind those words, even as Isao's corpse dangles above us, and the leopard guards her meal. Johnny suddenly seems as strange a beast as any I've yet encountered in this wild place, a man whose respect for this land runs as deep as the roots of these trees. I think of Richard, with his metallic-blue BMW and his black leather jacket and aviator glasses, things that made him seem masculine to me when we first met. But they were only trappings, to adorn a mannequin. That's what the word means, isn't it? A model of the human body, not real. Until now, it seems that I have known *only* mannequins who look like men, pretend to be men, but are merely plastic. I will never find another man like Johnny, not in London, not anywhere, and that is a heartbreaking thing to realize. That I will search for the rest of my life, and will always look back to this moment, when I knew exactly which man I wanted.

And would never be able to have him.

I reach toward him and whisper: "Johnny."

The rifle blast is so shocking I lurch backward, as if I've been struck. Johnny stands as frozen as a marksman's statue, his gun still aimed at the target. With a deep sigh he lowers the weapon. He bows his head as if praying for forgiveness, here in the church of the bush, where life and death are two halves of the same creature.

"Oh my God," I murmur and stare down at the leopard, which fell dead only two paces away from me, seemingly in mid-leap, her front claws a split second away from sinking into flesh. I cannot see the bullet hole; all I see is her blood, trickling into the grass, soaking into the hot soil. Her fur shines with the glossy elegance so coveted by the flashy tarts of Knightsbridge tycoons and I long to stroke it but it seems wrong, as if death has reduced her to nothing more than a harmless kitten. A moment ago she would have killed me, and she deserves my respect.

"We'll leave her here," Johnny says quietly.

"The hyenas will get her."

"They always do." He takes a deep breath and looks at the sycamore fig, but his gaze seems distant, as if he sees beyond the tree, even beyond this day. "I can get him down now."

"You told me you'd never kill a leopard. Not even to save your own life."

"I won't."

"But you killed this one."

"That wasn't for my life." He looks at me. "That was for yours."

• • •

THAT NIGHT I SLEEP in Mrs. Matsunaga's tent so she will not be alone. All day she has been nearly catatonic, hugging herself and whimpering in Japanese. The blondes have been trying to coax food into her, but Keiko has consumed nothing except a few cups of tea. She's retreated into some unreachable cave deep in her mind, and for the moment we're all relieved that she's quiet and controllable. We did not let her see Isao's body, which Johnny brought down from the sycamore fig and quickly buried.

But I saw it. I know how he died.

"A big cat kills by crushing your throat," Johnny told me as he dug the grave. He shoveled steadily, his spade cutting into the sun-baked earth. Though insects harassed us, he didn't wave them off, so intent was he on carving out Isao's resting place. "A cat goes straight for the neck. Clamps its jaws around your windpipe, ripping through arteries and veins. It's death by asphyxiation. You choke on your own blood."

Which is what I saw when I looked at Isao. Though the leopard had already begun to feast, tearing into abdomen and chest, it was the crushed neck that told me of Isao's final seconds, fighting for air as blood gurgled into his lungs.

Keiko knows none of these details. She knows only that her husband is dead and that we have buried him.

I hear her sigh in her sleep, one little whimper of despair, and she goes quiet again. She hardly moves but lies on her back, like a mummy wrapped in white sheets. The Matsunagas' tent smells different from mine. It has a pleasantly exotic scent, as if their clothes are impregnated with Asian herbs, and it is tidy and well organized. Isao's shirts, which he will never again wear, are neatly packed in his suitcase along with his gold wristwatch, which we retrieved from his body. Everything is in its place, everything is harmonious. So unlike my tent with Richard, which is the opposite of harmonious.

It's a relief to be away from him, which is why I so quickly volunteered to keep Keiko company. The last place I want to sleep tonight is in the tent with Richard, where the hostility hangs as thick as sulfurous fog. He's hardly spoken two sentences to me all day. Instead he spends his time huddled with Elliot and the blondes. The four of them seem to be a team now, as if this is a game of *Survivor Botswana,* and it's their tribe against my tribe.

Except I don't actually *have* anyone in my tribe, unless you count poor fractured Keiko—and Johnny. But Johnny belongs to no team, not really; he is his own man, and killing that leopard today has left him troubled and brooding. He's hardly spoken to me since.

So here I am, the woman no one talks to, lying in a tent beside a woman who talks to no one. Though it's silent in here, outside the tent the night symphony has begun, with its insect piccolos and hippo bassoons. I've grown to love those sounds, and I'll surely dream about them when I go home.

In the morning, I wake up to birdsong. For once there are no screams, no shouts of alarm, just the sweet melodies of dawn. Outside, the four members of Team Richard are huddled together at the campfire, sipping coffee. Johnny sits by himself under a tree. Exhaustion seems to drip off his shoulders, and his head bobs forward as he tries to fight off sleep. I want to go to him, to massage away his weariness, but the others are watching me. I join their circle instead.

"How's Keiko doing?" Elliot asks me.

"Still asleep. She was quiet all night." I pour myself coffee. "I'm glad to see we're all alive this morning." My quip is in poor taste, and I regret it as soon as the words are out of my mouth.

"I wonder if *he's* glad about it," Richard mutters, glancing at Johnny.

"What's that supposed to mean?"

"I just find it strange, how everything's gone so wrong. First Clarence gets killed. Then Isao. And the truck—how the hell does a truck just go dead like that?"

"You blame Johnny?"

Richard looks around at the other three, and I suddenly understand that he's not the only one who thinks Johnny's at fault. Is this why they've been huddling together? Exchanging theories, feeding their paranoia?

I shake my head. "This is ridiculous."

"Of course that's what she'd say," Vivian mutters. "I told you she would."

"Meaning what?"

"It's obvious to everyone that you're Johnny's favorite. I knew you'd stand up for him."

"He doesn't need anyone to stand up for him. He's the one keeping us alive."

"Is he?" Vivian glances warily in Johnny's direction. He's too far away to hear us, but she drops her voice anyway. "Are you sure of that?"

This is absurd. I search their faces, wondering who started this whispering campaign. "You're going to tell me Johnny killed Isao and dragged him up that tree? Or maybe he just delivered him to the leopard and let her take it from there?"

"What do we really know about him, Millie?" Elliot asks.

"Oh God. Not you, too."

"I gotta tell you, the things they're saying . . ." Elliot looks over his shoulder and even though he whispers, I can hear his panic. "It's freaking me out."

"Think about it," says Richard. "How did we all end up on this safari?"

I glare at him. "The only reason I'm here is because of *you. You* wanted your African adventure, and now you've got it. Is it not measuring up? Or has it gotten too adventurous even for *you*?"

"We found him on the Internet," says Sylvia, who has been silent up till now. I notice that her hands tremble around her coffee cup. Her grip is so unsteady she has to set the cup down to keep it from spilling. "Vivian and I, we wanted to do a camping trip in the bush, but we couldn't afford to spend a lot. We found his website, Lost in Botswana." She gives a half-hysterical laugh. "And so we are."

"I tagged along with *them,*" Elliot says. "Sylvia and Viv and I, we're sitting in a bar together in Cape Town. And they tell me about this *fabulous* safari they're going on."

"I'm so sorry, Elliot," Sylvia says. "I'm sorry you ever met us in that bar. I'm sorry we talked you into coming." She takes a shaky breath and her voice breaks. "God, I just want to go *home.*"

"The Matsunagas found this tour through the website, too," says Vivian. "Isao told me he was looking for a true African experience. Not some tourist lodge, but a chance to really explore the bush."

"That's also how we ended up here," Richard says. "That same fucking website. Lost in Botswana."

I remember the night Richard showed it to me on his computer. For days he'd been surfing the Web, drooling over images of safari lodges and tented camps and feasts spread across candlelit tables. I don't remember why Lost in Botswana was the site he finally settled on. Perhaps it was the promise of an authentic experience. True wilderness, the way Hemingway would have lived it, although Hemingway was more likely just a convincing bullshitter. I had no part in planning this holiday; it was Richard's choice, Richard's dream. Now a nightmare.

"What are you all saying, that his website's a fake?" I ask. "That he used it to lure us out here? Do you people even *hear* yourselves?"

"People come here from all around the world to hunt big game," says Richard. "What if this time, *we're* the game?"

If he's angling for a reaction, he certainly gets one. Elliot looks as if he might throw up. Sylvia claps her hand over her mouth, as though to stifle a sob.

But I respond with a snort of derision. "You think Johnny Posthumus is *hunting* us? God, Richard, don't turn this into one of your thrillers."

"Johnny's the one with the gun," Richard says. "He holds all the power. If we don't stick together, *every single one of us,* then we're all dead."

There it is. I hear it in his bitter voice. I see it in the wary looks they all give me. I'm the Judas in their midst, the one who'll run to

Johnny and tattletale. It's all so ridiculous I should laugh, but I'm too fucking angry. As I rise to my feet, I can scarcely keep my voice steady. "When this is over, when we're all on that plane back to Maun next week, I'm going to remind you of this. And you're all going to feel like idiots."

"I hope you're right," Vivian whispers. "I hope to God we *are* idiots. I hope we *are* on that plane, and not just a pile of bloody bones in the . . ." Her voice cuts off as a shadow suddenly looms over her.

Johnny has moved so quietly that they didn't hear his approach, and now he stands just behind Vivian and looks around at our gathering. "We need water and firewood," he says. "Richard, Elliot, come down to the river with me."

As both men stand up, I see fear in Elliot's eyes. The same fear that gleams in the eyes of the blondes. Johnny calmly cradles the gun across his body, the pose of a rifleman at ease, but just the presence of that gun in his arms tilts the balance of power.

"What about—what about the girls?" Elliot asks, nervously glancing at the blondes. "Shouldn't I, uh, stay and keep an eye on them?"

"They can wait in the truck. Right now, I need muscle."

"If you give me the gun," suggests Richard, "Elliot and I can get the firewood and water."

"No one leaves camp without me. And I don't leave the perimeter without this rifle." Johnny's face is grim. "If you want to stay alive, you'll just have to trust me."

TWELVE

BOSTON

GABRIEL'S STEAK WAS COOKED A PERFECT MEDIUM RARE, THE WAY HE always ordered it when they dined out at Matteo's. But tonight, as they sat at their favorite table in the restaurant, Jane could scarcely stomach the sight of blood oozing out when her husband sliced into the filet. It made her think of Debra Gomez's blood, dripping down the boulder. Of Gott's body, hanging like a side of beef. *Whether it comes from cow or human, we are all fresh meat.*

Gabriel noticed she'd scarcely touched her pork chop, and he gave her a searching look. "You're still thinking about it, aren't you?"

"I can't help it. Doesn't it happen to you? Scenes you can't get out of your head, no matter how hard you try?"

"Try harder, Jane." He reached across the table and squeezed her hand. "It's been far too long since our last dinner out together."

"I am trying, but this case . . ." She looked at his steak and shuddered. "It just might turn me into a vegetarian."

"As bad as that?"

"We've both seen some awful things. Spent too much time in

autopsy rooms. But this one, it freaks me out on some deeper level. Gutted and left hanging. Eaten by your own damn pets."

"That's why we shouldn't get a puppy."

"Gabriel, this isn't funny."

He reached for his glass of wine. "I'm just trying to lighten up date night. We don't get many of them, and this one is turning into another case review. As usual."

"It's the work we both do. What else are we supposed to talk about?"

"Our daughter, maybe? Where we should go on our next vacation?" He set down his wine and looked at her. "There's more to life than murder."

"It's what brought us together."

"It's not the only thing."

No, she thought as her husband again picked up his knife, wielding it with the cool, calm skill of a surgeon. The day they'd met, at a crime scene in Stony Brook Reservation, she'd found his unflappability intimidating. In the chaos of that afternoon, as cops and criminalists coalesced around the decomposing body, Gabriel had been a quietly commanding presence, the aloof observer taking it all in. She hadn't been surprised to learn he was FBI; she'd known at a glance that he was an outsider, and that he was there to challenge her authority. But what first pitted them against each other was also what later drew them together. Push and pull, the attraction of opposites. Even now, as she watched her maddeningly imperturbable husband, she knew exactly why she'd fallen for him.

He looked at her and gave a resigned sigh. "Okay, whether I like it or not, it seems we're going to talk about murder. So." He set down his knife and fork. "You really think Big Mouth O'Brien is the key to this?"

"Those nasty calls to his radio show were so eerily similar to the comments left on that article about Leon Gott. They talked about hanging and gutting."

"There's nothing particularly unique about that imagery. It's simply what hunters do. I've done it myself after bringing down a deer."

"The caller Suzy identifies herself as a member of the Vegan Action Army. According to their website, they claim to have fifty members in Massachusetts."

Gabriel shook his head. "That organization's not ringing any bells for me. I don't recall it popping up on any federal watchlists."

"Or Boston PD lists, either. But maybe they're smart enough to stay quiet. Not take credit for what they do."

"Hanging and gutting hunters? Does that sound like vegans?"

"Think of the Earth Liberation Front. They plant firebombs."

"But ELF tries its best to avoid killing anyone."

"Still, look at the symbolism. Leon Gott was a big-game hunter and taxidermist. *Hub Magazine* runs an article about him called 'The Trophy Master.' Months later, he's found hanging by his ankles, slashed from stem to stern and gutted. Suspended at just the right height to be eaten by his pets. What more fitting way to dispose of a hunter's body than to have it ripped apart by Fluffy and Fido?" She paused, suddenly aware that the restaurant had gone quiet. Glancing sideways, she saw the couple at the next table staring at her.

"Not the time or place, Jane," Gabriel said.

She stared down at her pork chop. "Nice weather we're having."

Only when the buzz of conversation around them had resumed did she say, more quietly: "I think the symbolism is obvious."

"Or it may have nothing to do with the fact he was a hunter. There's also theft as a motive."

"If it was theft, it was pretty specific. His wallet and cash were still in the bedroom, untouched. As far as we know, the only thing missing from his house is the snow leopard pelt."

"And you told me it was worth a lot."

"But a pelt that rare would be hard as hell to unload. It'd have to be for someone's private collection. And if robbery was the only motive, why go through the bloody ritual of gutting the victim?"

"It seems to me you have two specific symbolic features here. First, the taking of a rare animal pelt. Second, the way the victim's body was displayed." Gabriel frowned at the table candle as he mulled it over. He'd finally been dragged into the puzzle and now he was fully engaged. Tonight might be date night, the one evening a month when they vowed not to talk about work, but it always came back to murder. How could it not, when this was what they both lived and breathed? She watched the candlelight flicker on his face as he quietly sifted through the facts. How lucky she was to be able to share these facts with him. She thought of what it would be like to sit here with a spouse who was not in law enforcement, to be bursting to talk about what was gnawing away at her and unable to say a thing about it. Not only did they share a home and a child, they also shared the same grim knowledge of how instantaneously a life can change. Or end.

"I'll see what info we have on the Vegan Action Army," he said. "But I'd be inclined to focus on that leopard pelt, since it's the one item of value you know was taken." He paused. "What did you think of Jerry O'Brien?"

"Aside from his being a chauvinist jerk?"

"I mean, as a suspect. Any possible motive to kill Gott?"

She shook her head. "They were hunting buddies. He could just as easily shoot him in the woods and call it an accident. But yeah, I thought about O'Brien. And his personal assistant. Gott was such a loner, there aren't a lot of suspects to choose from. At least, none that we know of." But dig deep into someone's life and surprises always turned up. She thought of other victims, other investigations that had turned up secret lovers or hidden bank accounts or countless illicit cravings that only come to light when one's life is laid bare by a violent end.

And she thought of her own father, who had secrets of his own, whose affair with another woman had fractured his marriage. Even the man she thought she knew, the man with whom she'd shared every Christmas, every birthday, had turned out to be a stranger.

Later that evening, she was forced to confront that same stranger when she and Gabriel pulled up in front of Angela's house to pick up their daughter. Jane spotted the familiar car parked in the driveway and said: "What's Dad doing here?"

"This is his house."

"Used to be his house." She stepped out and eyed the Chevy, parked in its usual spot, as if it had never left. As if Frank Rizzoli could just step back into his old life and everything would be exactly the way it always was. The Chevy had a new dent in the left front fender; she wondered if Frank's bimbo had put it there, and whether he'd yelled at her about it, the way he'd once yelled at Angela when she'd scraped the car door. If you hung around any man long enough, even a shiny new lover would start to show his flaws. When had the bimbo noticed that Frank had nose hairs and morning breath like every other man?

"Let's just pick up Regina and go home," whispered Gabriel as they climbed the front porch.

"What do you think I'm going to do?"

"Not engage in the usual family drama, I hope."

"A family without drama," she said, ringing the bell, "would not be mine."

Her mother opened the door. At least, she *looked* like Angela, but this was a flat zombie version who greeted them with a lifeless smile as they walked in. "She's sound asleep, no trouble at all. Did you two have a nice dinner?"

"Yeah. Why's Dad here?" asked Jane.

Frank called out: "I'm sitting in my own house, that's what I'm doing. What kind of question is that?"

Jane walked into the living room and saw her father planted in his old easy chair, the wandering king back to reclaim his throne. His hair was a weird shoe-polish black—when had he dyed it? There were other changes too: the open-necked silk shirt, the fancy wristwatch. They made him seem like some Vegas version of Frank Rizzoli. Had she walked into the wrong house, entered an alternate universe with an android mom and a disco dad?

"I'll get Regina," said Gabriel, and he discreetly vanished down the hallway. *Coward.*

"Your mother and I have finally come to an understanding," Frank announced.

"Meaning?"

"We're going to patch things up. Go back to the way things were."

"Is that with or without Blondie?"

"What the hell's the matter with you? You trying to ruin things?"

"You did a pretty good job of it on your own."

"Angela! Tell her."

Jane turned to her mother, who stood staring at the floor. "Is this what you want, Ma?"

"It's gonna be okay, Janie," Angela said quietly. "It's gonna work."

"Like *that's* the voice of enthusiasm."

"I love your mom," said Frank. "We're a family, we've made a home, and we stay together. That's what matters."

Jane looked back and forth at her parents. Her father glared back, ruddy and pugnacious. Her mother didn't meet her gaze. There was so much she wanted to say, so much she *should* say, but it was late, and Gabriel was already standing by the front door, holding their sleeping daughter.

"Thanks for babysitting, Ma," Jane said. "I'll call you."

They walked out of the house to the car. Just as Gabriel finished buckling Regina into her car seat, the front door opened and Angela came out of the house, carrying Regina's stuffed giraffe.

"She'll scream bloody murder if you forget Benny," she said, handing the giraffe to Jane.

"Are you okay, Mom?"

Angela hugged herself and glanced back at the house, as if waiting for someone else to answer the question.

"Mom?"

Angela sighed. "It's the way things have to be. Frankie wants it. So does Mike."

"My brothers don't get a say in this. You're the only one who does."

"He never signed the divorce papers, Jane. We're still married, and that means something. It means he never really gave up on us."

"It means he wanted it both ways."

"He's your father."

"Yeah, and I love him. But I love you, too, and you don't look happy."

In the shadowy driveway, she saw her mother attempt a brave smile. "We're a family. I'll make this work."

"What about Vince?"

Just the mention of Korsak's name made her mother's smile suddenly crumple. She pressed her hands across her mouth and turned away. "Oh God. Oh God . . ." As she began to sob, Jane took her into her arms. "I miss him," said Angela. "I miss him every day. He doesn't deserve this."

"Do you love Vince?"

"Yes!"

"Do you love Dad?"

Angela hesitated. "Of course I do." But the real answer was in that pause, those silent seconds before she could contradict what her heart already knew. She pulled away from Jane, took a deep breath, and straightened. "Don't you worry about me. Everything's going to be fine. Now you go home and get that girl to bed, okay?"

Jane watched her mother walk back into the house. Through the window, she saw Angela settle onto the living room sofa opposite Frank, who was still planted in his armchair. Just like the old days, thought Jane. Mom in her corner. Dad in his.

THIRTEEN

MAURA PAUSED ON THE DRIVEWAY AND LOOKED UP AT THE SOUND OF a cawing crow. Dozens of them sat perched like ominous fruit in the tree above, their black wings flicking against the gray sky. *A murder of crows* was the correct term for this gathering, and it seemed appropriate on this cold gray afternoon, with thunderclouds moving in and a grim task awaiting her. Crime scene tape had been strung across the pathway leading to the backyard. She ducked under the strand and as she moved across the freshly disturbed soil, she felt the crows watching her, marking every step as they noisily discussed this new intruder in their kingdom. In the backyard, Detectives Darren Crowe and Johnny Tam stood beside a parked backhoe and a damp mound of dirt. As she approached, Tam waved to her with a purple-gloved hand. He was new to the homicide unit, an intense and humorless young detective who'd recently transferred from the Chinatown beat. To his misfortune, he'd been paired with Crowe, who'd driven his former partner Thomas Moore into a much-deserved retirement. *A match made in hell,* Jane had dubbed it, and the unit was taking bets on how long it would be before the tightly wound

Tam finally snapped and hauled off at Crowe. It would be a disastrous career move for Tam, to be sure, but everyone agreed it would be damn satisfying to watch.

Even here in the heavily wooded backyard, with no TV cameras in sight, Crowe was at his *GQ* best with his movie-star haircut and a suit well tailored to his broad shoulders. He was a man accustomed to sucking up all the attention in a room, and it would be easy to overlook the far quieter Tam. But Tam was the one Maura focused on because she knew she could count on him to deliver the facts, unfiltered and accurate.

Before Tam could speak, Crowe said with a laugh: "I don't think the homeowners expected to find *that* in their new swimming pool."

Maura looked down at a soil-stained skull and rib cage lying in a partially folded blue plastic tarp. One glance at the skull told her the bones were human.

She donned gloves. "What's the story here?"

"Supposed to be a new swimming pool. Owners bought the house three years ago, hired Lorenzo Construction to do the excavation. Two feet down, they scooped *that* up. Backhoe driver opened the tarp, freaked out, and called nine one one. Luckily it doesn't look like he caused much damage with his equipment."

Maura saw no clothing, no items of jewelry, but she needed neither to determine the sex of the deceased. Crouching down, she studied the skull's delicate supraorbital ridges. She peeled back the folded tarp, exposing a pelvis with widely flaring ilia. One glance at the femur told her the deceased was not tall, perhaps five foot three at the most.

"She's been here awhile," said Tam. He had not needed Maura's help to recognize that the remains were female. "How long, do you think?"

"Fully skeletonized. Spine no longer articulated," Maura observed. "These ligament attachments have already decayed."

"Meaning months? Years?" said Crowe.

"Yes."

Crowe gave a grunt of impatience. "That's as specific as you're gonna get?"

"I once saw full skeletonization in a shallow grave after only three months, so I can't give you a more specific answer. My best estimate for postmortem interval is a minimum of six months. The fact she's nude and the grave is pretty shallow would accelerate decay, but it was deep enough to protect her from scavenging carnivores."

As if in response, there was a loud caw overhead. She glanced up to see three crows perched on branches, watching them. She'd seen the damage that corvids could cause to a human body, how those beaks could shred ligaments and pluck eyes from sockets. In unison the birds rose in a flurry of spiky wings.

"Creepy birds. Like little vultures," said Tam, watching them flap away.

"And incredibly intelligent. If only they could talk to us." She looked at him. "What's the history of this property?"

"Belonged to some elderly lady for about forty years. She died fifteen years ago, it ended up in probate, and the house fell into disrepair. There were renters off and on, but it sat vacant for most of the time. Until this couple bought it around three years ago."

Maura looked around the perimeter. "No fences. And it backs up to woods."

"Yeah, it abuts Stony Brook Reservation. Easy access to anyone looking for a place to bury a body."

"And the current owners?"

"Nice young couple. They've been slowly fixing up the house, renovated the bathroom and kitchen. This was the year they decided to add an in-ground pool. Before they started digging for the pool, they said this part of the yard was pretty thick with weeds."

"So this burial probably predates their purchase of the house."

"What about our girl here?" Crowe cut in. "You see a cause of death?"

"Have a little patience, Detective. I haven't even finished unwrapping her." Maura peeled away the last of the blue tarp, exposing tibias and fibulae, metatarsals and . . . She froze, staring at orange nylon cord, still looped around the anklebones. An image instantly snapped into her head. Another crime scene. Orange nylon cord. A body hanging from its ankles, eviscerated.

Without a word, she moved back to the rib cage. Knelt closer and stared at the xiphoid process, where the ribs came together to join at the breastbone. Even on that overcast day, in the gloom of the woods, she could see the distinct nick in the bone. She pictured the body, suspended upside down by its ankles. Pictured a blade slicing downward through the belly, from pubis to sternum. That nick was right where the blade would land.

Her hands suddenly felt chilled inside the gloves.

"Dr. Isles?" Tam said.

She ignored him and looked at the skull. There on the frontal bone, where the forehead sloped down to the brow, were three parallel scratches.

She rocked back on her knees, stunned. "We need to call Rizzoli."

FIREWORKS AHEAD, THOUGHT JANE as she ducked under the bright strand of police tape. This was not her crime scene, not her turf, and she fully expected Darren Crowe to make that clear from the start. She thought of Leon Gott yelling *Get off my lawn* at the neighbor's kid. Imagined Crowe thirty years from now, an equally cranky old man, yelling *Get off my crime scene!*

But it was Johnny Tam who greeted her in the side yard. "Rizzoli," he said.

"How's his mood?"

"The usual. All sunshine and brightness."

"That good, huh?"

"He's not too happy with Dr. Isles at the moment."

"I'm not too happy, either."

"She insisted on bringing you in. And when she talks, I listen."

Jane eyed Tam, but as usual she couldn't read his face; she'd never been able to. Though he was new to the homicide unit, he'd already built a reputation as a man who went about his work with quiet and unassuming doggedness. Unlike Crowe, Tam was no glory hound.

"You agree with her that there's a link between these cases?" she asked.

"I know Dr. Isles isn't one to rely on hunches. Which is why it kind of surprised me, that she called you about this. Considering the predictable blowback."

They didn't need to say the name to know they were both talking about Crowe.

"So how bad is it, working with him?" she asked as they moved down the flagstone path toward the backyard.

"Aside from the fact I've already ripped through three punching bags in the gym?"

"Trust me, it won't get better. Working with him is like Chinese water tor—" She stopped. "You know what I mean."

Tam laughed. "We Chinese may have invented it, but Crowe perfected it."

They emerged into the backyard and she saw the object of their scorn standing with Maura. Everything about Crowe's body language screamed *pissed off,* from his rigid neck to his agitated gestures.

"Before you turn this into a three-ring circus," he said to Maura, "how about giving us a more specific time of death?"

"That's as specific as I can be," said Maura. "The rest is up to you. That *is* your job."

Crowe noticed Jane approaching and said, "I'm sure the all-powerful Rizzoli has the answers."

"I'm here at Dr. Isles's request," said Jane. "I'll just take a look and get out of your way."

"Yeah. Right."

Maura said, quietly, "She's over here, Jane."

Jane followed her across the yard, to where a backhoe was parked. The remains were lying on a blue tarp at the edge of a freshly dug pit.

"Adult female," said Maura. "About five foot three. No arthritic changes in the spine, epiphyses are closed. I estimate her age as somewhere between twenty and mid-thirties . . ."

"What the hell did you get me into?" Jane muttered.

"Excuse me?"

"I'm already on his shit list."

"So am I, but it doesn't stop me from doing my job." Maura paused. "Assuming I keep my job"—something that had been in doubt after Maura's testimony in court had sent a well-liked cop to prison. Maura's aloofness—some would call it strangeness—had never made her popular among Boston PD's rank and file, and now cops considered her a traitor to their brotherhood.

"I gotta be honest," said Jane. "What you told me over the phone didn't give me much of a tingle." She looked at the remains, stripped down by decay to nothing more than bones. "To start off with, this is a woman."

"Her ankles were bound with orange nylon cord. The same cord that was around Gott's ankles."

"That type of cord's common enough. Unlike Gott, this one's female and someone went to the trouble of burying her."

"There's a cut mark at the bottom of her sternum, just like Gott. I think she was quite possibly eviscerated."

"Possibly?"

"Without any remaining soft tissues and organs, I can't prove it. But that sternal cut is from a blade. The kind of nick you'd make when you slice open the abdomen. And there's one more thing." Maura knelt down to point at the skull. "Look at this."

"Those three little scratches?"

"Remember Gott's skull film, where I pointed out the three linear scratches? Like claw marks on the bone."

"These aren't linear. They're just tiny little nicks."

"They're spaced precisely apart. They might have been made by the same tool."

"Or by animals. Or that backhoe." Jane turned at the sound of voices. The crime scene unit had arrived, and Crowe was leading a trio of criminalists toward the remains.

"So what do you think, Rizzoli?" said Crowe. "You gonna call dibs on this?"

"I'm not fighting you for turf. I'm just checking out some similarities."

"Your vic was, what? A sixty-four-year-old guy?"

"Yeah."

"And this is a young female. Does that sound similar to you?"

"No," Jane admitted, feeling Maura's gaze on her.

"Your male victim—what did you find on autopsy? The cause of death?"

"There was a skull fracture, as well as crush injuries of the thyroid cartilage," said Maura.

"There's no obvious fractures on my gal's skull," said Crowe. *My gal.* As if she belonged to him, this nameless victim. As if he'd already claimed ownership.

"This woman was small and easier to control than a man," Maura said. "There'd be no need to stun her first with a blow to the head."

"But it is another difference," said Crowe. "Another detail that doesn't line up with the other case."

"Detective Crowe, I'm looking at the gestalt of these two cases. The overall picture."

"Which only you seem to be seeing. One vic is an older male, the other a younger female. One has a skull fracture, the other doesn't. One was killed and displayed in his own garage, the other was buried in a backyard."

"Both were nude, their ankles bound with cord, and they were very likely eviscerated. The way a hunter—"

"Maura," cut in Jane. "How 'bout we walk the property?"

"I've already walked it."

"Well, I haven't. Come on."

Reluctantly, Maura followed her away from the pit and they moved to the edge of the yard. There were overhanging trees here, which deepened the gloom of an already depressingly gray afternoon.

"You think Crowe's right, don't you?" said Maura, her voice tinged with bitterness.

"You know I always respect your opinion, Maura."

"But in this case, you don't agree with it."

"You have to admit, there are differences between these two victims."

"The cut marks. The nylon cord. Even the knots are similar, and—"

"A double square knot isn't unique. If I were a perp, it's probably what I'd use to tie up a victim."

"The gutting? How many recent cases have you seen of *that*?"

"You found a single nick in the sternum. It's not conclusive. These victims couldn't be more different. Age, sex, location."

"Until I ID this female, you can't say there's no connection with Gott."

"Okay," Jane conceded with a sigh. "True."

"Why are we arguing? You're always welcome to prove me wrong. Just do your job."

Jane stiffened. "When haven't I?"

That reply, so tight with tension, made Maura go still. Her dark hair, usually so smooth and sleek, was transformed by the chilly dampness into a wiry net that had trapped stray twigs. In the gloom of these trees, with her dirt-streaked pant cuffs and wrinkled blouse, she looked like a feral version of Maura, a stranger whose eyes glowed too brightly. Feverishly.

"What's really going on here?" Jane asked quietly.

Maura looked away, a sudden avoidance of gaze as if the answer was too painful to share. Over the years they had been privy to each other's miseries and missteps. They knew the worst of each other. Why now did Maura suddenly shrink from answering a simple question?

"Maura?" Jane prodded. "What's happened?"

Maura sighed. "I got a letter."

FOURTEEN

THEY SAT IN A BOOTH AT J. P. DOYLE'S, A FAVORITE BOSTON PD WATERing hole where, come five P.M., there would almost certainly be at least half a dozen cops at the bar, trading war stories. But three P.M. was a restaurant's witching hour, and that afternoon only two other booths were occupied. Although Jane had eaten countless lunches at Doyle's, this was Maura's first meal here, yet another reminder that despite their years together as colleagues and friends, a gulf remained between them. Cop versus doc, community college versus Stanford University, Adams Ale versus Sauvignon Blanc. As the waitress stood waiting, Maura scanned the menu with an expression of *What's the least disgusting thing I can order?*

"The fish-and-chips are good," suggested Jane.

"I'll take the Caesar salad," said Maura. "Dressing on the side."

The waitress left, and they sat for a moment in uneasy silence. In the booth across from them sat a couple who couldn't keep their hands off each other. Older man, younger woman. Sex in the afternoon, thought Jane, and no doubt illicit as hell. It made her think of her own father, Frank, and his blond chickie, the affair that had fractured his marriage and sent heartbroken Angela into Vince Korsak's arms. Jane wanted to yell: *Hey, mister, go back to your wife now, before you fuck up everyone's lives.*

As if men drunk on testosterone ever listened to reason.

Maura glanced at the passionately entwined couple. "Nice place. Do they rent rooms by the hour?"

"When you're on a cop's salary, this is the place for decent food and lots of it. Sorry it doesn't meet your standards."

Maura winced. "I don't know why I said that. I'm just not good company today."

"You said you got a letter. Who sent it?"

"Amalthea Lank."

The name was like a wintry breath, chilling Jane's skin, lifting the hairs on her neck. *Maura's mother.* The mother who'd abandoned her soon after birth. The mother who now resided in the women's prison in Framingham, where she was serving a life term for multiple homicides.

No, not a mother. A monster.

"Why the hell are you getting letters from her?" said Jane. "I thought you cut off all contact."

"I did. I asked the prison to stop forwarding her letters. I refused her phone calls."

"So how did you get this letter?"

"I don't know how she managed to slip it through. Maybe she bribed one of the guards. Or it was sent out in another inmate's letter. But I found it in my mail when I got home last night."

"Why didn't you call me? I would've handled the whole thing. One visit to Framingham, and I'd make damn sure she'll never bother you again."

"I couldn't call you. I needed time to think."

"What's to think about?" Jane leaned forward. "She's screwing around with your head again. It's the kind of thing she loves to do. Gives her a thrill to play mind games with you."

"I know. I know that."

"Open the door one tiny crack and she'll shove her way into your life. Thank God she didn't raise you. It means you don't owe her a thing. Not one word, not one thought."

"I carry her DNA, Jane. When I looked at her, I saw myself in her face."

"Genes are overrated."

"Genes determine who we are."

"Does that mean you're gonna pick up a scalpel and start slicing up people, like she did?"

"Of course not. But lately . . ." Maura paused and looked down at her hands. "Everywhere I look, I seem to see shadows. I see the dark side."

Jane snorted. "Of course you do. Look at where you work."

"When I walk into a crowded room, I'll automatically wonder whom I should be afraid of. Who needs to be watched."

"It's called situational awareness. It's smart."

"It's more than that. It's as if I can *feel* the darkness. I don't know if it comes from the world around me, or if it's already inside me." She was still staring at her hands, as if the answers were written there. "I find myself obsessed with looking for ominous patterns. Things that connect. When I saw that skeleton today, and I remembered Leon Gott's body, I saw a pattern. A killer's signature."

"It doesn't mean you're sliding into the dark side. It just means you're doing your medical examiner thing. Always looking for the gestalt, as you put it."

"You didn't see a signature. Why do I?"

"Because you're smarter than me?"

"That's a flippant answer, Jane. And it's not true."

"Okay, so using my *amazing* cop brain, let me make an observation. You've had a really rough year. You broke up with Daniel, and you probably still miss him. Am I right?"

"Of course I miss him." She added, softly: "And I'm sure he misses me."

"Then there was your testimony against Wayne Graff. You sent a cop to jail, and Boston PD gave you a rough time because of it. I've read about stress factors and how they make people sick. A broken love affair, conflict at work—hell, your stress score's so high, you should have cancer by now."

"Thank you for giving me one more thing to worry about."

"And now this letter. This goddamn letter from *her.*"

They fell silent as the waitress returned with their food. A club sandwich for Jane, the Caesar salad—dressing on the side—for Maura. Only after their server walked away did Maura ask, quietly:

"Do you ever get letters from *him*?"

She didn't have to say his name; they both knew whom she was talking about. Reflexively Jane clenched fingers over her scarred palms, where Warren Hoyt had plunged his scalpels. She had not laid eyes on him in four years, yet she could remember every detail of his face, a face so unremarkable that it could blend into any crowd. Incarceration and illness had no doubt aged him, but she had no interest in seeing the changes. She drew enough satisfaction knowing that she'd delivered justice with a single bullet to his spine, and his punishment would last a lifetime.

"He tried to send me letters from rehab," Jane said. "He dictates them to his visitors, and they mail them to me. I toss them right out."

"You've never read them?"

"Why would I? It's his way of trying to stay in my life. To let me know he's still thinking about me."

"The woman who got away."

"I didn't just get away. I'm the one who took him down." Jane gave a hard laugh and picked up her sandwich. "He's obsessed with me, but I won't waste one millisecond thinking about him."

"You really don't think about him at all?"

The question, asked so softly, hung unanswered for a moment. Jane focused on her sandwich, trying to convince herself that what she'd said was true. But how could it be? Trapped though he was in his paralyzed body, Warren Hoyt still wielded power over her because of their shared history. He'd seen her helpless and terrified; he was a witness to the moment she'd been conquered.

"I won't give him that power," Jane said. "I refuse to think about him. And that's what you should do."

"Even though she's my mother?"

"That word doesn't apply to her. She's a DNA donor, that's it."

"That's a powerful *it.* She's part of every cell in my body."

"I thought you'd decided this, Maura. You walked away from her, and swore you were never going to look back. Why are you changing your mind?"

Maura looked down at her untouched salad. "Because I read her letter."

"And I'm guessing she pressed all the right buttons. *I'm your only blood relative. We have unbreakable bonds.* Am I right?"

"Yes," Maura admitted.

"She's a sociopath and you don't owe her a thing. Tear up the letter and forget about it."

"She's dying, Jane."

"What?"

Maura looked at her, torment in her eyes. "She has six months, a year at the most."

"Bullshit. She's playing you."

"I called the prison nurse last night, right after I read the letter. Amalthea had already signed the release form, so they shared her medical information with me."

"She doesn't miss a trick, does she? She knew exactly how you'd respond and she laid the trap."

"The nurse confirmed it. Amalthea has pancreatic cancer."

"Couldn't happen to a more deserving candidate."

"My only blood relative and she's dying. She wants my forgiveness. She's begging me for it."

"And she expects you to give it to her?" Jane wiped mayonnaise from her fingers with swift, angry strokes of her napkin. "What about all the people she slaughtered? Who's gonna forgive her for that? Not you. You don't have the right."

"But I can forgive her for abandoning me."

"Abandoning you was the only good thing she ever did. Instead of being raised by a psycho mom, you got a chance at a normal life. Trust me, she didn't do it because it was *right.*"

"Yet here I am, Jane. Healthy and whole. I grew up with every advantage, raised by parents who loved me, so I have nothing to be bitter about. Why shouldn't I give some comfort to a dying woman?"

"So write a letter. Tell her she's forgiven, and then forget about her."

"She only has six months. She wants to see me."

Jane tossed down her napkin. "Let's not forget who she really is. You once told me you felt a chill when you looked into her eyes, because you didn't see a human being looking back at you. You said you saw a void, a creature without a soul. *You're* the one who called her a monster."

Maura sighed. "Yes, I did."

"Don't walk into the monster's cage."

Maura's eyes suddenly shimmered with tears. "And in six months, when she's dead, how do I deal with the guilt? The fact I turned down her last wish? It will be too late to change my mind. *That's* what I worry about most. That for the rest of my life, I'll feel guilty. And I'll never get the chance to understand."

"Understand what?"

"Why I am the way I am."

Jane looked into her friend's troubled face. "Meaning what? Brilliant? Logical? Too honest for your own damn good?"

"Haunted," said Maura softly. "By the dark side."

Jane's cell phone rang. As she dug it out of her purse, she said: "It's because of the job we do and the things we see. We both chose this work because we're not sunshine-and-ponies kind of gals." She hit the TALK button on her phone. "Detective Rizzoli."

"The carrier finally released Leon Gott's phone log," said Frost.

"Anything interesting?"

"*Really* interesting. On the day of his death he made several phone calls. One was to Jerry O'Brien, which we already knew about."

"About picking up Kovo's carcass."

"Yeah. He also made a phone call to Interpol in Johannesburg, South Africa."

"Interpol? What was he calling them about?"

"About his son's disappearance in Botswana. The investigator wasn't in the office, so Gott left a message saying he'd call again later. He never did."

"His son went missing six years ago. Why's Gott asking about it now?"

"I have no idea. But here's the *really* interesting item in his phone log. At two thirty P.M., he called a cell phone registered to Jodi Underwood, in Brookline. It lasted six minutes. That same night, at nine forty-six P.M., Jodi Underwood called Gott back. That call was only seventeen seconds long, so she might have just left a message on his answering machine."

"There *was* no message on his answering machine from that night."

"Right. And at nine forty-six, there's a good chance Gott was already dead. Since the next-door neighbor said she saw his lights get turned off between nine and ten-thirty."

"So who deleted this phone message? Frost, this is weird."

"It gets a lot weirder. I called Jodi Underwood's cell phone twice and it went straight to voice mail. Then it suddenly hit me that her name sounded familiar. You remember?"

"Hint, please."

"Last week's news. Brookline."

Jane's pulse suddenly kicked into a gallop. "There was a homicide . . ."

"Jodi Underwood was murdered in her home Sunday night. The same night as Leon Gott."

FIFTEEN

"I WENT ON HER FACEBOOK PAGE," SAID FROST AS THEY DROVE TO BROOKline. "Check out her profile."

For once he was the one driving as Jane played catch-up on Frost's iPad, tapping through webpages that he had already visited. She pulled up the Facebook page and saw a photo of a pretty redhead. According to her profile she was thirty-seven years old, single, and a high school librarian. She had a sister named Sarah and she was a vegetarian whose likes included PETA, animal rights, and holistic health.

"She's not exactly Leon Gott's type," said Jane. "Why would a woman who probably despised everything he stood for be talking to him on the phone?"

"I don't know. I went back four weeks on his phone log and there are no other calls between them. Just those two, on Sunday. He called her at two thirty, she called him back at nine forty-six. When he was probably dead."

Jane replayed the scenario as it must have unfolded that night. The killer still in Gott's house, the dead body already hanging in the garage, perhaps in the process of being gutted. The phone rings, the answering machine picks up, and Jodi Underwood leaves her message. What's on that message that compels the killer to delete it, leaving the bloody smear on the answering machine? What would make him drive to Brookline and commit a second murder that same night?

She looked at Frost. "We never did find a personal address book in his house."

"No. Searched all over, too, 'cause we wanted his contacts. No address book turned up."

She thought about the killer standing over that phone, seeing Jodi's number on display, a number that Gott had called earlier that day. A number that Gott must have stored in his personal directory, along with Jodi's mailing address.

Jane scrolled down through Jodi's Facebook page, reading the entries. The woman had posted fairly regularly, at least every few days. The last entry was on Saturday, the day before she died.

Check out this recipe for veggie pad Thai. I cooked it for my sister and her husband last night, and they didn't even miss the meat. It's healthy, tasty, and good for the planet!

Dining on rice noodles and tofu that night, did Jodi have any inkling it would be one of her last meals? That all her efforts to eat healthy would soon be irrelevant?

Jane scrolled back through Jodi's earlier entries, about books she'd read and movies she'd enjoyed, about friends' weddings and birthdays, about a gloomy day in October when she'd wondered about the point of life. Back another few weeks to September, more cheerful, the start of a new school year.

How nice to see familiar faces back in the library.

Then, in early September, she posted a photo of a smiling young man with dark hair, along with a melancholy entry.

Six years ago, I lost the love of my life. I will never stop missing you, Elliot.

Elliot. "His son," Jane said softly.

"What?"

"Jodi's Facebook entry is about a man named Elliot. She writes: *Six years ago, I lost the love of my life.*"

"Six years ago?" Frost looked at her with startled eyes. "That's when Elliot Gott vanished."

IN THE MONTH OF November, after clocks switch to standard time, the sun sets early in New England, and at four thirty on that gloomy afternoon it already felt like dusk. The sky had been threatening to rain all day, and a fine drizzle misted the windshield by the time Jane and Frost arrived at Jodi Underwood's residence. A gray Ford Fusion was parked in front of it, and on the driver's side they could see the silhouette of a woman's head. Even before Jane had her seat belt unbuckled, the Ford's door swung open and the driver stepped out. She was statuesque, her hair stylishly streaked with gray, and dressed in smart but practical attire: gray pants and suit jacket, a tan raincoat, and sturdy, comfortable flats. It was an outfit that could have come from Jane's closet, which wasn't surprising, since this woman, too, was a cop.

"Detective Andrea Pearson," the woman said. "Brookline PD."

"Jane Rizzoli, Barry Frost," said Jane. "Thanks for meeting us."

They shook hands but wasted no time lingering in the thickening drizzle, and Pearson immediately led them up the steps to the front door of the house. It was a modest residence, with a small front yard dominated by paired forsythia bushes, their branches stripped of leaves by autumn. A scrap of police tape still clung to the porch railing, a bright warning flag that announced: *Tragedy ahead.*

"I have to say, I was startled to get your call," Detective Pearson said as she pulled out the house key. "We haven't been able to pry Jodi Underwood's phone logs from her carrier yet, and her cell phone's missing. So we had no idea that she and Mr. Gott traded phone calls."

"You said her phone's missing," said Jane. "Was it stolen?"

"Along with other things." Detective Pearson unlocked the door. "Robbery was the motive here. At least, that's what we assumed."

They stepped into the house, and Detective Pearson switched on the lights. Jane saw wood floors, a living room furnished with sleek Swedish minimalism, but no bloodstains. The only evidence that a crime had been committed here were the smudges of fingerprint powder.

"Her body was lying right here, near the front door," said Detective Pearson. "After Jodi didn't show up for work Monday morning, the school called her sister Sarah, who drove straight over. She was found around ten A.M. The body was dressed in pajamas and a robe. The cause of death was pretty obvious. There were ligature marks around her neck, and the ME agreed it was strangulation. The victim also had a bruise on her right temple, maybe from an initial blow to stun her. There was no evidence of sexual assault. It was a blitz attack, a rapid takedown that probably happened right after she opened the door."

"You said she was wearing pajamas and a robe?" said Frost.

Pearson nodded. "The ME estimated time of death between eight P.M. and two A.M. If she made that phone call to Gott at nine forty-six P.M., that narrows down the time of death for us."

"Assuming the call actually came from her and not someone else using her phone."

Pearson paused. "That is a possibility, since her cell phone's missing. Every call made to her on Monday morning went straight to voice mail, so whoever has it seems to have turned it off."

"You said you thought that robbery was the motive. What else was taken?" asked Jane.

"According to her sister Sarah, the missing items include Jodi's MacBook Air laptop, a camera, cell phone, and her purse. There have been other break-ins in this neighborhood, but those happened while the occupants were away. The same sorts of valuables were taken, mostly electronics."

"Do you think this was the same perp?"

Detective Pearson didn't answer right away, but stared down at the floor, as if she could still see Jodi Underwood's body lying at her feet. A silvery curl of hair slid across her cheek, and she brushed it back. Looked at Jane. "I'm not sure. With the other burglaries, there were fingerprints left behind, obviously an amateur at work. But this crime scene, there was no evidence left behind. No fingerprints, no tool marks, no footwear evidence. It's so clean, so efficient, it almost seems . . ."

"Professional."

Detective Pearson nodded. "That's why I'm intrigued by her phone calls with Leon Gott. Did that crime scene look like a targeted killing?"

"I don't know about targeted," said Jane. "But it was definitely not clean and efficient, like this one."

"What do you mean?"

"I'll send you the crime scene photos. I'm sure you'll agree Leon Gott's murder was quite a bit messier. And more grotesque."

"So maybe there is no connection between these two cases," said Detective Pearson. "But do you know why they exchanged phone calls? How did they know each other?"

"I have a hunch, but I'll need to confirm it with Jodi's sister. You said her name is Sarah?"

"She lives about a mile from here. I'll give her a call and tell her we're coming. Why don't you follow me in your car?"

"MY SISTER HATED EVERYTHING that Leon Gott stood for. His big-game hunting, his politics, but most of all the way he treated his son," said Sarah. "I have no idea why he'd call Jodi. Or why she'd call *him*."

They sat in Sarah's tidy living room where the furniture was all blond wood and glass. It was apparent the two sisters shared similar tastes, right down to the Swedish-chic sensibilities. They resembled each other, too, both of them with curly red hair and swan necks. But unlike Jodi's smiling Facebook photo, Sarah's face was a snapshot of exhaustion. She'd brought out a tray of tea and cookies for her three visitors, but her own cup sat cooling and untouched. Though she was thirty-eight, in the gray light of the window she looked older, as if grief had exerted its own form of gravity on her face, drooping down the corners of her mouth, her eyes.

Detective Pearson and Sarah already knew each other and had bonded over Jodi's death, so Jane and Frost deferred to Pearson for the first few questions.

"These phone calls may have nothing to do with Jodi's murder, Sarah," said Pearson. "But the coincidence is certainly striking. Did Jodi mention Leon Gott at all in the past few weeks?"

"No. Not in the past months or years, either. After she lost Elliot, there was no reason to talk about his father."

"What did she say about Leon Gott?"

"She said he was the world's most despicable dad. Jodi and Elliot lived together for about two years, so she heard a lot about Leon. How he loved his guns more than his own family. How he took Elliot hunting one day, when Elliot was only thirteen. Told him to gut the deer, and when Elliot refused, Leon called him a faggot."

"How awful."

"Leon's wife left him right after that, taking Elliot with her. Best thing she could have done as a mother. Too bad she didn't do it earlier."

"And did Elliot have much contact with his father?"

"Sporadically. Jodi told me that the last call Leon made to Elliot was on his birthday, but it was a short conversation. Elliot tried to keep it civil, but he had to hang up when his dad started bad-mouthing his dead mother. A month later, Elliot left for Africa. It was his dream trip, something he'd planned for years. Thank God Jodi couldn't get vacation time to go with him, or she might be . . ." Sarah's head drooped and she looked down at her untouched cup of tea.

"After Elliot vanished," said Detective Pearson, "did Jodi have any contact with Leon?"

Sarah nodded. "A few times. It took losing his son for him to realize what an ass he'd been as a father. My sister was such a good soul and she tried to offer him some sort of comfort. They'd never gotten along, but after Elliot's memorial service, she wrote Leon a card. Even printed and framed the very last photo of Elliot, taken while he was in Africa. She gave that photo to Leon, and was surprised when she got a thank-you note from him. But after that, they fell out of touch. As far as I know, they hadn't spoken in years."

Up till now Jane had sat silent as Detective Pearson led the interview. Now she couldn't help but interject.

"Did your sister have other photos of Elliot in Africa?"

Sarah gave her a puzzled look. "A few. He sent them all from his cell phone while he was traveling. His camera was never found, so those cell phone shots are the only ones there are from his trip."

"Did you see them?"

"Yes. They were just typical travel shots. Photos of his flight, tourist spots in Cape Town. Nothing memorable." She gave a sad laugh. "Elliot wasn't a particularly good photographer."

Detective Pearson frowned at Jane. "Is there a reason you're asking about his Africa photos?"

"We spoke to a witness who was at Gott's house around two thirty on Sunday. He heard Gott talking on the phone, telling someone he wanted all of Elliot's photos from Africa. Based on the time of the call, that conversation would have been with Jodi." Jane looked at Sarah. "Why would Leon want those photos?"

"I have no idea. Guilt?"

"About what?"

"About all the ways he could have been a better father. All the mistakes he made, the people he hurt. Maybe he was finally thinking about the son he'd ignored all those years."

That's what Jerry O'Brien had told them as well, that Leon Gott had recently grown obsessed about his son's disappearance. With old age came regrets and thoughts of what one *should* have done, but for Leon there would never be a chance to heal the rift with Elliot. Alone in that house, with only a dog and two cats for company, did he suddenly realize what poor substitutes they were for the love of a son?

"That's all I can tell you about Leon Gott," said Sarah. "I met him just once, at Elliot's memorial service six years ago. I never saw him again."

The last glimmer of twilight had faded and it was now dark outside the window. In the warm glow of a lamp, Sarah's face seemed to have shed a few years and she looked younger, more animated. Perhaps it was because she'd moved beyond the role of grief-stricken sister and was now engaged in the puzzle of her sister's final hours and why they involved Leon Gott. "You said he called Jodi at two thirty," said Sarah, and she looked at Detective Pearson. "She would still have been down in Plymouth. At the conference."

Detective Pearson said to Jane and Frost: "We tried to reconstruct Jodi's last day. We know she was at a library conference on Sunday. It ended at five P.M., so she probably got home after dinnertime. Which may be why she called Gott back so late, at nine forty-six."

"We know he called her about the photos at two thirty," said Jane. "So I'm assuming she called him back that night about the same matter. Maybe to tell him she'd found Elliot's . . ." Jane paused. Looked at Sarah. "Where did your sister store those photos of Elliot's Africa trip?"

"They were digital files, so she would have kept them on her laptop."

Jane and Detective Pearson looked at each other. "Which is now missing," said Jane.

OUTSIDE, THE THREE DETECTIVES stood shivering in the dampness as they quietly conferred by their parked cars.

"We'll send you our notes, and we'd appreciate it if you send us yours," Jane said.

"Certainly. But I'm still not clear what it is we're chasing."

"Neither am I," admitted Jane. "But it feels like there's *something* here. Something to do with Elliot's photos in Africa."

"You heard how Sarah described them. They were typical tourist shots, nothing remarkable."

"To her, anyway."

"And they're from six years ago. Why would anyone care about them now?"

"I don't know. I'm just going on a . . ."

"Hunch?"

The word made Jane pause. She thought of her conversation with Maura earlier that day, when she had brushed off Maura's instincts about the newly excavated skeleton. When it comes to hunches, she thought, we only trust our own. Even if we're no better at defending them.

Detective Pearson brushed back a strand of rain-glistened hair and sighed. "Well, it can't hurt to share information. It's a nice change. Usually, the boys want to use *my* notes, but they won't share theirs." She looked at Frost. "Not to cast aspersions on the guys."

Jane laughed. "This guy's different. He shares everything, except his potato chips."

"Which you just steal anyway," said Frost.

"I'll email you what I've got as soon as I get home," said Detective Pearson. "You can get Jodi's autopsy report directly from the ME."

"Which doc did it?"

"I'm not familiar with all the pathologists there. It was a big man. Big voice."

"Sounds like Dr. Bristol," said Frost.

"Yes, that's his name. Dr. Bristol. He did her autopsy last Tuesday." Pearson took out her car keys. "There were no surprises."

SIXTEEN

THAT WAS THE THING ABOUT SURPRISES; YOU NEVER KNEW WHEN ONE would turn up that could change the course of an investigation.

Jane devoted the next afternoon to hunting for just such a surprise among the files that Andrea Pearson had emailed her. Sitting at her computer, the remains of her lunch scattered across her desk, she clicked through page after page of witness statements and Detective Pearson's notes. Jodi Underwood had lived in the same Brookline house for eight years, a house she'd inherited from her parents, and was known to be a quiet and considerate neighbor. She had no enemies and no current boyfriends. On the night of her murder, none of the neighbors recalled hearing any screams or loud noises, nothing to indicate someone was fighting for her life.

A blitz attack was what Pearson called it, a takedown so rapid that the victim had no chance to fight back. The crime scene photos supported Pearson's description. Jodi's body was found in the foyer lying on her back with one arm stretched toward the front door, as if to pull herself out and over the threshold. She was dressed in striped pajamas and a dark blue robe. One slipper was still on her left foot;

the other lay only a few inches away. Jane had slipper scuffs just like them, tan suede with fleece on the inside, ordered from L.L.Bean. She'd never again be able to wear them without thinking of this photo of a dead woman's feet.

She moved on to the autopsy report, dictated by Maura's colleague, Dr. Bristol. Abe Bristol was a larger-than-life personality with a loud laugh and big appetites and sloppy eating habits, but in the morgue he was every bit as detail-minded as Maura. Though the ligature was not found at the scene, the bruises on the victim's neck told Bristol that cord and not wire was used. Time of death was sometime between eight P.M. and two A.M.

Jane clicked through pages describing the internal organs (all healthy) and the genital exam (no evidence of trauma or recent sexual activity). No surprises yet.

She moved on to the list of clothing: women's striped pajamas, top and bottom, 100 percent cotton, size small. Bathrobe, dark-blue velour, size small. Women's fleece slipper scuffs, size seven, brand: L.L.Bean.

She clicked to the next page. Scanned down the list of trace evidence that had been turned over to the crime lab and saw the usual fingernail clippings, combed pubic hairs, orifice swabs. Then she focused on the items at the bottom of the page.

Three hair strands, white/gray, possibly animal, approximately three to four centimeters long. Collected from victim's bathrobe, near hem.

Possibly animal.

Jane thought of Jodi's stark wood floors and sleek Swedish furniture, trying to recall seeing any signs that a house pet lived there. A cat, perhaps, who'd brushed up against that blue velour bathrobe. She picked up the phone and called Jodi's sister.

"She loved animals, but she didn't have any pets, unless you count that goldfish who died a few months ago," Sarah said.

"She never had a dog or a cat?" Jane said.

"She couldn't. She was so allergic that if she just got near a cat, she'd start to wheeze." Sarah gave a sad laugh. "When she was a kid, she dreamed of being a veterinarian and she volunteered at the local animal hospital. That's when she got her first asthma attack."

"Did she own any fur coats? Maybe something with rabbit or mink?"

"Not a chance. Jodi belonged to PETA."

Jane hung up and stared at the words on her computer. *Three hairs, possibly animal.*

And she thought: Leon Gott had cats.

"THESE THREE HAIR STRANDS present an interesting puzzle," said Erin Volchko. A veteran Boston PD criminalist specializing in hair and fibers, Erin had tutored dozens of detectives over the years, guiding them through the intricate analysis of carpet fibers and hair strands, pointing out the differences between wool versus cotton, synthetic versus natural, plucked hair versus cut. Although Jane had peered into the microscope many times, examining strands from countless crime scenes, she would never have Erin's knack for distinguishing one strand from another; all blond hairs looked alike to Jane.

"I've got one of the hairs under the scope now," said Erin. "Have a seat and I'll show you my problem."

Jane settled on the lab stool and looked into the double-headed teaching microscope. Through the eyepieces, she saw a strand that stretched diagonally across the field of view.

"This is Strand Number One collected from Ms. Underwood's blue bathrobe," said Erin, looking through the other pair of eyepieces. "Color: white. Curvature: straight. Length: three centimeters. You can see the cuticle, cortex, and medulla very clearly. Focus first on the color. See how it's not quite uniform? It seems to get paler as you reach the tip, a feature that's called banding. Natural human hair tends to be of uniform color throughout the entire strand, so this is the first clue we're dealing with something that's not human. Now look at the medulla, the central pipeline running through the length of the strand. This medulla is wider than in human hair."

"So what kind of hair is this?"

"The outer layer of cuticle gives us a pretty good idea. I've taken photomicrographs. Let me show you." Erin swiveled around to the computer on her desk and tapped on the keyboard. A magnified image of the hair appeared on-screen. The surface of the strand was covered with slender triangular scales, layered like armor.

"I'd describe these scales as spinous," said Erin. "See how they lift up slightly, as if about to peel away, like little petals? I love how intricate everything looks under high magnification. A whole new universe that we can't see with the naked eye." Erin smiled at the screen as if viewing a foreign city she wished she could visit. Trapped all day in this windowless room, her crime beat was these microscopic landscapes of keratin and protein.

"So what does it mean?" asked Jane. "The fact it's got spinous scales?"

"It confirms my first impression that it's not human. As for species, this scale shape is characteristic of mink, seals, and house cats."

"Common things are common. So I'm guessing this is from a house cat."

Erin nodded. "I can't say it with one hundred percent certainty, but a cat is the most likely source. A single cat sheds hundreds of thousands of hairs in a single year."

"Holy cow. That's a lot of vacuuming."

"And if you've got more than one cat in the house, or dozens of them like some of those cat hoarders, imagine how many hairs that adds up to."

"I don't want to."

"I saw one forensic study that showed it's impossible to enter a residence where a cat lives without picking up some of its hair. Most American households have at least one cat or dog, so who knows how this particular hair got transferred to the victim's bathrobe? If she didn't have a cat herself, she could have been around a friend's cat."

"Her sister says the victim was severely allergic and avoided animals. I'm wondering if she picked up these hairs from a secondary source. The killer."

"And you think this killer transferred them from the Leon Gott crime scene."

"Gott had two cats and a dog, so his house was like a fur factory. I got covered in cat hair just walking through the place. The killer would have picked up hairs, too. If I collected a few hairs from Gott's cats, can you run DNA comparisons with these three strands?"

Erin sighed and slid her glasses up on her head. "I'm afraid DNA would present a bit of a problem. All three of these strands from Jodi Underwood's bathrobe were shed during the animals' telogen phase. These hairs have no root tags, ergo no nuclear DNA."

"What about under the microscope? Just a visual comparison?"

"That would only tell us we're looking at white hairs that *might* be from the same cat. Not good enough as proof in court."

"Is there any way I can prove these hairs were transferred from Gott's house?"

"Possibly. If you spend any time around cats, you'll notice how much they clean themselves. They're constantly grooming, and every time they lick their own hair, they shed epithelial cells from their mouths. We might be able to get mitochondrial DNA markers off these strands. I'm afraid it'll take weeks to get back the results."

"It would be proof, though?"

"Yes, it would be."

"Then I guess I need to collect some cat hairs."

"Pulled directly from the animal itself, so we can harvest root material."

Jane groaned. "That's not going to be easy, since one of the cats doesn't want to be caught. He's still somewhere in the victim's house, running loose."

"Oh dear. I hope someone's feeding him."

"Guess who goes over there every single day to leave food and water and change the litter box?"

Erin laughed. "Don't tell me. Detective Frost?"

"He claims he *can't stand* cats, but I swear he'd run into a burning building just to save a kitty."

"You know, I always liked Detective Frost. He's such a sweetie."

Jane snorted. "Yeah, makes me look like a bitch in comparison."

"What he needs is to find himself another wife," said Erin as she removed the microscope slide. "I wanted to set him up with one of my girlfriends, but she refuses to date cops. Says they have control issues." She placed a new slide under the microscope. "Okay, let me show you another hair collected from the same bathrobe. This is the one that's got me completely stumped."

Jane settled back onto the lab stool and peered into the eyepiece. "It looks like the first strand. What's different about it?"

"At first glance, it does seem similar. White, straight, about five centimeters. It has the same color banding that tells us this is probably not human. Initially I thought it was also from *Felis catus,* a house cat. But when you examine it at 1500X, you'll see it's from a very different origin." She swiveled back to her computer and opened a second window on the screen, showing a different photomicrograph. She arranged the two images side by side.

Jane frowned. "The second hair looks nothing like a house cat's."

"The cuticular scales are very different. They look like little flat-topped mountain peaks. Not at all like a housecat's spinous scales."

"What animal is this second hair from?"

"I've compared it to every animal hair in my database. But this is something I've never seen before."

A mystery creature. Jane thought of Leon Gott's house and its wall of mounted trophy heads. And she thought of his taxidermy workshop where he regularly scraped and dried and stretched the pelts of animals from around the world. "Could this hair be from a snow leopard?" she asked.

"That's pretty specific. Why a snow leopard?"

"Because Gott was working on a snow leopard pelt, and it's now missing."

"They're extremely rare animals, so I don't know where I'd get a hair sample to compare. But there is a way to determine species. Remember how we ID'd that weird hair from the Chinatown murder? The strand that turned out to be from a monkey?"

"You sent it to a lab in Oregon."

"Right, the Wildlife Forensics Lab. They have a database of keratin patterns from species around the world. With electrophoresis, you can analyze a hair's protein component and match it against known keratin patterns."

"Let's do it. If this hair came from a snow leopard, then it was almost certainly transferred from Gott's house."

"In the meantime," said Erin, "get me that house cat hair. If the DNA matches, you'll have the proof you need that these two murders are linked."

SEVENTEEN

"YOU WERE A BIG MISTAKE," SAID MAURA. "I NEVER SHOULD HAVE brought you home."

The cat ignored her and licked its paw, fastidiously cleaning up after devouring a meal of imported Spanish tuna packed in olive oil. An extravagance at ten dollars a serving, but he'd refused to touch the dry cat food, and Maura had forgotten to pick up more cans of gourmet cat food on her way home that afternoon. A search of her pantry had turned up that one precious can of tuna, which she'd intended to use in a nice salade Niçoise with crisp green beans and red potatoes. But no, her greedy little houseguest lapped up every tasty morsel and sauntered out of the kitchen, making it clear that Maura's services were no longer needed.

So much for companionship. I'm just the maid. Maura rinsed the cat bowl in hot soapy water and placed it in the dishwasher for a thorough, microbe-blasting scrub. Could you catch *Toxoplasma gondii* from a cat in just a week? Lately she'd been obsessed with toxoplasmosis, because she'd read it could lead to schizophrenia. Crazy cat ladies were crazy *because* of their cats. This is how these crafty animals control us, she thought. They infect us with a parasite that makes us serve them ten-dollar cans of tuna.

The doorbell rang.

She washed and dried her hands thinking *Die, microbes!* and walked to the front door.

Jane Rizzoli stood on the porch. "I'm here for the cat hair," she said and pulled tweezers and an evidence bag from her pocket. "You do the honors."

"Why don't you?"

"He's your cat."

With a sigh, Maura took the tweezers and went into the living room, where the cat now sat on the coffee table, staring at her with suspicion in his green eyes. They'd been together for a week and she had not yet bonded with the animal. Was it possible to actually bond with a cat? At the Gott crime scene, he had lavished affection on Maura, mewing and rubbing against her until she'd been seduced into adopting him. Since she'd brought him home, his attitude had been sheer indifference, even though she'd lavished him with tuna and sardines. It was the universal lament of disappointed wives: *He charmed me, wooed me, and now I'm his maid.*

She knelt down beside the cat, who promptly jumped off the coffee table and strolled toward the kitchen with an attitude of sleek disdain.

"It has to be plucked straight from the animal," said Jane.

"I know, I know." Maura followed the cat down the hallway, muttering: "Why do I feel so ridiculous?"

Maura found the cat sitting where his bowl should be and his eyes fixed on hers with an accusing glare.

"Maybe he's hungry," said Jane.

"I just fed him."

"So feed him again." Jane opened the refrigerator and took out a carton of heavy cream.

"I need that for a recipe," said Maura.

"I need cat hair." Jane poured the cream into a bowl and set it down. The cat instantly started lapping it up. He never even noticed when Jane plucked three hairs from his back. "When all else fails, try bribery," said Jane, sealing the hairs in the evidence bag. "Now I just need to get a sample from that other cat."

"No one's been able to catch the other cat."

"Yeah, that's gonna be a problem. Frost's been to the house every day this week and hasn't even spotted it."

"Are you sure it's still in the house? It hasn't escaped?"

"Something's eating the cat food, and that house has a lot of places to hide. Maybe I can trap him. You got a cardboard box I can use?"

"You'll also need gloves. Do you have any idea how many nasty infections you can get from a cat scratch?" Maura went to the hall closet and found a pair of brown leather gloves. "Try those."

"Gee, these look really expensive. I'll try not to ruin them." She turned toward the front door.

"Hold on. I need a pair. I know I've got some more in here."

"You're coming, too?"

"That cat doesn't want to be caught." Maura reached into a coat pocket and found a second pair of gloves. "This is definitely a two-woman job."

THE SMELL OF DEATH still lingered in the house. Though the body and entrails had been removed days ago, decomposition releases its chemical signature into the air, a ripe bouquet of scents that find their way into every closet and crevice, seeping into furniture and carpets and drapes. Like smoke after a fire, the stench of decay does not easily surrender its quarters, and it stubbornly clung to Gott's home, like a ghost of the man himself. No cleaning service had yet come to mop and scrub, and bloody pawprints still tracked across the floor. A week ago, when Maura had entered, she'd been in the company of detectives and criminalists whose voices had echoed throughout the rooms. Today she heard the stillness of an abandoned house, the silence broken only by the hum of one lone fly circling aimlessly in the living room.

Jane set down the cardboard box. "Let's go room by room. Downstairs first."

"Why am I suddenly thinking about that dead zookeeper?" said Maura.

"This is a house cat, not a leopard."

"Even cute little house cats are predators, deep down in their DNA." Maura pulled on gloves. "One study I read estimates that pet cats kill almost four billion birds a year."

"Billions? For real?"

"It's what they're designed to do. Silent, agile, and fast."

"In other words, hard to catch." Jane sighed.

"Unfortunately." Maura reached into the box and pulled out a bath towel that she'd brought from home. Her plan was to toss it over the fugitive kitty and bundle him into the box without getting clawed. "This has to be done eventually anyway. Poor Frost can't spend the rest of his life delivering cat food and kitty litter. Once we catch it, do you think Frost wants it?"

"If we take it to the pound, he'll never speak to us again. Trust me, when I drop it off at his house, it's there to stay."

They both pulled on gloves. Mounted animal heads stared down at them as they began their hunt. Jane got down on hands and knees and peered under the sofa and armchair. Maura searched cabinets and cubbyholes where the cat might have retreated. Clapping dust from her hands, she straightened and suddenly focused on the mounted African lion head, its glass eyes agleam with such life-like intelligence that she half expected the animal to leap from the wall.

"There he is!" Jane shouted.

Maura spun around and saw something white streak across the living room and dart up the stairs. She snatched up the cardboard box and followed Jane to the second floor.

"Master bedroom!" Jane yelled.

They stepped into the room and shut the door behind them.

"Okay, we've got him trapped," said Jane. "I know he came in here. So where the hell is he hiding?"

Maura scanned the furniture. Saw a queen bed, twin nightstands, and a massive chest of drawers. A mirror on the wall reflected their flushed and frustrated faces.

Jane dropped to her knees and looked under the bed. "Not here," she announced.

Maura turned to the walk-in closet, its door hanging ajar. It was the only other hiding place in the room. They glanced at each other and simultaneously took deep breaths.

"A hunting we will go," Jane sang softly and flipped on the closet light. They eyed jackets and sweaters and far too many plaid shirts. Jane nudged aside a heavy parka to peer deeper into the closet. Flinched back as the cat came flying out, yowling.

"Shit!" Jane stared at her right arm, where her sleeve had been clawed open. "I now officially *hate* cats. Where the fuck did it go?"

"It ran under the bed."

Jane stalked toward her feline nemesis. "No more Mrs. Nice Cop. Cat, you are *mine.*"

"Jane, you're bleeding. I've got alcohol swabs in my purse downstairs."

"First we catch him. Go to the other side of the bed. Scare him toward me."

Maura dropped to her knees and looked under the bed frame. A pair of yellow eyes glared back at her, and the growl that rumbled from the animal's throat was so feral it made the hairs lift on Maura's arms. This was no nice little kitty. This was Demon Fluffy.

"Okay, I'm ready with the towel," said Jane. "Chase him my way."

Maura gave a timid swipe at the animal. "Shoo."

The cat bared its teeth and hissed.

"Shoo?" Jane snorted. "Seriously, Maura, that's the best you can do?"

"Okay, then. Move, cat!" Maura waved her arm and the cat backed away. Maura pulled off her shoe and swung it at the animal. *"Go!"*

The cat shot out from under the bed. Though Maura couldn't see the struggle that ensued, she heard the yowling and hissing and Jane's muttered oaths as she wrestled her prey. By the time Maura was back on her feet, Jane had Demon Fluffy securely bundled in the bath towel. Jane dumped the struggling cat and towel into the cardboard box and closed the flaps. The box rattled and shook with fifteen pounds of angry cat.

"Do I need a rabies shot?" Jane asked, looking at her clawed arm.

"What you need first is soap and antiseptic. Wash your arm. I'll go downstairs and get those alcohol swabs."

The old Boy Scout motto of *Be Prepared* was one that Maura also shared, and in her purse she had latex gloves, alcohol swabs, tweezers, shoe covers, and plastic evidence bags. Downstairs, she found her purse on the coffee table where she'd left it. She dug out the bundle of alcohol wipes and was turning to go back upstairs when she suddenly noticed the bare nail in the wall. Surrounding the empty spot were framed photos of Leon Gott on various hunting expeditions, posing with his rifle and his lifeless trophies. Deer, a buffalo, wild boar, a lion. Also framed was the printed article about Gott from *Hub Magazine:* "The Trophy Master: An Interview with Boston's Master Taxidermist.' "

Jane came down the stairs, into the living room. "So *should* I worry about rabies?"

Maura pointed to the bare nail. "Was something removed from here?"

"I'm worried about my arm falling off, and you're asking about an empty spot on the wall."

"There's something missing here, Jane. Was it like this last week?"

"Yeah, it was. I noticed that nail before. I can check the crime scene videos to confirm." Jane paused, suddenly frowning at the exposed nail. "I wonder . . ."

"What?"

Jane turned to her. "Gott called Jodi Underwood, asking for Elliot's photos from Africa." She pointed to the empty space on the wall. "You think this has to do with why he called her?"

Maura shook her head, perplexed. "A missing photo?"

"That same day, he also called Interpol in South Africa. Again, it was about Elliot."

"Why would he focus on his son now? Didn't Elliot vanish years ago?"

"Six years ago." Once again Jane turned to look at the naked spot where something had been removed. "In Botswana."

EIGHTEEN

BOTSWANA

HOW LONG CAN A MAN STAY AWAKE, I WONDER AS I WATCH JOHNNY nodding off in the firelight, his eyes half closed, his torso slumping forward like a tree on the verge of collapse. Yet his fingers are still wrapped around the rifle in his lap, as if the weapon is part of his body, an extension of his limbs. All evening the others have been watching him, and I know Richard's tempted to wrestle control of that gun, but even a half-asleep Johnny is too formidable to tangle with. Since Isao's death, Johnny has caught only snatches of sleep during the day and he's determined to stay awake all night. If he keeps this up, in another few days he will be either catatonic or insane.

Either way, he'll be the one with the gun.

I look at the faces around the fire. Sylvia and Vivian huddle together, their blond hair equally tangled, faces equally tight with worry. It's strange, what the bush does to even beautiful women. It strips them of all superficial gloss, dulls their hair, scours away makeup, erodes them down to flesh and bone. That's what I see when I look at them now: two women slowly being eroded to their bare elements.

Already it has happened to Mrs. Matsunaga, who's been worn down to her fragile, fractured core. She is still not eating. The plate of meat I gave her sits untouched at her feet. To coax some sort of nutrition into her, I added two spoonfuls of sugar to her tea, but she immediately spat it out, and now she looks at me with distrust, as if I tried to poison her.

In fact, everyone now looks at me with distrust, because I haven't joined their *blame-Johnny* team. They think I've gone to the dark side, and I'm Johnny's spy, when all I'm trying to do is figure out the most likely way for us to stay alive. I know Richard's no outdoorsman, even though he thinks he is. Clumsy, terrified Elliot hasn't shaven in days, his eyes are bloodshot, and any minute now I expect him to start babbling like a madman. The blondes are falling apart even as I watch. The only person who still has it together, who actually knows what he's doing out here, is Johnny. I vote for him.

Which is why the others no longer look at me. They look past me or through me, shooting furtive glances at one another in some silent eyelid-flickering Morse code. We're living the real-life version of TV's *Survivor,* and it's clear I've been voted off the island.

The blondes are off to bed first, huddling together and whispering as they leave the firelight. Then Elliot and Keiko slip away to their respective tents. For a moment it's just Richard and me sitting by the fire, too wary of each other to say a word. That I once loved this man is almost impossible to believe. These days in the bush have added a handsomely rugged edge to his good looks, but now I see the petty vanity underneath it all. The real reason he dislikes Johnny is that he can't measure up. It's all come down to who's more of a man. Richard always has to be the hero of his own story.

He seems about to say something when we both realize that Johnny's awake, his eyes gleaming in the shadows. Without a word, Richard rises to his feet. Even as I watch him stalk off and duck into our tent, I'm aware of Johnny's gaze on me, can feel the heat of it on my face.

"Where did you meet him?" Johnny asks. He sits so still against the tree that he seems to be part of the trunk itself, his body like one long, sinuous root.

"A bookshop, of course. He came in to sign copies of his book *Kill Option.*"

"What was that one about?"

"Oh, the usual R. Renwick thriller. The hero finds himself trapped on a remote island with terrorists. Uses his wilderness skills to take them down one by one. Men eat up the books like candy, and we had a full house for the signing. Afterward, he and the bookshop staff went out to the pub for drinks. I thought for certain he had his eye on my colleague Sadie. But no, he went home with me."

"You sound surprised."

"You haven't seen Sadie."

"And how long ago was this?"

"Almost four years ago." Long enough for Richard to get bored. Long enough for the various hurts and grievances to pile up and make a man wonder about better options.

"Then you should know each other pretty well," says Johnny.

"We should."

"You're not certain?"

"Can one ever be?"

He looks at Richard's tent. "Not about some people. The way you can't ever be sure about some animals. It's possible to tame a lion or an elephant, even learn to trust them. But you can't ever trust a leopard."

"What kind of animal do you think Richard is?" I ask, only half serious.

Johnny doesn't crack a smile. "You tell me."

His answer, spoken so quietly, forces me to consider my almost four years with Richard. Four years of a shared bed and shared meals, but always with a distance between us. He was the one who's held back, the one who scoffed at the idea of marriage, as if it was beneath us, but I think I knew all along why he never married me; I just refused to admit it to myself. He was waiting for *the one.* And I'm not her.

"Do you trust him?" Johnny says softly.

"Why are you asking this?"

"Even after four years, do you really know who he is? What he's capable of?"

"You don't think *Richard's* the one who—"

"Do you?"

"That's what the others are saying about *you.* That we can't trust you. That you deliberately stranded us here."

"Is that what you think?"

"I think if you wanted to kill us, you'd have done it already."

He stares back at me, and I'm keenly aware of the rifle at his side. As long as he controls the gun, he controls us. Now I wonder if I've made a fatal mistake. If I've confided in the wrong man.

"Tell me what else they're saying," he says. "What are they planning?"

"No one's planning anything. It's just that they're scared. We're *all* scared."

"There's no reason to be, as long as no one does anything rash. As long as you trust me. No one but me."

Not even Richard is what he implies, although he doesn't say it. Does he really think that Richard's to blame for what's happened? Or is this part of Johnny's game to divide and conquer, by planting the seeds of suspicion?

Already the seeds are taking root.

Later, as I lie beside Keiko in her tent, I think about all the evenings when Richard came home late. Out with his literary agent, he'd tell me. Or dinner with his publishing team. My biggest fear used to be that he was having a fling with another woman. Now I wonder if I suffered from a lack of imagination and his reasons were darker, more horrifying than mere infidelity.

Outside the tent, the nightly chorus of insects sings as predators circle our camp, held off only by the fire. And by a lone man with a gun.

Johnny wants me to trust him. Johnny promises he'll keep us safe.

That's what I cling to as I finally fall asleep. Johnny says we'll live through this and I believe him.

Until daybreak, when everything changes.

THIS TIME, IT'S ELLIOT who's screaming. His panicked yelps of *Oh my God! Oh my God!* wrench me awake and toss me back into the nightmare of real life. Keiko's gone, and I'm alone in the tent. I don't even bother to struggle into my trousers, but roll out of my tent in T-shirt and underwear, pausing only to shove bare feet into boots.

The whole camp is awake and everyone has converged on Elliot's tent. The blondes cling to each other, their hair greasy and disheveled, their legs bare in the chill dawn. Like me, they'd rushed out of their tents in only their underwear. Keiko's still wearing pajamas, her feet clad in tiny Japanese sandals. Only Richard is fully dressed. He stands gripping Elliot's shoulders, trying to calm him down, but Elliot keeps shaking his head, blubbering.

"It's gone," says Richard. "It's not there anymore."

"It could be hiding in my clothes! Or in the blankets."

"I'll look again, okay? But I didn't see it."

"What if there's another one in there?"

"Another what?" I ask.

They all turn to look at me and I see wariness in their eyes. I'm the one no one trusts, because I threw in my lot with the enemy.

"A snake," says Sylvia, and she hugs herself, shivering. "Somehow it got into Elliot's tent."

I glance down at the ground, half expecting to see a serpent slither toward my boots. In this land of spiders and biting insects, I've learned never to walk barefoot.

"It was hissing at me," says Elliot. "That's what woke me up. I opened my eyes and it was *right there,* coiled on top of my legs. I thought for certain . . ." He wipes a trembling hand across his face. "Oh God. We're not going to make it another week!"

"Elliot, stop," Richard commands.

"How can I sleep after this? How can *any* of you sleep, when you don't know what might be crawling into your bed?"

"It was a puff adder," says Johnny. "That would be my guess."

Once again, he's managed to startle me with his silent approach. I turn and see him toss wood into the dying fire.

"You saw the snake?" I ask.

"No. But Elliot said it hissed at him." Johnny moves toward us, carrying the ever-present rifle. "Was it yellow-brown? Speckled, with a triangular head?" he asks Elliot.

"It was a snake, that's all I know! You think I bothered to ask its name?"

"Puff adders are common out here in the bush. We'll probably see more of them."

"How poisonous are they?" Richard asks.

"Left untreated, the venom can be fatal. But if it makes you feel any better, their bites are often dry and carry no venom at all. It probably just crawled into Elliot's bed to get warm. That's what reptiles do." He looks around at us. "That's why I warned you all to keep your tents zipped up."

"It *was* zipped up," Elliot says.

"Then how did it get into your tent?"

"You know how freaked out I am about malaria. I *always* zip up to keep the mosquitoes out. I didn't think a fucking *snake* could get inside!"

"It could have gotten in during the day," I suggest. "While you weren't in the tent."

"I'm telling you, I *never* leave it unzipped. Even during the day."

Without a word, Johnny circles to the other side of Elliot's tent. Is he searching for the snake? Does he think it's still lurking somewhere under the canvas, waiting for another chance to invade? Suddenly Johnny drops down where we can't see him. The silence is unbearable.

Sylvia calls out in an unsteady voice: "Is the snake still there?"

Johnny doesn't answer. He rises to his feet and when I see his expression, my hands turn to ice.

"What is it?" Sylvia asks. *"What is it?"*

"Come see this for yourselves," he says quietly.

Almost hidden by scrubby grass, the slit runs along the lower edge of the tent. Not a mere rip, this is a clean, straight cut in the canvas, and the significance is instantly clear to us all.

Elliot looks around at us in disbelief. "Who did this? Who the hell cut open my tent?"

"You all have knives," points out Johnny. "Anyone could have done it."

"Not anyone," says Richard. "*We* were asleep. *You* were the one out here all night, *keeping watch* as you call it."

"I left at first light to get firewood." Johnny looks Richard up and down. "And how long have *you* been up and dressed?"

"You see what he's doing, don't you?" Richard turns to look at us. "Don't forget who has control of the gun. Who's been in charge here, while everything's gone straight to hell."

"Why *my* tent?" Elliot's voice has gone shrill, infecting us all with his panic. "Why *me*?"

"The men," says Vivian softly. "He's taking out the men first. He killed Clarence. Then Isao. And now it's Elliot . . ."

Richard takes a step toward Johnny and the rifle instantly snaps up, its barrel pointed straight at Richard's chest. "Back away," Johnny orders.

"So this is how it's going to be," says Richard. "He'll shoot me first. Then he'll kill Elliot. And what about the women, Johnny? You may have Millie on your side, but you can't take the rest of us down. Not if we all fight back."

"It's you," says Johnny. "You're the one doing this."

Richard takes another step toward him. “I’m the one who’ll stop you.”

“Richard,” I plead. “Don’t do this.”

“It’s time to choose sides, Millie.”

“There are no sides! We have to talk about this. We have to be rational.”

Richard takes another step toward Johnny. It’s a dare, a contest of nerves. The bush has stripped him of reason, and he’s acting on raw fury now, at Johnny his rival. At me, the traitor. Time slows down and I register every detail with painful clarity. The sweat on Johnny’s brow. The snap of the twig under Richard’s boot as he rocks forward. Johnny’s hand, his muscles twitching taut, preparing to fire.

And I see Keiko—small, frail Keiko—as she slips silently behind Johnny. I see her raise her arms. I see the rock slam into the back of Johnny’s head.

He is still alive.

Minutes after the blow, his eyes flicker open. The rock sliced open his scalp, and he’s shed an alarming amount of blood, but the look he gives us is clear-eyed and fully aware.

“You’re making a mistake, all of you,” he says. “You have to listen to me.”

“No one’s listening to you,” says Richard. His shadow moves across Johnny, and he stands staring down at him. He’s the one with the rifle now, the one in control.

Groaning, Johnny tries to rise, but it’s a struggle for him just to sit up. “Without me, you’re not going to make it.”

Richard looks at the others, who stand in a circle around Johnny. “Shall we take a vote?”

Vivian shakes her head. “I don’t trust him.”

“Then what are we going to do with him?” says Elliot.

“Tie him up. That’s what.” Richard nods to the blondes. “Go find some rope.”

“No. *No.*” Johnny staggers to his feet. Even though he’s swaying, he's still too intimidating for anyone to tackle. "Shoot me if you want, Richard. Right here, right now. But I won't be tied up. I won't be left helpless. Not out here."

"Go on, tie him up!" Richard snaps at the blondes, but they stand frozen. "Elliot, you do it!"

"Just try it," Johnny growls.

Elliot blanches and backs away.

Turning to Richard, Johnny says: "So you've got the gun now, hey? Proved you're the alpha male. Was that the whole point of the game?"

"Game?" Elliot shakes his head. "No, we're all just trying to stay the fuck *alive.*"

"Then don't trust *him,*" says Johnny.

Richard's hands tighten on the rifle. Oh God, he's going to fire it. He's going to kill an unarmed man in cold blood. I lunge for the barrel to yank it downward.

Richard's slap sends me sprawling. "You want to get us killed, Millie?" he screams. "Is that what you're trying to do?"

I touch my throbbing cheek. Never before has he hit me; if this were anywhere else, I'd be on the phone to the police, but out here there's no escape, no authority to call. When I look around at the others, I see no sympathy in their faces. The blondes, Keiko, Elliot—they all side with Richard.

"All right," says Johnny. "You have the firepower, Richard. You can use it anytime. But if you're going to shoot me, you'll have to do it in the back." He turns and starts to walk away.

"If you come back to camp, I'll kill you!" yells Richard.

Johnny calls over his shoulder: "I'd rather take my chances in the bush."

"We'll keep watch! If we see you anywhere near us—"

"You won't. I'd as soon trust the animals." Johnny pauses, looks back at me. "Come with me, Millie. *Please,* come."

I glance back and forth between Richard and Johnny, paralyzed by the choice.

"No, stay with us," says Vivian. "There'll be a plane looking for us any day."

"By the time the plane comes back, you'll be dead," says Johnny. He holds his hand out to me. "I'll take care of you, I swear it. I won't let anything happen. I'm *begging* you to trust me, Millie."

"Don't be crazy," says Elliot. "You can't believe him."

I think of everything that's gone wrong: Clarence and Isao, their flesh ripped from their bones. The truck, suddenly and mysteriously out of commission. The viper in Elliot's newly slashed tent. I remember what Johnny revealed only a few days ago, about how he'd collected snakes as a boy. Who else but Johnny knows how to catch and handle a pit viper? None of what's happened has been merely bad luck; no, we were *meant* to die out here, and only Johnny could execute such a plan.

He can read the decision in my eyes, and he reacts with a look of pain, as if I have delivered a mortal blow. For a moment he stands defeated, his shoulders slumped, his face a mask of sorrow. "I would have done anything for you," he says to me softly. Then, with a shake of his head, he turns and strides away.

We are all still watching as he vanishes into the bush.

"Do you think he'll come back?" says Vivian.

Richard pats the rifle lying beside him, the rifle that's now never out of his reach. "If he tries, I'll be ready for him."

We're sitting around the campfire, which Elliot has built into a raging inferno against the darkness. The flames are too high and too hot for comfort, and a foolish waste of firewood, but I understand why he felt compelled to feed it so extravagantly. Those flames hold off the predators that even now are watching us. We've spotted no other campfires, so where is Johnny on this black, black night? What tricks does he have to stay alive when teeth and claws are everywhere?

"We'll keep watch in pairs," says Richard. "No one should be out here alone at any time. Elliot and Vivian will take the first watch.

Sylvia and I will take the second. That will get us through the night. We keep this up, keep our wits about us, and we'll be fine until the plane comes looking for us."

That he's left me out of the watch schedule is painfully obvious. I understand why Keiko's not expected to contribute; after her startling takedown of Johnny, she's retreated once again into silence. At least she's eating now, a few spoonfuls of tinned beans and a handful of crackers. But here I am, able-bodied and ready to help, and no one even glances my way.

"What about me?" I ask. "What should I do?"

"We'll handle this, Millie. You don't need to do a thing." The tone of his voice allows no protest, certainly not from the woman who once dared to take Johnny's side. Without a word, I leave the fire and slink into our tent. Tonight I'm back with Richard because Keiko doesn't want me in her tent anymore. I'm the pariah, the traitor who might stab you while you're sleeping.

When Richard crawls in beside me an hour later, I'm still awake.

"It's over between us," I say.

He doesn't bother to argue. "Yes. Obviously."

"So which one are you going to choose? Sylvia or Vivian?"

"Does it matter?"

"No, I guess not. Whatever her name, it all boils down to screwing someone new."

"What about you and Johnny? Admit it, you were ready to leave me and join *him.*"

I turn to Richard, but all I see is his silhouette, framed by the glow of firelight through canvas. "I stayed, didn't I?"

"Only because we control the gun."

"And that makes you the winner, does it? King of the bush?"

"I'm fighting for our fucking *lives.* The others understand that. Why can't you?"

My breath comes out in a long, sad sigh. "I do understand, Richard. I know you *think* you're doing the right thing. Even if you have no clue what to do next."

"Whatever our problems, Millie, we need to stick together now, or we won't make it. We've got the gun and the supplies, and the numbers are on our side. But I can't predict what Johnny will do. Whether he'll just escape into the bush, or come back and try to finish us off." He pauses. "We're witnesses, after all."

"Witnesses to what? We never saw him kill anyone. We can't prove he did anything wrong."

"Then let the police prove it. After we get out of here."

We lie silent for a moment. Through the canvas, I hear Elliot and Vivian talking by the fire as they keep watch. I hear the shrill screech of insects, the far-off cackle of hyenas, and I wonder if Johnny's still alive out there, or if his corpse is even now being ripped apart and devoured.

Richard's hand brushes against my hand. Slowly, tentatively, his fingers link with mine. "People move on, Millie. It doesn't mean these last three years were wasted."

"Four years."

"We're not the same people we were when we met. It's just the way life goes, and we need to be grown up about it. Figure out how to divide our things, how to tell our friends. Do it all without drama."

These things are so much easier for him to say. I may have been the first to declare it over between us, but he's the one who actually did the leaving. I realize now that he's been in the act of leaving me for a long, long time. It's Africa that finally brought it to a head, Africa that showed us how unsuited we are to each other.

I may have loved him once, but now I think I never really liked him. Certainly I don't like him now, as he talks so matter-of-factly about the terms of our breakup. How I should find a new flat as soon as we get back to London. Would my sister take me in while I search for the right place? And then there's all the things we've acquired together. The cookware can go with me, the CDs and electronics stay with him, fair enough? And what a good thing we have no pets to fight over. What a far cry from the night we huddled on the sofa, planning this trip to Botswana. I'd imagined starry skies and cocktails around the campfire, not these bloodless terms of dissolution.

I roll onto my side, turning away from him.

"All right," he says. "We'll talk about it later. Like civilized people."

"Right," I mutter. "Civilized."

"Now I need to get some sleep. Have to be up in four hours for my watch."

Those are the last words he ever says to me.

I WAKE IN DARKNESS, and for a moment I'm confused about which tent I'm in. Then it all slams into me, with a pain that's physical. My breakup with Richard. The lonely days ahead. It is so black inside the tent that I can't tell if he's lying beside me. I reach out to touch him, but find only emptiness. This is the future; I will have to get used to sleeping alone.

Twigs snap as someone—or something—walks past my tent.

I strain to see through the canvas, but it's so dark that I can't make out even the faintest glow of the campfire. Who has let the fire burn down? Someone needs to add wood before it dies altogether. I pull on trousers and reach for my boots. After all this talk about staying alert and keeping watch, these useless idiots could not maintain even our most basic safeguard.

Just as I unzip the tent flap, the first gunshot explodes.

A woman is screaming. Sylvia? Vivian? I can't tell which one; all I hear is her panic.

"He's got the gun! Oh God, he's got the—"

I hunt blindly in the dark for my knapsack, where I keep my torch stashed. My hand closes around the strap just as the second shot explodes.

I scramble out of the tent, but see only shadows upon shadows. Something moves past the dying coals of the fire. *Johnny. He's here to take revenge.*

A third shot thunders and I dart toward the blackness of the bush, am almost to the perimeter wire when I stumble over something and go down on my knees. I feel warm flesh, long tangled hair. And blood. *One of the blondes.*

Instantly I'm back on my feet, fleeing blindly into the night. Hear bells clang as my boot snags the perimeter wire.

The next bullet comes so close I can hear it whistle past.

But I'm cloaked in darkness now, a target that Johnny can't see. Behind me, there are shrieks of terror and one final, thunderous gunshot.

I have no choice; I plunge alone into the night.

NINETEEN

BOSTON

"ALWAYS TRYING TO PROVE HE'S HOT STUFF. YOU'D THINK HE'D AT least make the effort to show up on time," said Crowe, scowling at his watch. "Should've been here twenty minutes ago."

"I'm sure Detective Tam has a good reason for being late," said Maura. As she laid Jane Doe's right femur in its correct anatomical position, the stainless-steel table gave an ominous clang. Under the coldly clinical glare of the morgue lights, the bones looked plastic and artificial. Strip away a young woman's skin and flesh, and this was all that remained: the bony latticework on which that flesh was mounted. When human skeletons arrived in the morgue they were often incomplete, missing the small bones of the hands and feet, which are so easily carried off by scavengers. But this Jane Doe had been wrapped in a tarp and buried just deep enough to protect her from claws and teeth and beaks. Instead it was insects and microbes that had feasted on flesh and viscera, scouring the bones clean. Maura positioned those bones on her table with the precision of a master strategist preparing for a game of anatomical chess.

"Everyone assumes he's some kind of egghead, just because he's Asian," Crowe said. "Well, he's not as smart as he thinks he is."

Maura had no desire to engage in this conversation—or indeed, in any conversation with Detective Crowe. When he launched into one of his many rants about the incompetence of others, it was usually lawyers and judges who caught the brunt of it. That he was ragging about his own partner, Tam, made Maura particularly uncomfortable.

"There's something sneaky about him, too. You ever noticed? He's going behind my back about something," said Crowe. "I caught sight of a document on his laptop yesterday and asked him about it. Just like that, he hits ESCAPE and shuts down the file. Says it's something he's digging into on his own. Huh."

Maura matched the left fibula to its paired tibia and laid them down side by side like bony railroad tracks.

"I saw it was a VICAP file on his computer. I didn't request any VICAP search. What the hell's he trying to hide from me? What's his game?"

Maura didn't look up from the bones. "That's hardly illegal, requesting a VICAP search."

"Without telling his partner? I'm telling you, he's sneaky. And it's distracting him from *our* case."

"Maybe it is about your case."

"Then why's he keeping it under wraps? So he can whip it out at the right moment to impress everyone? Surprise, the genius detective Tam solves the case! Yeah, he'd love to show me up."

"That doesn't seem like something he'd do."

"You haven't figured him out yet, Doc."

But I've figured *you* out, thought Maura. Crowe's rant was a classic example of projection. If anyone was hungry for attention it was Crowe himself, known to his colleagues as Cop Hollywood. Place a TV news crew anywhere in the vicinity, and there he'd be, tanned and camera-ready in his tailored suit. As Maura laid the last bone on the table, Crowe was back on his cell phone, leaving Tam another pissed-off voice mail. How much simpler it was to deal with the silence of the dead. While Jane Doe waited so patiently on the table, Crowe was pacing the room, radiating a toxic cloud of hostility.

"Do you want to hear about Jane Doe's remains, Detective? Or would you prefer to wait for my written report?" she asked, hoping he'd opt for the latter and leave her in peace.

He shoved the cell phone in his pocket. "Yeah, yeah. Go ahead. What've we got?"

"Fortunately, we have a complete skeleton, so we shouldn't have to extrapolate. This is a female between eighteen and thirty-five years of age. I estimate her height, based on the length of her femur, to be about five foot three or four. Facial modeling will give us an idea of her appearance, but if you look at her skull . . ." Maura picked up the cranium and examined the nasal bones. Turned the skull upside down to look at the upper teeth. "Narrow nasal cavity, high nasal root. Smooth maxillary incisors. These are all consistent with Caucasoid features."

"White girl."

"Yes, with good dentition. All four wisdom teeth have been extracted and she has no dental caries. Her teeth are in perfect alignment."

"Rich white girl. Not from England."

"Trust me, the English *have* discovered orthodontics." Trying to ignore his annoying comments, she turned her attention to the rib cage. Once again her gaze went straight to the cut mark in the xiphoid process. She tried to think of other ways the nick could have been carved into the breastbone, but only a knife blade made sense to her. Slice a line up the abdomen, and that was where your blade would strike, against the bony shield that guards the heart and lungs.

"Maybe it's a stab wound," said Crowe. "Maybe he was going for the heart."

"I suppose that's possible."

"You still think she was gutted. Like Leon Gott."

"I think all theories are still on the table."

"Can you give me a better time of death?"

"There is no *better* time of death. Just a more accurate one."

"Whatever."

"As I told you at the burial site, complete skeletonization can take months or years, depending on burial depth. Any estimate would be imprecise, but the fact there's significant disarticulation here tells me . . ." She paused, suddenly focusing on one of the thoracic ribs. At the burial site, she had missed seeing this detail, and even now, under bright morgue lights, the marks were barely visible. Three equidistant nicks, in the back of the rib. Just like the nicks in this woman's skull. *The same tool did this.*

The morgue door swung open and Detective Tam walked in.

"Forty-five minutes late," snapped Crowe. "Why do you even bother to show up?"

Tam gave his partner barely a glance; his attention was on Maura. "I've got your answer, Dr. Isles," he said and handed her a file folder.

"What, are you working for the ME now?" said Crowe.

"Dr. Isles asked me to do her a favor."

"Funny you didn't bother to tell me."

Maura opened the folder and stared at the first page. Flipped to the next page, and the next.

"I don't like secrets, Tam," said Crowe. "And I *really* don't like partners who keep things from me."

"Have you told Detective Rizzoli about this?" Maura abruptly cut in, looking at Tam.

"Not yet."

"We'd better call her now."

"Why are you bringing Rizzoli into this?" said Crowe.

She looked at the bones on the table. "Because you and Detective Rizzoli are going to be working this case together."

FOR A COP WHO'D joined the homicide unit only a month ago, Johnny Tam was already lightning-quick at navigating the FBI's online Violent Criminal Apprehension Program, otherwise known as VICAP.

With a few rapid keystrokes, Tam logged onto the Law Enforcement Enterprise portal, giving him access to the FBI database of over 150,000 violent cases around the country.

"It's a pain to file these crime analysis reports," said Tam. "No one wants to answer two hundred questions and write an essay just to add your case to the data bank. So I'm sure this is just a partial list. But what *does* turn up on VICAP is fairly disturbing." He turned his laptop around so that the others seated at the conference table could see his screen. "Here's the result of my preliminary search, based on my initial set of criteria. All these cases occurred within the last decade. You'll find a summary in those folders I gave you."

Sitting at one end of the conference table, Maura watched Jane, Frost, and Crowe page through the stack of papers that Tam had distributed. Through the closed door she heard laughter in the hall and the ding of the elevator, but in this room there was only the sound of shuffling pages and skeptical grunts. Only rarely did she join the detectives at a case conference, but this morning Tam had asked her to sit in as consultant. Her place was in the morgue, where the dead didn't argue with you, and she felt uneasy in this room of cops, where disagreement was always on the tip of someone's tongue.

Crowe tossed a page down on his stack of papers. "So you think there's *one* perp running around the country doing all these victims? And you're going to track him down while sitting at your desk, playing VICAP bingo?"

"The first list was just a starting point," said Tam. "It gave me a preliminary database to work with."

"You've got murders in eight states! Three females, eight males. Nine whites, one Hispanic, one black. Ages all over the place, from twenty to sixty-four. What kind of a screwy pattern is that for a killer?"

"You know how much I hate to agree with Crowe," said Jane, "but he's got a point. There's too much variability in these victims. If it is a single perp, why did he choose these particular victims? They have nothing in common, as far as I can see."

"Because the common factor we started with was what Dr. Isles first focused on when she saw Jane Doe: the orange nylon cord around the ankles. Same as Gott."

"She and I have already discussed that," said Jane. "I didn't think it was enough of a link."

Maura noticed that Jane didn't look at her as she spoke. Because she's annoyed with me? she wondered. Because she thinks I shouldn't play cop when my job is in the morgue, holding a scalpel?

"That's all you have linking these dozen homicides? *Tied by cord?*" said Crowe.

"For both victims, orange solid-braid three-sixteenth-inch nylon was used," said Tam.

"Available at every hardware store in the country." Crowe snorted. "Hell, I might have some in my garage right now."

"Nylon cord was not my *only* search term," said Tam. "These dozen victims were all found suspended upside down. Some from trees, others from rafters."

"It's still not enough to make it a killer's signature," said Crowe.

"Let him finish, Detective Crowe," said Maura. Up till now she'd hardly said a word, but she could hold her tongue no longer. "Maybe you'll see what we're getting at. There really may be a connection between our two cases and others around the country."

"And you and Tam are going to pull the rabbit out of the hat." Crowe took a handful of pages from the folder and spread them across the table. "Okay, let's look at what you came up with. Victim number one, fifty-year-old white attorney in Sacramento. Six years ago, found hanging upside down in garage, hands and ankles bound, throat slashed.

"Victim number two, twenty-two-year-old Hispanic male truck driver, found hanging upside down in Phoenix, Arizona. Hands and feet bound, burn and cut marks all over his torso, genitals removed. Huh. Nice. Let me guess: drug cartel.

"Victim number three, thirty-two-year-old white male, record of petty theft, found dangling upside down from a tree in Maine, abdomen sliced open, internal organs scavenged. Oops, we already know the perp on that one. An arrest warrant's been issued for his former buddy. So scratch that one from the list." He looked up. "Need I go on, Dr. Isles?"

"There's more to this than just the bound ankles and the cord."

"Yeah, I know. There's those three cut marks, maybe made with a knife, maybe not. This is just a distraction. Maybe Tam will play fetch for you, but I've got my own case to focus on. And you still can't tell me when Jane Doe died."

"I gave you an estimated time of death."

"Yeah, somewhere between two and twenty years ago. *Really* specific."

"Detective Crowe, your partner has put hours of work into this analysis. The least you can do is hear him out."

"Okay." Crowe tossed down his pen. "Go, Tam. Tell us how the dead people on this list are all connected to our Jane Doe."

"Not all of these are," said Tam. Tempers might be rising in the room, but he appeared as unruffled as ever. "The first list you saw was just our initial set of flagged homicides, based on type of cord and the fact they were found hanging upside down. Then I did a separate search, using the term *evisceration,* because we know it was done to Gott. And Dr. Isles suspects it was also done to Jane Doe, based on the cut mark in her sternum. VICAP gave us a few additional names, of victims who were merely eviscerated, but not hung by a rope."

Jane looked at Frost. "There's a phrase you don't hear every day. *Merely eviscerated.*"

"While I was reading through those cases of evisceration, there was one in particular that caught my eye, from four years ago. The victim was a thirty-five-year-old female backpacker in Nevada, camping with friends. There were two women and two men in the group, but she was the only one who was ever found. The others are still missing. Based on insect evidence, she'd been dead between three and four days. The body was still intact enough for the ME to determine that evisceration had occurred."

"Three to four days outdoors in the wild, and there was enough left of her to see that?" said Crowe.

"Yes. Because she wasn't left on the ground. The body was found up in a tree, draped over a branch. Evisceration *and* elevation. I wondered if *that* combination was the key. It's what a hunter would do with wild game. Hang it and gut it. Which brought me right back to Leon Gott and his connection to hunting and hunters. I went on the VICAP database again and started all over. This time, I looked for open cases in wilderness areas. Any victims who had sternal cut marks or anything else compatible with evisceration. And that's when I found something interesting. Not just a single victim, but another missing group, just like those four backpackers in Nevada. Three years ago, in Montana, a trio of elk hunters vanished. All three were men. One man was later found partially skeletonized, and wedged up in a tree. A second man's jawbone turned up months later—just the jawbone—near a cougar den. A bear or cougar attack was the ME's theory, but a bear wouldn't drag a body up a tree. Which led the ME to conclude it might have been a cougar attack. Although I'm not sure if cougars would drag a kill up a tree."

"You said they were hunters, so they would have been armed," said Frost. "How does a killer take down three men with guns?"

"Good question. One rifle was never found. The other two firearms were still in the men's tents. The victims must have been taken by surprise."

Up till now, Jane had looked skeptical. Now she leaned forward, her full attention on Tam. "Tell me more about that woman backpacker in Nevada. What did the ME say about manner of death?"

"In that case, a cougar attack was also considered a possibility. But we're talking about *four* backpackers, and two of them were men. The manner of death was left 'undetermined.' "

"Could a cougar take down four adults all by itself?"

"I don't know," said Tam. "We'd have to consult with a big-cat specialist. Even if a cougar *did* kill all four backpackers, there's one detail that bothered the ME. It's the reason why the female victim was added to the VICAP database."

"A sternal cut mark?"

"Yes. And three bullet casings. They were found nearby, on the ground. The backpackers weren't armed, but obviously someone else in the area was." Tam looked around the table at the three detectives. "I started off looking at nylon cord, and ended up with a completely different set of common denominators. Evisceration. Elevation. And areas where hunters might be found."

"What about that petty thief in Maine, the one found sliced open and hanging in a tree?" asked Frost. "You said they identified a suspect for that case."

Tam nodded. "The suspect's name is Nick Thibodeau, the victim's so-called buddy. White male, six foot two, two hundred pounds. He has prior convictions of breaking and entering, theft, assault and battery."

"So a history of violence."

"Definitely. And get this: Thibodeau's an avid deer hunter." Tam rotated his laptop to show them a photo of a young man with close-cropped hair and a direct gaze. He stood beside his trophy, a partially skinned buck that hung suspended by its back legs from a tree. Even in bulky hunting garb, it was obvious that Nick Thibodeau was muscular and powerful, with a thick neck and beefy hands.

"This photo was taken about six years ago, so picture him a little older now," said Tam. "He grew up in Maine, knows the wilderness, and knows his way around a gun. Based on this photo, he also knows how to take apart a deer."

"And maybe other large game," said Maura. "There's our common thread: hunting. Maybe deer got boring for Thibodeau. Maybe killing a man gave him such a thrill, he decided to pursue more challenging prey. Consider the timing of these kills. Five years ago, Thibodeau's buddy is killed, hung, and gutted. Thibodeau vanishes. A year later, four unarmed backpackers are attacked in Nevada. A year after that, it's three armed hunters in Montana. This killer keeps raising the stakes, making the challenge more exciting. And maybe the risks as well."

"Leon Gott would have been a challenging target, too," Frost agreed. "He was armed to the teeth and well known to the hunting crowd. The killer would have heard about him."

"But why would this hunter go after Jane Doe?" Crowe said. "A woman? Where's the challenge in that?"

Jane snorted. "Yeah, 'cause we're such weak, helpless creatures. For all you know, she could have been a hunter herself."

"Don't forget Jodi Underwood. She was a woman," said Frost. "And her murder seems connected to Gott's."

"I think Jane Doe's the one we should focus on," said Tam. "If she was killed more than six years ago, she might be one of the very first victims. Identifying her could be key to cracking this case."

Jane closed the folder and regarded Tam. "You and Maura seem to be quite the team. When did that happen?"

"When she asked me to search VICAP for any similar cases," said Tam. "I took it from there."

Jane looked at Maura. "You could've called me."

"I could have," admitted Maura. "But all I had to go on were my instincts. And I didn't want to waste your time." She stood to leave. "Thank you, Detective Tam. You covered all the bases, and there's nothing I have to add. So I'll get back to the morgue." The place where I really belong, among the obedient dead, she thought, and walked out of the conference room.

As she stepped into the elevator, Jane slipped in beside her.

"Talk to me," Jane said as the door slid shut, leaving no escape from this conversation. "Why'd you go to Tam?"

Maura stared straight ahead at the floor light indicator. "He was willing to help me."

"And I wasn't?"

"You didn't agree with me about the similarities."

"Did you ever ask me *specifically* to do a database search for you?"

"Tam was filing a VICAP report anyway, for Jane Doe. He's new to homicide, and he's eager to prove himself. He was open to my theory."

"And I'm just a jaded cynic."

"You're a skeptic, Jane. I'd have to talk you into doing it, and that was too much effort."

"Too much effort? Between friends?"

"Even between friends," Maura said and stepped out of the elevator.

Jane wasn't ready to be shaken off and kept pace as Maura walked out of the building and headed to the parking garage. "You're still ticked off that I didn't agree with you."

"No."

"Yes you are, or you'd have asked me, and not Tam."

"You refused to see the parallels between Gott and Jane Doe, but they're there. I feel it."

"*Feel* it? Since when did you start listening to hunches instead of evidence?"

"You're the one who always talks about instinct."

"But you never do. You're always about facts and logic, so what's changed?"

Maura halted beside her car but did not unlock it. Just stood beside the door, staring at her own reflection in the window. "She wrote me again," she said. "My mother."

There was a long silence. "And you didn't just toss the letter away?"

"I couldn't, Jane. There are things I need to know before she dies. Why she gave me up. Who I really am."

"You know who you are, and it has nothing to do with her."

"How do you know that?" She took a step toward Jane. "Maybe you're only seeing what I let you see. Maybe I've hidden the truth."

"What, that you're some kind of monster like her?" Maura had moved so close they were now standing eye to eye, but Jane merely laughed. "You're the *least* scary person I know. Well, except for Frost. Amalthea's a freak, but she didn't pass that on to you."

"She did pass on one thing. We both see the darkness. Where everyone else sees sunshine, we notice what's in the shadows. The child with bruises, the wife who's too afraid to speak. The house where the curtains are always shut. Amalthea called it a *gift* for recognizing evil." Maura pulled an envelope out of her purse and handed it to Jane.

"What's this?"

"Items she collects from newspapers. She saves everything where I'm mentioned and follows every case I'm working on."

"Including Gott and Jane Doe."

"Of course."

"Now I know where this is coming from. Amalthea Lank tells you there's a connection, and you believe her." Jane shook her head. "Didn't I warn you about her? She's playing you."

"She sees things no one else does. Spots the clues lost among all the details."

"How can she? She doesn't have access to the details."

"Even in prison, she hears things. People tell her, or write her, or send her news clippings. She sees connections, and she was right about this one."

"Yeah. If she weren't a convicted killer, she'd make a great crime analyst."

"Maybe she would. After all, she is my mother."

Jane raised both hands, a gesture of surrender. "Okay. You want to give her that power, I can't stop you. But I know a mistake when I see one."

"And you're always so happy to point it out."

"Who else is going to say it? That's what a friend does, Maura. She stops you before you screw up your life again."

Again. Maura could offer no retort and she stared back in silence, stung by the truth of what Jane had said. *Again.* She thought of all the times Jane had tried to stop her from making the mistake that still haunted her all these months later. As she and Father Daniel Brophy had circled closer and closer, drawn into a love affair with no possible happy ending, Jane had been the voice of reason, warning her of heartbreak ahead. A voice that Maura had ignored.

"Please," Jane said quietly. "I just don't want you to be hurt." She reached for Maura's arm with the stalwart grasp of a friend. "You're so smart in every other way."

"Except when it comes to people."

Jane laughed. "People *are* the problem, aren't they?"

"Maybe I should stick to cats," Maura said as she opened her car door and slid inside. "With them, at least you know exactly where you stand."

TWENTY

LOBSTER AND MOOSE AND WILD BLUEBERRIES. THAT'S WHAT MOST PEOple imagined when they thought about the state of Maine, but Jane's images were far grimmer. She thought of dark woods and murky bogs and all the hidden places where a human being could vanish. And she thought of the last time she and Frost had made this drive north, only five months earlier, on a night that had ended in a mist of blood and death. For Jane, Maine was no Vacationland; it was a place where bad things happened.

Five years ago, a bad thing happened to a petty thief named Brandon Tyrone.

The rain turned to icy pellets as they drove north on Coastal Route 1, Frost at the wheel. Even with the heater blowing, Jane's feet were chilled and she wished she'd pulled on boots that morning, instead of the thin flats she was now wearing. As much as she hated to acknowledge that summer was over, all it took was a glance out the car window at bare trees and gunmetal-gray skies to see that the darkest season had arrived. It seemed they were driving into winter itself.

Frost slowed down as they passed two hunters in blaze orange, hefting a gutted doe into a parked pickup truck. He gave a sad shake of his head. "Bambi's mom."

"November. It's that time of year."

"With all these guns blasting away, it makes me nervous crossing the state line. *Bang! Bagged another Masshole!*"

"You ever hunted?"

"Never wanted to."

"Because of Bambi's mom?"

"It's not like I'm against hunting. I just don't see the fun of it, lugging a rifle into the woods. Freezing your ass off. And then . . ." He shuddered.

"Having to gut a deer?" She laughed. "Naw, I can't see you doing it."

"Well, could you?"

"If I had to. It is where meat comes from."

"No, meat comes from the supermarket, where it's wrapped in plastic. No guts involved."

Outside their car, bare branches dripped icy water and dark clouds hung on the horizon. It was a miserable day to be tramping in the woods, and when they finally arrived at the trailhead parking lot two hours later, she was not surprised to find no other cars. They sat for a moment, eyeing the gloomy woods and leaf-littered picnic tables.

"Well, we're here. So where is he?" she said.

"He's only ten minutes late." Frost pulled out his cell phone. "No signal. How we gonna reach him?"

Jane pushed open her door. "Well, I can't wait. I'm going to take a little walk in the woods."

"You sure you want to go out there? Hunting season?"

She pointed to the NO HUNTING sign nailed to a nearby tree. "This area's posted. Should be safe."

"I think we should wait in the car for him."

"No, I really can't wait. I gotta pee." She climbed out and started toward the woods. The wind cut right through her thin trousers, and her bladder ached in the cold. She tramped a few yards into the trees, but November had stripped them of leaves, and through the bare branches, she could still see the car. She kept walking, and the silence of the woods made every snap of a twig sound like a startling explosion. Ducking behind a clump of evergreen saplings, she unzipped her pants and squatted, hoping that no one would hike by and see her in all her bare-assed glory.

A gunshot echoed.

Before she could jump back to her feet, she heard Frost calling her name. Heard footsteps crashing toward her through the underbrush. Suddenly there he was, and he was not alone; a few steps behind him was a beefy man who eyed her in amusement as she yanked up her pants.

"We heard a gunshot," said a red-faced Frost, quickly averting his eyes. "I'm sorry, I didn't mean to—"

"Forget about it," Jane snapped as she finally managed to zip up. "It's posted for no hunting. Who the hell's shooting?"

"Sound could've come from up the valley," said the heavyset man. "And you folks shouldn't be out in the woods without blaze orange." Certainly no one could miss the neon-bright vest he was wearing over his parka. "You must be Rizzoli." He glanced down at where she'd been squatting and didn't offer a handshake.

"This is Detective Barber, Maine State Police," said Frost.

Barber gave her a curt tip of the head. "I was surprised when you folks called yesterday. Never thought Nick Thibodeau would end up in Boston."

"We're not saying he did," said Jane. "We just want to get a better handle on him. Who he is, and whether he might be the guy we're looking for."

"Well, you wanted to see where we found Tyrone's body five years ago. So let me show you."

He led the way, tramping confidently through the underbrush. Within a few steps, Jane snagged her trouser leg on a spiky blackberry cane and had to stop to disentangle herself. When she looked up again, Barber's blaze-orange vest was already bobbing far ahead, beyond a tangle of bare branches.

Another gunshot thundered in the distance. *And here I am wearing black and brown, just like a bear.* She scrambled after Barber, anxious to reach the safety of that neon orange. By the time she caught up, Barber had steered them onto a groomed trail.

"Pair of campers from Virginia found Tyrone's body," said Barber, not bothering to glance back to see if she'd kept up. "They had a dog with 'em, and he led 'em straight to it."

"Yeah, it's always the dogs who find 'em out here," said Frost, suddenly sounding like an expert on bodies in the wilderness.

"It was late summer, so the trees were leafed out, hid it from view. Might've smelled it themselves if the wind was blowing the right way. But things are always dying out in the woods, so you expect to come across a dead animal now and then. What you don't expect is some guy hanging upside down with his belly slit open." He nodded ahead at the trail. "We're coming up on the spot."

"How do you know?" said Jane. "These trees all look alike to me."

"Because of that." He pointed to a NO HUNTING sign posted alongside the trail. "Past this sign, it's just a few dozen paces into the woods."

"You think the location's significant? Was this sign meant as some kind of message?"

"Yeah. It's a big *fuck you* to authority."

"Or maybe this *is* the message: No hunting. Because one of our victims in Boston was a hunter and we're wondering if the killer is making a political point."

Barber shook his head. "Then you're looking for the wrong man here. Nick Thibodeau was no animal rights nut. Hunting was his thing." He headed off the trail, into the woods. "Let me show you the tree."

With every step, the cold seemed to deepen. Jane's shoes were damp, and the chill was now seeping through the leather. The dead leaves were calf-deep here, and they hid mudholes and ankle-snagging roots. On that warm day in August five years ago, the killer would have had a far pleasanter stroll through these woods, although mosquitoes might have swarmed, stirred up by his passage. Was the victim still alive, walking willingly beside him, unaware of his companion's intentions? Or was Brandon Tyrone already dead, slung like a gutted deer across the killer's shoulders?

"This is the tree," said Barber. "He was hanging upside down from that branch."

Jane looked up at the branch where a few brown leaves still clung quivering to the twigs. She saw nothing to distinguish this particular oak from any other tree, no hint of what had dangled from that branch five years ago. It was an ordinary tree that told no secrets.

"Tyrone had been dead about two days, according to the ME," said Barber. "Hanging up there, the only wildlife that could reach him was birds and insects, so he was still in one piece." He paused. "Except for the guts, which would've been scavenged right away." He stared up at the branch, as if he could see Brandon Tyrone still suspended there, shaded by the summer canopy of leaves. "We never found his wallet or his clothes. Probably disposed of, to make him harder to ID."

"Or he took them as a trophy," said Jane. "The way hunters take an animal's skin, to remind them of the thrill."

"Naw, I doubt he meant it as any kind of ritual. Nicko was just being practical, as usual."

Jane looked at Barber. "You sound like you know the suspect."

"I do. We grew up in the same town, so I know him and his brother Eddie."

"How well?"

"Enough to know those boys were trouble from way back. At twelve, Nick was already stealing loose change out of the other kids' jackets. At fourteen, he was breaking into cars. At sixteen, it was houses. The victim, Brandon Tyrone, was the same story. Nick and Tyrone, they'd come out here together, steal stuff out of campers' tents and cars. After Nick killed Tyrone, we found a bag of stolen items hidden in Tyrone's garage. Maybe that's why they had a falling-out. There was some nice stuff in that bag. Cameras, a silver cigarette lighter, a wallet full of credit cards. I think they got in a fight over how to divide it, and Tyrone lost. Mean little bastard. Couldn't happen to a nicer guy."

"And where do you think Nick Thibodeau is now?"

"I assumed he took off out west. California, maybe. Didn't think he'd end up as close as Boston, but maybe he doesn't want to be too far from his brother Eddie."

"Where's Eddie live?"

"He's about five miles from here. Oh, we hit Eddie hard with the questions, but to this day he refuses to tell us where Nick is."

"Refuses? Or doesn't know?"

"Swears he doesn't know. But these Thibodeau boys, in their minds, it's them against the world. You gotta remember, Maine is the northern tip of Appalachia, and some of these families value loyalty above all. Stand by your brother, no matter what he's done. I think that's exactly what Eddie did. Came up with a plan to get Nick outta here and help him disappear."

"For five years?"

"Not so hard if you have help from your brother. That's why I still keep tabs on Eddie. I know where he goes and who he calls. Oh, he's sick of me all right, because he knows I'm not gonna let it go. He knows I have my eye on him."

"We need to talk to Eddie Thibodeau," said Jane.

"You won't get the truth out of him."

"We'd still like to try."

Barber glanced at his watch. "Okay, I've got a free hour. We can head over to his house now."

Jane and Frost looked at each other. Frost said, "Maybe it'd be better if we saw him on our own."

"You don't want me there?"

"You two have a history," said Jane, "obviously not a friendly one. If you're there, it'll put him on guard."

"Oh, I get it. I'm the bad cop and you want to be the good cops. Yeah, that makes sense." He looked at the weapon strapped to Jane's waist. "And I see you're both carrying. That's good."

"Why? Is Eddie a problem?" asked Frost.

"He's unpredictable. Think about what Nick did to Tyrone, and stay alert. Because these brothers are capable of anything."

A GUTTED FOUR-POINT BUCK hung upside down in Eddie Thibodeau's garage. Cluttered with tools and spare tires, trash cans and fishing gear, it looked like any suburban garage in America, except for the animal dangling from a ceiling hook, dripping blood into a puddle on the concrete floor.

"I don't know what else I can say 'bout my brother. Already told the police everything there is to say." Eddie raised a knife to the buck's hind leg, slit around the ankle joint, then sliced through skin from ankle to groin. Working with the efficiency of a man who'd broken down many a deer, he grasped the pelt with both hands and grunted with effort as he peeled it down, baring purplish muscle and sinew cloaked in silvery fascia. It was cold in the open garage, and he exhaled clouds of steam as he paused to catch his breath. Like the photo of his brother Nick, Eddie had broad shoulders and dark eyes and the same stony expression, but he was an unkempt version of his brother, dressed in bloodstained overalls and a wool cap, his beard stubble already peppered with gray at the ripe age of thirty-nine.

"After they found Tyrone hanging in that tree, the state police kept hassling me, asking the same damn questions. Where would Nick go to ground? Who was hiding him? I kept telling 'em they got it all wrong. That something must've happened to Nick, too. If he was on the run, he'd never leave without his bug-out bag."

"What kind of bag?" said Frost.

"Don't tell me you've never heard of a bug-out bag." Eddie frowned at them across the splayed rear legs of the deer.

"What is it, exactly?"

"It's where you keep your essentials for survival. For when the system goes all to hell. See, if there's some kind of catastrophe like a dirty bomb or a terrorist attack, people in big cities are gonna be in a world of hurt. No power, folks in a panic. That's why you need a bug-out bag." Eddie peeled more of the pelt, and the smell of bloody deer meat, raw and gamy, made Frost grimace and step away.

Eddie glanced at him in amusement. "Not a fan of venison?"

Frost stared at the glistening flesh, streaked with fat. "I tried it once."

"Didn't like it?"

"Not really."

"Then it wasn't prepared right. Or killed right. For the meat to taste good, the deer has to go down quick. One bullet, no struggle. If it's only wounded and you have to chase it down, that meat's gonna taste like fear."

Frost stared at exposed muscles that had once propelled this buck through fields and woods. "And how does fear taste?"

"Like scorched flesh. Panic sends all kinds of hormones through the animal and you taste the struggle. Ruins the flavor." He cleanly sliced a fist-sized hunk of meat from the haunch and tossed it into a stainless-steel bowl. "This onc was killed right. Never knew what hit him. Gonna make a tasty stew."

"You ever go hunting with your brother?" asked Jane.

"Nick and I grew up hunting together." He sliced off another hunk. "I miss that."

"Was he a good shot?"

"Better than me. Real steady, always took his time."

"So he could survive out there, in the woods."

Eddie gave her a cold stare. "It's been five years. What, you think he's still out there, living like some mountain man?"

"Where do *you* think he is?"

Eddie dropped his knife in a bucket, and bloodstained water splashed onto the concrete. "You're looking for the wrong man."

"Who's the right man?"

"Not Nick. He's no killer."

She eyed the dead buck, its left leg now stripped down to bone. "When they found Nick's buddy Tyrone, he was gutted and hanging just like this deer."

"So?"

"Nick was a hunter."

"So am I, and I haven't killed anyone. I'm just feeding my family, something you people are so far removed from, you've probably never even used a boning knife." He took the rinsed knife from the bucket and held it out to Jane. "Let's see you give it a try, Detective. Go on, take it. Slice off a chunk and see how it feels to harvest your own dinner. Or are you afraid of a little blood on your hands?"

Jane saw the disdain in his eyes. Oh no, a city girl would never dirty her hands. It was men like the Thibodeau brothers who hunted and farmed and butchered so that she could have her steak on a plate. She might view his kind in contempt, but so, too, did he view hers.

She took the knife, stepped toward the buck, and sliced deep, all the way to bone. As chilled flesh peeled open, she smelled all that the deer had once been: fresh grass and acorns and forest moss. And blood, wild and coppery. The meat came away from bone, a dense, purple wedge of it, which she tossed into the bowl. She didn't glance at Eddie as she started carving off the next chunk.

"If Nick didn't kill his friend Tyrone," she said, her knife gliding through flesh, "who do you think did?"

"I don't know."

"Nick has a history of violence."

"He was no angel. He got in a few fights."

"Did he ever get in a fight with Tyrone?"

"Once."

"That you know of."

Eddie picked up another knife and reached deep inside the carcass to strip out a tenderloin. His blade was at work barely an arm's length away from her but she calmly carved another chunk from the leg.

"Tyrone was no angel, either, and they both liked to drink." Eddie pulled out the bloody tenderloin, slippery as an eel, and tossed it into the bowl. Swished the blade in the bucket of icy water. "Just because a man loses control once in a while doesn't make him a monster."

"Maybe Nick did more than just lose control. Maybe an argument led to something way worse than a fight."

Eddie looked straight at her. "Why would he leave him hanging from a tree, out in the open, where everyone could find him? Nick's not stupid. He knows how to cover his tracks. If he killed Tyrone, he'd drag him into the woods and bury him. Or scatter his parts for the animals. What was done to Tyrone, that was something else, something sick. That *wasn't* my brother." He crossed to a workbench to hone his blade, and all conversation was cut off by the whine of the sharpener. The steel bowl was now mounded high with meat, at least twenty pounds' worth, and half the deer had yet to be butchered. Outside the open garage, an icy drizzle was falling. On this lonely country road there were few houses, and in the last half hour she'd seen no cars pass by. And here they were, in the middle of nowhere, watching an angry man sharpen his knife.

"Did your brother go down to Boston much?" she called out over the screech.

"Sometimes. Not a lot."

"He ever mention a guy named Leon Gott?"

Eddie glanced up at her. "That's what this is about? Leon Gott's murder?"

"You knew him?"

"Not personally, but I knew his name, of course. Most hunters do. I could never afford his work, but if you wanted your kill stuffed and mounted, Gott was the man to go to." Eddie paused. "Is that why you're up here, asking about Nick? You think *he* did Gott?"

"We're just asking if they knew each other."

"We read Gott's articles in *Trophy Hunter.* And we went down to Cabela's, to check out some of the big game he mounted. But as far as I know, Nick never met the guy."

"He ever go to Montana?"

"Years ago. We both went, to see Yellowstone."

"How many years ago?"

"Does it matter?"

"Yes, it does."

Eddie set down the knife he'd been sharpening and said, quietly, "Why are you asking about Montana?"

"Other people have been killed, Mr. Thibodeau."

"You mean, like Tyrone was?"

"There were similarities."

"Who are these other people?"

"Hunters, in Montana. It happened three years ago."

Eddie shook his head. "My brother disappeared five years ago."

"But he has been to Montana. He's familiar with the state."

"It was one fucking trip to Yellowstone!"

"What about Nevada?" said Frost. "He ever been there?"

"No. What, did he supposedly kill someone there, too?" Eddie looked back and forth at Jane and Frost and snorted. "Any other murders you want to pin on Nick? He can't defend himself, so you might as well throw your whole cold-case file at him."

"Where is he, Eddie?"

"I wish I knew!" In frustration, he slapped away an empty bowl and it hit the concrete floor with an ear-ringing clang. "I wish you fucking cops would do your fucking jobs and come up with answers! Instead you keep harassing me about Nick. I haven't seen or heard from him in five years. The last time I did see him, he was on the porch, drinking with Tyrone. They were haggling over some crap they'd picked up at the campground."

"Picked up?" Jane snorted. "You mean, stolen."

"Whatever. But it wasn't a fight, okay? It was a . . . lively negotiation, that's all. They left for Tyrone's place, and that's it. The last time I saw them. Few days later, state police shows up here. They found Nick's truck parked at the trailhead. And they found Tyrone. But they never found any trace of Nick." As if too weary to stand any longer, Eddie sank onto a bench and huffed out a breath. "That's what I know. That's all I know."

"You said Nick's truck was parked at the trailhead."

"Yeah. Police figured he took off into the wild. That he's somewhere in the woods like Rambo, living off the land."

"What do you think happened?"

For a moment, Eddie was silent, staring down at his callused hands, the nails crusted with blood. "I think my brother's dead," he said softly. "I think his bones are scattered somewhere, and we just haven't found him yet. Or he's hanging from some tree, like Tyrone."

"So you think he was murdered."

Eddie raised his head and looked at her. "I think they met someone else out there, in the woods."

TWENTY-ONE

BOTSWANA

WHEN THE SUN COMES UP, I AM ALONE IN THE WILDERNESS. I HAVE stumbled for hours in the darkness, and I have no idea how far I've traveled from camp; I only know that I am somewhere downstream, because all night I kept the sound of the river to my left. As the sky brightens from pink to gold I am so thirsty I drop to my knees at the water's edge and drink like a wild animal. Only yesterday, I would have insisted the water be boiled or purified with iodine first. I would have fretted over all the microbial terrors I'm ingesting, a fatal dose of bacteria and parasites with every gulp. None of that matters now, because I am going to die anyway. I scoop up water in my palms, drink so greedily that it splashes my face, streams from my chin.

When at last I've had my fill, I rock back on my haunches and gaze across a clump of papyrus to the trees and waving grasses beyond the river. To the creatures who inhabit this green and alien world, I am but a walking source of meat, and everywhere I look, I imagine teeth waiting to devour me. With sunrise came the noisy chatter of birds, and when I look up, I see vultures tracing lazy loops in the sky. Have they already marked me for their next meal? I turn upriver, toward camp, and see the clear trail of footprints I've left along the bank. I remember how easily Johnny tracked even the faintest paw prints. My trail will be as glaring as neon for him to follow. Now that it's daylight, he'll be hunting me because he can't afford to let me live. I'm the only one left who knows what happened.

I rise to my feet and continue to flee downstream.

I can't allow myself to think of Richard or the others. All I can focus on is staying alive. Fear keeps me moving, pushes me deeper into the wild. I have no clue where this river leads. I recall from the guidebook that the rivers and streams of the Okavango Delta are fed by rainfall in the Angola highlands. All this water, which annually floods these lagoons and swamps from which so much wildlife magically springs, will eventually empty into the parched Kalahari Desert. I glance up to gauge the direction of the sun, which is only now lifting over the treetops. I am walking south.

And I am hungry.

In my knapsack I find six PowerBars, 240 calories each. I remember tucking them into my suitcase in London, just in case I couldn't abide the food in the bush, and I remember how Richard mocked my unadventurous palate. In an instant I devour one of the PowerBars and have to force myself to leave the remaining five for later. If I stay near the river, at least I'll have water, an endless supply of it, even though it surely carries a host of diseases I can't even pronounce. But the water's edge is a dangerous zone where predator and prey so often meet, where life and death converge. At my feet is an animal's skull, bleached by the sun. Some deer-like creature that met its end here on the riverbank. A line of ripples disturbs the water, and a crocodile lifts beady eyes to the surface. This is not a good place to be. I veer away into the grass and find a pathway has already been trampled here. Tracks stomped in the dust tell me that I am following in the footsteps of elephants.

When you are afraid, everything zooms into sharp focus. You see too much, hear too much, and I'm overwhelmed by a rapid click-click of images and sounds, any one of which might be the only warning of something that will kill me. That must all be processed at once. That swaying of the grass? Merely the wind. The blur of wings swooping above the reeds? A fish eagle. The rustling in the underbrush is merely a warthog rambling by. Tawny impala and the darker shapes of Cape buffalo move along the horizon. Everywhere I see life, flying, chattering, swimming, feeding. Beautiful and hungry and dangerous. And now the mosquitoes have found me and are feasting on my blood. My precious pills are back in my tent, so add malaria to the list of ways to die, along with being mauled by a lion, trampled by a buffalo, drowned by a crocodile, and crushed by a hippo.

As the heat builds, the mosquitoes become relentless. I wave at them maniacally as I walk, but they thicken into a biting cloud that I cannot escape. In desperation, I'm driven back to the riverbank where I scoop up handfuls of mud and slather my face and neck and arms. The silt is slimy with decaying vegetation and the smell makes me gag, but I slap on thicker and thicker layers until I'm encased in it. I rise to my feet, a primeval creature emerging from the muck. Like Adam.

I continue on the elephant path. They, too, prefer to travel alongside the river, and as I walk I spot other prints that tell me this route is used by a multitude of different creatures. This is the bush equivalent of a superhighway, all of us traveling in the footsteps of elephants. If impala and kudu walk this way then surely lions do as well.

Here is yet another killing zone, where predator and prey find each other.

But the tall grass on either side of me hides just as many threats, and I don't have the energy to thrash my own path through dense bush. I must move quickly, because somewhere behind me is Johnny, the most relentless predator of all. Why did I refuse to see it? As the others were taken down one by one, their flesh and bones fed to this hungry land, I was blind to his game. Every look Johnny gave me, every kind word, was merely a prelude to a kill.

As the sun reaches its height, I am still trudging the elephant path. The mud dries to a hard crust on my skin and clumps of it crumble into my mouth as I eat a second PowerBar, and I devour it, grit and all. I know I should conserve my food supply, but I'm already famished and the ultimate tragedy would be to collapse dead, with food still in my knapsack. The trail veers back toward the water's edge, where I come to a lagoon so black and still that a twin sky is reflected in its waters. The heat of midday has silenced the bush; even the birds have gone quiet. At the water's edge is a tree where dozens of strange, pendulous sacs hang like Christmas balls. In my heat-crazed exhaustion, I wonder if I've stumbled upon a colony of alien cocoons, left to incubate where no one will discover them. Then a bird flutters past and vanishes into one of the sacs. Weaver-bird nests.

The water of the lagoon stirs, as if something has just awakened. I back away, sensing evil here, waiting to trap the unwary. I feel its chill at my back as I retreat, once again, into the grass.

THAT EVENING, I WALK straight into the elephant herd.

In bush this thick, even something as large as an elephant can take you by surprise, and as I stumble out of a stand of acacia trees, suddenly *there she is* in front of me. She seems just as startled as I am and gives a trumpet of alarm so loud that it seems to blast straight through me. I'm too shocked to run. I stand frozen, the acacias at my back, the elephant facing me, standing just as still. As we stare at each other, I see massive gray shapes moving all around me. A whole herd of them are rattling the branches, snapping off twigs. They know I am here, of course, and they pause in their feeding to warily eye the mud-caked intruder. How little effort it would take for any one of them to kill me. A swat of the trunk, one massive foot on my chest, would rid them of this threat. I feel them all studying me, weighing my fate. Then one elephant calmly reaches up, breaks off a twig, and slides it into her mouth. One by one, they resume feeding. They have judged me, and issued their reprieve.

Quietly I slip back into the brush and move toward the cover of a majestic tree that towers above the acacias. I clamber up the massive trunk until I'm high enough to perch safely above the herd, and I settle into the crook of a branch. Like my primate ancestors, I find safety in the trees. In the distance, hyenas cackle and lions roar, a warning of the coming battle at nightfall. From high in my perch, I watch the sun set. In the shadows below my tree, elephants continue to feed, rustling and shuffling. Reassuring sounds.

The whole night comes alive with screams and roars. The stars wink on, crystalline bright in a black sky. Through arching branches I spy the constellation Scorpio, which Johnny pointed out to me on the first night. It's just one of the many things he taught me about living in the bush, and I wonder why he bothered. To give me a fighting chance and make me more worthy as prey?

Somehow I have outlasted all the others. I think of Clarence and Elliot, the Matsunagas and the blondes. Most of all I think of Richard and what we once had together. I remember the promises we made, and the nights when we'd fall asleep with our arms around each other. Suddenly I am weeping for Richard, for all that we once had, and my sobs are like one more animal call in this noisy nocturnal chorus. I cry until my chest aches and my throat is raw. Until I am so exhausted that I am limp.

I fall asleep the way my ancestors did a million years ago, in a tree, under the stars.

AT DAWN ON THE fourth day, I unwrap the final PowerBar. I eat it slowly, each bite an act of reverence for the holy power of food. Because it is my last meal, every nut, every flake of oat is a joyous explosion of flavor that I never truly appreciated before. I think of the many holiday feasts I've gorged on, but none was as sacred as this meal, eaten in a tree as the sky blooms gold with the rising sun. I lick the last crumbs from the wrapper, then clamber down to the riverbank, where I drop to my knees as though in prayer, and drink from the rushing water.

When I rise to my feet, I feel strangely sated. I can't remember when the plane is due back at the landing strip, but it hardly matters now. Johnny will tell the pilot that there was a terrible calamity and there is no one left alive to search for. No one will ever come looking for me. To the world, I am dead.

I scoop up mud from the river and anoint my face and arms with a fresh layer. Already I feel the sun's heat beating down on my neck and swarms of biting insects rise from the reeds. The day has scarcely begun, and I am already exhausted.

I force myself to my feet. Once again, I trudge south.

BY THE AFTERNOON OF the next day, I am so hungry that I double over with stomach cramps. I drink from the river, hoping that water will ease the pangs, but I gulp down too much, too fast, and it all comes up again. I kneel in the mud, retching, weeping. How easy it would be to give up now! To lie down and let the animals take me. My flesh, my bones, will be devoured by the wilderness, forever joined to Africa. From this land we all arose, and to this land I return. It is a fitting place to die.

Something splashes in the water, and I lift my head to see two ears flicking on the surface. A hippo. I'm close enough to alarm it, but I'm beyond fear, beyond caring if I live or die. Though it knows I'm here, it continues to bask unconcerned. The murky water ripples with small fish and insects, and cranes splash down from the sky. In this place where I am dying, there is so much life. I watch an insect flutter toward a thicket of papyrus reeds, and suddenly I'm hungry enough to eat even that dragonfly. But I'm not fast enough, and all I catch is a handful of reeds, thick and fibrous. I don't know if they'll poison me; I don't care. I just want something to fill my stomach and ease the cramps.

With the pocketknife from my knapsack, I slash a handful of reeds and bite down on the stems. The rind is soft, the flesh starchy.

I chew and chew until all that's left in my mouth is a hard wad of fibers, which I spit out. My cramps are easing. I cut another handful of papyrus reeds and gnaw on them, like an animal. Like the hippo, who calmly grazes nearby. Slash and chew, slash and chew. With every mouthful, I take the bush into me, feel it become one with me.

The woman I once was, Millie Jacobson, has reached the end of her journey. On my knees, at the river's edge, I surrender her soul.

TWENTY-TWO

BOSTON

MAURA COULD NOT SEE HIM, BUT SHE KNEW HE WAS WATCHING HER.

"There, up on the ledge," said Dr. Alan Rhodes, the zoo's large-cat specialist. "He's just behind that clump of grass. He's hard to make out because he blends so perfectly into the rocks."

Only then did Maura spot the tawny eyes. They were fixed on her and only her, with the cold, laser focus that binds predator to prey. "I would have missed him completely," she murmured. Already shivering in the cold wind, she felt her chill deepen as she met the cougar's unrelenting stare.

"He didn't miss *you,*" said Rhodes. "He's probably been tracking you since we walked around that bend, into his field of view."

"You say he's tracking me. But not you?"

"For a predator, it's all about identifying the most accessible prey, the easiest one to bring down. Before he'd attack a full-grown man, a cougar will choose a child or a woman. Look, do you see that family coming toward us? Watch what the cougar does. Watch his eyes."

Up on the ledge, the cougar's head suddenly swiveled and he snapped to full alertness, his muscles rippling as he rose to a crouch.

His gaze was no longer on Maura; instead those laser eyes were fixed on a new target, which was now scampering toward his enclosure. A child.

"It's both movement and size that attract him," said Rhodes. "When a kid goes running by this enclosure, it's like flipping a switch inside a cat's head. Instinct takes over." Rhodes turned to her. "I'm curious why you're suddenly interested in cougars. Not that I mind answering questions," he added quickly. "In fact, I'd be happy to tell you a lot more over lunch sometime, if you'd like."

"I find big cats fascinating, but I'm actually here because of a case we're working on."

"So it's about work."

Was that disappointment she heard in his voice? She couldn't read his face, because he'd turned toward the enclosure, his elbows propped on the guardrail, his gaze back on the cougar. She considered what it might be like to have lunch with Alan Rhodes. Interesting conversation with a man who was clearly passionate about his work. She saw intelligence in his eyes, and although he wasn't particularly tall, his work outdoors kept him tanned and fit. This was the solid, reliable sort of man she *should* have fallen in love with, but the spark wasn't there. Chasing that damn spark had brought her nothing but sorrow; why did it never ignite with a man who could make her happy?

"How does cougar behavior relate to an ME's case?" he asked.

"I want to know more about their hunting patterns. How they kill."

He frowned at her. "Has there been a cougar attack in the state? That would certainly support the rumors I've been hearing."

"What rumors?"

"About cougars in Massachusetts. There are reported sightings throughout New England, but right now they're the equivalent of ghosts, sighted but never confirmed. Except for the one killed in Connecticut a few years ago."

"Connecticut? Was he an escaped pet?"

"No, that animal was definitely wild. It was hit by an SUV on a highway in Milford. According to DNA analysis, he migrated here from a wild cougar group in South Dakota. So these cats have definitely made it to the East Coast. They're probably right here, in Massachusetts."

"I find that scary. But you sound almost thrilled by the prospect."

He gave a sheepish laugh. "Shark experts love sharks. Dinosaur guys are nuts about tyrannosaurs. It doesn't mean they want to run into one, but we all share that sense of wonder about big predators. You know, cougars used to own this continent, coast to coast, before we chased them out. I think it's pretty exciting that they're coming back."

The family with the child had left the exhibit and moved on down the zoo path. Once again the cougar's gaze turned to Maura. "If they're here in the state," she said, "there goes any thought of a peaceful walk in the woods."

"I wouldn't get freaked out about it. Look how many cougars there are in California. Night-motion cameras have caught them wandering around in LA's Griffith Park. It's rare that you hear about an incident, although they have attacked joggers and bicyclists. They're primed to chase fleeing prey, so movement catches their eye."

"Then we should stand and face them? Fight back?"

"To be honest, you'd never see one coming. By the time you're aware he's there, he's already sinking his jaws in your neck."

"Like Debbie Lopez."

Rhodes paused. Said quietly: "Yes. Like poor Debbie." He looked at her. "So *has* there been a cougar attack here?"

"It's a case from Nevada. The Sierras."

"These cats are definitely there. What were the circumstances?"

"The victim was a female backpacker. Her body had been scavenged by birdlife by the time she was found, but several details made the ME consider cougar attack. First, the victim was disemboweled."

"A not-infrequent finding in a large-cat kill."

"The other thing that puzzled the ME was where the body was found. It was up in a tree."

He stared at her. "A tree?"

"She was draped over a branch about ten feet above the ground. The question is, how did she get up there? Could a cougar have dragged her?"

He thought about this for a moment. "It's not classic cougar behavior."

"After the leopard killed Debbie Lopez, he dragged her up onto the ledge. You said he did it out of instinct, to protect his kill."

"Yes, that behavior's typical of an African leopard. In the bush, they face competition from other large carnivores—lions, hyenas, crocodiles. Hauling a large kill up a tree is how they keep it away from scavengers. Once the kill is safely cached in the branches, the leopard can feed at its leisure. In Africa, when you see a dead impala up in a tree, there's only one animal who could have put it there."

"What about cougars? Do they use trees?"

"The North American cougar doesn't face the same scavenger competition that carnivores do in Africa. A cougar might haul prey into heavy brush or into a cave before feeding. But drag it up a tree?" He shook his head. "It would be unusual. That's more like African leopard behavior."

She turned toward the enclosure again. The cat's eyes were still riveted on her, as if only she could satisfy his hunger. "Tell me more about leopards," she said softly.

"I highly doubt there's a leopard running around in Nevada, unless it escaped from some zoo."

"Still, I'd like to know more about them. Their habits. Their hunting patterns."

"Well, I'm most familiar with *Panthera pardus,* the African leopard. There are also a number of subspecies—*Panthera orientalis, Panthera fusca, Panthera pardus japonensis*—but they're not so well studied. Before we hunted them nearly to extinction, you could find leopards across Asia, Africa, even as far west as England. It's sad to see how few of them are left in the world. Especially since we owe them a debt for boosting us up the evolutionary ladder."

"How did they do that?"

"There's this theory that early hominids in Africa fed themselves not by hunting, but by stealing meat that leopards had stored in trees. It would have been the equivalent of a fast-food outlet. No need to chase down an impala yourself. Just wait for the leopard to make the kill and drag it up a tree. He'll eat his fill and leave for a few hours. That's when you snatch the rest of the carcass. That ready supply of protein might have boosted the brainpower of our ancestors."

"The leopard wouldn't stop you?"

"Radio collar monitoring confirms that leopards don't stay with their kills during the day. They'll gorge, leave for a while, then return hours later to feed again. Since the carcasses are often disemboweled, the meat stays good for a few days. It gave us hominids a chance to sneak in and steal dinner. But you're right, it wouldn't have been a risk-free proposition. You find plenty of prehistoric hominid bones in ancient leopard caves. While we were stealing their dinner, they sometimes made us *theirs.*"

She thought of the cat in her own home, and how it watched her as intently as this cougar was doing now. The connection between felines and humans was more complex than between mere predator and prey. A house cat might sit in your lap and eat from your hand, but it still had the instincts of a hunter.

As do we.

"They're solitary animals?" she asked.

"Yes, like most felids. Lions are the exception. Leopards in particular are solitary. Females leave their cubs alone for periods up to a week, because they prefer to hunt and forage by themselves. By a year and a half, those cubs have left Mom and they're off to establish their own home range. Except when they breed, they keep to themselves. Very secretive, very hard to spot. They're nocturnal hunters with a reputation for stealth, so you can see why they held such a powerful place in mythology. It would have made the darkness terrifying for ancient man, knowing that, on any given night, you might find a leopard's jaws clamped around your throat."

She thought of Debra Lopez, for whom that terror would have been the last thing she registered. She glanced toward the leopard enclosure just a few yards away. Since the zookeeper's death, a temporary screen had been erected to hide the cage, but two zoo visitors stood there now, snapping cell phone photos. Death was a rock star who always drew an audience.

"You said big cats disembowel their kills," she said.

"It's just a consequence of how they feed. Leopards will rip open the body cavity from the rear. That releases the entrails, which they'll consume within the first twenty-four hours. It keeps the meat from decaying too quickly, so the cat can take its time feeding." He paused as his cell phone rang. With an apologetic look, he answered the call. "Hello? Oh God, Marcy, I completely forgot about it. I'll be right there." He hung up with a sigh. "Sorry, but they're expecting me at a board meeting. It's the eternal hunt for funds."

"Thank you for seeing me. You've been a big help."

"Anytime." He started down the path, then turned and called: "If you ever want a private after-hours tour, let me know!"

She watched him hurry away around the bend, and suddenly she was alone, shivering in the wind.

No, not entirely alone. Through the bars of the empty leopard's cage, she glimpsed blond hair, tawny as a lion's mane, and broad shoulders clad in a brown fleece jacket. It was the zoo's veterinarian, Dr. Oberlin. For a moment they eyed each other like two wary creatures who have unexpectedly come face-to-face in the bush. Then he gave a brusque nod, a wave, and vanished back into the camouflaging shrubbery.

As invisible as a cougar, she thought. I never even knew he was there.

TWENTY-THREE

"IF INDEED THESE VARIOUS ATTACKS IN DIFFERENT STATES ARE LINKED, then we're dealing with a set of highly complex ritual behaviors," said Dr. Lawrence Zucker. A criminal psychologist who served as consultant to Boston PD, Zucker's pale, hulking figure was a familiar sight in the homicide unit. From his seat at the head of the table, he eyed Maura and the four detectives who'd gathered in the conference room that morning. There was something disturbingly reptilian about Zucker, and as his gaze swept past Maura, it felt like the cold flick of a lizard's tongue on her face.

"Before we get ahead of ourselves," said Detective Crowe, "we haven't yet established that these attacks *are* linked. Dr. Isles came up with that theory, not us."

"And we're still digging into it," said Jane. "Frost and I drove up to Maine yesterday to look into the case that happened five years ago. A victim named Brandon Tyrone, who was found gutted and hanging from a tree."

"And what do you think?" asked Zucker.

"I can't say the picture's any clearer. Maine State Police are focused on only one suspect, a man named Nick Thibodeau. He and the victim knew each other. They may have had a falling-out, which triggered the killing."

Crowe said, "I called Montana and Nevada, spoke to detectives about their cases. They believe cougar attacks could explain both incidents. I don't see how the out-of-state cases connect to ours, or to the homicide in Maine."

"It's the *symbolism* that connects them all," said Maura, unable to hold her silence. Neither a cop nor a psychologist, she was once again the intruder at this meeting, and had come at the invitation of Dr. Zucker. As they all turned to look at her, she felt the wall of skepticism looming in her way. A wall she'd have to batter down. Crowe had all force fields up. Both Frost and Jane were trying to look open-minded, but she'd heard the lack of enthusiasm in Jane's voice. As for Johnny Tam, he remained as opaque as ever, keeping his opinions to himself.

"After I spoke to Dr. Rhodes about leopard biology, I realized *that* was the common thread. The way a leopard hunts, the way it feeds, the way it elevates its kill. We see it in all these victims."

"So who are we looking for?" Crowe sniggered. "Leopard Man?"

"You make light of it, Detective Crowe," said Zucker. "But don't dismiss Dr. Isles's theory out of hand. When she called me about this yesterday, I was doubtful, too. Then I reviewed those out-of-state homicides."

"Nevada and Montana weren't necessarily homicides," Crowe pointed out. "Again, the ME's say those *could* have been cougar attacks."

"Dr. Rhodes said cougars don't normally drag their kills into trees," said Maura. "And what happened to the other members of both parties? There were four backpackers in the Nevada group. Only one was found. There were three hunters in Montana, and the remains of only two were found. Cougars couldn't have wiped them *all* out."

"Maybe a family of cougars."

"It wasn't a cougar at all," said Maura.

"You know, Dr. Isles, I'm having a little trouble keeping up with all your changing theories." Crowe looked around the table. "First, we hear this killer hates hunters and that's why he hangs and guts them. Now it's, what? Some crazy guy who thinks he's a leopard?"

"He's not necessarily insane."

"Hey, if I went around pretending I was a leopard," said Crowe, "you'd call the guys in white coats to have me shut away."

Jane muttered: "Please, could we arrange that now?"

Dr. Zucker said, "You need to hear what Dr. Isles has to say." He looked at Maura. "Why don't you describe for us, once again, the condition of Mr. Gott's body."

"We've all read the autopsy report," said Crowe.

"Nevertheless, let her describe his wounds again."

Maura nodded. "There was a depressed fracture of the right parietal bone, compatible with a blow from a blunt object. There were also multiple parallel lacerations of the thorax, probably inflicted postmortem. There were crush injuries of the thyroid cartilage, which most likely resulted in asphyxiation. A single incision extended from the sternum's xiphoid process all the way to the pubis, and viscera of both the thoracic and abdominal cavities were removed." She paused. "Would you like me to continue?"

"No, I'd say that paints a sufficient picture. Now let me read you all a doctor's description. It's from another crime scene." Zucker slipped on his glasses. " 'The victim is a woman, about eighteen years of age, found dead in her hut at daybreak. Her throat was crushed and her face and neck were torn open by what seem to be multiple claw marks, the flesh so horribly mutilated that it appears partially devoured. The intestines and liver are missing, but here I note the peculiar detail of how cleanly one end of the intestine was incised. Upon further examination, I note that the abdomen has been sliced open with a peculiarly straight and clean incision—a wound that no wild creature I am familiar with could inflict. Thus, despite my initial impression that this poor soul was a victim of leopard or lion attack,

I must conclude that the perpetrator, without a doubt, was human.'" He set down the page he'd been reading. "Surely you all agree the report bears an uncanny resemblance to what Dr. Isles just described?"

"Which case was that?" asked Frost.

"It was written by a German missionary doctor working in Sierra Leone." Zucker paused. "In the year 1948."

The room went dead silent. Maura looked around the table and saw astonishment in Frost's and Tam's faces, skepticism in Crowe's. *And what's Jane thinking? That I've finally gone over the edge and I'm chasing phantoms?*

"Let me get this straight," said Crowe. "You think we're dealing with a killer who was doing this in *1948*? Which would make him, what? About eighty-five years old?"

"That's not at all what we're suggesting," said Maura.

"Then what *is* your new theory, Dr. Isles?"

"The point is, there's historical precedent to these ritual murders. What's happening today—the parallel slash marks, the evisceration—it's an echo of what's been happening for centuries."

"Are we talking about a cult? Ghosts? Or are we back to Leopard Man?"

"For God's sake, let her talk, Crowe," Jane looked at Maura. "I just hope you've got more than supernatural woo-woo."

Maura said, "This is very real. But first it requires a little history lesson, going back almost a century." She turned to Zucker. "Do you want to give them the background?"

"I'm happy to. Because the history *is* fascinating," said Zucker. "Around the time of World War One, in West Africa, there were numerous reports of mysterious deaths. The victims were men, women, and children. They were found with what appeared to be claw marks on their bodies, their throats slashed, their bellies eviscerated. Some of them had been partially consumed. These were all hallmarks of big-cat attacks, and one witness saw what he thought was a leopard fleeing into the bush. Some monstrous cat was thought to be on the prowl, invading villages, attacking people as they slept.

"But local authorities soon realized a real leopard wasn't behind the attacks. The killers were human, members of an ancient cult that goes back centuries. A secret society that identifies so strongly with leopards, its members believe they actually transform into the animal if they drink the victim's blood or eat the victim's flesh. They kill to make themselves powerful, to take on the strength of their totemic animal. To perform these ritual killings, the believer dons a leopard skin and uses steel claws to slash his victim."

"A *leopard* skin?" said Jane.

Zucker nodded. "The theft of that snow leopard pelt takes on new significance, doesn't it?"

"Does this leopard cult still exist in Africa?" asked Tam.

"There are rumors," said Zucker. "During the 1940s, there were dozens of murders in Nigeria attributed to leopard men, a few even committed in broad daylight. Authorities cracked down by bringing in hundreds of additional police officers, who ultimately arrested and executed a number of suspects. The attacks ceased, but was the cult actually wiped out? Or did it simply go underground—and spread?"

"To Boston?" said Crowe.

"Hey, we've had cases involving voodoo and satanists here," said Tam. "Why not leopard men?"

"Those killings by the leopard cult, in Africa," said Frost. "What was the motive?"

"Some of it may have been political. The elimination of rivals," Zucker said. "But that doesn't explain the apparently random killing of women and children. No, there was something else behind it, the same thing that's inspired ritual murder cults around the world. Vast numbers of people have been sacrificed for a variety of beliefs. Whether you kill to terrify your enemies or to appease gods like Zeus or Kali, it all gets down to one thing: *power.*" Zucker looked around the table, and once again Maura felt that cold reptilian kiss. "Add up the peculiarities of these murders and you start to see the common thread: hunting as power. This killer may look perfectly ordinary and work at an ordinary job. These things don't give him the thrill or the sense of power that killing does. So he travels in search of prey, and he has the means and freedom to do so. How many more deaths have been misclassified as wilderness accidents? How many hikers or campers who've gone missing were actually his victims?"

"Leon Gott wasn't hiking or camping," said Crowe. "He was killed in his own garage."

"Perhaps to steal that leopard pelt," said Zucker. "It's this killer's totemic symbol, to be used for ritual purposes."

Frost said, "We know Gott bragged about the snow leopard in online hunting forums. He announced to everyone that he was commissioned to work on one of the rarest animals on earth."

"Which again points to a hunter as your suspect. It makes sense, both symbolically and practically. This killer identifies with leopards, nature's most perfect hunter. He's also comfortable in the wild. But unlike other hunters, his quarry isn't deer or elk; he chooses humans. Hikers or outdoorsmen. It's the ultimate challenge, and he favors wilderness areas to stalk his prey. The mountains of Nevada. The Maine woods. Montana."

"Botswana," said Jane softly.

Zucker frowned at her. "Pardon?"

"Leon Gott's son vanished in Botswana. He was with a group of tourists on safari in a remote area."

At the mention of Elliot Gott, Maura's pulse jolted into a gallop. "Just like the backpackers. Just like the hunters," she said. "They go into the wild, and they're never seen again." *Patterns. It's all about seeing the patterns.* She looked at Jane. "If Elliot Gott was one of his victims, that means this killer was stalking prey six years ago."

Jane nodded. "In Africa."

THE ELECTRONIC FILE HAD been sitting in Jane's laptop for days, sent to her from the Interpol National Central Bureau for Botswana. It was nearly a hundred pages long and contained reports from the Botswana Police Service in Maun, the South African Police Service, and the Johannesburg branch of Interpol. When she'd first received the file, she'd been unconvinced of its relevance to Leon Gott's murder six years later, and had only skimmed through it. But the disappearance of the hikers in Nevada and the hunters in Montana had unsettling parallels to Elliot Gott's doomed safari, and now she settled down at her desk and clicked open the file. As phones rang in the homicide unit and Frost noisily crinkled sandwich wrappers at his desk, Jane once again read the file, but this time more carefully.

The report from Interpol contained a concise summary of the events and the investigation. On August 20 six years ago, seven tourists from four different countries boarded a bush plane in Maun, Botswana, and flew into the Okavango Delta. They were dropped off at a remote airstrip, where they were met by their bush guide and his tracker, both from South Africa. The safari would bring them deep into the Delta, where they would camp at a different location each night, traveling by truck, sleeping in tents, eating wild game. The bush guide's website promised a "true wilderness adventure in one of the last remaining Edens on earth."

For six of those seven unfortunate tourists, the adventure had been a journey into oblivion.

Jane clicked to the next page, a list of the known victims, their nationalities, and whether the remains had been recovered.

Sylvia Van Ofwegen (South Africa). Missing, presumed dead. No remains found.

Vivian Kruiswyk (South Africa). Deceased. Partial remains recovered, confirmed by DNA.

Elliot Gott (USA). Missing, presumed dead. No remains found.

Isao Matsunaga (Japan). Deceased, remains found buried at campsite. Confirmed by DNA.

Keiko Matsunaga (Japan). Missing, presumed dead. No remains found.

Richard Renwick (UK). Missing, presumed dead. No remains found.

Clarence Nghobo (South Africa). Deceased. Partial remains recovered. Confirmed by DNA.

She was about to click to the next page when she suddenly paused, her eye on one particular name on that victim list. A name that stirred a faint memory. Why did it seem familiar? She struggled to retrieve the image it conjured up. Saw, in her mind's eye, another list, with the same name.

She swiveled around to Frost, who was happily devouring his usual turkey sandwich. "You have the Brandon Tyrone file from Maine?"

"Yeah."

"Have you read it yet?"

"Yeah. Not much more to it than what Detective Barber told us."

"There was a list of stolen items they found stashed in Tyrone's garage. Can I see it again?"

Frost set down the sandwich and picked through the stack of files on his desk. "Don't remember anything worth noting on it. Few cameras. Credit cards and an iPod . . ."

"Wasn't there a silver cigarette lighter?"

"Yeah." He pulled out a folder and handed it to her. "So?"

She flipped through the file until she found the list of items that Brandon Tyrone and Nick Thibodeau had stolen from tents and cars at the Maine campground. Scanning down the list, she came to the item she'd remembered. *Cigarette lighter, sterling silver. Engraved with name: R. Renwick.* She looked at her laptop. At the names of the victims in Botswana.

Richard Renwick (UK). Missing, presumed dead.

"Holy shit," she said, and reached for the phone.

"What is it?" said Frost.

"Maybe nothing. Maybe everything." She punched in a phone number.

After three rings a voice answered: "Detective Barber."

"Hey, it's Jane Rizzoli, Boston PD. You know that file you gave us on Brandon Tyrone's murder? There's a list of items that you recovered from Tyrone's garage."

"Yeah. The stuff he and Nick stole from the campground."

"Did you track down the owners of all these items?"

"Most of them. The credit cards, stuff with names attached were easy. After the news broke that we'd recovered stolen goods from the campground, a few other owners filed claims."

"I'm interested in one item in particular. A sterling silver lighter with a name engraved on it."

Barber said, without hesitation: "Nope. Never found the owner."

"You're sure no one claimed it?"

"Yep. I interviewed everyone who came in to claim property, just in case they'd witnessed something at the campground. Maybe saw Nick and Tyrone at the scene. No one ever came for the lighter, which surprised me. It's sterling silver. Someone obviously paid a lot of money for it."

"Did you try tracking down the name engraved on it? R. Renwick?"

Barber laughed. "Try doing a Google search on R. Renwick. You'll turn up about twenty thousand results. All we could do was put it out on the news and hope the owner would call us. Maybe he didn't hear about it. Maybe he never noticed he'd lost it." Barber paused. "Why're you asking about the lighter?"

"That name, R. Renwick. It turned up in another case. A victim, named Richard Renwick."

"Which case?"

"Multiple murders, six years ago. In Botswana."

"Africa?" Barber snorted. "That's a stretch. Don't you think the name's more likely to be a coincidence?"

Maybe, thought Jane as she hung up. Or maybe it was the one thing that tied all these cases together. Six years ago, Richard Renwick was murdered in Africa. A year later, a cigarette lighter with the name *R. Renwick* turned up in Maine. Did it come to the US in a killer's pocket?

"You want to tell me what's going on?" said Frost as she dialed the phone again.

"I need to track someone down."

He looked over her shoulder at the page displayed on her laptop. "The Botswana file? What does it have to do with—"

She held up a hand to silence him as she heard her husband's usual brusque greeting. "Gabriel Dean."

"Hey, Mr. Special Agent. Can you do me a favor?"

"Let me guess," he said with a laugh. "We're out of milk."

"No, I need you to put on your Bureau cap. I want to find someone, and I have no idea where in the world she is. You've got that buddy at Interpol, in South Africa. Henk something."

"Henk Andriessen."

"Yeah, maybe he can help me."

"This is an international case?"

"Multiple murders in Botswana. I told you about it. Those tourists who vanished on safari. The problem is, it's been six years and I'm not sure where this person is now. I'm guessing she's back in London."

"What's her name?"

"Millie Jacobson. The sole survivor."

TWENTY-FOUR

SOUTH AFRICA

EVERY MORNING FOR THE PAST FIVE DAYS, A CARMINE BEE-EATER HAS been visiting the bottlebrush tree. Even as I step into my back garden with a cup of coffee, the bird sits unruffled, a bright red ornament perched among the cheerful tangle of shrubs and flowers. I have worked hard on this garden, digging and composting, weeding and watering, transforming what was once a patch of scrub into my own private retreat. But on this warm November day, I scarcely register the summery blooms or the visiting bee-eater. Last night's phone call has left me too shaken to think of anything else.

Christopher comes out to join me, and wrought iron scrapes across the patio stones as he sits down with his coffee at the garden table. "What are you going to do?" he asks.

I breathe in the scent of flowers and focus on the trellis, gloriously engulfed by vines. "I don't want to go."

"So you've decided."

"Yes." I sigh. "No."

"I can handle this for you. I'll tell them to leave you alone. You've answered all their questions, so what more can they expect?"

"A little courage, maybe," I whisper.

"Good God, Millie. You're the bravest woman I know."

That makes me laugh, because I don't feel brave at all. I feel like a quivering mouse afraid to leave this home where I've felt so safe. I don't want to leave because I know what's out there in the world. I know *who* is out there, and my hands shake at the mere thought of seeing him again. But that is what she's asking me to do, that policewoman who called from Boston. *You know his face. You know how he thinks and how he hunts. We need you to help us catch him.*

Before he kills again.

Christopher reaches across the table to grasp my hands. Only then do I notice how cold I am. How warm he is. "You had the nightmare last night, didn't you?"

"You noticed."

"It's not hard when I'm sleeping right next to you."

"I haven't had the dream in months. I thought I was over it."

"That bloody phone call," he mutters. "You know they don't have anything solid. It's just their theory. They could be looking for someone else entirely."

"They found Richard's lighter."

"You can't be sure it's the same lighter."

"Another R. Renwick?"

"It's a common enough name. Anyway, if it *is* the same lighter, it means the killer's far away. He's moved on, to a different continent."

Which is why I want to stay here, where Johnny can't find me. I'd be insane to go in search of a monster. I drain my coffee cup and stand, the chair squealing across the stones. I don't know what I was thinking, buying wrought-iron garden furniture. Perhaps it was the sense of permanence, the feeling that I could always count on it to last, but the chairs are heavy and hard to move. As I walk back into the house I feel as if I'm hauling yet another burden, heavy as wrought iron, fear-forged and anchoring me to this place. I go to the sink to wash cups and saucers, and tidy up a countertop that is already pristine.

You know how he thinks. And how he hunts.

An image of Johnny Posthumus's face suddenly rears up in my mind, as real as if he's standing right outside my kitchen, staring through the window. I flinch and a spoon clatters to the floor. He's always there, haunting me, just a stray thought away. After I left Botswana, I felt certain he would one day track me down. I'm the only one who lived through it, the one witness he couldn't kill. Surely that's a challenge he can't ignore. But the months became years and I heard nothing from either the Botswana or the South African police, and I began to hope that Johnny was dead. That his bones lie scattered somewhere in the wilderness, like Richard's. Like the others'. That was the only way I could feel safe again, by imagining him dead. These past six years, no one has seen or heard from him, so it was reasonable to believe he'd met his end and couldn't hurt me.

The call from Boston changes everything.

Footsteps thump lightly down the stairs and our daughter Violet comes dancing into the kitchen. At four years old, she's still fearless because we have lied to her. We've told her the world is a place of peace and light and she does not know that monsters are real. Christopher scoops her into his arms, swirls her around, and carries her laughing into the living room for their Saturday-morning ritual of cartoons. The dishes are washed, the coffeepot rinsed, and everything is as it should be, but I pace the kitchen looking for new tasks, anything to distract me.

I sit down at the computer and see a batch of emails that have popped into my inbox since last night, from my sister in London, from the other mothers in Violet's playgroup, from some Nigerian who wants to wire a fortune into my bank account, if only I will give him my number.

And there's one from Detective Jane Rizzoli in Boston. It was sent last night, barely an hour after our phone conversation.

I hesitate to open it, already sensing that this is the point of no return. Once I cross this line, I cannot retreat behind my solid wall of denial. In the next room, Christopher and Violet are laughing at cartoon mayhem while here I sit, my heart pounding, my hand frozen.

I click the mouse. I might as well have lit the fuse on a stick of dynamite, because what shows up on my screen hits me like an explosion. It is a photograph of the sterling silver cigarette lighter that the police found in a bag of stolen goods in Maine. I see the name R. RENWICK, in the Engraver's Bold font that Richard liked so much. But it's the scratch that rivets my gaze. Though faint, it is clearly there, like a single claw mark marring the gloss, slicing across the top of the R. I think of the day it happened, the day it fell out of Richard's pocket in London and hit the pavement. I think of how often I saw him use that lighter, and how pleased he was when I presented it to him on his birthday. Such a vain and pretentious gift that he'd requested, but that was Richard, always wanting to mark his territory, even if that territory is a shiny bit of sterling silver. I remember how he used it to light his Gauloises by the campfire, and the smart click of it snapping shut.

I have no doubt this lighter is indeed his. Somehow the lighter made its way out of the Okavango Delta, carried in a killer's pocket, and across the ocean to America. Now they are asking me to follow in his footsteps.

I read the message that Detective Rizzoli sent along with the photo. *Is this the same lighter? If so, we urgently need to discuss this further. Will you come to Boston?*

The sun shines brightly outside my kitchen window and my garden is at its glorious summer best. In Boston, winter is approaching and I imagine it is chilly and gray, even grayer than London. She has no idea what she's asking of me. She says she knows the facts of what happened, but facts are cold, bloodless things, like bits of metal welded together into a statue, but missing a soul. She can't possibly understand what I went through in the Delta.

I take a deep breath and type my response. *I'm sorry. I can't go to Boston.*

TWENTY-FIVE

As a Marine, Gabriel had acquired more than a few survival skills, and one of the skills that Jane envied was her husband's ability to quickly snatch a few precious hours of sleep whenever the opportunity presented itself. Minutes after the flight attendants dimmed the cabin lights, he reclined his seat, closed his eyes, and dropped off straight into dreamland. Jane sat wide awake, counting the hours until landing, and thinking about Millie Jacobson.

The sole survivor of the doomed safari was not back in London, as Jane had assumed, but was now living in a small town in South Africa's Hex River Valley. After two nightmarish weeks fighting to survive in the bush, caked in mud and eating nothing but reeds and grass, the London-bred bookseller hadn't returned to the city, but had chosen to settle on the same continent that had nearly killed her.

The photos of Millie Jacobson after she'd emerged from the bush made it clear just how hewn to the bone she'd become by the end of her ordeal. Her UK passport photo had shown a dark-haired young woman with blue eyes and a heart-shaped face, pleasantly ordinary, neither pretty nor plain. The photo taken in the hospital during her recovery was of a woman so transformed that Jane could scarcely believe it was the same person. Somewhere in the wild, what had once been Millie Jacobson was cast off like snakeskin, to reveal a bony, sun-blackened creature with haunted eyes.

While everyone else on the plane seemed to be sleeping, Jane once again reviewed the police file of the Botswana safari murders. At the time there'd been substantial publicity in the UK about the case, where Richard Renwick was a popular thriller novelist. In the United States he was not well known and Jane had never read his books, which were described in the London *Times* as "action-packed" and "testosterone-driven." The *Times* article focused almost entirely on Renwick, devoting only two paragraphs to his live-in girlfriend Millie Jacobson. But it was Millie who now captured Jane's full attention, and she stared transfixed at the Interpol file photo of the young woman. It had been taken soon after the ordeal, and in Millie's face Jane saw a reflection of herself not that many years ago. Both of them had been touched by the cold hand of a killer, and survived. That touch was something you never forgot.

She and Gabriel had left Boston on a day of wind-driven sleet and rain, and the weather during their brief stopover in London had been no less gray and wintry. So it was a shock to walk off the plane hours later, into the summery warmth of Cape Town. Here the seasons seemed upside down, and in an airport where everyone else was garbed in shorts and sleeveless dresses, Jane was still wearing the turtleneck and wool sweater that she'd donned in Boston. By the time they claimed their luggage and walked out of immigration, she was sweltering and desperate to strip down to her tank top.

She had just peeled the turtleneck over her face when she heard a man's voice boom out: "Dean the Machine! You've finally made it to Africa!"

"Henk, thanks for meeting us," said Gabriel.

Jane yanked off the turtleneck to find her husband and a blond, buffalo-sized man exchanging back slaps, that peculiarly male greeting that's both attack and embrace.

"Long flight, hey?" Henk said. "But now you'll get to enjoy some warm weather." He turned to Jane with a gaze that made her feel exposed in her thin tank top. His eyes seemed unnaturally pale in the floridly sunburned face, the same silvery shade of blue that she'd once seen in a wolf's eyes. "And you're Jane," he said, holding out a damp and meaty hand. "Henk Andriessen. I'm glad to finally meet the woman who landed the Machine. I didn't think anyone could."

Gabriel laughed. "Jane's not just any woman."

As they shook hands, she could feel Henk taking her measure and she wondered if he'd expected Dean the Machine to have landed someone prettier, someone who didn't walk off the plane looking like a wrung-out rag. "I've heard about you, too," she said. "Something about a boozy night in the Hague twelve years ago."

Henk glanced at Gabriel. "I hope you told her the redacted version."

"You mean there's more to the story than *two men walk into a bar?*"

Henk laughed. "That's *all* you need to know." He reached for her suitcase. "Let me show you to my car."

As they left the terminal, Jane lagged a few paces behind the men, letting them catch up on the latest news in each other's lives. Gabriel had slept almost all the way from London, and he walked with the energetic spring of someone eager to tackle the day. She knew that Henk was a good ten years older than Gabriel, that he was thrice divorced, originally from Brussels, and had worked with South Africa's Interpol branch for the past decade. She also knew of his reputation as a heavy drinker and a ladies' man, and she wondered what sort of trouble he'd dragged Gabriel into on that notorious night in the Hague. Surely Henk was the one who'd done the dragging, because she couldn't imagine her straitlaced husband as a hell-raiser. Just looking at them from behind, she knew which man had discipline in his favor. Gabriel had the lean build of a runner, and he walked with direction and purpose, while Henk's bloated waistline was the mark of uncontrollable appetites. Yet they clearly got on well together, a friendship forged in the heat of murder investigations in Kosovo.

Henk led them to a silver BMW, the favored automotive mascot of every man on the prowl, and he waved at the front seat. "Jane, would you like to ride shotgun?"

"No, I'll let Gabriel have the honors. You two have a lot of mischief to catch up on."

"Not as good a view back there," said Henk as they all buckled their seat belts. "But I guarantee you'll love the view where we're going."

"Where are we going?"

"Table Mountain. You're here for such a short time, and it's the one place you really don't want to miss. Your hotel room probably isn't ready yet anyway, so why don't we head straight for the mountain?"

Gabriel turned to her. "You feel up for it, Jane?"

What she really longed for was a shower and a bed. Her head ached from the blinding sunlight and the inside of her mouth felt like a tar pit, but if Gabriel could launch straight into a day of sightseeing, she'd damn well do her best to keep up with the boys. "Let's do it," she said.

An hour and a half later, they pulled into the parking lot of Table Mountain's lower cableway station. Stepping out of the car, Jane stared up at aerial lines that soared up the side of the mountain. She was not particularly afraid of heights, but the idea of swooping up to that dizzying mountaintop made her stomach drop. Suddenly she was no longer exhausted; all she could think about was cables snapping apart and a two-thousand-foot plunge to death.

"And up there is the view I promised you," said Henk.

"Jesus. There are people hanging off the side of that cliff!" said Jane.

"Table Mountain's a favorite place for rock climbers."

"Are they out of their frigging minds?"

"Oh, we lose a few climbers every year. After you fall from that height, it's not a rescue. It's a body recovery."

"And that's where we're going? Up *there*?"

"Are you afraid of heights?" Those pale wolf eyes turned to her in amusement.

"Trust me, Henk," Gabriel said with a laugh. "Even if she were, she'd never admit it."

And one of these days, pride is going to be the death of me, she thought as they crowded into the cable car with dozens of other tourists. She wondered when the system had last been inspected. Stared hard at the Cableway workers, searching for anyone who was drunk or high or psycho. She counted heads, to be sure they weren't over the posted passenger limit, and hoped they'd made generous weight allowances for men as big as Henk.

Then the cable car swooped into the sky, and all she could focus on was the view.

"Your first look at Africa," said Henk, leaning in to murmur in her ear. "Does it surprise you?"

She swallowed. "It's not what I imagined."

"What did you imagine? Lions and zebras running around everywhere?"

"Well, yeah."

"That's the way most Americans picture Africa. They watch too many nature shows on TV, and when they walk off the plane wearing bush jackets and khaki, they're surprised to find a modern city like Cape Town. Not a zebra in sight, except at the zoo."

"I was kind of hoping to see a zebra."

"Then you should take a few extra days and fly out to the bush."

"I wish we could," she said with a sigh. "But our agencies are keeping us on a tight leash. No time for fun."

The cable car glided to a stop and the doors opened.

"Then let's get some work done, shall we?" said Henk. "There's no reason we can't enjoy the view at the same time."

From the edge of the Table Mountain plateau, Jane stared in wonder as Henk pointed out the landmarks of Cape Town: the rocky outcroppings known as Devil's Peak and Signal Hill, Table Bay, and Robben Island to the north, where Nelson Mandela was imprisoned for nearly two decades.

"So much history here. So many stories I could tell you about this country." Henk turned to her. "But now we get down to business. The Botswana murders."

"Gabriel told me you had a part in the case."

"Not the initial investigation, which took place in Botswana. Interpol became involved only after Botswana police learned that the killer had crossed the border, into this country. He used the credit cards of two of his victims in border towns, at businesses that didn't require PIN numbers. The safari truck was found abandoned outside Johannesburg. Although the crimes were committed in Botswana, Johnny Posthumus is a citizen of South Africa. The case spans multiple countries, which is why Interpol was brought in. We issued a Red Notice for the arrest of Posthumus, but we still have no clue of his whereabouts."

"Has there been any progress at all on the case?"

"Nothing significant. But you have to understand the challenges we face here. There are about fifty murders a day in this country—that's six times the homicide rate in the US. Many cases remain unsolved, the police are overwhelmed, and evidence labs are underfunded. Also, these murders took place in Botswana, a different country. Coordinating between different jurisdictions adds to the difficulties."

"But you're certain that Johnny Posthumus is your man," said Gabriel.

Andriessen paused, and those few seconds of silence spoke louder than any words that might follow. "I have . . . reservations."

"Why?"

"I've delved thoroughly into his past. Johnny Posthumus was born in South Africa, the son of farmers. At age eighteen, he went off to work at a game lodge, in Sabi Sands. He moved on to Mozambique and Botswana, and eventually went solo as an independent guide. There were never any complaints. Through the years, he built a reputation as a reliable man. Except for one drunken brawl, he had no criminal record and no history of violence."

"That you're aware of."

"True, there could be incidents that were never reported. Kill someone in the bush, and the body may never be found. It just troubles me that there were never any warning signs. Nothing in his earlier behavior to indicate that one day, he would bring eight people deep into the Delta and slaughter seven of them."

"According to the sole survivor, that's exactly what happened," said Jane.

"Yes," Henk conceded. "That's what she said."

"Do you have doubts about her?"

"She identified Posthumus based only on a two-year-old passport photo, which was shown to her by the Botswana police. There aren't many other photos of him in existence. Most were lost when his parents' farmhouse burned down seven years ago. Remember, Ms. Jacobson walked out of the bush half dead. After such an ordeal, and with only a passport photo to go on, can her identification of him really be trusted?"

"If the man wasn't Johnny Posthumus, who was he?"

"We know he used his victims' credit cards. He took their passports, and in the few weeks before they were reported missing, he could have assumed their identities. It would allow him to be anyone, to go almost anywhere in the world. Including America."

"And the real Johnny Posthumus? Do you think he's dead?"

"It's only a theory."

"But is there any evidence to back it up? A body? Any remains?"

"Oh, we have thousands of unidentified human remains, from crime scenes around the country. What we lack are the resources to ID them all. Because of the DNA backlog in crime labs, identifying a victim can take months, even years. Posthumus might be among them."

"Or he could be alive and living right now in Boston," said Jane. "He may not have a criminal record, only because he's never made a mistake until Botswana."

"You mean Millie Jacobson."

"He let her escape."

Henk was silent for a moment as he looked out over Table Bay. "At the time, I doubt he considered that a problem. Letting her escape."

"The one woman who could identify him?"

"She was as good as dead. If you stranded any other tourist in the Delta, man or woman, they wouldn't last two days, much less two weeks. She *should* have died out there."

"Why didn't she?"

"Grit? Luck?" He shrugged. "A miracle."

"You've met the woman," said Gabriel. "What did you think of her?"

"It's been a few years since I interviewed her. Her name's not Jacobson now, but DeBruin. She married a South African. I remember her as . . . utterly unremarkable. That was my impression, and to be honest I was surprised. I'd read her statement and I knew what she supposedly survived. I was expecting Superwoman."

Jane frowned. "You don't think her statement was true?"

"That she walked among wild elephants? That she traveled for two weeks through the bush with no food and no weapon? That she survived on nothing more than grass and papyrus stems?" He shook his head. "No wonder the police in Botswana doubted her story at first. Until they confirmed that seven foreigners hadn't boarded their scheduled international flights home. They spoke to the pilot who'd flown the tourists into the bush, asked him why he didn't report them missing. He said he got a call that they were all traveling back to Maun by road instead. It took a few more days before it finally dawned on the Botswana police that Millie Jacobson was telling the truth."

"Yet you seem doubtful."

"Because, when I met her, she struck me as a bit, well . . . troubled."

"How?"

"Reclusive. Not entirely forthcoming. She lives in a small town out in the countryside, where her husband has a farm. She almost never ventures out of her district. She refused to come to Cape Town for the interview. I had to drive to Touws River to meet her."

"We're headed there tomorrow," said Gabriel. "It's the only way she'd agree to see us."

"It's a beautiful drive. Lovely mountains and farms and vineyards. But it *is* a drive. Her husband's a big stern Afrikaner who keeps everyone at bay. Trying to be protective I suppose, but he makes it clear he doesn't want the police upsetting his wife. Before you can talk to her, you'll have to pass muster with him."

"I understand that completely," said Gabriel. "It's what any husband would do."

"Isolate his wife in the middle of nowhere?"

"Keep her safe, in any way he can. Assuming she cooperates." He glanced at Jane. "Because, God knows, not every wife does."

Henk laughed. "Obviously you two have wrestled with that issue."

"Because Jane takes too many damn chances."

"I'm a cop," said Jane. "How am I supposed to take down bad guys if you've got me locked up for safekeeping? Which is what it sounds like this guy's done to his wife. Hidden her away in the country."

"And you'll have to deal with him first," said Henk. "Explain how vital it is that his wife assists you. Convince him that this won't place her in any danger, because that's *all* he cares about."

"It doesn't bother him that Johnny Posthumus might be killing other people right now?"

"He doesn't know those victims. He's protecting his own, and you need to earn his trust."

"Do you think Millie will work with us?" said Gabriel.

"Only to a point, and who can blame her? Think about what it took for her to walk out of the Delta alive. When you survive an ordeal like that, you don't come out the same."

"Some people would come out stronger," said Jane.

"Some are destroyed." Henk shook his head. "Millie, I'm afraid, is now little more than a ghost."

TWENTY-SIX

DESPITE ALL THAT MILLIE JACOBSON HAD ENDURED IN THE BUSH, SHE had not returned to the familiar comforts of London, but had settled in a small town in the Hex River Valley of the Western Cape. If Jane had been the one to survive two hellish weeks in the wilderness, dodging lions and crocodiles, caked in mud, and eating roots and grass, she would have headed straight home to her own bed, in her own neighborhood, with all its urban conveniences. But Millie Jacobson, London bookseller, born and raised in the city, had forsaken everything she'd known, everything she'd been, to live in the remote town of Touws River.

Looking out the car window, Jane could certainly see what might have attracted Millie to this countryside. She saw a landscape of mountains and rivers and farmland, painted in the lush colors of summer. Everything about this country seemed off-kilter to her, from the upside-down season to the northerly direction of the sun, and as they rounded a curve, she suddenly felt dizzy, as if the world had turned on its head. She closed her eyes, waiting for everything to stop spinning.

"Gorgeous countryside. Makes you not want to go home," said Gabriel.

"It's a long way from Boston," she murmured.

"A long way from London, too. But I can see why she might not want to go back."

Jane opened her eyes and squinted at rows and rows of grape-vines, at fruits ripening in the sun. "Well, her husband does come from this area. People do crazy things for love."

"Like packing up and moving to Boston?"

She looked at him. "Do you ever regret it? Leaving Washington to be with me?"

"Let me think about that."

"Gabriel."

He laughed. "Do I regret getting married and having the most adorable kid in the world? What do you think?"

"I think a lot of men wouldn't have made the sacrifice."

"Just keep telling yourself that. It never hurts to have a grateful wife."

She looked out again at the passing vineyards. "Speaking of grate-ful, we're going to owe Mom big-time for babysitting. Think we should ship her a case of South African wine? You know how much she and Vince love . . ." She paused. There was no Vince Korsak in Angela's life anymore, now that her dad was back. She sighed. "I never thought I'd say it, but I miss Korsak."

"Obviously your mom does, too."

"Am I a bad daughter, wishing my dad would go back to his bimbo and leave us alone?"

"You are a good daughter. To your mother."

"Who won't listen to me. She's trying to make everyone happy except herself."

"It's her choice, Jane. You need to respect it, even if you don't understand it."

Just as she didn't understand Millie Jacobson's choice to retreat to this remote corner of a country so far from everything and everyone she'd ever known. On the phone, Millie had made it clear that she would not come to Boston to aid the investigation. She had a four-year-old daughter and a husband who needed her, the standard acceptable excuses that a woman could trot out when she doesn't want to admit her real reasons: that she's terrified of the world. Henk Andriessen had called Millie a ghost, and had warned them that they would never coax her out of Touws River. Nor would Millie's husband ever allow it.

That husband was the first to greet them on the porch when she and Gabriel pulled up to the farmhouse, and a glance at his florid face told Jane they had a challenge ahead. Christopher DeBruin was as burly and intimidating as Henk had described him. He was older than Millie by a decade, his blond hair already half gray, and he stood with arms crossed, an immovable wall of muscle holding off the invaders. As Jane and Gabriel stepped out of their rental car, he did not come down the steps to greet them, but waited for his unwelcome guests to approach.

"Mr. DeBruin?" said Gabriel.

A nod, nothing more.

"I'm Special Agent Gabriel Dean with the FBI. This is Detective Jane Rizzoli, Boston PD."

"They sent two of you all this way, did they?"

"This investigation crosses both state and international borders. A number of different agencies are involved."

"And you think it all leads to my wife."

"We think she's key to the case."

"And this concerns me how?"

Two men and too much damn testosterone, thought Jane. She stepped forward and DeBruin frowned at her, as if not certain how to rebuff a woman.

"We've come a long way, Mr. DeBruin," she said quietly. "Please, may we speak to Millie?"

He eyed her for a moment. "She went to pick up our daughter."

"When will she be back?"

"A while." Grudgingly he opened the front door. "You might as well come in. Some things need to be said first."

They followed him into the farmhouse, and Jane saw wide-plank floors and massive ceiling beams. This home had history in its bones, from the hand-hewn banister to the antique Dutch tiles on the hearth. DeBruin offered them neither coffee nor tea, but brusquely waved them toward a sofa. He settled into the armchair facing them.

"Millie feels safe here," he said. "We've made a good life together on this farm. We have a daughter. She's only four years old. Now you want to change everything."

"She could make all the difference in our investigation," said Jane.

"You don't know what you're asking of her. She hasn't slept through the night since your first phone call. She wakes up screaming. She won't even leave this valley, and now you expect her to go all the way to Boston?"

"Boston PD will look after her, I promise. She'll be perfectly safe."

"Safe? Do you have any idea how hard it is for her to feel safe even here?" He snorted. "Of course you don't. You don't know what she went through in the bush."

"We read her statement."

"Statement? As if a few typed pages can tell the whole story? I was there, the day she walked out of the bush. I was staying at a game lodge in the Delta, spending my holiday watching elephants. Every afternoon, we were served tea on the veranda, where we could watch the animals drinking at the river. That day, I saw a creature I'd never seen before come out of the bush. So thin, it looked like a bundle of twigs caked in mud. As we watched, not believing our eyes, it crossed the lawn and came up the steps. There we were, with our fine china cups and saucers, our fussy little cakes and sandwiches. And this creature walks up to me, looks me straight in the eye, and says: 'Are you real? Or am I in heaven?' I told her, if this is heaven, then they've sent me to the wrong place. And that's when she dropped to her knees and started weeping. Because she knew her nightmare was over. She knew she was safe." DeBruin gave Jane a hard, penetrating look. "I swore to her that I'd keep her safe. Through thick and thin."

"So will Boston PD, sir," said Jane. "If we can just convince you to let her—"

"It's not me you need to convince. It's my wife." He glanced out the window as a car pulled into the driveway. "She's here."

They waited in silence as a key grated in the lock, then footsteps pattered into the house and a little girl came running into the living room. Like her father she was blond and sturdy, with the healthy pink cheeks of a child who lives her life in sunshine. She gave the two visitors scarcely a glance and ran straight into her father's arms.

"There you are, Violet!" DeBruin said, lifting his daughter onto his lap. "How was riding today?"

"He bit me."

"The pony did?"

"I gave him an apple and he bit my finger."

"I'm sure he didn't mean to. That's why I tell you to keep your hand flat."

"I'm not giving him any more apples."

"Yah, that will teach pony a lesson, hey?" He looked up, grinning, and suddenly went still as he saw his wife standing in the doorway.

Unlike her husband and daughter, Millie had dark hair and it was pulled back in a ponytail, making her face appear startlingly thin and angular, her cheeks hollow, her blue eyes smudged by shadows. She gave their visitors a smile, but there was no disguising the apprehension in her gaze.

"Millie, these are the people from Boston," said DeBruin.

Both Jane and Gabriel stood to introduce themselves. Shaking Millie's hand was like grasping icicles, so stiff and chilled were her fingers.

"Thank you for seeing us," said Jane as they all sat down again.

"Have you been to Africa before?" Millie asked.

"First time for both of us. It's beautiful here. So is your home."

"This farm's been in Chris's family for generations. He should give you a tour later." Millie paused, as if the effort to keep up even trivial conversation exhausted her. Her gaze dropped to the empty coffee table and she frowned. "Did you not offer them tea, Chris?"

At once DeBruin jumped to his feet. "Oh yah, sorry. Completely forgot about that." He took his daughter's hand. "Violet, come help your silly dad."

In silence Millie watched her husband and daughter leave. Only when she heard the faint clang of the teakettle and water running in the kitchen did she say: "I haven't changed my mind about going to Boston. I suppose Chris told you that."

"In so many words," said Jane.

"I'm afraid this is a waste of your time. Coming all this way, just to hear me repeat what I told you on the phone."

"We needed to meet you."

"Why? To see for yourselves that I'm not a lunatic? That everything I told the police six years ago actually happened?" Millie glanced at Gabriel, then back at Jane. The phone calls had already established a link between the women, and Gabriel stayed silent, allowing Jane to take the lead.

"We have no doubt it happened to you," said Jane.

Millie looked down at her hands, folded in her lap, and said softly: "Six years ago, the police didn't believe me. Not at first. When I told them my story, from my hospital bed, I could see the doubt in their eyes. A clueless city girl, surviving two weeks alone in the bush? They thought I'd wandered away from some other game lodge and gotten lost and delirious in the heat. They said the pills I took for malaria might have made me psychotic or confused. That it happens to tourists all the time. They said my story didn't ring true because anyone else would have starved to death. Or been torn apart by lions or hyenas. Or trampled by elephants. And how did I know that I could stay alive eating papyrus reeds, the way the natives do? They couldn't believe I survived because of pure dumb luck. But that's exactly what it was. It was luck that I chose to head downriver and ended up at the tourist lodge. Luck that I didn't poison myself on some wild berry or bark, but ate the most nutritious reed I could have chosen. Luck that after two weeks in the bush, I walked out alive. The police said it wasn't possible." She took a deep breath. "Yet I did it."

"I think you're wrong, Millie," said Jane. "It wasn't luck, it was *you.* We read your account of what happened. How you slept in the trees every night. How you followed the river and kept walking, even when you were beyond exhausted. Somehow you found the will to survive when almost everyone else would have given up."

"No," said Millie softly. "It was the bush that chose to spare me." She gazed out the window at a majestic tree, its branches spread like protective arms embracing all who stood beneath it. "The land is a living, breathing thing. It decides if you should live or die. At night, in the dark, I could hear its heartbeat, the way a baby hears the heartbeat of its mother. And every morning, I woke up wondering if the land would let me live through the day. That's the only way I could have walked out alive. Because it let me. It protected me." She looked at Jane. "From him."

"Johnny Posthumus."

Millie nodded. "By the time they finally started searching for Johnny, it was too late. He'd had plenty of time to vanish. Weeks later, they found the truck parked in Johannesburg."

"The same truck that wouldn't start in the bush."

"Yes. A mechanic explained to me later how it could be done. How to temporarily disable a car without anyone spotting the problem. Something about the fuse box and plastic relays."

Jane looked at Gabriel, and he nodded.

"Unplug the start or fuel pump relay," he said. "It wouldn't be easy to detect. And it's reversible."

"He made us think we were stranded," said Millie. "He trapped us there, so he could kill us one by one. First, Clarence. Then Isao. Elliot would have been next. He was taking out the men first, leaving the women for last. We thought we were on safari, but we were really on Johnny's hunting trip. And we were the game." Millie took a breath and it came out a shudder. "The night he killed the others, I ran. I had no idea where I was going. We were miles from the nearest road, miles from the airstrip. He knew there was no chance I'd survive, so he simply packed up camp and drove away, leaving the bodies to the animals. Everything else, he took. Our wallets, cameras, passports. The police say he used Richard's credit card to buy petrol in Maun. And Elliot's card to buy supplies in Gaborone. Then he crossed the border into South Africa, where he vanished. Who knows where he went next. With our passports and credit cards, he could have dyed his hair brown and passed for Richard. Could have flown to London and breezed straight through immigration." She hugged herself. "He could have turned up on my doorstep."

Gabriel said: "The UK has no record of Richard Renwick reentering the country."

"What if he's killed other people, taken other identities? He could go anywhere, be anyone."

"Are you certain your guide was actually Johnny Posthumus?"

"The police showed me his passport photo, taken just two years earlier. It was the same man."

"There are very few verified photos of him in existence. You saw only that one."

"You think I made a mistake?"

"You know how people can look different, sometimes completely different, from one photo to the next."

"If it wasn't Johnny, who else would he be?"

"An impostor."

She stared at Gabriel, struck dumb by the possibility.

They heard the clatter of china as DeBruin returned from the kitchen with the tea tray. Noticing the silence in the room, he quietly set the tray down on the coffee table and gave his wife a searching look.

"Can I pour the tea, Mummy?" said Violet. "I promise I won't spill it."

"No, darling. Mummy needs to pour it this time. Maybe you and Daddy can go watch some TV." She gave her husband a pleading look.

DeBruin took their daughter's hand. "Let's go see what's on, hey?" he said and led her out.

A moment later they heard the TV come on in the next room with a blast of jarringly cheerful music. Though the tea tray sat on the table in front of her, Millie made no move to pour, but sat with arms wrapped around herself, still chilled by this new uncertainty.

"Henk Andriessen from Interpol told us that you were still hospitalized when the police showed you the photo. You were still weak, still recovering. And it had been weeks since you'd last seen the killer."

"You think I made a mistake," she said softly.

"Witnesses frequently make mistakes," said Gabriel. "They misremember details or they forget faces."

Jane thought of all the well-meaning eyewitnesses who'd so confidently pointed to the wrong suspects, or offered descriptions that later proved wildly inaccurate. The human mind was expert at filling in missing details and confidently turning them into facts, even if those facts were merely imagined.

"You're trying to make me doubt myself," said Millie. "But the photo they showed me *was* Johnny. I remember every detail of his face." She looked back and forth at Jane and Gabriel. "Maybe he goes by a different name now. But wherever he is, whatever he calls himself, I know he hasn't forgotten me, either."

They heard Violet give a squeal of laughter as the TV played its relentlessly cheerful music. But in here, a chill had settled so deeply into the room that even the afternoon sunlight streaming in the window could not dispel it.

"That's why you didn't return to London," said Jane.

"Johnny knew where I lived, where I worked. He knew how to find me. I couldn't go back." Millie looked toward the sound of her daughter's laughter. "And there was Christopher."

"He told us how you met."

"After I walked out of the bush, he was the one who stayed with me. Who sat by my hospital bed day after day. He's the one who made me feel safe. The only one." She looked at Jane. "Why would I go back to London?"

"Isn't your sister there?"

"But this is my home now. It's where I belong." She looked out the window, at the tree with the all-embracing branches. "Africa changed me. Out there, in the bush, I lost bits and pieces of myself. It wears you away like a grinding stone, makes you shed everything that's unnecessary. It forces you to face who you really are. When I first got there, I was just a silly girl. I fussed over shoes and purses and face creams. I wasted years, waiting for Richard to marry me. I thought all I needed was a wedding ring to make me happy. But then, just when I thought I was dying, I found myself. My real self. I left the old Millie out there, and I don't miss her. This is my life right here, in Touws River."

"Where you still have nightmares."

Millie blinked. "Chris told you?"

"He told us you've been waking up screaming."

"Because you called me. That's why it all started again, because *you* brought it back."

"Which means it's still there, Millie. You haven't really left it behind."

"I was doing fine."

"Were you?" Jane looked around the room at the neatly arranged books on the shelves, at the vase of flowers precisely centered on the mantelpiece. "Or is this just a place to hide from the world?"

"After what happened to me, wouldn't you hide?"

"I'd want to feel safe again. The only way to do that is to find this man and lock him away."

"That's your job, Detective. Not mine. I'll help you as much as I'm able to. I'll look at whatever photos you've brought. I'll answer all your questions. But I won't go to Boston. I won't leave my home."

"And there's no way we can change your mind?"

Millie looked straight at her. "None whatsoever."

TWENTY-SEVEN

THEY ARE STAYING IN OUR GUEST BEDROOM TONIGHT. IF ANYTHING should make me feel safe, it would be having both a policewoman and a US federal agent under my roof, yet once again I cannot fall asleep. Chris lies breathing deeply beside me, a warm, reassuring hulk in the darkness. What luxury to sleep so soundly every night, to awake refreshed in the morning, free of the smothering cobwebs of bad dreams.

He doesn't stir as I climb out of bed, reach for a robe, and slip out of our room.

Down the hall, I pass the guest bedroom where Detective Rizzoli and her husband are staying. Odd that I did not immediately pick up on the fact they were married to each other, until after I'd spent the whole afternoon with them. They'd shown me photo after photo of possible suspects on a laptop computer. So many faces, so many men. By the time it was dinner hour, the photos were all blending together. I rubbed my tired eyes and when I opened them again, I saw Agent Dean's hand resting on Detective Rizzoli's shoulder. It was not just a platonic pat, but the caress of a man who cared about this woman.

That's when the other details came into focus: the matching wedding rings. The way they finished each other's sentences. The fact he didn't have to ask, but simply stirred a teaspoon of sugar into her coffee before handing it to her.

On the surface, they'd been strictly business, especially the aloof and chilly Gabriel Dean. But over dinner, after a few glasses of wine, they started to talk about their marriage and their daughter and the life they shared in Boston. A complicated life, I think, because of their demanding jobs. Now their work has brought them all the way to my remote corner of the Western Cape.

I tiptoe past their closed door into the kitchen and pour a generous splash of scotch into a glass. Just enough to make me drowsy, but not drunk. I know by experience that while a little scotch will help me fall asleep, too much will make me wake up in a few hours with nightmares. I settle into a chair at the kitchen table and slowly nurse the drink as the clock ticks loudly on the wall. If Chris were awake, we'd take our drinks outside to the garden and sit together in the moonlight to enjoy the scent of night-blooming jasmine. I never go out in the dark by myself. Chris tells me I'm the bravest woman he knows, but courage wasn't what kept me alive in Botswana. Even the lowliest creature does not want to die and will fight to stay alive; in that way, I am no braver than any rabbit or sparrow.

A noise behind me makes me bolt straight in my chair. I turn to see Detective Rizzoli walk barefoot into the kitchen. Her uncombed hair looks like a wild crown of black thorns and she's dressed in an oversized T-shirt and men's boxer shorts.

"Sorry if I startled you," she says. "I just came out for a glass of water."

"I can offer you something stronger, if you'd like."

She eyes my glass of scotch. "Well, I wouldn't want you to drink alone." She pours herself a glass, adds an equal part of water, and settles into the chair across from me. "So do you do this often?"

"Do what?"

"Drink alone."

"It helps me fall asleep."

"Having trouble with that, huh?"

"You already know I do." I take another sip, but it doesn't help me relax because she's watching me with dark, probing eyes. "Why aren't *you* asleep?"

"Jet lag. It's six P.M. Boston time, and my body refuses to be fooled." She takes a sip and doesn't flinch in the least at the bite of the scotch. "Thank you again for offering your guest room."

"We couldn't have you driving all the way back to Cape Town tonight. Not after the hours you spent with me. I hope you don't have to fly back to the States right away. It'd be a shame if you didn't see some of the country."

"We get one more night in Cape Town tomorrow."

"Only one?"

"I had a tough enough time convincing my boss to approve this trip. We're all about cost cutting these days. God forbid we have any fun on their dime."

I look down at my scotch, which gleams like liquid amber. "Do you actually like your work?"

"It's what I always wanted to do."

"Catch killers?" I shake my head. "I don't think I'd be able to stomach it. Seeing the things you see. Coming face-to-face every day with what people are capable of."

"That's something you've already seen firsthand."

"And I never want to see it again." I tip the rest of the drink into my mouth and swallow it in one gulp. Suddenly it's not enough, not nearly enough to settle my nerves. I get up to pour myself a refill.

"I used to have nightmares, too," she says.

"No wonder, with your line of work."

"I got over them. You can, too."

"How?"

"The same way I did. Slay the monster. Put him away where he can't hurt you or anyone else."

I laugh as I recork the bottle. "Do I look like a policewoman?"

"You look like a woman who's terrified of just going to sleep."

I set the bottle down on the counter and turn to her. "You didn't live through what I did. You may hunt killers, but they aren't hunting *you.*"

"You're wrong, Millie," she says quietly. "I know exactly what you're living through. Because I've been hunted, too." She fixes me with a steady gaze as I sink back into the chair.

"What happened?" I ask.

"It was several years ago, around the time I met my husband. I was searching for a man who'd killed a number of women. Considering what this killer did to them, I'm not sure I'd call him human, but some other species. A creature who fed off pain and fear. Who took pleasure in their terror. The more afraid you were, the more he desired you." She lifts the glass to her lips, takes a deep swallow. "And he knew I was afraid."

I'm surprised she admits it, this woman who projects such fearlessness. Over dinner she'd described how she'd kicked down her first door, how she had chased killers across rooftops and into dark alleys. Now, sitting in her T-shirt and boxer shorts, with her messy mop of dark hair, she looks like any other woman. Small, vulnerable. Defeatable.

"You were his target?" I ask.

"Yeah. Lucky me."

"Why you?"

"Because he'd trapped me once before. Had me right where he wanted me." She raises her hands and shows me her scarred palms. "He did this. With scalpels."

Earlier today, I had noticed those peculiarly placed scars, like healed wounds of a crucifixion. I stare at them in horror because I now know how those wounds were inflicted.

"Even after he went to prison, even though I knew he couldn't reach me, I had nightmares about what he almost did to me. How could I forget, when I carry these permanent reminders of him on my hands? The bad dreams did start to fade, though. After a year, I hardly dreamed of him at all, and that should have been the end of it. It *would* have been the end of it."

"Why wasn't it?"

"Because he escaped." She meets my gaze, and I see my own fear reflected in her eyes. I see a woman who knows what it means to live in a killer's crosshairs, without any idea when the trigger will be pulled. "That's when my nightmares started again."

I stand up and get the bottle of scotch. Bring it back to the table and set it between us. "For the nightmares," I offer.

"You can't drink them away, Millie. No matter how many bottles you guzzle."

"What do you suggest I do?"

"The same thing I did. Hunt down the monster who's been chasing you in your dreams. Cut him to pieces and bury him. Then, and only then, will you sleep soundly again."

"And do you sleep soundly?"

"Yes. But only because I chose not to run and hide. I knew that as long as he was out there, circling me, I'd never rest easy. So *I* became the hunter. Gabriel knew I was putting myself at risk and he tried to keep me off the case, but I had to be part of it. For my own sanity, I had to be in the fight, not hiding behind locked doors, waiting for the attack."

"And your husband didn't try to stop you?"

"Oh, we weren't married then, so he couldn't stop me." She laughs. "Not that he can now, either. Though he tries his hardest to keep me in line."

I think of Chris, peacefully snoring in our bed. How he bundled me up and brought me to this farm to keep me safe. "That's what my husband tries to do."

"Keep you behind a locked door?"

"To protect me."

"Yet you don't feel safe. Even six years later."

"I do feel safe here. At least, I did. Until *you* brought it back into my life."

"I'm just doing my job, Millie. Don't blame me. I didn't put those nightmares in your head. I'm not the one who made you a prisoner."

"I'm *not* a prisoner."

"Aren't you?"

We stare at each other across the table. She has dark, luminous eyes. Dangerous eyes that see straight through my skull, to the deepest folds of my brain where I hide my secret terrors. I can't deny anything she's said. I *am* a prisoner. I'm not merely avoiding the world; I'm cowering from it.

"It doesn't have to be this way," she says.

I don't answer at first. Instead I look down at the glass, which I'm cradling with both hands. I want to take another sip, but I know it will ease the fear for only a few hours. Like anesthesia, it eventually wears off.

"Tell me how you did it," I say. "How you fought back."

She shrugs. "I didn't have a choice, in the end."

"You chose to fight."

"No, I mean I *really* didn't have a choice. You see, after he escaped from prison, I knew I had to hunt him down. Gabriel, my colleagues at Boston PD, they all tried to keep me out of it, but I couldn't be sidelined. I knew that killer better than anyone else did. I'd looked into his eyes, and I'd seen the beast. I understood him—what thrilled him, what he craved, how he stalked his prey. The only way I'd sleep soundly again was to hunt him down. The problem was, he was also hunting *me.* We were two enemies locked in mortal combat, and one of us had to go down." She pauses, takes a sip of scotch. "He struck first."

"What happened?"

"I was cornered when I least expected it. Taken to a place where no one would ever find me. The worst part was, he wasn't alone. He had a friend."

Her voice is so soft I have to lean in to hear her. Outside, insects sing in the night garden, but in my kitchen it is quiet, so quiet. I think of all my fears multiplied by two. Two Johnnys hunting me. I don't know how this woman can sit here so calmly and tell me her story.

"They had me where they wanted me," she says. "There was no one to rescue me, no one who'd swoop in to save the day. It was me against them." She took a breath and straightened in her chair. "And I won. Just like you can, Millie. You can kill that monster."

"Is that what *you* did?"

"He might as well be dead. My bullet severed his spinal cord, and now he's trapped in a place he'll never escape—his own body. Paralyzed from the neck down. And his friend is rotting in a grave." Her smile is weirdly at odds with what she's just described, but when you've triumphed over monsters, you deserve a grin of victory. "And that night, I slept better than I had in a year."

I hunch at the table, saying nothing. Of course I know why she's told me her story, but it doesn't work on me. You can't force a person to be brave if they don't already have it in them. I'm alive merely because I was too terrified to die, which makes me a coward, really. The woman who kept walking and walking, past elephants and crocodiles, the woman blessed with a sturdy pair of legs and more than her share of luck.

She yawns and stands up. "I think I'll head back to bed. I hope we can talk more about this tomorrow."

"I won't change my mind. I can't come to Boston."

"Even though you could make a difference? You *know* this killer better than anyone else does."

"And he knows me. I'm the one who escaped, the one he's searching for. I'm his unicorn, the creature doomed to be hunted into extinction."

"We'll keep you safe. I promise."

"Six years ago, in the bush, I found out what it's like to die." I shake my head. "Don't ask me to die again."

DESPITE ALL THE SCOTCH I downed, or maybe because of it, I dream once again about Johnny.

He stands before me, reaching out to me with both hands, begging me to run to him. All around us are lions closing in for the kill, and I must make my choice. How I want to trust Johnny, as I trusted him once before! I never truly believed he was a killer, and now he stands before me, broad-shouldered and golden-haired. *Come to me, Millie. I'll keep you safe.* In joy I run to him, hungry for his touch. But just as I step into his arms, his mouth transforms into jaws that open wide, baring bloody teeth ready to devour me.

I lurch awake, screaming.

I sit up on the side of the bed, my head in my hands. Chris rubs my back, trying to calm me. Even as the sweat cools, chilling my skin, my heart is still hammering inside my chest. He murmurs, "You're fine, Millie, you're safe," but I know I am not fine. I am a cracked porcelain doll ready to shatter apart with the lightest tap. The passage of six years has not made me whole again, and it's clear to me that I will never be whole. Not until Johnny is in prison—or dead.

I lift my head and look at Chris. "I can't go on like this. *We* can't."

He gives a deep sigh. "I know."

"I don't want to, but I have to do this."

"Then we'll all go with you to Boston. You won't be alone."

"No. *No.* I don't want Violet anywhere near him. I want her right here, where I know she's safe. And you're the only one I trust to take care of her."

"But who'll take care of *you*?"

"They will. You heard them say they won't let anything happen to me."

"And you trust them?"

"Why shouldn't I?"

"Because you're just a tool for them, a means to an end. They don't care about you. They only want to catch *him.*"

"That's what I want, too. I can help them do it."

"By letting him catch a whiff of your scent? What if they can't capture him? What if he turns the tables and follows you back here?"

That's a possibility I hadn't considered. I think of the nightmare I just awoke from. Johnny beckoning, promising safety, just before his jaws open wide. It's my subconscious warning me to stay away. But if I do stay away, nothing changes, nothing heals. I will always be that cracked porcelain doll.

"I have no choice," I say. "I have to trust them."

"You can choose not to go."

I reach for his hand. It's a farmer's hand, large and callused, strong enough to wrestle sheep to the ground and gentle enough to comb a little girl's hair. "I need to finish this, darling. I'm going to Boston."

CHRISTOPHER HAS A LIST of demands, and he presents them to Detective Rizzoli and Agent Dean with the glow of brimstone in his eyes.

"You will check in with me every day, so I know she's fine," he orders them. "I want to know that she's healthy and safe. I want to know if she's homesick. I want to know if she sneezes."

"Please, Chris." I sigh. "I'm not going to the moon."

"The moon might be safer."

"You have my word, we'll look after her, Mr. DeBruin," says Detective Rizzoli. "We're not asking her to strap on a gun. She's merely consulting with our team of detectives and our forensic psychologist. She'll be away for a week, maybe two at the most."

"I don't want her sitting alone in some hotel room. I want her to stay with someone. A proper home, where she won't feel isolated."

Detective Rizzoli glances at her husband. "I'm sure we can come up with some sort of arrangement."

"Where?"

"I need to make a phone call first. Find out if the home I'm thinking of will work out."

"Whose home?"

"Someone I trust. A friend."

"Before Millie gets on that plane, I want you to confirm it."

"We'll have all the details arranged before we leave Cape Town."

Chris studies their faces for a moment, searching for reasons not to trust them. My husband is innately skeptical of people; it comes from growing up with an unreliable father and a mother who abandoned him when he was seven. He always fears he'll lose the people he loves, and now he's afraid of losing me.

"Everything will be fine, darling," I say, sounding more confident than I actually feel. "They know exactly what they're doing."

TWENTY-EIGHT

BOSTON

MAURA SET A VASE OF YELLOW ROSES ON THE DRESSER AND TOOK one last glance around her guest bedroom. The white duvet was freshly laundered, the Turkish rug thoroughly vacuumed, and the bathroom supplied with fluffy white towels. The last time anyone had slept in this room was in August, when seventeen-year-old Julian Perkins had visited during his summer break from school. Since his departure, she'd hardly stepped into this room. Now she gave it a critical once-over, to confirm that all was ready for her houseguest. The window had a view of her back garden, but on this late-November afternoon, what she saw was a dreary landscape of bare perennials and brown grass. At least there was a bright touch of spring in the painting of luscious pink peonies hanging over the bed, and on the dresser with that vase of yellow roses. A cheerful welcome for a guest on a grim mission.

Jane had emailed to explain the situation, and Maura had read Millie's file, so she knew what to expect. But when the doorbell rang and she laid eyes on Millie for the first time, she was taken aback by how haggard the woman looked. It was a long journey from Cape Town and

Jane looked bedraggled as well, but Millie appeared frail as ectoplasm, her eyes hollow, her thin frame almost lost in her oversized sweater.

"Welcome to Boston," said Maura as they came into the house, Jane carrying Millie's suitcase. "I apologize for the weather."

Millie managed a wan smile. "I didn't expect it to be so cold." She looked down sheepishly at her enormous sweater. "I bought this at the airport. I think I could fit another woman in here."

"You must be exhausted. Would you like a cup of tea?"

"That would be lovely, but first I think I need to use the toilet."

"Your room's down the hall, on the right, and you have your own bathroom. Please, take your time to get settled in. The tea can always wait."

"Thank you." Millie took her suitcase. "I'll be a few minutes."

Maura and Jane waited until they heard Millie's bedroom door close. Then Jane said: "You sure this is okay? I tried to come up with another solution, but our apartment's too small."

"It's perfectly fine, Jane. You said it's only for a week, and you can't stick that poor woman in a hotel."

"Well, I do appreciate it. The only alternative was my mom's house, but it's a loony bin these days, with Dad driving her nuts."

"How *are* things with your mother?"

"Besides her being psychotically depressed?" Jane shook her head. "I'm waiting for her to get up the nerve and kick him out. The trouble is, she tries so hard to make everyone else happy, she forgets all about herself." Jane sighed. "My mom, the saint."

Something my mother will never be, thought Maura. She thought about the last time she'd visited Amalthea in prison. Remembered the woman's soulless eyes, her calculating gaze. Even then the tumor must have been incubating inside Amalthea, evil within evil, like poisonous nesting dolls. With cancer now consuming her, had she come to feel remorse? For such a creature, was redemption even possible? In a few months, six at the most, those eyes would go dark forever. *And I will always wonder.*

Jane looked at her watch. "I've got to go. Tell Millie I'll pick her up around ten tomorrow, for the team meeting. I've asked Brookline PD to send a cruiser by your house every so often, to keep an eye on things."

"Is that necessary? No one knows she's here."

"It's all about making her feel safe. It was a struggle just to get her here, Maura. As far as she's concerned, we've brought her straight to the beast's lair."

"It may be true."

"But we need her. We just have to keep her comfortable, so she doesn't jump on a plane home."

"I don't mind a houseguest," said Maura. She glanced down at the cat, who chose that instant to jump onto the coffee table. "Although *this* particular houseguest I'd love to get rid of." She plucked up the cat and dropped him back on the floor.

"You two still not bonding, huh?"

"Oh, he's bonded all right. To my can opener." In disgust, Maura clapped cat hair from her hands. "So what do you make of her?"

Jane glanced toward the hallway and said quietly: "She's scared, and I can't blame her. She's the only one who walked out alive, the only one who can ID him in court. Six years later, he's still giving her nightmares."

"It's not hard to understand. You and I have been in her shoes." She didn't need to elaborate; they both knew what it was like to be hunted, to lie sleepless in your own bed, listening for the shattering of a window, the turn of the doorknob. They were part of the same unfortunate sisterhood of women who have been stalked by killers.

"She's going to face a lot of questions tomorrow, be asked to relive some painful memories," said Jane. "Make sure she gets a good night's sleep." As she stepped out the front door to leave, her cell phone rang and she paused on the porch to answer it. "Hey, Tam, we just got in. I'm heading over to catch up on . . ." She halted on the porch. "What? Are you sure?"

Maura watched as Jane hung up and stood staring at the phone as if it had just betrayed her. "What is it?"

Jane turned to face her. "We have a problem. Remember Jane Doe?"

"The bones from the backyard?"

"You had me convinced she was killed by Leopard Man."

"I still believe it. The claw marks on her skull. The evidence of evisceration. The nylon cord. It all fits the picture."

"The problem is, she's just been identified, and it's confirmed by DNA. Her name was Natalie Toombs, twenty years old. She was a coed at Curry College. White female, five foot three."

"That's all consistent with the skeletal remains I examined. What's the problem?"

"Natalie vanished fourteen years ago."

Maura stared at her. "Fourteen years? Do we know where Johnny Posthumus was then?"

"Working at a bush lodge in South Africa." Jane shook her head. "He couldn't have killed Natalie."

"THIS SHOOTS YOUR ALL-POWERFUL Leopard Man theory all to hell, Rizzoli," said Darren Crowe. "Fourteen years ago, when Natalie Toombs vanished in Boston, this guy was working in Sabi Sands, South Africa. It's all documented in the Interpol report. His employee records from the bush lodge, a log of his hours and pay stubs. Obviously, he didn't kill Natalie. Which means you brought that witness all the way here from South Africa for nothing."

Still groggy from a bad night's sleep, Jane tried to focus on her laptop. She'd awakened disoriented that morning, had downed two cups of coffee to kick-start her brain before this team conference, but the deluge of new facts left her struggling to catch up. She felt the other three detectives watching her as she clicked through pages that confirmed what Tam had told her yesterday over the phone. Natalie Toombs, formerly referred to as Jane Doe, had been a twenty-year-old English major at Curry College, barely two miles from where her bones were found buried. Natalie had lived in an off-campus rental house with two other coeds, who described her as outgoing, athletic, and a nature lover. She was last seen on a Saturday afternoon, her backpack full of books, leaving for a study date with someone named Ted, whom neither housemate had ever met.

The next day, the housemates reported her missing.

For fourteen years, the case had languished in the national missing persons database, along with thousands of other unsolved disappearances. Her mother, who'd since passed away, had provided the FBI with a DNA sample, in the event her daughter's remains ever turned up. It was this DNA that confirmed the bones dug up in the backyard construction site were indeed Natalie's.

Jane looked at Frost, who gave an apologetic shake of the head. "It's hard to argue with the facts," he said, sounding pained. It always hurt to admit when Crowe was right.

"You wasted a nice chunk of Boston PD change, flying that witness here from South Africa," said Crowe. "Good job, Rizzoli."

"But there's physical evidence linking at least *one* murder to Botswana," she pointed out. "That cigarette lighter. We know it belonged to Richard Renwick. How did it get from Africa to Maine, unless the killer carried it?"

"Who knows how many hands it's passed through in the last six years? It could've gotten here in the pocket of some innocent tourist who picked it up God knows where. Any way you look at it, it's clear that Natalie Toombs wasn't killed by Johnny Posthumus. Her death predates all these other cases by nearly a decade. I'm calling it quits on our joint investigation. You keep looking for your Leopard Man, Rizzoli, and we'll look for our perp. 'Cause I don't think there's any connection between our cases." He turned to his partner. "Come on, Tam."

"Millie DeBruin came all the way from Cape Town," said Jane. "She's waiting with Dr. Zucker right now. At least listen to her."

"Why?"

"What if there *is* only one killer? What if he moves across states, across international borders, by assuming other identities?"

"Wait. Is this some *new* theory?" Crowe laughed. "An impostor who kills under other people's names?"

"Henk Andriessen, our contact at Interpol, was the first person to suggest the possibility. Henk was bothered by the fact that Johnny Posthumus had no criminal record, no history of violence. He had a reputation as a top-notch safari guide, respected by his colleagues. What if the man who took those seven tourists into the bush *wasn't* Johnny? None of these tourists had ever met him before. The African tracker had never worked with him before. Another man could have taken the real Johnny's place."

"An impostor? Then where's the real Johnny?"

"He'd have to be dead."

There was silence at the table as her three colleagues digested this new possibility.

"I'd say this puts you back at square one," said Crowe. "Looking for a killer with no name, no identity. Good luck."

"Maybe we don't have a name," said Jane, "but we do have a face. And we have someone who's seen it."

"Your witness identified Johnny Posthumus."

"Based on a single passport photo. We all know that photos can lie."

"So can witnesses."

"Millie isn't a liar," Jane shot back. "She went through hell and she didn't even want to come here. But she's sitting out there with Dr. Zucker right now. The least you can do is listen to her."

"Okay." Crowe sighed, sinking back into his chair. "I'll play along for now. Might as well hear what she has to say."

Jane went to the intercom. "Dr. Zucker, can you bring Millie in?"

Moments later Zucker escorted Millie into the conference room. She was dressed in a wool skirt suit with an oxford shirt, but her outfit was a size too large, as if she'd recently lost weight, and she looked more like a girl masquerading in her mother's clothes. Meekly she sat down in the chair that Zucker pulled out for her, but she kept her gaze on the table, as if too intimidated to look at the detectives who were now studying her.

"These are my colleagues in homicide," said Jane. "Detectives

Crowe, Tam, and Frost. They've read the file and they know what happened to you in the Delta. But they need more."

Millie frowned at her. "More?"

"About Johnny. The man you knew as Johnny."

"Tell them what you just told me, about Johnny," suggested Dr. Zucker. "Remember how I said that every killer has his own technique, his own signature? These detectives want to know what makes Johnny unique. How he works, how he thinks. What you tell them might be the one detail they need to catch him."

For a moment Millie thought about this. "We trusted him," she said softly. "It all came down to that. We—I—believed he'd take care of us. In the Delta, there are dozens of different ways to die. Every time you step out of the jeep, step out of the tent, there's something waiting to kill you. In a place like that, the one person you have to believe in is your bush guide. The man with the experience, the man with the rifle. We had every reason to trust him. Before Richard booked the trip, he'd done some research. He said Johnny had eighteen years of experience. He said there were testimonials from other travelers. People from all over the world."

"And he got this all off the Internet?" said Crowe, eyebrow arched.

"Yes," Millie admitted, flushing. "But everything seemed perfectly fine when we arrived in the Delta. He met us at the airstrip. The tents were basic but comfortable. And the Delta was beautiful. Truly wild, in a way you can't believe still exists." She paused, eyes unfocused, lost in the memories of that place. She took a breath. "For the first two nights, it all went as promised. The camping, the meals, the game drives. Then . . . everything changed."

"After your tracker was killed," said Jane.

Millie nodded. "At dawn, we found Clarence's body. Or . . . parts of it. The hyenas had fed, and there was so little left of him, we had no idea what happened. By then we were way out in the bush, too far to use the radio. Anyway, it was dead. So was the truck." She swallowed. "We were stranded."

The room had gone silent. Even Crowe refrained from his usual smart-ass remarks. The mounting horror of Millie's story had gripped them all.

"I wanted to believe it was just a string of bad luck. Clarence getting killed. The truck not starting. Richard still thought it was a grand adventure, something he could write into his book. His hero Jackman Tripp, stranded in the wild, surviving against all odds. We knew we'd be rescued eventually. The plane would come looking for us. So we decided to make the best of it and enjoy the bush experience." She swallowed. "Then Mr. Matsunaga was killed, and it wasn't an adventure anymore. It was a nightmare."

"Did you suspect Johnny was behind it?" asked Frost.

"Not yet. At least, I didn't. Isao's body was found up in a tree, like a classic leopard kill. It seemed like another accident, another case of bad luck. But the others were whispering about Johnny. Wondering if he was behind it. He'd promised to keep us safe, and two people were dead." Millie looked down at the table. "I should have listened to them. I should have helped them bring down Johnny, but I couldn't believe it. I refused to believe it, because . . ." She stopped.

"Why?" Dr. Zucker asked gently.

Millie blinked away tears. "Because I was halfway in love with him," she whispered.

In love with the man who tried to kill her. Jane looked around the table at her colleagues' startled expressions, but she herself found nothing shocking about Millie's confession. How many other women had been killed by husbands and boyfriends, by men they adored? A woman in love is a poor judge of character. No wonder Millie was so deeply haunted; she had been betrayed not just by Johnny, but by her own heart.

"I've never admitted that before. Not even to myself," said Millie. "But out there, in the wild, everything was so different. Beautiful and strange. The sounds at night, the way the air smelled. You wake up every morning feeling a little bit scared. On edge. *Alive.*" She looked at Zucker. "That was Johnny's world. And he made me feel safe in it."

The ultimate aphrodisiac. In the face of danger, there's no one more desirable than the protector, thought Jane. It was why women fell in love with cops and bodyguards, why singers crooned about *someone to watch over me.* In the African bush, the most desirable man is the one who can keep you alive.

"The others were talking about overpowering Johnny and taking control of the gun. I wouldn't go along with it, because I thought they were paranoid. And Richard was egging them on, trying to play the hero, because he was jealous of Johnny. There we were, surrounded by animals that could eat us, but the real battle was *inside* our camp. It was Johnny and me, against everyone else. They stopped trusting me, stopped telling me their plans. I thought we could all just ride it out till we got rescued, and then they'd see how ridiculous they were. I thought we just needed to calm down and wait it out. And then . . ." She swallowed. "He tried to kill Elliot."

"The snake in the tent," said Jane.

Millie nodded. "That's when I knew I had to make a choice. Even then, I couldn't quite believe it was Johnny. I didn't want to believe it."

"Because he made you trust him," said Zucker.

Millie wiped her eyes, and her voice cracked. "That's how he does it. He makes you trust him. He chooses the one person who *wants* to believe in him. Maybe he looks for the wallflower, the utterly ordinary woman. Or the woman whose boyfriend is leaving her. Oh, he knows which one she is. He smiles at her, and for the first time in her life she feels truly alive." Again she wiped her eyes. "I was the weakest gazelle in the herd. He knew it."

"Hardly the weakest," Tam said gently. "You're the one who lived."

"And she's the one who can identify him," said Jane. "Whatever his real name is. We have his description. We know he's about six foot two or three, muscular build. Blond hair, blue eyes. He may have changed his hair color, but he can't disguise his height."

"Or his eyes," said Millie. "The way he looks at you."

"Describe it."

"As if he's looking straight at your soul. Reading your dreams, your fears. As if he can see exactly who you are."

Jane thought of another man's eyes, eyes that she'd once stared into as she prepared to die, and gooseflesh rippled across her arms. We've both felt a killer's gaze, she thought. But I knew it when I saw it. Millie didn't, and her shame was apparent in the drooping shoulders, the bowed head.

Jane's cell phone rang, shrill and startling. She stood and left the room to answer it.

It was criminalist Erin Volchko calling. "You know those animal hairs they found on Jodi Underwood's blue robe?"

"The cat hairs," said Jane.

"Yeah, two of them are definitely from a domestic cat. But there was that third hair I couldn't ID. The one I sent off to the wildlife lab in Oregon. We just got back the result on the keratin."

"A snow leopard?"

"No, I'm afraid not. It's from the species *Panthera tigris tigris.*"

"That sounds like a tiger."

"A Bengal tiger, to be specific. Which is a complete surprise to me. Maybe you can explain how a tiger hair got on a victim's bathrobe."

Jane already had the answer. "Leon Gott's house was a Noah's Ark of mounted animals. I seem to remember a tiger head on his wall, but I have no idea if it was a Bengal tiger."

"Can you get me a few strands off that mounted head? If we can match those hairs to this tiger hair, it tells us there was transfer from Leon Gott's house to Jodi Underwood's robe."

"Two victims. The same killer."

"It's certainly starting to look that way."

TWENTY-NINE

HE IS HERE, SOMEWHERE IN THIS CITY. AS WE SIT IN AFTERNOON TRAFfic, I look out the car window and watch pedestrians trudge past, heads bowed against the wind that whips between buildings. I have lived so long on the farm that I've forgotten what it's like to be in a city. I don't care for Boston. I don't like how cold and gray it is here, and these tall buildings cut off any view of the sky, trapping me in eternal shadow. I don't like the brusqueness of the people, who are so direct and hard-edged. Detective Rizzoli seems distracted as she drives, and she makes no effort at conversation, so we sit in silence. Outside is a cacophony of honking horns and distant sirens and people, so many people. Like the bush, this, too, is a wilderness, where the wrong move—a careless step off the curb, an exchange of words with an angry man—can prove fatal.

Where, in this giant maze of a city, is Johnny hiding?

Everywhere I look, I imagine I see him. I glimpse a towering blond head and a pair of broad shoulders, and my heart gives a lurch. Then he turns and I see it's not him. Nor is the next tall, fair-haired man who catches my eye. Johnny is simultaneously everywhere, and nowhere.

We halt at another stoplight, boxed in between two lanes of cars. Detective Rizzoli looks at me. "I need to make one quick stop before I take you to Maura's. Is that okay?"

"That's fine. Where are we going?"

"A house. The Gott crime scene."

She says it so casually, but this is what she does for a living. She goes to places where they find bodies. She is like Clarence, our tracker in the Delta, who was always hunting for signs of game. The game that Detective Rizzoli hunts for are those who kill.

At last we escape heavy city traffic and enter a much quieter neighborhood of single-family houses. There are trees here, although November has stripped them of their leaves, which tumble like brown confetti on the streets. The house where we pull up has all its shades closed, and a single strand of police tape flutters on a tree, the lone bright accent in the autumnal gloom.

"I'll only be a few minutes," she says. "You can wait in the car."

I glance around at the deserted street and spy a silhouette in a front window, where someone stands watching us. Of course people *would* be watching. A killer has visited their neighborhood, and they worry he'll make a second appearance.

"I'll come in with you," I say. "I don't want to sit out here by myself."

As I follow her to the front porch, I'm nervous about what I'm going to find. I've never been inside a house where someone was murdered, and I imagine blood-spattered walls, a chalk figure drawn on the floor. But when we step inside I see no blood, no signs of violence—unless you count the ghastly display of animal heads. There are dozens of them mounted on the walls, with eyes so life-like they seem to be staring at me. An accusatory gallery of victims. The overwhelming smell of bleach makes my eyes water, my nose sting.

She notices my grimace and says, "The cleaners must have doused the whole house in Clorox. But it's a lot better than what it used to smell like."

"Did it happen . . . was it in this room?"

"No, it was in the garage. I don't need to go in there."

"What are we doing here, exactly?"

"Hunting for a tiger." She scans the trophy heads displayed on the walls. "And there he is. I knew I saw one in here."

As she drags over a chair to reach the tiger, I imagine the souls of these dead animals murmuring among themselves, passing judgment on us. The African lion looks so alive that I'm almost afraid to approach him, but he draws me like a magnet. I think of the real lions I saw in the Delta, remember their muscles rippling beneath tawny coats. I think of Johnny, golden-haired and just as powerful, and imagine his head staring down at me. The most dangerous creature on this wall.

"Johnny said he'd kill a man before he'd ever shoot a big cat."

Rizzoli pauses in the midst of plucking hairs from the mounted tiger and looks at me. "Then this house would definitely piss him off. All these cats, killed for sport. Then Leon Gott went bragging about it in a magazine." She points to the gallery of photos hanging on the opposite wall. "That's Elliot's dad."

In all the pictures, I see the same middle-aged man, posing with a rifle next to his various kills. There is also a framed magazine article: "The Trophy Master: An Interview with Boston's Master Taxidermist."

"I had no idea Elliot's father was a hunter."

"Elliot never told you?"

"Not a word. He didn't talk about his father at all."

"Probably because he was ashamed of him. Elliot and his dad had a falling-out years before. Leon liked to blast away at animals. Elliot wanted to save the dolphins, the wolves, and the field mice."

"Well, I know he loved birds. On safari, he was always pointing them out to us, trying to identify them." I look at the photos of Leon Gott with his dead-animal conquests and shake my head. "Poor Elliot. He was everyone's punching bag."

"What do you mean?"

"Richard was always putting him down, making him the butt of jokes. Men and their testosterone, always trying to one-up each other. Richard had to be king, and Elliot had to bow. It was all about impressing the blondes."

"The two South African girls?"

"Sylvia and Vivian. Elliot had such a crush on them, and Richard never lost a chance to show how much more of a man *he* was."

"You still sound bitter about it, Millie," she observes quietly.

I'm surprised that I *am* bitter. That even after six years, it still stings to remember those nights around the campfire, Richard's attention all on the girls.

"And during this battle for male dominance, where was Johnny in all this?" she asks.

"It's odd, but he didn't really seem to care. He just stood back and watched the drama. All our petty battles and jealousies—none of it seemed to matter to him."

"Maybe because he had other things to think about. Like what he had planned for all of you."

Was he thinking about those plans as he sat beside me at the fire? Was he imagining how it would feel to spill my blood, watch life drain from my eyes? Feeling suddenly cold, I hug myself as I look at the photos of Leon Gott and his conquered animals.

Rizzoli comes to stand beside me. "I hear he was an asshole," she says, looking at Gott's picture. "But even assholes deserve justice."

"No wonder Elliot never mentioned him."

"Did he ever talk about his girlfriend?"

I look at her. "Girlfriend?"

"Jodi Underwood. She and Elliot were together for two years."

This surprises me. "He was so busy mooning over the blondes, he never mentioned any girlfriend. Have you met her? What is she like?"

She doesn't answer right away. Something's troubling her, something that makes her hesitate before responding.

"Jodi Underwood is dead. She was killed the same night Leon was."

I stare at her. "You didn't tell me. Why didn't you tell me?"

"It's an active investigation so there are things I can't tell you, Millie."

"You brought me all this way to help you, yet you keep things from me. Important things. You should have told me *that.*"

"We don't know that their deaths are connected. Jodi's murder looks like a robbery, and the method of killing was entirely different from Leon's. That's why I came for these hair samples. We're looking for a physical link between the attacks."

"Isn't it obvious? The connection is *Elliot.*" The realization hits me with such force that for a moment I can't speak, can't even breathe. I whisper: "The connection is *me.*"

"What do you mean?"

"Why did you contact me? Why did you think I could help you?"

"Because we followed the links. They led us to the Botswana murders. And you."

"Exactly. Those links led you to *me.* For six years I've been hiding in Touws River, living under a different name. I've stayed away from London because I was afraid Johnny would find me. You think he's here, in Boston. And now, so am I." I swallow hard. "Right where he wants me."

I see my alarm reflected in her eyes. She says quietly: "Let's go. I'm taking you back to Maura's."

As we step out of the house, I feel as vulnerable as a gazelle in open grass. I imagine eyes everywhere, watching me from the houses, from the passing cars. I wonder how many people know that I'm in Boston. I remember the crowded airport where we landed yesterday, and I think of all the people who might have seen me in the Boston PD lobby or in the cafeteria or waiting for the elevator. If Johnny was there, would I have spotted him?

Or am I like the gazelle, blind to the lion until the moment he springs?

THIRTY

"IN HER MIND, HE'S GROWN INTO A MONSTER OF MYTHICAL PROPORTIONS," said Maura. "For six years, she's been obsessed with him. It's only natural she thinks this hunt is all about her."

From the living room, Jane could hear the sound of the shower running in the guest bathroom. While Millie was out of earshot, this was their chance to talk about her in private, and Maura was quick to offer her opinion.

"Think about how preposterous her idea is, Jane. She thinks superhuman Johnny killed Elliot's father, killed Elliot's girlfriend, *and* had the miraculous foresight to plant a silver cigarette lighter as a clue five years ago? All this, to lure her out of hiding?" Maura shook her head. "Even for a master chess player, it's too elaborate."

"But it's possible this *is* about her."

"Where's your proof that Jodi Underwood and Leon Gott were killed by the same perp? He was strung up and gutted. She was strangled in a quick, efficient blitz attack. Unless there's a DNA match with those cat hairs—"

"The tiger hair's pretty convincing."

"What tiger hair?"

"The forensic lab called me just before we left to come here. You know that unidentified third strand on Jodi's blue bathrobe? It came from a Bengal tiger." Jane pulled the plastic evidence bag from her pocket. "Leon Gott just happens to have a tiger head mounted on his wall. What are the chances there are two different killers running around who've both been in contact with a tiger?"

Maura frowned at the hairs in the evidence bag. "Well, that does make your case a lot more convincing. Outside of a zoo, you're not going to find many . . ." She paused, looked at Jane. "The zoo has a Bengal tiger. What if that hair was from a live animal?"

The zoo.

A memory suddenly sprang into Jane's head. The leopard cage. Debra Lopez, mauled and bleeding at her feet. And the veterinarian, Dr. Oberlin, crouched over Debra's body, his hands pumping on her chest as he desperately tried to restart her heart. Tall, blond, blue eyes. *Just like Johnny Posthumus.*

Jane pulled out her cell phone.

HALF AN HOUR LATER, Dr. Alan Rhodes called back. "I'm not sure why you want this, but I was able to find you a photo of Greg Oberlin. It's not a very good one. It was taken at our fund-raiser a few weeks ago. What's this all about, anyway?"

"You didn't tell Dr. Oberlin about this, right?" said Jane.

"You asked me not to. Frankly, I don't feel comfortable going behind his back. Is this some sort of police matter?"

"I can't share the details, Dr. Rhodes. It needs to stay confidential. Can you email that photo?"

"You mean, right now?"

"Yes right now." Jane called out: "Maura, I need to use your computer. He's sending the photo."

"It's in my study."

By the time Jane sat down at Maura's desk and signed into her email account, the photo was already in her inbox. Rhodes had said it was taken during a zoo fund-raiser, and the event was clearly a black-tie affair. She saw half a dozen smiling guests posed in a ballroom, wineglasses in hand. Dr. Oberlin was at the edge of the image, partly turned away as he reached toward the canapé tray.

"Okay, I'm looking at it now," she said to Rhodes over the phone. "But it's not the best shot of him. Do you have any others?"

"I'd have to hunt around. Or I could just ask him for one."

"No. Do *not* ask him."

"Can you please tell me what this is all about? You're not investigating Greg, are you, because he's as straight-arrow as they come."

"Do you know if he's ever been to Africa?"

"What does that have to do with anything?"

"Do you know if he's visited Africa?"

"I'm sure he has. His mother's originally from Johannesburg. Look, you need to ask Greg yourself. This is making me uncomfortable."

Jane heard footsteps and swiveled around to see Millie standing behind her. "What do you think?" Jane asked her. "Is it him?"

Millie didn't answer. She stood with eyes rooted on the photo, hands clutching the back of Jane's chair. Her silence stretched on so long that the computer screen went black, and Jane had to reawaken it.

"Is it Johnny?" she asked.

"It . . . it could be," Millie whispered. "I'm not sure."

"Rhodes," said Jane into the phone. "I need a better photo."

She heard him sigh. "I'll ask Dr. Mikovitz. Or maybe his secretary has something in the PR office."

"No, that's too many people in the loop."

"Look, I don't know how else you're going to get one. Unless you want to come here with your own camera."

Jane looked at Millie, whose eyes were still fixed on the screen image of Dr. Gregory Oberlin. And she said: "That's exactly what I'm going to do."

THIRTY-ONE

SHE PROMISES I'LL BE SAFE. SHE SAYS I'LL NEVER HAVE TO FACE HIM DIrectly because it will all be done with video, and multiple police officers will be on the premises. I sit with Detective Frost in the zoo parking lot, and from his car I watch families and children funneling through the entrance. They look happy and excited about a day at the zoo. It's Saturday, at last the sun is shining, and everything looks different—clean and bright and crisp. I feel the difference in myself as well. Yes, I'm nervous, and more than a little scared, but for the first time in six years I think the sun is about to rise in my own life, and soon all the shadows will be washed away.

Detective Frost answers his ringing cell phone. "Yeah, we're still in the parking lot. I'll bring her in now." He looks at me. "Rizzoli's interviewing Dr. Oberlin in the animal care facility. That's at the south end of the zoo, and we won't go anywhere near there. You don't have a thing to worry about." He opens the door. "Let's go, Millie."

He's right beside me as we head toward the entrance. None of the ticket takers is aware there's a police operation under way, and we walk in the same way every other visitor does, by handing over tickets and pushing through the turnstile. The first exhibit I see is the flamingo lagoon, and I think of my daughter, Violet, who has witnessed the spectacle of thousands of flamingos in the wild. I feel sorry for these city children, for whom flamingos will always be represented by a dozen listless birds in a concrete pond. I get no chance to glimpse any other animals, because Detective Frost leads me straight down the walkway to the administrative building.

We wait in a conference room, which is furnished with a long teak table, a dozen comfortable chairs, and a media cart stocked with video equipment. On the walls are framed honors and awards for the Suffolk Zoo and its staff. EXCELLENCE IN DIVERSITY. EXCELLENCE IN MARKETING. R. MARLIN PERKINS AWARD. BEST EXHIBIT, NORTHEAST. This is their bragging room, to show visitors how distinguished an institution it is.

On the opposite wall, I see the curricula vitae of various staff members, and my eyes go straight to Dr. Oberlin's. Forty-four years old. Bachelor of science degree, University of Vermont. Doctor of veterinary medicine, Cornell University. There is no photograph.

"This may take a while, so we have to be patient," says Detective Frost.

"I've waited six years," I tell him. "I can wait a little longer."

THIRTY-TWO

AT SIX FOOT THREE, BLOND WITH BLUE EYES, DR. GREGORY OBERLIN bore a striking resemblance to Johnny Posthumus's passport photo. He had the same square jaw and the same broad forehead, which was now wrinkled in puzzlement as he watched Jane press RECORD on the video camera.

"Do you really need to record this?" he asked.

"I want to have an accurate record. Plus, this frees me from having to take notes, so I can focus on the interview." Jane smiled as she sat down. There were distracting noises in the background, animal sounds from the veterinary cages just outside Dr. Oberlin's office, but this setting would have to do. She wanted him in familiar surroundings, where he'd be relaxed. An interview at Boston PD would almost certainly alarm him.

"I'm glad you're following up on Debra's death," he said. "It's been bothering me. A lot."

"What about it, in particular?" asked Jane.

"An accident like that shouldn't have happened. Debra and I worked together for years. She was not a careless person, and she knew her way around big cats. I can't see her forgetting something as simple as latching the leopard's night cage."

"Dr. Rhodes says that even experienced zookeepers have done it."

"Well, that's true. There have been accidents in very good zoos, by veteran keepers. But Debra was the sort of person who wouldn't leave the house without checking all the burners and making sure the windows were latched."

"So what are you saying happened? Someone else opened the night cage?"

"That must be what you're thinking, isn't it? I assume that's why you wanted to interview me."

"Was there any reason Debra might have been careless that day?" Jane asked. "Anything that could've distracted her?"

"We'd broken up a few months before, but she seemed to be doing fine. I'm not aware of anything that was bothering her."

"You told me she instigated the breakup."

"Yes. I want children, and she didn't. There's no way to compromise on that issue. There were no bitter feelings between us, and I never stopped caring about her. That's why I really need to know if we've missed anything."

"If she didn't leave the gate unlatched, then who do you think did it?"

"That's just it, I don't know! The staff area is out of public view, so theoretically anyone could have sneaked back there unseen."

"Did she have enemies?"

"No."

"A new boyfriend?"

A pause. "I don't think so."

"You don't sound too sure."

"We hadn't really talked much lately, except about issues at work. I know she was upset the day that I euthanized Kovo, but I really had no choice. We tried to keep that cat alive for as long as we could. In the end, it was cruel to let him suffer."

"So Debra was upset about something."

"Yes, and pissed off, too, that Kovo was going to be stuffed and mounted for some rich asshole. Especially when she found out the asshole was Jerry O'Brien."

"You're not a fan, I take it."

"The man considers Africa his personal slaughterhouse. He brags about it on his radio show. So yes, she was pissed, and so am I. Part of our mission here is wildlife conservation. I'm supposed to go to Johannesburg next month, for a conference on rare species protection. And here we made a deal with the devil, all for money."

"So you're going to Africa," she said. "Been there before?"

"Yes. My mother's from Johannesburg, and we have family there."

"What about Botswana? I've been thinking of going. Have you ever been?"

"Yes. You should definitely go."

"When were you there?"

"I don't know. Seven, eight years maybe. It's beautiful, one of the last wild places on earth."

She shut off the RECORD button. "Thank you. I think that's all the information I need for now."

He frowned. "That's all you wanted to know?"

"If I have other questions, I'll be in touch."

"You will keep pursuing this, won't you?" he said as she packed up the video camera. "It bothers me that it's automatically dismissed as an accident."

"At the moment, Dr. Oberlin, it's difficult to call it anything but an accident. Everyone keeps telling me that big cats are dangerous."

"Well, let me know what else you need from me. I'll do everything I can to help."

You already have, she thought as she walked out of his office, carrying the camera. Sunny weather and Saturday had brought crowds into the zoo, and she had to weave her way down the busy pathway. Now things could start to move fast. Four plainclothes officers were already on the premises, waiting for her call to arrest Oberlin. A tech team would swoop in to seize his computer and electronic files, and Maura was already collecting samples from the zoo's Bengal tiger for the hair and fiber lab. The trap was ready to spring, and all Jane needed to deploy it was a positive ID from Millie.

By the time she walked into the administrative building's conference room, where Frost and Millie were waiting for her, Jane felt electricity sizzling through every nerve. Like the hunter who's sighted his prey, she could already smell her quarry's blood in the air.

Jane connected the camera to the video monitor and turned to Millie, who stood gripping the back of a chair, her hands so tense the tendons looked ready to snap. For Jane, this was merely a hunt; for Millie, this could be the moment her nightmares ended, and she faced the video monitor like a prisoner begging for reprieve.

"Here we go," Jane said, and pressed PLAY.

The screen flickered to life, and Dr. Oberlin appeared, frowning at the camera.

Do you really need to record this?

I want to have an accurate record. Plus, this frees me from having to take notes, so I can focus on the interview.

As the video played, Jane kept her eyes fixed on Millie. The only sound in the room was the recording of Jane's questions, Oberlin's responses. Millie stood rigid, hands still gripping the chair as if it were the only solid anchor in the room. She didn't move, didn't even seem to breathe.

"Millie?" said Jane. She pressed PAUSE, and the face of Gregory Oberlin remained frozen on-screen. "Is it him? Is it Johnny?"

Millie looked at her. "No," she whispered.

"But you saw his photo yesterday. You said it might be him."

"I was wrong. It's not him." Millie's legs crumpled beneath her and she sank into a chair. "It's not Johnny."

Her answer seemed to suck all the air out of the room. Jane had been so certain they had the killer in their trap. Now, instead of Leopard Man, it appeared they'd caught Bambi. This was her reward for gambling everything on one shaky witness with an unreliable memory.

"Jesus," muttered Jane. "So we're back to *nothing.*"

"Come on, Rizzoli," said Frost. "She was never really sure."

"Marquette's already on my back about the Cape Town trip. Now this."

"What did you expect?" said Millie. She looked up at Jane with sudden anger. "For you, it's just a jigsaw puzzle, and you thought I had the missing piece. What if I don't?"

"Look, we're all tired," said Frost, playing the mediator as always. "I think we should take a deep breath. Maybe get something to eat."

"I did what you asked. I don't know what else I can do for you!" said Millie. "Now I want to go home."

Jane sighed. "Okay. I know it's been a rough day for you. We'll have a patrolman drive you back to Maura's."

"No, I mean *home.* To Touws River."

"Look, I'm sorry I snapped at you. Tomorrow, we'll review everything again. Maybe there's something—"

"I'm done with this. I miss my family. I'm going home." Millie shoved back the chair and stood, eyes bright with a fierceness Jane hadn't seen in her before. *This* was the woman who'd survived against all odds in the bush, the woman who'd refused to kneel down and die. "I'm leaving tomorrow."

Jane's cell phone rang. "We can talk about it later."

"There's nothing to talk about. If you won't get me a flight, I'll do it myself. I'm *done* with this." She walked out of the room.

"Millie, wait," Frost said, following her into the hallway. "Let me get someone to drive you back."

Jane reached for her ringing cell phone and snapped: "Rizzoli."

"Sounds like this is not a good time," said criminalist Erin Volchko.

"As a matter of fact, it's a lousy time. But go ahead. What's up?"

"This may or may not improve your mood. It's about those hair samples you collected from the mounted Bengal tiger. The one in the Gott residence."

"What about them?"

"They're brittle and degraded, with thinning and fusion of the surface cuticle. I suspect that tiger was killed and mounted decades ago, because these hairs show changes due to age and UV radiation. That's a problem."

"Why?"

"The tiger hair pulled from Jodi Underwood's bathrobe showed no signs of degradation. It's fresh."

"You mean, like from a live tiger?" Jane sighed. "Too bad. We just crossed the zoo veterinarian off our list."

"You told me there were two other zoo employees in the Gott residence earlier that day, delivering the snow leopard carcass. Their clothes are probably covered with all sorts of animal hairs. Maybe they shed hairs in the house, and the killer picked it up on his clothes. Tertiary transfer could explain how tiger hair got onto Jodi's bathrobe."

"So we could still be talking about the same killer, both murders."

"Yes. Is that good news or bad?"

"I don't know." Jane hung up with a sigh. *I don't have a freaking clue how it all fits together.* In frustration she unplugged the video camera from the monitor, coiled up the cables, and shoved everything into the carrying case. She thought about the questions she'd face at tomorrow's case conference, and how to defend her decisions, not to mention her expenses. Crowe would pick at her bones like the vulture he was, and what was she going to say?

At least I got a trip to Cape Town out of it.

She rolled the media cart back to the side of the room where she'd found it and shoved it against the wall. Paused as something on that wall caught her eye. Hanging there were the names and qualifications of the Suffolk Zoo's staff. Dr. Mikovitz, the veterinarians, and the various experts in birds, primates, amphibians, and large mammals. It was Alan Rhodes's curriculum vitae that she focused on.

DR. ALAN T. RHODES.

BACHELOR OF SCIENCE, CURRY COLLEGE. PHD, TUFTS UNIVERSITY.

Natalie Toombs had also attended Curry College.

Alan Rhodes would have been a senior student the year Natalie vanished. She'd left her house to go on a study date with a man named Ted, and was never seen again. Until fourteen years later, when her bones turned up wrapped in a tarp, the ankles bound with orange nylon cord.

Jane dashed out of the conference room and bounded up the stairs to the zoo's administrative offices.

The secretary glanced up with an arched eyebrow as Jane burst into the room. "If you're looking for Dr. Mikovitz, he left for the afternoon."

"Where's Dr. Rhodes?" Jane asked.

"I can give you his cell phone number." The secretary opened her drawer and pulled out the zoo directory. "Just let me look it up."

"No, I want to know where he *is.* Is he still here at work?"

"Yes. He's probably over at the tiger enclosure. That's where they arranged to meet."

"Meet?"

"That woman from the medical examiner's office. She wanted tiger hair for some study she's doing."

"Oh God," said Jane. *Maura.*

THIRTY-THREE

"HE'S SUCH A BEAUTY," SAID MAURA, STARING INTO THE ENCLOSURE.

From the other side of the bars, the Bengal tiger stared back, his tail flicking. Camouflaged perfectly, he was almost invisible except for those alert eyes peering through the grass, and the sinuously waving tail.

"Now, this is a true man-eater," said Alan Rhodes. "There are only a few thousand of them left in the world. We've encroached so deeply into their habitat, it's inevitable they sometimes take a few people down. When you look at this cat, you can see why hunters prize them so much. Not just for the pelt, but for the challenge of defeating such a formidable predator. It's perverse, isn't it? How we humans want to kill the animals we most admire?"

"I'm perfectly happy to admire him from afar."

"Oh, we won't need to get any closer. Like any cat, he sheds plenty of hair." He looked at her. "So why do you need it?"

"It's for forensic analysis. The lab needs a sample of Bengal tiger hair, and I just happened to know someone with access to it. Thank you for this, by the way."

"Is this for a criminal case? It's not something to do with Greg Oberlin, is it?"

"I'm sorry, but I can't talk about it. You understand."

"Of course. The curiosity's killing me, but you have a job to do. So let's go around to the staff entrance. You should be able to find hair in his night cage. Unless you were expecting to pluck it straight off his back. In which case, Doc, you are on your own."

She laughed. "No, hair that's recently been shed will be fine."

"That's a relief, because you definitely don't want to go near this fellow. He's five hundred pounds of muscle and teeth."

Rhodes led her down a path marked STAFF ONLY. Hidden from the public eye by thick plantings, the employee walkway cut like a canyon between the walls of the neighboring tiger and cougar enclosures. Those walls blocked any view of the animals, but Maura could almost feel their power radiating through the concrete, and she wondered if the cats could sense her presence as well. Wondered if they were even now tracking her progress. Though Rhodes seemed perfectly at ease, she kept glancing up at the walls, half expecting to see a pair of yellow eyes peering down at her.

They reached the rear entrance to the tiger enclosure, and Rhodes unlocked the gate. "I can bring you through, into the night cage. Or you can wait out here and I'll collect the hair samples for you."

"I need to do this myself. It's for chain of custody."

He stepped inside the enclosure and unlatched the inner gate to the night room. "All yours. The cage hasn't been cleaned yet, so you should find plenty of hair. I'll wait outside."

Maura entered the night cage. It was an indoor space, about twelve feet square, with a built-in waterer and a concrete ledge for sleeping. A tree log in the corner bore savage gashes where the animal had sharpened his claws, a stark reminder of the tiger's power. Crouching over the log, she remembered the parallel lacerations on Leon Gott's body, so similar to these. A tuft of animal hair clung to the log, and she reached into her pocket for tweezers and evidence bags.

Her cell phone rang.

She let the call go to voice mail and focused on her task. She plucked the first sample, sealed it, and scanned the room. Spotted more hairs on the concrete sleeping ledge.

The phone rang again.

Even as she collected the second sample, the phone kept ringing, shrill and urgent, refusing to be ignored. She sealed the hair in a separate bag and reached for her cell phone. She'd barely managed to say "Hello" when Jane's voice cut in.

"Where are you?"

"I'm collecting tiger hair."

"Is Dr. Rhodes with you?"

"He's waiting right outside the cage. Do you need to talk to him?"

"No. Listen to me. I need you to get away from him."

"What? Why?"

"Stay calm, stay friendly. Don't let him know there's anything wrong."

"What's going on?"

"I'm heading your way now, and I've called the rest of the team to meet us. We'll be there in a few minutes, tops. Just get away from Rhodes."

"Jane—"

"*Do it,* Maura!"

"Okay. Okay." She took a deep breath, but it did nothing to calm her. As she ended the call, her hands were unsteady. She looked down at the evidence bag she was holding. She thought of Jodi Underwood and the strand of tiger hair clinging to her blue robe. Hair that was transferred from her attacker. An attacker who worked with big cats, who knew how they hunted and how they killed.

"Dr. Isles? Is everything all right?"

Rhodes's voice was shockingly close. He'd moved so quietly into the night cage that she hadn't realized he was standing right behind her. Close enough to have heard her conversation with Jane. Close enough to see that her hands were trembling as she slid the phone back in her pocket.

"Everything's fine." She managed a smile. "I'm all through here."

He stared at her so intently that she could feel his gaze penetrating her skull, tunneling into her brain. She made a move to leave, but he stood firmly planted between her and the cage door, and she could not squeeze past him.

"I have what I need," she said.

"Are you sure?"

"If you'll excuse me, I'd like to leave now."

For a moment he seemed to be weighing his options. Then he stepped aside and she slipped past, close enough for their shoulders to brush. Surely he could smell the fear on her skin. She didn't meet his eyes, didn't dare glance back as she exited the enclosure. She just kept walking down the employee pathway, her heart leaping in her throat. Was he following her? Was he even now closing in?

"Maura!" It was Jane, calling from somewhere beyond the screen of shrubbery. "Where are you?"

She took off running toward that voice. Pushed through a tangle of bushes into the open, and saw Jane and Frost, flanked by police officers. All their weapons simultaneously rose and Maura halted as half a dozen barrels pointed straight at her.

"Maura, *don't move*!" Jane commanded.

"What the hell are you doing?"

"Come toward me. Slowly. *Don't. Run.*"

They still had their guns pointed in her direction, but their gazes weren't focused on her. They were staring at something behind her. Every hair instantly stood up on her neck.

She turned and looked straight into amber eyes. For a few heartbeats she and the tiger regarded each other, predator and prey, locked in a stare. Then Maura realized she was not the only one facing him. Jane had stepped forward, was even now moving past her, to place herself between Maura and the tiger.

Confused by this new aggressor, the animal took a step back.

"Do it, Oberlin!" yelled Jane. "Do it now!"

There was a sharp *pop*. The tiger flinched as the tranquilizer dart pierced his shoulder. He didn't retreat but stood his ground, eyes fixed on Jane.

"Hit him again!" ordered Jane.

"No," said Oberlin. "I don't want to kill him! Give the drug time to work."

The tiger sagged sideways, caught himself. Began to stagger in a drunken circle.

"There, he's going down!" said Oberlin. "A few more seconds and he'll—" Oberlin stopped as screams erupted from the public pathway. People sprinted past, scattering in panic.

"Cougar!" came a shriek. "The cougar's out!"

"What the fuck is going on?" said Jane.

"It's Rhodes," said Maura. "He's letting the cats loose!"

Frantically Oberlin reloaded his tranquilizer gun. "Get everyone out! We need to evacuate!"

The public didn't need to be coaxed. Already they were fleeing toward the exits in a stampede of hysterical parents and screaming children. The Bengal tiger was down, collapsed in a heap of fur, but the cougar—where was the cougar?

"Get to the exit, Maura," Jane ordered.

"What about you?"

"I'm staying with Oberlin. We need to find that cat. *Go.*"

As Maura joined the exodus, she kept glancing over her shoulder. She remembered how intently the cougar had watched her on her last visit, and he could be tracking her now, tracking anyone. She almost stumbled over a toddler who lay screaming on the pavement. Scooping him up, she glanced around for his mother and spotted a young woman who was frantically scanning the crowd as she juggled an infant and a diaper bag.

"I've got him!" Maura called out.

"Oh my God, there you are! Oh my God . . ."

"I'll carry him. Just keep moving!"

The exit was mobbed with people shoving through the turnstiles, vaulting across barriers. Then a zoo employee hauled open a gate and the crowd surged out, spilling like a tidal wave into the parking lot. Maura handed the toddler to his mother and stationed herself by the turnstiles to wait for news from Jane.

Half an hour later, her phone rang.

"You okay?" Jane asked.

"I'm standing at the exit. What about the cougar?"

"He's down. Oberlin had to hit him with two darts, but the cat's back in his cage. Jesus, what a disaster." She paused. "Rhodes got away. In all the chaos, he slipped out with the crowd."

"How did you know it was him?"

"Fourteen years ago, he attended the same college that Natalie Toombs did. I don't have the proof yet, but I'm guessing Natalie was one of his early kills. Maybe his very first one. You were the one who saw it, Maura."

"All I saw was—"

"The gestalt, as you called it. The big picture. It was all about the pattern of his kills. Leon Gott. Natalie Toombs. The backpackers, the hunters. God, I should have listened to you."

Maura shook her head, confused. "What about the Botswana murders? Rhodes doesn't look anything like Johnny Posthumus. How is that connected?"

"I don't think they are."

"And Millie? Does she fit into the picture at all?"

Over the phone, she heard Jane sigh. "Maybe she doesn't. Maybe I've been wrong about the whole thing."

THIRTY-FOUR

"BREAK IT," JANE SAID TO FROST.

Glass shattered, shards flying into the house, spilling across the tiled floor. In seconds she and Frost were through the door and inside Alan Rhodes's kitchen. Weapon drawn, Jane caught rapid-fire glimpses of dishes stacked in the drying rack, a pristine countertop, a stainless-steel refrigerator. Everything looked orderly and clean—too clean.

She and Frost moved down the hallway, into the living room, Jane in the lead. She looked left, looked right, saw no movement, no signs of life. She saw bookshelves, a sofa and coffee table. Not a thing out of place, not even a stray magazine. The home of a bachelor with OCD.

From the foot of the stairway she peered up toward the second floor, trying to listen through the pounding of her own heart. It was quiet upstairs, as silent as the grave.

Frost took the lead as they moved up the stairs. Though the house was chilly, her blouse was already damp with sweat. The most dangerous animal is the one who's trapped, and by now Rhodes must realize this was the end game. They reached the second-floor landing. Three doorways ahead. Glancing through the first, she saw a bedroom, sparsely furnished. No dust, no clutter. Did a real human actually live in this house? She eased toward the closet, yanked it open. Empty hangers swayed on the rod.

Back into the hallway, past a bathroom, to the last doorway.

Even before she stepped through, she already knew Rhodes wasn't there. He was probably never coming back. Standing in his bedroom, she looked around at blank walls. The queen bed had a stark white cover. The dresser was bare and dust-free. She thought of her own dresser at home, a magnet for keys and coins, socks and bras. You could tell a lot about people by looking at what migrated to their dressers and their countertops, and what she saw here, on Alan Rhodes's dresser, was a man without an identity. *Who are you?*

From the bedroom window, she looked down at the street, where yet another Danvers PD patrol car had just pulled up. This neighborhood was outside Boston PD's jurisdiction, but in their rush to capture Rhodes she and Frost had not wasted time waiting for Danvers detectives to assist. Now there'd be bureaucratic hell to pay.

"There's a trapdoor up here," said Frost, standing in the closet.

She squeezed in beside him and looked up at the ceiling panel, where a pull rope dangled. It probably led to attic storage space, where families stash boxes they never open, filled with items they couldn't bring themselves to throw out. Frost tugged on the rope and the panel swung open, revealing a drop-down ladder and a shadowy space overhead. They shot a tense glance at each other, then Frost climbed the ladder.

"All clear!" he called down. "Just a bunch of stuff."

She followed him through the trapdoor and turned on her pocket flashlight. In the gloom she glimpsed a row of cardboard boxes. This could be anyone's attic, a depository for clutter, for the reams of tax documents and financial papers you fear you might need someday when the IRS comes calling. She opened one box and saw bank statements and loan documents. Moved on to the next and the next. Found copies of *Biodiversity and Conservation.* Old sheets and towels. Books and more books. There was nothing here to tie Rhodes to any crimes at all, much less murder.

Have we made another mistake?

She climbed back down the ladder, into the bedroom with its bare walls and spotless bedspread. Her uneasiness grew as another car pulled up outside. Detective Crowe climbed out, and she felt her blood pressure shoot up as he strutted toward the house. Seconds later, someone pounded on the front door. She went downstairs and found Crowe grinning at her from the front porch.

"So, Rizzoli, I hear the city of Boston's not big enough for you. You breaking down doors in the suburbs now?" He walked in and made a lazy stroll around the living room. "What've you got on this guy Rhodes?"

"We're still looking."

"Funny, 'cause he's got a clean record. No arrests, no convictions. You sure you tagged the right guy?"

"He ran, Crowe. He released two large cats to cover his escape, and he hasn't been seen since. It makes the death of Debra Lopez look less and less like an accident."

"Murder by leopard?" Crowe shot her a skeptical look. "Why would he kill a zookeeper?"

"I don't know."

"Why did he kill Gott? And Jodi Underwood?"

"I don't know."

"That's a lot of *don't knows.*"

"There's trace evidence linking him to Jodi Underwood. That tiger hair on her bathrobe. We also know he was a student at Curry College, the same year Natalie Toombs vanished, so there's a link to her as well. Remember how Natalie was last seen leaving for a study date with someone named Ted? Rhodes's middle name is Theodore. According to his bio at the zoo, before he started college, he spent a year in Tanzania. Maybe that's where he learned about the leopard cult."

"A lot of circumstantials." Crowe waved his arm at the sterile-looking living room. "I gotta say, I don't see anything here that screams *Leopard Man.*"

"Maybe that's significant. There's not a whole lot here, period. There are no photos, no pictures, not even a DVD or a CD to tell us about his personal tastes. The books and magazines are all related to his work. The only medicine in his bathroom is aspirin. And you know what's missing?"

"What?"

"Mirrors. There's only one small shaving mirror in the upstairs bathroom."

"Maybe he doesn't care how he looks. Or are you going to tell me he's a vampire?"

She turned away at his laughter. "A giant blank, that's what this house is. It's like he tried to keep it a sterile zone, a place just for show."

"Or this is exactly who he is. A totally dull guy with nothing to hide."

"There's *got* to be something here. We just haven't found it yet."

"And if you don't?"

She refused to consider the possibility, because she knew she was right. She *had* to be right.

But as the afternoon slid into evening and a team of criminalists scoured the house for evidence, her stomach knotted tighter and tighter with uncertainty. She could not believe she'd made a mistake, but it was beginning to look like one. They'd invaded the home of a man with no known criminal past. They'd broken a window, pulled apart his house, and found nothing to tie him to the murders, not even a fragment of nylon cord. They'd also attracted the attention of keenly curious neighbors, and those neighbors had nothing bad to say about Alan Rhodes, although no one admitted to knowing him well. *He was quiet and polite. Never seemed to have any girlfriends. Liked to garden, always hauling home bags of mulch.*

That last remark sent Jane out to take another look at Rhodes's backyard. She had already walked the entire property, which was nearly three-quarters of an acre and abutted a wooded conservation easement. In the darkness she scanned the ground by flashlight, her beam moving across shrubs and grass. She tramped to the far edge of the lot, where a fence marked the property line. Here a sharply sloping hillock had been planted with rosebushes, their canes now spindly and bare. She stood frowning at that odd landscaping feature, wondering about that hillock. In a yard that was otherwise level, it stood out like a volcano thrust up from a plain. She was so focused on that peculiar mound that she didn't notice Maura crossing toward her until the flashlight beam flared in her eyes.

"Have you found anything?" said Maura.

"No dead bodies for you to look at, anyway." She frowned at Maura. "So what brings you here?"

"I couldn't stay away."

"You have got to get yourself a better social life."

"This *is* my social life." Maura paused. "Which is pathetic."

"Well, nothing's happening here," Jane said in disgust. "As Crowe keeps pointing out to me."

"It's got to be Rhodes, Jane. I know he's the one."

"Based on what? Are you talking gestalt again? Because I don't have a damn thing to use in court."

"He would have been only twenty when he killed Natalie Toombs. She may have been his only Boston victim until he killed Gott. The reason we had trouble seeing the pattern is because he's too intelligent to hunt in the same place. Instead he expanded his territory, to Maine. To Nevada and Montana. It made his signature almost impossible to spot."

"How do we explain Leon Gott and Jodi Underwood? Those were reckless killings, both in the same day. Within ten miles of each other."

"Maybe he's accelerating. Losing control."

"I don't see any sign of that in this house. Did you look around inside? Everything's in perfect order. There's no hint of the monster."

"Then he has another place. A lair, where that monster lives."

"This is the only property Rhodes owns, and we can't even find a piece of rope here." In frustration, Jane kicked at the mulch and frowned at the rosebush that she'd just knocked askew. She gave the bare bush a tug, and felt only minimal resistance from the roots. "This was planted recently."

"It's odd, this mound of dirt." Maura swept her flashlight around the yard, across grass and shrubs and a gravel walkway. "There don't seem to be any other recent plantings. Just here."

Jane stared at the hillock and suddenly felt a chill when she realized what it represented. *Dirt. Where did all this dirt come from?* "It's here, under our feet," she said. "His lair." She moved onto the lawn, searching for an opening, a seam, anything that might indicate a hatchway leading underground, but the yard was obscured by shadow. It could take them days to dig it all up, and what if they found nothing? She could imagine the ridicule from Crowe about *that.*

"Ground-penetrating radar," said Maura. "If there's a chamber under here, that would be the quickest way to locate it."

"Let me check with CSU. See if we can get a GPR unit here in the morning." Jane walked back to the house and had just stepped inside when she heard the chime announcing a text message on her phone.

It was from Gabriel, who was in DC and wouldn't be home till tomorrow. CHECK YOUR EMAIL. INTERPOL REPORT.

She'd been so focused on searching Rhodes's house, she hadn't read her email all afternoon. Now she scrolled through an inbox stuffed with the trivial and annoying before she found the message. It had arrived three hours earlier, sent by Henk Andriessen.

She squinted at a screen filled with dense text. As she scanned the document, words leaped out at her. *Skeletonized remains found, outskirts of Cape Town. White male, multiple skull fractures. DNA match.*

She stared at the newly identified name of the deceased. This makes no sense, she thought. This cannot be true.

Her phone rang. Gabriel again.

"Did you read it?" he asked.

"I don't understand this report. It's *got* to be a mistake."

"The man's remains were found two years ago. They were fully skeletonized, so the bones could have been lying there much longer. It took them a while to finally run the DNA and make the ID, but now there's no doubt about who he is. Elliot Gott didn't die on safari, Jane. He was murdered. In Cape Town."

THIRTY-FIVE

I AM NO LONGER OF INTEREST TO THE POLICE. THE KILLER THEY'RE HUNTing for isn't Johnny, but a man named Alan Rhodes, who has always lived in Boston. This is what Dr. Isles told me just before she left the house this evening, to join Detective Rizzoli at a crime scene. What a different world these people inhabit, a twisted universe that we ordinary people aren't aware of until we read about it in the newspapers, or see it on the TV news. While most of us go about our everyday lives, someone, somewhere, is committing an unspeakable act.

And that's when Rizzoli and Isles go to work.

I'm relieved to be escaping their world. They needed something from me, but I couldn't deliver, so tomorrow I go home. Back to my family and Touws River. Back to my nightmares.

I pack for the morning flight, tucking shoes into the corner of my suitcase, folding wool sweaters that I won't need when I land in Cape Town. How I've missed the bright colors of home and the smell of flowers. My time here has felt like hibernation, bundled in sweaters and coats against the cold and the gloom. I lay a pair of pants on top of the sweaters and as I fold a second pair, the gray cat suddenly jumps into my suitcase. During my entire stay, this cat has completely ignored me. Now here he is, purring and rolling around on my clothes, as if he wants me to bring him home. I pick him up and drop him on the floor. He climbs right back into the suitcase and begins meowing.

"Are you hungry? Is that what you want?" Of course it is. Dr. Isles was in and out of the house so quickly, she didn't have a chance to feed him.

I head into the kitchen and he's right beside me, rubbing against my leg as I open a can of cat food and empty it into his bowl. As he slurps up chunks of chicken in a savory sauce, I realize I'm hungry as well. Dr. Isles gave me full run of her house, so I go into her pantry and search the shelves for something quick and satisfying. I find a package of spaghetti, and I remember seeing bacon and eggs and a block of Parmesan cheese in the refrigerator. I'll make spaghetti carbonara, the perfect meal for a cold night.

I've just pulled the package of spaghetti off the shelf when the cat suddenly gives a loud hiss. Through the partly open pantry door, I see him staring at something that I can't see. His back is arched, his fur electric. I don't know what has alarmed him; I only know that every hair on the back of my neck is suddenly standing up.

Glass cracks and clatters like hail across the floor. One bright shard glistens like a tear right outside the doorway.

Instantly I flick off the pantry light and stand trembling in the darkness.

The cat yowls and darts out of view. I want to flee with him, but I hear the door bang open, and heavy footsteps are crunching across broken glass.

Someone is in the kitchen. And I'm trapped.

THIRTY-SIX

JANE FELT THE ROOM SUDDENLY SPIN AROUND HER. SHE HADN'T EATEN since noon, had been on her feet for hours, and this revelation was enough to make her sag against a wall for support. "This report can't be right," she insisted.

"DNA doesn't lie," said Gabriel. "The remains found near Cape Town were matched to DNA that was already in the Interpol database. DNA that Leon Gott submitted to them six years ago, after his son vanished. The bones are Elliot's. Based on skeletal trauma, his death was classified a homicide."

"And these were found two years ago?"

"In parkland on the city outskirts. They can't be specific about date of death, so he could have been killed six years ago."

"When we *know* he was alive. Millie was with him on safari in Botswana."

"Are you absolutely certain about that?" Gabriel said quietly.

That made her go silent. *Are we absolutely certain Millie told the truth?* She pressed a hand to her temple as thoughts swirled like a windstorm in her head. Millie couldn't be lying, because known facts supported her. A pilot *did* deliver seven tourists to a landing strip in the Delta, among them a passenger with Elliot Gott's ID. Weeks later, Millie *did* stumble out of the wild, with a horrifying tale of massacre in the bush. Animal scavenging had scattered the remains of the dead, and the bones of four of the victims were never found. Not Richard's. Not Sylvia's. Not Keiko's. Not Elliot's.

Because the real Elliot Gott was already dead. Murdered in Cape Town before the safari even began.

"Jane?" said Gabriel.

"Millie wasn't lying. She was *wrong.* She thought Johnny was the killer, but he was a victim, like the others. Killed by the man who used Elliot's ID to book the safari. And after it was all over, after he'd enjoyed his ultimate bush hunt, he went home. Back to who he really was."

"Alan Rhodes."

"Since he traveled with Elliot's ID, there'd be no record of him entering Botswana, nothing at all to connect him to the safari." Jane focused on the living room where she was standing. On the blank walls, the impersonal collection of books. "He's an empty shell, like his house," she said softly. "He can't afford to reveal the monster he really is, so he becomes other people. After he steals their identities."

"And leaves no record of himself."

"But in Botswana, he made a mistake. One of his victims escaped, and she can identify . . ." Jane suddenly turned to Maura, who had just stepped inside and was now watching her with questions in her eyes. "Millie's all by herself," Jane said to her.

"Yes. She's packing to go home."

"Oh God. We left her alone."

"Why does that matter?" asked Maura. "Isn't she now irrelevant to our case?"

"No, it turns out she's the *key* to it. She's the only one who can identify Alan Rhodes."

Maura shook her head in bewilderment. "But she's never met Rhodes."

"Yes she has. In Africa."

THIRTY-SEVEN

THE FOOTSTEPS MOVE CLOSER. I SHRINK BEHIND THE PANTRY DOOR, my heart banging as loud as drums. I can't see who has just broken into the house; I can only hear him, and he's lingering in the kitchen. I suddenly remember that I left my purse on the counter, and I hear him unzipping it now, hear coins clatter onto the floor. Oh God, please let him be just a thief. Let him take my wallet and then be on his way.

He must have found what he wanted, because I hear my purse thud onto the countertop. Please leave. Please leave.

But he doesn't. He moves, instead, across the kitchen. He will have to pass the pantry to get to the rest of the house. I stand frozen in the shadows, not daring to breathe. As he walks past the doorway crack, I glimpse his back and see curly dark hair, thick shoulders, a squarish head. There is something shockingly familiar about him, but it isn't possible. No, that man is dead, his bones scattered somewhere in the Okavango Delta. Then he turns toward the cracked doorway and I see his face. Everything I believed these past six years, everything I *thought* I knew, flips on its axis.

Elliot is alive. Poor, awkward Elliot, who pined after the blondes, who stumbled around in the bush, who was always the butt of Richard's jokes. Elliot, who claimed he found a viper in his tent, a viper that no one else saw. I think back to the last night my companions were alive. I remember darkness, panic, gunshots. And a woman's last scream: *Oh God, he has the gun!*

Not Johnny. It was never Johnny.

He keeps walking past the pantry, and his footsteps fade away. Where is he? Is he standing still, just out of sight, waiting for me to show myself? If I step out of the pantry and try to slip out the kitchen door, will he spot me? Frantically I try to picture the backyard beyond that door. It's fully fenced, but where is the gate? I can't remember. I could get boxed in by that fence, trapped in a killing yard.

Or I could stay right here in the pantry and wait for him to find me.

I reach for a jar on the shelf. Raspberry jam. It feels solid and heavy in my hand; not much, but it's the only weapon I have. I ease around from behind the pantry door and peer out.

No one there.

I creep out of the pantry, into the brightly lit kitchen, where I'm painfully exposed in the glare. The back door is maybe ten paces away, across a floor littered with broken glass.

The phone rings, loud as a shriek. I freeze in place and the answering machine picks up. I hear Detective Rizzoli's voice on the line: *Millie, please pick up. Millie, are you there? This is important . . .*

Through the urgent sound of her voice, I listen desperately for other sounds in the house, but I can't hear him.

Go. Go now.

Terrified of betraying my presence, I tiptoe around the broken glass. Nine paces to the door. Eight. I make it halfway across the kitchen when the cat shoots into the room, claws sliding across the slick tiles, loudly scattering shards.

The noise alerts him, and heavy footsteps move toward me. I'm out in the open, with nowhere to hide. I make a dash for the door. Just manage to grasp the knob when hands grab my sweater and wrench me backward.

I whirl around, blindly swinging the jar at him. It slams into the side of his head and shatters, releasing a spray of raspberry jam, bright as blood.

He howls in rage and loses his grip. Just for an instant I'm free, and again I lurch for the door. Again, I almost make it.

Then he tackles me and we both go sprawling to the floor, sliding across glass and raspberry jam. The trash can topples, spilling out dirty wrappers and coffee grounds. I struggle to my knees, desperately crawling through scattered garbage.

A cord loops around my neck, goes taut, and yanks my head back.

I reach up, clawing at the cord, but it's tight, so tight it cuts like a blade into my flesh. I hear his grunt of effort. I can't loosen the cord. I can't breathe. The light starts to dim. My feet no longer work. So this is how I die, so far from home. From everyone I love.

As I sag backward, something sharp bites into my hand. My fingers close around the object, which I can barely feel because everything is going numb. *Violet. Christopher. I should never have left you.*

I fling my arm backward, slashing at his face.

Even through my darkening fog, I can hear his shriek. Suddenly the cord around my neck goes limp. The room brightens. Coughing, gasping, I release the object I've been holding and it clatters to the floor. It's the open cat-food can, its exposed lid sharp as a razor.

I haul myself to my feet and the countertop block of kitchen knives is right in front of me. He's moving in, and I turn to face him. Blood streams from his slashed brow, a waterfall of it, dripping into his eyes. He lunges, hands reaching for my throat. Partly blinded by his own blood, he doesn't see what I'm holding. What I bring up just as our bodies collide.

The butcher knife sinks into his belly.

The hands grappling at my throat suddenly fall away, limp. He drops to his knees where, just for an instant he remains upright, his eyes open, his face a bloody mask of surprise. His body tilts sideways, and I close my eyes as he hits the floor.

Suddenly I myself am wobbling. I stagger across the blood and glass and I sink into a chair. I drop my head in my hands, and through the roaring of blood in my ears I hear another sound. A siren. I have no strength to lift my head. I hear banging on the front door, and voices shouting: *Police!* But I cannot seem to move. Only when I hear them step in through the back door, and one of them utters a startled oath, do I finally look up.

Two policemen loom in front of me, both of them staring at the carnage in the room. "Are you Millie?" one of them asks. "Millie DeBruin?"

I nod.

He says, into his radio: "Detective Rizzoli, she's here. She's alive. But you're not gonna believe what I'm looking at."

THIRTY-EIGHT

A DAY LATER, THEY UNCOVERED HIS LAIR.

After ground-penetrating radar detected the underground chamber in Alan Rhodes's backyard, it took only a few minutes' shovel work to locate the entrance, a wooden hatch cover hidden under an inch of mulch.

Jane was the first to climb down the steps, descending into a chilly blackness that smelled of damp earth. At the bottom she reached a concrete floor and stared at what her flashlight revealed: the snow leopard pelt, mounted on the wall. Dangling from a hook beside it were steel claws, the razor-sharp tips polished to a gleaming brightness. She thought of the three parallel slashes on Leon Gott's torso. She thought of Natalie Toombs and the three nicks on her skull. Here was the tool that had left those marks in flesh and bone.

"What do you see down there?" called Frost.

"Leopard Man," she said softly.

Frost came down the stairs and they stood together, their flashlight beams slashing the darkness like sabers.

"Jesus," he said as his light fixed on the opposite wall. On the two dozen drivers' licenses and passport photos tacked to corkboard. "They're from Nevada. Maine. Montana . . ."

"It's his trophy wall," said Jane. Like Leon Gott and Jerry O'Brien, Alan Rhodes also displayed his kills, but on a wall that was for his eyes only. She focused on a page ripped from a passport: *Millie Jacobson,* the trophy Rhodes thought he'd won, but this prize had been prematurely claimed. Next to Millie's photo were other faces, other names. Isao and Keiko Matsunaga. Richard Renwick. Sylvia Van Ofwegen. Vivian Kruiswyk. Elliot Gott.

And Johnny Posthumus, the bush guide who had fought to keep them alive. In Johnny's direct gaze, Jane saw a man ready to do whatever was necessary, without fear, without hesitation. A man prepared to face any beast in the wild. But Johnny had not realized that the most dangerous animal he would ever encounter was the client smiling back at him.

"There's a laptop in here," said Frost, crouched over a cardboard box. "It's a MacBook Air. You think it was Jodi Underwood's?"

"Turn it on."

With gloved hands, Frost lifted the computer and pressed the POWER button. "Battery's dead."

"Is there a power cord?"

He reached deeper into the box. "I don't see one. There's some broken glass in here."

"From what?"

"It's a picture." He pulled out a framed photo, its protective glass shattered. He shone his flashlight on the image, and for a moment neither one of them said a word as they both registered its significance.

Two men stood together, the sun in their faces, the bright light defining every feature. They looked enough alike to be brothers, both with dark hair and squarish faces. The man on the left smiled straight into the lens, but the second man appeared caught by surprise just as he'd turned to face the camera.

"When was this taken?" said Frost.

"Six years ago."

"How do you know?"

"Because I know where this is. I've been there. It's Table Mountain, in Cape Town." She looked at Frost. "Elliot Gott and Alan Rhodes. They knew each other."

THIRTY-NINE

DETECTIVE RIZZOLI STANDS AT DR. ISLES'S FRONT DOOR, HOLDING A laptop case. "It's the last piece of the puzzle, Millie," she says. "I think you'll want to see it."

It's been almost a week since I survived Alan Rhodes's attack. Although the blood and glass are now gone, and the window has been replaced, I'm still reluctant to go into the kitchen. The memories are too vivid, and the bruises around my neck still too fresh, so instead we move into the living room. I settle onto the sofa between Dr. Isles and Detective Rizzoli, the two women who have been hunting the monster, and who tried to keep me safe from him. But in the end, I'm the one who had to save myself. I'm the one who had to die twice, in order to live again.

The gray tabby crouches on the coffee table and watches with a look of unsettling intelligence as Rizzoli opens her laptop and inserts a flash drive. "These are the photos from Jodi Underwood's computer," she says. "This is the reason Alan Rhodes killed her. Because these pictures tell a story, and he couldn't afford to let anyone see them. Not Leon Gott. Not Interpol. And certainly not you."

The screen fills with image tiles, all of them too small to make out any details. She clicks on the first tile and the photo blooms on-screen. It's a smiling, dark-haired man of about thirty, dressed in jeans and a photographer's vest, a backpack slung over his shoulder. He is standing in an airport check-in line. He has a squarish forehead and gentle eyes, and there is a happy innocence about him, the innocence of a lamb who has no idea he's headed for slaughter.

"This is Elliot Gott," says Rizzoli. "The *real* Elliot Gott. It was taken six years ago, just before he boarded the plane in Boston."

I study his features, the curly hair, the shape of his face. "He looks so much like . . ."

"Like Alan Rhodes. That may be why Rhodes chose to kill him. He picked a victim who resembled him, so he could pass himself off as Elliot Gott. He used Gott's name when he met Sylvia and Vivian at the nightclub in Cape Town. He used Elliot's passport and credit cards to book the flight to Botswana."

Which is where I met him. I think of the day I first laid eyes on the man who called himself Elliot. It was in the satellite air terminal in Maun, where the seven of us waited to board the bush plane into the Delta. I remember how nervous I was about flying on a small plane. I remember how Richard complained that I wasn't in the spirit of adventure, and why couldn't I be more cheerful about it, like those cute blond girls giggling on the bench? About that first meeting with Elliot, I remember almost nothing at all, because my focus was entirely on Richard. How I was losing him. How he seemed so bored with me. The safari was my last-gasp effort to salvage what we had together, so I scarcely paid attention to the awkward man who was hovering over the blondes.

Rizzoli advances to the next photo. It is a "selfie," taken aboard the airline flight. The real Elliot grins from the aisle coach seat as the female passenger on his right lifts a wineglass to the camera.

"These are all cell phone photos that Elliot emailed to his girlfriend, Jodi. It's a day-by-day chronicle of what he saw and who he met," says Rizzoli. "We don't have the emailed text that accompanied these pictures, but they document his trip. And he took a lot of them." She clicks through the next photos, of his airline meal. The sunrise through the plane's window. And another selfie, where he's wearing a goofy grin as he leans into the aisle to show the cabin behind him. But this time, it's not Elliot I focus on; it's the man in the seat behind him, a man whose face is clearly visible.

Alan Rhodes.

"They were on the same flight," says Rizzoli. "Maybe that's how they met, on the plane. Or maybe they'd met earlier, in Boston. What we do know is, by the time Elliot arrived in Cape Town, he had a friend to hang out with."

She clicks another image icon, and a new photo glows on-screen. Elliot and Rhodes, standing together on Table Mountain.

"This picture is the last known photo taken of Elliot. Jodi Underwood had it framed and she gave it to Elliot's father. We believe it was hanging in Leon's house the day Alan Rhodes delivered the snow leopard. Leon recognized Rhodes from the photo. He probably asked Rhodes how he knew Elliot, and how they both happened to be in Cape Town. Later, Leon made phone calls. To Jodi Underwood, asking for all her photos from Elliot's trip. To Interpol, trying to reach Henk Andriessen. That photo was the catalyst for everything that followed. Leon Gott's murder. Jodi Underwood's murder. Maybe even the zookeeper, Debra Lopez, because she was there in Gott's house and heard the whole exchange. But the one person Rhodes was most afraid of was *you.*"

I stare at the laptop screen. "Because I'm the only one who knew which of these men actually went on safari."

Rizzoli nods. "He had to keep you from ever seeing this picture."

Suddenly I can't bear to look at Rhodes's face any longer and I turn away. "Johnny," I whisper. That's the only word I say, just *Johnny.* A memory springs into my head, of him in the sunlight, his hair tawny as a lion's. I remember how he stood, with feet planted as firmly as a tree in its native African soil. How he'd asked me to trust him, told me that I must also learn to trust myself. And I think of the way he looked at me as we sat by the fire, the light of the flames flickering on his face. If only I'd listened to my heart; if only I'd put my faith in the man I wanted to believe in.

"So now you know the truth," Dr. Isles says gently.

"It could have turned out so differently." I blink, and a tear slides down my cheek. "He fought to keep us alive. And we all turned against him."

"In a way, Millie, he did keep you alive."

"How?"

"Because of Johnny—your fear of him—you stayed hidden in Touws River, where Alan Rhodes couldn't find you." Dr. Isles glances at Rizzoli. "Until we, unfortunately, brought you to Boston."

"Our fault," admits Rizzoli. "We had our eye on the wrong man."

So did I. I think of how Johnny has stalked me through my nightmares, when he was never the one I should have feared. Those bad dreams are fading now; last night I slept better than I have in six years. The monster is gone, and I'm the one who defeated him. Weeks ago, Detective Rizzoli told me it was the only way I'd ever sleep soundly again, and I'm confident that soon the nightmares will vanish entirely.

She closes the laptop. "So tomorrow you can fly home knowing it really *is* over. I'm sure your husband will be glad to have you back."

I nod. "Chris has been calling me about three times a day. He says this has made it into the news there."

"You'll go home a hero, Millie."

"I'm just happy to go home."

"Before you do, there's something I thought you might want to have." She reaches into the laptop bag and pulls out a large envelope. "Henk Andriessen emailed that to me. I printed it up for you."

I open the envelope and pull out a photograph. My throat closes over, and for a moment I can't make a sound. I can only stare at the picture of Johnny. He stands in knee-high grass, a rifle at his side. His hair is gilded by sunlight and his eyes are crinkled in mid-laugh. This is the Johnny I fell in love with, the real Johnny who was temporarily eclipsed by the shadow of a monster. This is how I must remember him, at home in the wild.

"It's one of the few good photos that Henk could find. It was taken by another bush guide around eight years ago. I thought you'd like it."

"How did you know?"

"Because I know what a mental whiplash it must be to find out that everything you believed about Johnny Posthumus was wrong. He deserves to be remembered for who he really was."

"Yes," I whisper as I caress the smiling face in the photo. "And I will."

FORTY

CHRISTOPHER WILL BE WAITING FOR ME AT THE AIRPORT. VIOLET WILL be there too, almost certainly holding a big bouquet of flowers. I'll be swept into their arms and then we'll drive home to Touws River, where there'll be a welcome-home party this evening. Chris has already warned me about it, because he knows I don't like surprises, nor do I much like parties. But I feel it's finally time to celebrate, because I am reclaiming my life. I'm rejoining the world.

I'm told that half the town will be there because everyone's curious. Until they saw the story on the news, few of them had any idea of my past, or why I've been such a recluse. I could never risk the exposure before. Now they all know, and I'm the town's new celebrity, the ordinary mum who went to America and defeated a serial killer.

"It'll be utter madness here," Chris told me during our phone call just before I boarded the plane. "The newspaper keeps calling, and the TV station. I've told them to leave us alone, but you need to be ready for this."

In half an hour, my plane will touch down. These final moments of the flight will be my last chance at solitude. As we start our descent toward Cape Town, I take out the photograph one last time.

Six years have passed since I last saw him. Every year I grow older, but Johnny never will. He will always stand straight and tall, the grass waving at his feet, the sunlight reflected in his smile. I think about all the things that could have been if things had turned out differently. Would we now be married and blissful in our rustic hut in the bush? Would our children have his wheat-colored hair, and grow up running barefoot and free? I will never know, because the real Johnny lies somewhere in the Delta, his bones crumbling into the soil, his atoms forever bound to the land he loved. The land he'll always belong to. All I own are my memories of him, and these I'll guard as my secret. They belong to no one but me.

The plane touches down and rolls to the gate. Outside, the sky is a brilliant blue, and I know the air will be soft with the scent of flowers and the sea. I slip Johnny's photo back into the envelope and tuck it inside my purse. Out of sight, but never forgotten.

I rise to my feet. It's time to go back to my family.

ACKNOWLEDGMENTS

I will never forget the thrill of my first glimpse of a leopard in the wild. For that treasured memory, I thank the wonderful staff at the Ulusaba Safari Lodge in Sabi Sands. I owe special thanks to ranger Greg Posthumus and tracker Dan Ndubane for introducing me to the beauty of the African bush—and for keeping my husband alive.

I owe a huge debt of gratitude to my literary agent, Meg Ruley, who has been my stalwart friend and ally through the years, and to my editors, Linda Marrow (US) and Sarah Adams (UK), for their invaluable help in making this book shine.

Most of all I thank my husband, Jacob, for sharing this journey. The adventure continues.

rizzoli & isles
THE COMPLETE FIRST SEASON
rizzoli & isles
THE COMPLETE SECOND SEASON

ABOUT THE AUTHOR

TESS GERRITSEN is a physician and an internationally bestselling author. She gained nationwide acclaim for her first novel of suspense, the *New York Times* bestseller *Harvest.* She is also the author of the bestsellers *Rizzoli & Isles: Last to Die, The Silent Girl, Ice Cold, The Keepsake, The Bone Garden, The Mephisto Club, Vanish, Body Double, The Sinner, The Apprentice, The Surgeon, Life Support, Bloodstream,* and *Gravity.* Tess Gerritsen lives in Maine.

www.tessgerritsen.com
Facebook.com/TessGerritsen
@tessgerritsen

ABOUT THE TYPE

The text of this book was set in Life, a typeface designed by W. Bilz and jointly developed by Ludwig & Mayer and Francesco Simoncini in 1965. This contemporary design is in the transitional style of the eighteenth century. Life is a versatile text face and is a registered tradmark of Simoncini S.A.